HEART
on
FIRE

AMANDA
BOUCHET

piatkus

PIATKUS

First published in the US in 2018 by Sourcebooks, Inc.
First published in Great Britain in 2018 by Piatkus

1 3 5 7 9 10 8 6 4 2

Copyright © 2018 by Amanda Bouchet

The moral right of the author has been asserted.

A CIP catalogue record for this book
is available from the British Library.

ISBN 978-0-349-41262-7

Printed and bound in Great Britain by
Clays Ltd, St Ives plc

Papers used by Piatkus are from well-managed forests
and other responsible sources.

Piatkus
An imprint of
Little, Brown Book Group
Carmelite House
50 Victoria Embankment
London EC4Y 0DZ

An Hachette UK Company
www.hachette.co.uk

www.littlebrown.co.uk

For my mother, the most generous heart I know.

CHAPTER 1

"Do you see what I see?"

What normal person doesn't look up at *that*? Not that I'm entirely normal, but at least Griffin's question snaps me from unpleasant thoughts of giant metallic birds, Cyclopes, fire, and blood.

"I see…Piers?" And there's another person riding alongside Griffin's brother on a large gray horse. Nondescript traveling clothes flap on a tall, lean frame. There's an odd, lumpy hat. I frown. "Kaia?"

"Then I'm not hallucinating." My husband does not sound happy, and seeing as he thinks everyone he loves should be protected by his own army and safe behind thick walls, finding his baby sister on the road to Tarva City disguised as a boy must come as an Olympian shock.

With a muttered oath, Griffin urges Brown Horse into a gallop. Squeezing his sides, I direct Panotii to follow, my newly healed ribs aching in mild protest at the increase in speed. Another day of rest would have done them good. Not heaving up my pregnant guts after breakfast every morning for the last few days might have helped, too.

We reach Piers and Kaia and rein in, four sets of hooves kicking up clumps of half-dried mud in the road. Kaia doesn't bother to dismount but launches herself directly into Griffin's arms, landing mostly across his lap. He grunts and grabs her, keeping her from slipping to the ground.

"What are you doing here?" he practically growls. "This is no place for you."

She clings to him, crawling up his chest until his chin knocks her hat askew. A long ribbon of dark hair tumbles loose. Kaia gulps down a breath, but then her face crumples, and she lets out a huge sob.

My heart goes into painful overdrive. Did something happen at home?

"What's wrong? Is everyone all right?" Griffin echoes my worries, anxiety sharpening his words. A deep crease forms between his eyebrows as he takes in his brother's grim face.

Piers looks haggard. *And angry?*

"Is everyone all right?" Kaia repeats, her voice rising shrilly before breaking on a hiccup. Almost violently, she knocks her hat all the way off, getting it out of her face. "I thought you were going to die. Over and over. All of you." She twists her fingers in the front of Griffin's tunic, holding on tight. "Blood. Fire." She turns and spears me with a bloodshot gaze. "Spiders."

My stomach hollows so fast it leaves a gaping hole in my middle. She was at the Games? Fifteen-year-old, sheltered, innocent Kaia was at the Agon Games? How in the name of Zeus and his pet Pegasus did *that* happen?

"But then you didn't. Die, I mean. You just kept going, no matter what. But Carver, I thought he did. He looked so…dead." Sniffling, she wipes the back of her wrist under her nose. Her hand shakes. "And then the news spread that you'd taken over Tarva, but we couldn't get to you. Your new guards didn't know us and wouldn't let us in. *They wouldn't let us in!*"

Kaia balls up her fist and thumps it hard against Griffin's chest. She hits him again, pouring her fear and frustration into her punch rather than into a new rush of tears—tears she seems to be only barely holding back.

I shift uncomfortably in my saddle. We did this to her. And it was my idea to compete in the Games to gain access to the previous Tarvan royals. Because of me, nearly everyone Kaia loves was almost massacred on more than one occasion. Worse, she obviously witnessed the most recent ones.

His jaw flexing, Griffin looks up from his sister's tearstained face. His somber gaze flicks to Piers. "Did you ask the guards to bring us a message?"

Piers nods, keeping his eyes trained solely on Griffin, as if I'm too unsavory to look at. "But so did about a hundred other people every hour, using all sorts of incentives. Saying they were family. Offering bribes." He makes no effort to disguise the bitterness in his voice. "Everyone wants a look at the glorious winners of the Agon Games—and the new Tarvan Alpha couple."

I glance at Griffin. He catches my quick look and frowns. The reason we're out alone, and in our dingiest old traveling gear, is because disguising ourselves and slipping away was the only way past the crowd chanting *"Elpis"* at our new front gate. The meaning behind the name we gave our team in the Agon Games has been spreading, reminding Thalyrians of the ancient and mostly forgotten spirit and personification of Hope: Elpis. And now, the indomitable idea of hope in a world full of ills appears to be contagious. It's expanding far and wide.

If people were so ready for change in Thalyria, it's hard to believe they waited for me to come along to do it. Or, more accurately, for Griffin to push me into doing something about it. No expectations at all seem to have turned into too much expectation overnight, and now all that growing excitement is camped out on our doorstep and serving as a loud and constant reminder that I have a lot to figure out—and soon.

At any rate, we went out the back.

Piers finally looks at me, his expression going from hard to harder. As if reading my mind, he says, "Elpis. How fitting."

So why the irony? I narrow my eyes on the one member of Griffin's family—*my* family—that I just can't seem to like. "You're the only one with something against hope."

"I'm the only one with something against leading my family and friends into bloodbaths!" Piers snaps.

"We're not dead!" I snap back.

"Where's Cassandra?"

The blood drains from my face so fast it leaves my head numb and my hearing dull.

Piers's eyes turn as chilling as winter frost. "They told me she went to fight alongside you in the Games, but then I saw Jocasta, *my sister*, in that terror pit of an arena instead."

I open my mouth to respond, although I don't know what to say. Still, it's my responsibility, just like Cassandra was. But before I can form the awkward words scraping at my tongue, Griffin steps in, his voice even and strong.

"Cassandra left our rooms at night to do unsanctioned reconnaissance. She made that decision herself, and it cost her her life before the Games even started. It wasn't Cat's fault."

Piers pales, his face turning the same shade as the knuckles on the fists clenching his reins. He looks sick, and in that moment, I realize he still hoped, maybe even believed, that Cassandra was alive. She could simply have been somewhere in Castle Tarva with us, off limits, protected behind high walls and slightly overzealous guards.

But she's not. She never saw either of our victories—winning the brutal Agon Games or the successful takeover of Tarva—and it *was* my fault. Partially, at least. My plan to enter the tournament brought her to Kitros. To the arena.

She came because she believed in Griffin and me, to fight for us, for a new Thalyria, and she was the first casualty on our side since I joined this cause.

Slowly, Piers looks away from Griffin. His dark-gray eyes land on me and spark like flint on steel.

The heavy dose of guilt weighing on my chest makes it hard to breathe. "I'm sorry. She was very nice."

The moment I say it, I want to shove the weak platitude back down my throat. Two bright spots appear high on Piers's pale cheeks, and I think he wants to shove my words back down my throat, too, along with his fist. I can hardly blame him.

The muscles in Piers's face twitch, and I think he's just barely holding back the colossal tongue-lashing he wants to give me. Clearly struggling for control, he still urges his horse forward until he's uncomfortably close. When he finally speaks, his voice is so tense and low that it vibrates like the first ominous tremors before a volcano belches up destruction from below.

"Let me get this clear, *Cat*. You stole my second-in-command when I wasn't there to stop it, got her killed, and then replaced a solid, seasoned warrior on your team with my completely untrained sister?"

I swallow. *Gods, I'd hate me, too.* "Jocasta handled herself well in the ring."

"She should never have been in the ring!"

"She wouldn't have been if Cassandra had stayed put!" *Damn it! I want to take that back, too.*

Piers's nostrils flare. "You're blaming a dead woman for putting my sister's life in danger?"

"Your sister volunteered," I answer through gritted teeth. "We needed six people in order to compete. She was courageous and strong."

"She'd be dead if Carver hadn't intervened in the final round. For days, we thought he'd died saving her."

Painful memories filled with heartache and fear hit me like a series of hard punches to the gut, nearly winding me. It was so close. If Selena wasn't frighteningly powerful and a healer beyond compare, we could never have brought Carver back from the brink of death.

Piers drops his reins and balls both his hands into fists, grinding them hard against his thighs. His hands are big and strong, but they don't scare me. Sometimes, I wish he'd go ahead and hit me. Then I could show him just how unfriendly I can be.

"I could have lost three siblings because of your impossible, insane scheme," he bites out.

My eyebrows fly up. "Impossible? It worked! As the victors, we got an audience with the Tarvan royals. In their own home." Ours now, hard won, but without a long and bloody war and with only a handful of lives lost. I'll only regret two casualties: Cassandra and Appoline, the seer princess who protected my unborn child and me at the cost of her own life.

"I'd think my brother was dead right now if I hadn't finally heard otherwise from news at the castle gate!" Piers seethes.

I'm truly sorry for his loss, and his worry, but indignation starts to seethe back. Doesn't he realize what we've accomplished? How many lives we've saved? What we've gained?

"We sent a message home." Griffin's too-even tone means to tread carefully. He's still holding Kaia on his lap, and his fingers flex with tension against her back. "If you'd been where you were supposed to be—*both* of you—you would have known we were all right. And

Cassandra made her own choices. So did Jocasta. So did Carver, for that matter."

"And you sanctioned it! Every part of it. Cat says jump, and you all march blindly to your deaths!"

Griffin's face darkens with anger. I can tell he's barely holding on to his temper, and his tolerance far exceeds mine. Personally, I feel like my head is a geyser, and steam is about to explode from my ears. I understand that Piers is protective and angry, and he has every right to be, but this is about a lot more than losing his second-in-command, or even Jocasta competing in the Games. He's never liked me. At first, it was because I didn't support Griffin's ambitions, or fall blindly into his arms. Now it's because I do? And because I have? I've become an integral part—no, *the lynchpin*—of Griffin's grand design for Thalyria, but that's still not good enough. Or maybe it's too much.

Gods! I can't win with Piers!

Kaia pushes up from Griffin's chest, straightening as she wipes her lingering tears away. Her face is splotched with red. "But they're not dead." She bites her lower lip hard enough to turn it white. Glancing down, she quietly adds, "Except for Cassandra."

Piers flinches. So do I. Then his eyes blaze with anger so fierce I feel it like a physical blow. "You turned my sister into a murderer."

Rage rises up in me, lifting my chin a notch. "She turned herself into a warrior. You should be proud."

"You should be ashamed," Piers shoots back. "Making innocent people fight your war."

My war? I open my mouth to argue, because really, how can I not respond to *that*? But Griffin has apparently heard enough.

"You're talking to my wife and your Alpha," he says.

"The Queen of two realms. Jocasta showed great bravery. And Cassandra wasn't forced into anything. She came by choice, and we lost *one* life instead of thousands. As the person actively recruiting our army for us, you should see the bigger picture, and you should definitely respect your friend's sacrifice."

"As the person recruiting your army, I feel useless. You don't even need it," Piers spits out, glaring at me as if I've single-handedly undermined his life's work.

"We do," Griffin counters. "There's no taking Fisa without a huge fighting force."

"Fisa." Piers huffs a bitter laugh. "So this is all about Cat and her mother? You'll drag all of Thalyria into a war to settle your wife's family squabble? To feed her need for power?"

My jaw drops. Acid coats his every word, and Piers makes everything about me, when I never initiated any of this. Without Griffin, and apparently a few meddling Gods to push me along, I'd still be telling fortunes at the circus, occasionally filling in for the acrobats, lying about my past, ignoring my future, and living as far away from my cruel tyrant of a mother as humanly possible.

"This has nothing to do with a family squabble or any-one's need for power," Griffin answers harshly. "And you know it."

Piers doesn't meet Griffin's eyes. Instead, he and I glare daggers at each other. I have a lot to say, but I somehow keep my mouth shut. I don't want to make things worse.

Kaia slides to the ground between Griffin and me. I back Panotii up a few steps to give her more room. There's the added benefit of putting some distance between Piers and myself without looking like I'm backing down. Because I'm not.

"Why are you out here alone?" Kaia looks around, as

if half expecting the rest of Beta Team to come galloping down the road.

Alpha Team?

Nope. I'll never get used to that.

"Where's everyone else?" she asks.

"Back at the castle," Griffin answers. "They're fine. Cat's friend Selena told us to go see what was on the West Road."

Griffin and I exchange a look. Apparently, we found it.

"We're on the West Road," Kaia says, brightening. "Piers finally gave up. We were leaving for Sinta City, but I convinced him to turn around and try again. I had this… feeling." She wrinkles her nose, scrunching together the few sun-induced freckles she must have picked up over the last couple of weeks.

A feeling? Like the sight? Or a nudge from a God?

With Griffin's immunity to harmful magic, Carver's incredible skill with a sword, and Kaia's "feeling," I have to wonder if this family is as Hoi Polloi as I've always believed. Sometimes magic is a sort of intuition, and their instincts are usually spot-on.

I dismount next to Kaia, feeling stiff and heavy and kind of out of breath, even though I wasn't really moving. All that seems to be a permanent condition at the moment. It started a few days ago, along with the copious vomiting.

"You did the right thing," I tell her. "You should always listen to your gut." I loop my arm around Kaia's waist and squeeze, attempting a casual display of affection. It goes well, I think.

Joining us on the ground, Griffin plants his hands on his hips and gives Kaia a stern look from under lowered brows. She immediately starts shifting from foot to foot. I squeeze her again in encouragement and then drop my arm, stepping back.

"And what, exactly, are *you* doing here?" Griffin demands, his eyes narrowing on his sister. "And why in the name of the *Gods* were you at the Agon Games?"

Griffin is nearly old enough to be Kaia's father and just as authoritative. She moves closer to me and hangs her head, duly intimidated and apparently mute.

"She followed me," Piers says tightly, dismounting as well. "I don't know how she got out of Castle Sinta—dressed like that and with a horse—and I only realized she was on my trail when I was nearly to Kitros."

Resourceful girl. I nudge her arm, smiling a little. And good for her for not giving Piers her secrets.

With a quick flash of a grin, Kaia smiles back, her head still ducked.

If Piers could kill me with the evil eye alone, he would. Griffin doesn't look happy, either, but I don't know if it's because of my nudge and smile, or because Kaia spent time on the road alone.

"I didn't have time to take her back," Piers says in grudging explanation, "so I took her with me."

"To the bloody Agon Games? What were you thinking!" Griffin explodes.

"I didn't know what they'd be like!"

I snort, and Piers has the good sense to try again.

"I didn't know they'd be quite like *that*. It was more horrible and violent than I ever imagined."

I stare at him in disbelief, the fear and pain still fresh in my mind and muscles. *Horrible and violent* doesn't even begin to describe it.

Piers swings his gaze back to me again. "And then there was your victory visit to Castle Tarva. That worked out well for you, didn't it?"

There's a snide undercurrent in Piers's words again,

as if confronting dangerous enemy royals and taking over Tarva were just to satisfy some little whim of mine.

I cross my arms, mainly to keep from reaching out and smacking him. "Would you rather it hadn't worked out, and we'd all died?"

His jaw clenches hard, a muscle bouncing out on one side. "That's not what I said."

"Just what you implied."

He shakes his head, his features tightening in anger once again. "There were other, less dangerous ways to go about it."

"Like what? Throwing nameless, faceless soldiers at Galen Tarva instead of ourselves? He would have opened up a chasm in the ground that swallowed them whole, which is exactly what he tried to do to me in his own throne room. Who's expendable, then? Anyone you don't know?" I glare at Piers, disgusted now. "That's leadership for you."

"Cat…" Griffin's voice holds a hint of warning, urging me to back down. I understand. Soldiers have an important role, and I shouldn't forget it. Griffin knows what armies can do. He's led them.

"Leadership is making wise decisions based on rational thought," Piers snaps.

"Leadership is actually *leading*, not using others as a shield while you shout orders and hop around in the back."

Piers's eyes widen in obvious shock. *Ha!*

Griffin grips my arm above my elbow, squeezing lightly. "Piers fought alongside me. Alongside *us*." By us, he means Carver, Kato, and Flynn. My friends. My team. "And there was no hopping around in the back."

His censorious tone rankles, but I guess I did just shoot my mouth off about something I wasn't there for and didn't really know about.

Frowning slightly, I extract my arm from Griffin's hold. "I know Piers rides out on patrol. I know he can fight." And that's as much of an apology as he'll get.

"How do you plan to hold on to Tarva?" Piers asks. "Taking over a realm isn't the same thing as keeping it."

If you ask me, we've already done the hard part.

"The army you're building might come in useful." *There. Another concession.*

I hear the sarcasm that creeps into my voice, though. So does Griffin. He looks at me sharply, probably disapproving of my hostility.

I almost roll my eyes. If Piers weren't his brother, Griffin would have knocked him senseless by now for speaking to me the way he has.

For Griffin's sake, I attempt a more neutral tone. "Honestly? I don't think it'll be much of an issue if all the Tarvans cheering at the castle gate are any indication. Then again, their last Alpha was a mass-murdering megalomaniac, so it's hard to do worse."

Piers laughs a little—dryly. Does he think I'm worse? *Please.* Galen Tarva leveled an entire neighborhood in his own backyard just to send a message to my mother. He scared her enough that she offered up my unique skills— and me—just to keep him off her back. And when one psychotic monster is frightened of the other... Well, that's saying something.

Piers breathes deeply, the long inhale making his chest expand. His slate-colored eyes meet mine. "Can I speak with you for a moment? Alone."

Wariness tingles up my spine and then sweeps down my arms, making my knife hand twitch. I glance at Griffin. His brow furrows, but he nods, not seeming overly worried about Piers's request. I have no idea what Piers could have to say to me that he can't say in front of Griffin and Kaia. Their presence hasn't exactly been holding him back.

"All right." My reluctant agreement comes with a quick and automatic inventory of any magic I could use to defend myself—none. The magic I absorbed during the Agon Games was lost to injuries and exhaustion afterward, and Piers already knows I can detect lies and turn invisible, so popping out of sight won't even surprise him.

There are always physical weapons. I've got my knives, and a sword, but I doubt Griffin would appreciate my taking a blade to his brother, no matter how annoying Piers might get. Betrayal and backstabbing just aren't done. Not in his family, anyway.

CHAPTER 2

Piers leads me fifty paces from the road. The distance seems excessive to me, but what do I know? I've never had a private argument with him before. I have to skirt tumble bumbles and low-lying scrub that he can just step over with his prowling, long-legged strides. The trek over uneven terrain leaves me winded, and I have to wonder how baby Eleni, who I wasn't even feeling a week ago and who's probably only the size of a little bean, could be so damn heavy all of a sudden.

I'll have to scold her when she comes out. Gently. Maybe. Or maybe not at all?

"Far enough, Piers." I try to mask my shortness of breath with a brusque tone. "What do you want?"

"Give it up," he says plainly. "Stop here."

"Stop here?" I look at my feet.

He scowls, irritated by my deliberate obtuseness. "You've got two realms. Stop before anyone else dies. Anyone *you* care about."

That was low. And hit hard. "I'm not the one orchestrating this. This comes straight from Olympus."

"The Gods have decided that *you* should rule all of Thalyria?" Snide. Again.

"Do you think I can't?" *Do I think I can?* No choice, really. Not anymore.

"I think you're a hotheaded egomaniac, and I have no idea why Griffin puts up with you."

"Awww. I'm blushing." I fan myself because I need to.

The little bean in my belly seems to be heating me from the inside out. "I like you, too."

Piers's face contorts into something rather unattractive for an attractive man. Physically, at least. "You're unbelievable."

I shrug. "I can't help being special."

His face pinches even more. "Stop for a moment and think about what you're doing. You could propel Thalyria into an endless war. It could go on for generations. Is that really the legacy you want?"

"That's already been going on for generations. It's beyond ridiculous to blame me for it."

"The only wars I've seen in my lifetime have been started by you and Griffin."

Actually, that's all Griffin. He took Sinta with an army. He fought battles and won. Then we took over Tarva together with our own blood, sweat, and agony.

"That's only because you hadn't seen a Power Bid yet. And what went on in between realm wars wasn't much better," I point out. "Raids. Thievery. Abuse. There hasn't been lasting peace in centuries."

"There might have been, at least for Sinta."

I shake my head. "All our sources say Sinta was about to get invaded by Acantha Tarva and her endless supply of snakes, and we wouldn't have been able to stop her without the Ipotane."

"Ipotane you risked your lives to ensnare and then didn't even use. Now we have horse-people crawling all over our border for no reason because you took it a step farther before anyone even attacked."

"Isn't that the goal in life?" I ask. "People don't generally say, 'Good job! You took a step back.' We took care of the Tarvan threat and gained a realm in the process. I have no idea why you're being such a prick about it instead of patting us on the backs."

Piers's evil eye turns epic. "The army isn't fully trained or equipped yet, but it's big enough to deter an invasion. Instead, you went ahead with a half-cocked plan that risked my family's safety. And before that, you traded Cassandra's life on a what-if."

No one means more to me than my husband and my team, and if Piers throws Cassandra's death in my face one more time, I swear I'll throw something back.

"Since you were at the Games," I say through gritted teeth, "I'm sure you know she's not the only one who paid in blood."

"She's the only one who's dead." Piers's livid stare cuts straight through me. "And you could have stopped it."

I take a slow, deep breath, striving to control my baser impulses. "What is this really about? Your family? Thalyria? Me? The fact that you don't agree with my choices but other people do?" I scoff. "Pick something and stick to it. Or let's just agree to disagree. I don't have all day."

His eyes narrow. "Too busy being a queen?"

"Yes, actually. And I'm not *a* queen. I'm *the* Queen." I wave my hands around. "There's a lot to do."

"Like invade Fisa?"

His hostile tone is really starting to grate on me, and my patience is far from legendary. That's something I'll have to work on before Little Bean makes her grand appearance.

"Among other things," I answer dryly. Here I am, defending something I don't even want to do. If I never see Mother again, it'll still be too soon. "Are you with us, or against us?" In the end, that's all that really matters.

Piers stiffens all over. "I'm never against my family."

My Kingmaker Magic flares to life with a blast of scorching heat. I feel the exclusion in his words, the truth pummeling me almost as hard as a lie would. To Piers, I'm not part of his family.

Even coming from someone I've never gotten along with, being so clearly set apart stings.

"Griffin wants to unite the three realms. That was *his* idea. You know that, and it was Poseidon who pushed him in my direction. Zeus, Hades, Athena, and Artemis have all helped us in some way. They're backing us, and all we want is to make Thalyria a place worth living in again, like it used to be before the kingdom split and the Alphas turned all greedy and demented. Working against me means working against Griffin and everything he hopes to accomplish." I study Piers, looking for some sign of the reason and intelligence on which he prides himself. "You must see that."

"Then why did he crown you? Why is he putting the power in your hands instead of his own?"

Frankly, I wish he wasn't. Griffin knows that. So does everyone we're close to—I thought. But I've learned the hard way that the Fates don't just go away. They dog your heels and bite you in the back. Destiny isn't something you can ignore, and in my case, Griffin made sure of it.

Piers wasn't there when we told the rest of Griffin's family about our time on the Ice Plains. They must have filled him in, but I say it again. "Artemis told us I'm the Origin. In essence, the new beginning. That means what-ever we construct—hopefully a unified Thalyria where people aren't living in fear of their royals most of the time—somehow starts with me. But Griffin and I will rule together. Of course we will."

"Until you decide you want all the power for yourself."

I look at him, completely taken aback. Is Piers blind? Deaf? "When have I ever given any indication of wanting that?"

"It's in your blood," he says flatly. "You won't be able to stop yourself."

"Oh, that's fair." I toss up my hands. "If your father was a murderer, I should just assume you're one, too?"

His eyes narrow. "You are a murderer."

My jaw drops in outrage. "I am *not* my mother."

"Yet. And you're still a murderer."

He's completely convinced. My magic only used to detect lies, except on very rare occasions. Truths mainly came to me as a natural by-product of falsehoods. Since I met Griffin, my magic can also flare hot and painful for truly strong, heartfelt honesty. Right now, the burn in my bones is telling me that Piers means every word.

"I've only ever killed in self-defense. Or in the defense of others," I say past the knot forming in my chest. "You've fought in a war. How is that any different from what I've done?"

"I saw you in the Games. That's killing for sport."

"We didn't go there for fun. Or glory." Anger and emotion are starting to get the upper hand and staying calm takes a real effort. "We went hoping to win the opportunity to confront Galen and Acantha Tarva without putting anyone in danger but ourselves. And we spared anyone we reasonably could in the arena, even the creatures. More people made it out of those Agon Games alive than they have in centuries."

Piers sneers. "Oh, yes. *Elpis*. I forgot."

That's it. Fury heats my blood to the boiling point, and if it were possible to actually see red, I would. "I've had enough. Go home. Don't help. Be impartial if you want to, just don't get in my way."

"*My* way?" Piers loads enough scorn into his voice to sink a ship. "See? It's starting already."

The urge to pummel him rocks me hard. I curl my hands

into fists, but I turn on my heel and walk away before I do something I'll regret.

"Bloody sanctimonious bastard," I mutter as I start back toward Griffin and Kaia. Being moved to physical violence is the easy and natural path for me, and my whole body almost vibrates with the need to pounce and pound. I'm trying to control myself and learn better habits, but Piers is making it hard.

He suddenly grabs my wrist from behind and jerks me to a stop. I swing around, just barely stopping myself from punching him with my free hand. My lips draw back in a snarl, baring my teeth, and I have to hold on to my thigh to keep my fist from flying up. I'm too filled with rage to hear what he's saying at first, but then I realize the pattern is a chant, and the words are familiar.

No! Dread slams into me, replacing my fury with fear. I've heard those ancient words before, on the Ice Plains. Only there, different rules applied. Here...

"Stop!" I cry, trying to break his grip on my wrist. "You don't know what you're doing!"

Piers talks faster, louder. He's Hoi Polloi, but that doesn't matter. You don't need to be Magoi to make this work.

His stone-cold eyes glint with determination, and I let my fist fly, trying to punch him in the throat. I get him, but not hard enough to shut him up. His next words come out hoarse but still too distinct to break the flow of the chant. He starts a new, treacherous repetition, bringing us all closer to terrible danger.

Jerking hard on the wrist he's holding, I pull him closer and plant my foot in his groin. Or try to. He's quick and pivots. I hit his hip, jarring the bones in my foot and ankle. Piers hardly moves, absorbing the blow in the same way Griffin would have. He keeps chanting.

"Cat!" Griffin shouts my name from the road. Panic wells up, making my heart pump double time. He can't be here for this.

I shift my stance and send a quick and powerful knee toward Piers's gut. He swipes his free arm down and blocks me with his forearm, throwing me off-balance. Before I can recover, he spins me around and pulls me up against his chest, limiting my mobility.

"Cat!"

I look up and see Griffin coming for me at a dead sprint. Piers wraps both his arms around my torso, squeezing and lifting me to my toes. My leverage is gone, and I can hardly breathe with my chest flattened under muscles that are thicker and stronger than I ever thought. I grab for my knives, but I have to reach over Piers's arms, and my fingers just barely graze the hilts. There's no way I'll get them out of my belt loops like this.

"Stop chanting!" I claw at his arms, digging my fingernails into his skin. Blood slicks the backs of his forearms and coats my palms. "It's not too late!"

The old words keep tumbling into my ears, fast and low. I bang him in the shins with my boot heels, but Piers ignores me, my thumping feet, and my scraping nails. He begins another repetition.

Part of me knows I'm not fighting him as hard as I could. Respect and affection for Griffin's family hold me back. And Piers will stop. This is just to scare me, to get me to back off. *Isn't it?*

I use my head to crack him in the jaw. His chant stumbles, but only for a moment, and I see stars.

Griffin is almost on top of us now, a look of absolute fury twisting his face. Kaia isn't far behind.

"Run!" I shout to him. "Take Kaia and run!"

My voice holds enough of the panic I'm feeling to make him hesitate. He slows, his near-wild eyes swinging back and forth between his sister and me.

"Get her out of here!" I scream with the last of my breath.

Piers's grip tightens painfully, and he starts backing away from them, dragging me with him. He shows no sign of abandoning his folly, forcing me to trade his safety for ours. I stop hesitating and try to muster the lightning that would definitely—and possibly permanently—shut him up.

Nothing happens. No lightning. Not even a spark. The Olympian magic in my blood has a fickle mind of its own, and it fails me yet again. Only panic leaps through my veins, along with an icy current of dread.

"Let. Cat. Go." Griffin's demand is low and furious. He stalks forward in a rage.

Horror floods me anew. *Why doesn't anyone listen to me? When I say* run, *you run!*

Piers continues to drag me back. One step. Two. Crushing my lungs. I struggle to breathe.

"What are you chanting?" Griffin keeps advancing on us, but he holds out a hand to keep Kaia back. "What's going on?"

I try in vain to reach my lightning again. Even though he doesn't fully understand what's happening, I know from Griffin's expression that he'll fight his own brother down to blood and bone in order to set me free.

As a last, desperate resort, I twist furiously in Piers's arms and scream like a lunatic. It stops Griffin in his tracks and seems to startle Piers into loosening his grip. Feeling the change in pressure around my ribs, I stop thrashing and drop. My deadweight breaks his hold. I land in a crouch and then take off at a sprint, yelling for Griffin and Kaia to *run!*

Thank the Gods, they spin and run without question, knowing I'm not far behind. I'm fast, but Griffin and Kaia quickly outdistance me. Griffin looks back, hesitating, and I gesture frantically for him to keep going. I don't look back, and I don't slow down, even when my lower belly tightens, and the muscles there feel like they're turning to stone. Piers is chasing me, and I'm guessing he's as swift as the rest of his family. I run faster than I ever have in my life, my legs flying and my chest burning.

I'm halfway to the road when Piers hits my back. Everything tilts, I go weightless for a sickening second, and then we both hit the ground with a bone-jarring thud. I just barely keep my head up, and the ground scrapes my bare arms raw from palms to elbows as we skid across the dirt. Piers ends up sprawled flat-out across my back, and I wheeze a frightened sound, terrified of having knocked little Eleni loose, even though I know she's been through worse.

Griffin shouts my name again, and every protective instinct in me rebels. *Don't come back!*

Footsteps thunder in my direction. Piers is as heavy and solid as a Centaur. He's somehow still chanting as he pushes me into the hard-packed earth. Fright chokes off what little air I have left. He's almost done, and I can't let this happen. Griffin and Kaia are too close.

I free an elbow and swing back wildly, hitting some-where that makes Piers grunt the last word of the final repetition, sealing our fates forever. *Ares.*

He just summoned the God of War.

CHAPTER 3

PIERS SPRINGS OFF ME, SPITTING A CURSE AS HE BACKS AWAY. I flip over and surge to my feet. Air flows more freely into my lungs again, but I still feel like I can't breathe.

"What in the name of the Gods is going on?" Griffin bellows, charging the last few feet to me. He came back. He'll always come for me, and Kaia is right behind.

I throw out my hands. "No, Griffin! Stop!"

A deafening roar sets off a series of explosions in my head, painful, like magic punches to the brain. Then the ground shakes as a man—no, *Ares*—drops from the sky like a meteorite, hitting the ground with a colossal boom.

The earth cracks all around him. Fissures branch out in an enormous web that tangles beneath our feet. We lurch, trying to steady ourselves as the ground rattles with the force of Olympus itself.

Griffin grabs my arm, keeping me upright. With his other hand, he latches on to Kaia. I gasp, reeling from the staggering amount of power suddenly saturating the air around us. This is no ethereal, regal entrance like Artemis made on the Ice Plains. The stealthy and light-footed Goddess of the Hunt wove through our senses like moonbeams on a melody. This is the God of War landing like a thunderclap in our midst.

Griffin's eyes widen, turning frantic with growing comprehension. He shoves both Kaia and me behind him with such a hard thrust that we bang together like two hands clapping. Then Griffin backpedals, forcing us to move back with him.

I twist enough to peer around my husband's arm. Piers is on the far side of Ares, facing him in awe—and apparent satisfaction. The God is looking back at him, at the person who did the summoning, and all we see is the broad and muscled back of the most enormous male I've ever laid eyes on. He's bare from the waist up and wearing a wide, bronze-studded belt that's fully loaded with weapons of all shapes and sizes. The flat sides of multiple blades, each one more lethal-looking than the previous, brush his thick, leather-clad legs.

"No one has summoned me in an age." Ares's voice is rich and deep. So is the chuckle that washes over me like a warm wave. It reminds me of a dangerous ocean swell, the kind with an unpredictable undertow. It'll drag you under and dash you against the rocks if you don't know how to swim the waters.

And this right here? I don't think any of us knows how to navigate this.

Ares speaks again. "This promises to be interesting."

I wince. *Or heartbreaking.*

I tap Griffin's arm, and he angles his head enough that our eyes catch for a split second while I hold a finger to my lips. If we're silent and still, maybe Ares won't notice us?

Before Griffin's gaze turns back around, I see the same haunted fear I'm feeling building in his eyes. He knows what his brother did.

Call a God, lose a soul. One of us isn't leaving here with the others.

Ares dips his head, and hair the color of polished olive wood glints in the sun. It brushes his massive shoulders, the thick locks a tawny blond liberally streaked with darker tones. "I see. This is about the woman you call a warmonger."

An explosive jolt of adrenaline sends my heart

slamming against my ribs. My pulse leaps in response to the accelerated beat. The Gods aren't joking when they say they know everything.

My lower belly tightens again, suddenly feeling like lead.

Piers nods and then jerks his head at me. The ratter. So much for staying quiet and hidden. "She's violent and a brute. She'll fit right in with you."

Violent and a brute? Fit right in with you? Did he just insult an enormous God? He certainly offended me.

The muscles across Ares's back stiffen. "That's your only request? To take her away?"

Terror beats through me. I can't leave Griffin. There's baby Eleni on the way!

But if it's not me, then it's Griffin or Kaia. That simply can't happen. I won't let it.

Griffin's grip digs into my arm as he goes impossibly rigid. I feel more than hear his breath hitch and know the sickening whoosh of betrayal is sweeping through his body like an ax cleaving him in two.

"Only request?" The slightly baffled look on Piers's face makes me think he translated the old parchments wrong. You don't call a God just to get rid of someone. There are weapons for that, sometimes bare hands, and if you're a sneak and a cheat, there's always poison. You don't call a God to do that kind of dirty work. You call a God to request something epic, something you can't possibly accomplish on your own. Losing a soul close to you is the consequence, a payment of sorts—one people finally caught on to. That's why they eventually hid the scrolls, burying them deep in the archives of the knowledge temples.

Clearly, they should have buried them even deeper.

"Believe me, she's enough," Piers finally says with enough acidity to practically slap me in the face.

I stare, horrified on so many levels. He's unbelievable. And criminally shortsighted. Piers has done the unthinkable, so he might as well at least help the brother whose heart he's tearing out. I can hardly believe it; it's so unconscionable. He doesn't even want *the God of War's* assistance to help Griffin conquer Fisa?

Ares folds his arms across his chest, making his monstrous biceps bulge. Something in the Olympian's expression must make Piers think the God needs some convincing.

"She'll fight well for you wherever she goes." Piers's eyes connect with mine from across a space of cracked ground and palpable power. "She's like a wild animal when she smells blood. Unstoppable."

I snort. I can't help it. That's probably the most insulting compliment I've ever heard.

"Do you mean to say that you called me from Olympus for no reason?" Ares demands.

Oh, he has a reason. Piers wants me permanently removed from Thalyria—and from his brother's life—without having to kill me himself. He'd rather I become a slave to War and battle across the worlds until my inevitable, lonely, and possibly quick demise. *Gah! What a prince.*

For the first time, Piers looks uncertain. "I'm giving her a chance to do what she does best—fight. She left me no choice. She's vicious, power-hungry, and won't see reason. She's placing everyone I care about in danger."

I'm not any of those things! Well, I can be a little savage. And maybe I don't always see reason…

"Piers…" Griffin chokes out his brother's name. I've never heard a sound like that come out of his mouth before, and it breaks my heart. A horrible pressure clamps down on my chest as what's about to happen really sinks in, but it's Griffin's total devastation that nearly brings me to my knees.

Piers glances over at us. We must look like a trio of ghosts. His chin lifts, and his shoulders go back. From his stiff, self-righteous body language alone, I know he's utterly convinced he's doing the right thing. Saving Griffin from me. Saving everyone.

Does he really think that passing off the responsibility to Ares means passing off the guilt and blame? Griffin will *never* forgive him for this. And neither will I. When I die, I swear to the Gods I'll haunt the banks of the Styx until Piers gets there. I'll make him pay for ripping Griffin and me apart. He'll pay forever, in this world, and in the next.

Tucked behind Griffin with me, Kaia takes a shuddering breath. Visibly shaking, she looks at me with tears tracking down her face. "How could he?"

Sudden heat bursts behind my eyes. "Be brave," I whisper, for her sake as well as mine.

Nodding, she presses her lips together and blinks her tears away. I force mine not to come.

"You're Hoi Polloi," Ares states. He still hasn't turned around. Our insignificance couldn't be more obvious.

Piers's hands clench at his sides. "I may not have magic in my blood, but I knew what that chant did. I understood."

"You understood too much. And not enough." Ares steps toward Piers. "Even Magoi don't use that incantation anymore. And definitely not below the Ice Plains. Those scrolls were hidden centuries ago. There might have been a good reason for that, don't you think?"

Piers's eyes flick toward us again, over his brother and sister. His throat bobs, and some of the certainty and color drain from his face. Does he finally comprehend the danger he's put them in? Is he feeling some of our dread?

Actually, I don't care how he feels. My sympathy for Piers died a fiery death and became nonexistent the moment he decided to rip me from my husband and toss me from this world.

"I don't see a warmonger here." The pervasive rumble of power in Ares's almost cavernous voice seems to hold all the knowledge and secrets of shifting time and earth. For some reason, it strikes me as oddly familiar. "If anyone courts war, it's your brother. Should I take him? Or your young sister? Shall I take her across the worlds and throw her into endless battles? See how long she lasts?"

"No!" Piers's denial is immediate and heartfelt. His eyes shoot wide open in alarm.

Now he gets it. He summoned Ares, and a soul has to go with the God, but Piers doesn't get to choose which one.

"You want me to take Catalia Fisa?"

Piers nods stiffly, and I can only imagine how deeply his actions cut into Griffin's loyal heart. I can hardly believe Piers's animosity toward me extends this far. He constantly rubs me the wrong way, but I never once thought about eliminating him. And he thinks *I'm* vicious and unreasonable?

"You would deprive your brother of his wife?" Ares asks.

Griffin's hold slides to my wrist and then turns painful, as if the strength of his fingers alone could keep me from being torn away from him. I grip his forearm back with my free hand, anchoring myself to him. But if Ares decides to take me, there'll be no stopping him.

And it will be me. It has to be. I won't let him take Griffin or Kaia.

Trembling violently now, Kaia looks at me again. Her lips are white, her eyes huge. She's monstrously frightened. I wonder if I look the same.

Ares takes another step toward Piers, ignoring us

completely. "You would deprive him of his unborn child, growing right now inside his wife's womb?"

Piers's gaze snaps back to us. His nostrils flare on a sharp inhale, and his expression changes entirely, turning first blank with shock and then flooding with undisguised horror. He takes a step back, almost stumbling. His body language sends a whole new message now. Family does mean something to him, maybe everything. He can convince himself it's okay to get rid of me, the Fisan Magoi warmonger, even if it hurts his brother, but he'd never banish someone of his own blood.

I narrow my eyes, charging my expression with biting accusation. *Thanks, Uncle Piers. You're doing a fabulous job of welcoming little Eleni into the family.*

His mouth opens. Closes. His boots scrape backward through the dirt. "Perhaps I was…hasty."

You think? I want to scream at him. Words of disgust and blame almost detonate in my mouth, but I don't want to draw Ares's attention to us.

In silence, Griffin and I hold on to each other desperately. I know he must be gripping Kaia just as hard. Despite Piers's sudden turnaround, no hope lifts my leaden heart. You don't cast the dice in a gambling game with the Gods and then hope to back out before play is done.

Kaia must know that as well as anyone. Her erratic breathing turns so loud it snaps my focus back to her. She's staring at my belly.

"Too late," Ares says flatly, confirming my worst fears. "Call a God, lose a soul. But I can't take Talia."

He can't? But that means… *No. No. No! Not Griffin!*

Griffin seems to unbend a fraction. His hold on my wrist changes, but probably only to shift his tighter grip to Kaia. She flinches in reaction, but I don't know if it's because her arm hurts under Griffin's iron hand, or because her chances of being taken away by Ares just went from one in three to a full fifty percent.

My throat closes up until I can barely swallow. *Gods, this can't be happening.*

Wait? Did Ares just call me Talia? A new ripple of unease tingles the length of my spine. Only people from my past and my blood family—or what's left of them—call me that.

"The laws of Olympus forbid me to take two souls at once. She's with child, and therefore carrying a second soul inside her. But I wouldn't take her anyway. Not after we spent years putting her in place."

He's talking about my destiny. *Destroyer of realms.* I thought I was finally coming to terms with my fate, but the churning inside me says otherwise. Or maybe that's Little Bean. Right now, it's hard to tell.

"Years' worth of people and events carefully watched and nudged in order to urge the Origin toward her throne. All that effort undermined in an instant because you can't see farther than your own nose? Because you can't compete in your brother's eyes with his wife's power and knowledge? Because they are both so much more than you will ever be?"

Ares's anger seems to rip all the air from around us. Suddenly, I can't breathe, and then there's a fist-like tightening in my gut.

I grab my lower belly. "Griffin?"

He looks down at me just as my womb seizes, contracting painfully. I can deal with the pain. It's the abrupt terror that's hard to take. I let out a deep groan that doesn't help me at all but that makes Griffin go even paler than before. He lets go of Kaia, instinctively reaching for me.

At the same time, cool fingers land on the back of my neck, pushing down. Strong currents of magic nip at my hairline and then spread out through the rest of me.

"Bend over." Selena's familiar voice joins her healing touch. "Breathe."

The moment she touches me, some of the pain and panic subside. Confusion takes their place. We left her at Castle Tarva hours ago. I have no idea how she got here, but her presence brings instant comfort and soothing relief. Griffin grunts something in surprise, probably at her sudden appearance, but I keep my head down, letting the blood flow back into it.

"Where did you come from?" I brace my hands on my knees as another wave of tightness grips my belly. Selena is shockingly powerful and probably the best healer of our time—not to mention Hades's lover—but even after eight years of being more-or-less mothered by her, I had no idea she could appear out of thin air.

Selena doesn't answer, which doesn't surprise me. Her hand tightens on my nape, keeping my head down. "Breathe," she says again.

Griffin squats down next to me, peering into my face. A deep groove settles into the space between his eyebrows. His color isn't good. "*Agapi mou?*"

"What's happening?" I ask him, my voice reedy with fear.

A shadow flits through Griffin's eyes. He shakes his head, looking anxious and at a loss. He doesn't know, either. Or maybe we both do, and neither of us wants to admit it.

His wide mouth flattens, whitening, and then he touches my face with a light caress that brings an instant sting to my eyes. The rough tips of his fingers slide gently over my cheek to carefully tuck a dangling twist of hair behind my ear. I take a shuddering breath, and his frown deepens. I can tell he wants to reassure me, but Griffin won't lie to me. Or to himself.

I blink hard, just barely holding back tears. I think Eleni is in trouble. What if I lose her?

Selena smooths her hand down my spine and then back up to my neck, making a shushing sound. "She'll be fine. If I had to guess, which I don't, I'd say your little Eleni is protesting her uncle's idiocy." She rubs my back again in a slow, even rhythm. As she does, healing magic seeps into me, and the worst of the cramping starts to subside. I breathe more easily with each stroke of her power-charged hand.

"But she's still tiny." My voice wavers. I can't stop the tremor in it. "Like a bean."

Selena makes a low sound that's not quite a laugh. "Look at her parents. She may be tiny, but she's a pow-erhouse and not to be underestimated, even at this stage."

Really? Oh my Gods. Am I going to have to figure out disciplining her before she's even out? I can't have her making me sick every time someone does something stupid. Okay, incredibly stupid, but still…

"You were just as aware early on as she is. You simply don't remember it now."

"But *this* early?" I shake my head. "That's not possible."

Selena sighs, her hand stopping on my nape. "Everything is possible. And I thought you were finally past denial as your knee-jerk reaction."

I try to straighten, feeling better now. Physically, at least. There's still a whole lot to worry about—namely, Ares—but Selena keeps my head down.

"Don't mince your words or anything. And let me up," I demand.

She gives my neck a quick squeeze before lifting her hand. Under other circumstances, the gesture might have felt reassuring.

"I suppose it's finally time to have this out." Selena sounds like she's grumbling, and I've never known her to do something as churlish as grumble before.

I push my hair back from my face as I slowly straighten up. "Have what ou—"

The word dies on my lips, and my insides lurch in a way that has nothing to do with Little Bean's lingering protests. Ares finally turned around.

"Thanos?" I breathe, not believing my eyes.

The weight inside me lifts, bubbling up like air under water. Elation and bewilderment leave me dizzy, like I've been knocked senseless, even though I'm somehow still standing. A giddy spiral of emotion sweeps me backward in time. Memories flit like colorful mosaics through my mind, some good, some bad, some painful, some messy and chaotic. All with a constant—Thanos. The broad cheekbones, strong nose, deep-set eyes, and multiple scars are the same as I remember, but everything else is bigger. More. This incredibly potent male is taller, more muscled, broader—and my childhood protector was already gigantic to begin with.

Ares flashes me the rare grin I saw only occasionally as a girl. "Hello, little monster." Even his voice is fuller, richer, round with power.

I stop breathing and simply stare, incapable of anything else. When I blink, he's still there, still Thanos, and yet he's not. He's a *God*.

Swaying on my feet, I stumble forward. Griffin reaches for me, maybe to stop me, maybe to steady me. I don't know because I brush past his hand and keep going,

suddenly running. I don't stop. I can't. I crash into the God
of War and throw my arms around his Titan-sized waist,
burying my face in the center of his bare torso. He smells of
iron, fire, and wind, just like he always did. Arms the size
of tree trunks close around me, engulfing my entire upper
body. My shaky inhale shudders between us. I barely hold
back a sob.

The fear and dread crushing my chest disappear, and
whatever Selena did with her healing touch seems to have
calmed Little Bean. Ares is Thanos. *My* Thanos. He practically raised me. Everything will be all right. Before I ever
knew Selena's fresh rain and budding leaves perfume or
Griffin's light citrus and sunshine scent, Thanos's unique
blend of warrior male and primal elements was the smell
of rescue and refuge, of my invincible house.

I pull back, ball up my fist, and then pound Thanos on
his bulging pectoral. "You left me!"

"You walked out of Castle Fisa on your own two feet."
He looks down at me with a warm expression that does
little to dispel the hurt I've been carrying around inside me
for more than eight years.

I thump his chest again as hard as I can. "And you
refused to come with me."

Thanos's expression sours as he shoots a heated glare at
Selena. "It was her turn. It was decided."

"Decided?" I echo. "By whom?"

He turns back to me, half his face in shadow. The other
half is bronzed, battered, and beautiful. "And you were getting far too pretty and grown up to stay in my care."

His voice gives nothing away. Neither does his expression, but my heart starts galloping like someone just hit it
with a whip. When I begged him to run away with me, did
he want to?

"From birth, you were spoken for," he adds quietly, as if reading my thoughts. "As am I."

I swallow. Ares and Aphrodite. Thanos is Ares. If the legends are true, Aphrodite is the only one of the Gods who can stand him. I don't know why. He's powerful, protective, and discriminately violent. In my eyes, perfect.

I glance at Griffin. The man I married. The father of my child. *From birth, you were spoken for.*

Griffin has always felt so right. I love him. I had no hope of resisting him, even though I tried. He's always saying I was made for him, *meant* for him, but from the shocked and almost stricken look on his face, I think he's more focused on my obvious adoration of the God of War and on my running into another male's arms than on the fact that he was right about us all along.

I step back from Ares. Whatever romantic feelings I had for him are long gone, leaving only the reality that for the first fifteen years of my life, he saved me every time I truly needed it. He also let me get hurt. A lot.

A sliver of pain pricks my heart. And he let me walk off, alone and utterly devastated by my sister's death, without seeming to care what happened next.

Ares looks at me sharply, his wide brow furrowing.

My nostrils flare. *Is* he reading my thoughts?

"How are you feeling now?" Selena's voice is back to being like a mist-cloaked stream on a spring morning—slightly lilting, cool, mysterious. It soothes me.

I glance at my belly, as if the still-flat surface should reveal something of note. "Fine. I guess she's over her outburst. Or sleeping."

"Good." Selena very pointedly inserts herself between Ares and me.

Does she think Thanos would hurt me?

The God's tawny eyebrows slam down. The same glinting, bluish-green eyes I remember from my childhood flare with anger, but now, tiny bursts of light skip along their power-bright surfaces. "Lightning bolts on Olympus, woman! What do you think I'm going to do to her?" Ares growls.

Selena shrugs, looking him up and down with visible distaste. "Squash her? You're not exactly delicate."

"She used to fit in the palm of my hand. I bounced her on my knee and tickled her. If I didn't crush her then, there's no chance of my doing it now."

So that just exponentially increased the weird factor of my one-time crush. In my defense, it didn't develop until later, along with breasts and hips.

I glance at Griffin again. His jaw is bulging so much that it looks like he's trying to break his own teeth, but I appreciate his silence. Maybe he's still absorbing all this. Maybe he's overwhelmed. I know I am, and I grew up with these two.

Ares roughly shoves Selena aside to get a clear view of me again. I've never seen anyone manhandle Selena, and it startles a gasp out of me. But with the ease of an Amazon warrior, she recovers her lost ground and then retaliates with a hard hit of her own. Ares lowers his head, getting ready to charge. Selena shifts her balance, magic swells in the air, biting at my skin, and I see a clash of epic proportions coming that could knock us all into the next realm.

"Stop!" I cry, jumping between them. These two are the closest I've ever had to a real mother and father, despite both my parents still being alive, and it's surprisingly painful to see them at odds. It's probably not a good idea to get between them when they're angry and primed for a fight, but if there's one person in this world I don't think either of them will hurt—at least not on purpose—it's me.

"What in the name of the Gods is going on?" Piers demands.

I snap my head around to glare at him. In fact, we all do.

"I thought he was the smart one." Ares gestures impatiently toward Piers. His words probably make Griffin bristle even more. I don't know. I don't look.

Okay, I look. Griffin appears to be more intensely worried than angry. He's frozen in place and keeping Kaia behind him, looking like he's not sure what to do—something I know must not sit well with him.

"You. Summoned. Me." Ares's drawn-out, mocking tone calls into question Piers's vaunted intelligence. "Now I have to take someone off to endless war. Very. Good. Plan."

The God coats each word in layers of sarcasm, but I see no humor anywhere. In fact, I feel sick again.

Piers lifts his arm and points at Selena. "Take her!"

Selena makes an incredulous sound. Part laugh. Part snort. I hardly hear it because blood roars in my ears, and something inside of me snaps. My relief was so potent, so profound. But now that reassurance has been ripped away again, and it's all Piers's fault.

I lunge at Piers so fast he doesn't see me coming. My fist hits his nose. While his head is still snapping back and crimson beads are flying through the air in a perfect, gory arc, I get behind him and smash one foot into the back of his knee, ignoring the flare of pain just hitting my knuckles now. The leg buckles, and he drops.

I have no idea how I moved so fast. It's unnatural, like a blur. I don't stop there. I slam the flat of my hand down between his shoulder blades and send him sprawling face-first into the dirt. I checked myself at the last second, a tiny shift. If I'd hit him any higher, I might have broken his neck. Part of me wonders why I didn't.

Power springs from deep within, snapping and rolling through my veins. I feel it connecting every part of me. Blood. Flesh. Bone. My hair vibrates at the roots, rising on a tide of unchecked magic. Lightning webs down my arms. It bursts from my palms and chars the ground at my feet. The earsplitting crack of thunder seems to come straight from the hollow in my chest and shatter outward, annihilating what little restraint I have left.

Piers twists and looks up at me. His eyes widen. His jaw drops. I see him through a haze of magic—his shocked expression, his broken nose, the sudden fear in his eyes.

My ire grows, swelling along with my magic. He chose the wrong Magoi to cross. I am descended from Gods. I have ichor in my veins. Olympian power. He's a threat to me, to my family, to all the people I love. I'm about to lose control all over him, and frankly, I don't give a damn.

CHAPTER 4

I POUNCE ON PIERS, READY TO DO SOME SERIOUS DAMAGE, BUT Griffin grabs me around the waist and drags me back. I wrench in his hold. Violence pumps through my veins like liquid fire. Lightning coats my entire body, and the magic storm jumps to Griffin, crackling around us both until we're lit up like a pair of blazing torches.

I snarl. *Stupid, unpredictable magic. Now it works? Earlier would have been better!*

"Hold, Cat." Utterly immune to any magic that could harm him, Griffin is like a grounding rod, and all that deadly, flashing power crashes straight down. The ground under our feet begins to smoke and stink.

"Calm yourself," he grates in my ear, his implacable grip immobilizing me.

"But he just condemned Selena!" She might frustrate the magic out of me sometimes with her vagueness and secrecy, but I love her. I rely on her. She gave me shelter and a home. And now she'll be gone!

I buck and growl, twisting furiously in Griffin's steely arms. Lightning cracks, and thunder echoes back at me.

"Think of little Eleni." The stubble on Griffin's jaw scratches my temple as he curls me inward against him, squeezing. "And remember, it's not Piers who decides. There are no good choices here. And don't prove him right by turning into exactly what he thinks you are."

He thinks I'm a vicious killer. Who enjoys it.

Like the quick, startling sting of a whip, shame lashes

me. I stop thrashing. Griffin is right. I shouldn't have attacked Piers. I should have been more mindful of Eleni.

Out of the corner of my eye, I catch Kaia's terrified gaze. She's looking at me like you do when you come across something both so dreadful and so astonishing that you don't know whether to watch in fascination or to run for your life.

That's me—dreadful and fascinating. *What a mix.*

Lightning abruptly stops leaping from my body, settling roughly back into whatever mostly inaccessible well it resides in.

"She wouldn't be half as belligerent if she'd grown up with me." Selena crosses her arms, apparently wholly unconcerned by her potential impending doom.

Ares scowls. "She wouldn't be half as *alive* if she'd grown up with you."

"I beg to differ," Selena responds coolly.

"Beg all you want. I'm still right."

"I'm very effective."

"You make rainbows and heal people."

"You make war and kill people."

"I taught her well." Pride gleams in Ares's eyes. "She just brought down a man a head taller than she is and twice as heavy without even trying."

Selena scoffs. "Her exceptional reflexes are hardly your doing."

"Or yours," Ares says with narrowed eyes.

I'm not sure what they mean by that, but I glance at Piers, not proud of myself. To Griffin, I say, "You can let me go now."

Griffin's arms drop away, but he dips his dark head toward mine and rumbles, "I don't blame you for protecting the people you love." His words absolve me to a certain extent, and the stony expression he turns on Piers would make any man quake.

Piers pushes himself up from the ground. His nose is out of alignment. There's blood everywhere and a raw scrape down his jaw. He spits out crimson saliva and then shoves his nose back into place. Mostly. And with barely a wince. He doesn't look entirely steady, but he doesn't look like he's about to fall down, either. Maybe I should have hit him harder.

Training his eyes on Ares, Piers flicks his blood-stained fingers toward Selena. "I called you, and I say she should go."

I shake my head, my lip curling in disdain at how easily he throws people away. There's also no doubt in my mind that if it weren't for the baby, he'd still wish it were me.

Great. Even in a family where I thought I was finally safe and welcome, there's a brother to stab me in the back. Disappointed as I am, far worse than stabbing me in the back is the fact that Piers has just cut out Griffin's heart and placed both my husband and Kaia in grave danger.

Ares's huge hands land hard on his hips. He shakes his head. "He really is an idiot. I can't take Persephone."

There's a single beat of my heart, a breath, before I understand what Ares just said. My eyes widen, and I turn to look at Selena so fast I nearly fall down. I leave my jaw somewhere on the ground behind me. "Persephone?"

"Finally." With a deep breath, Selena lifts her hands and tilts her head back, as if offering praise to Olympus. "Really, Cat. You should have figured that out."

"I should... I-I..." I gape at her, my heart pounding like a thousand feet marching into the unknown. The rest of me goes numb with shock. Even Little Bean seems stunned. Well, she doesn't react, anyway. Maybe she already knew? "But Persephone has to spend six months of the year in the Underworld."

Selena raises perfect blonde eyebrows, her expression turning incredulous. "But I do."

"But...but...you..." I shut up. I'm incoherent at this point.

Selena—*Persephone*—takes pity on me at last. "It's a common misconception that they have to be six *consecutive* months. I have half a dozen worlds in which to start the springtime. I can't do them all at once. They're staggered. Besides..." She leans in, adding, "You can't possibly think I'd share Hades with another female."

I blink. No. I've always had trouble imagining that.

Before our eyes, Selena sheds whatever magic was making her look human all this time. She's still her, with delicate features; high, arching brows; startling blue eyes; thick, silky hair; and obvious innate power. But now she's *more*. Just like Thanos, she's taller, stronger, and even more awe-inspiring in every way.

She rolls her shoulders and moves her neck from side to side, as if adjusting to her new dimensions. "Ah. Better." The Goddess spears Piers with an irate look. "Cat has a clear destiny here in Thalyria. Ares can't take her, and not only because of the two-souls thing. And despite his faults, I doubt Ares is interested in ripping her husband from her. So, not only did you betray your brother in the worst possible way, but you've doomed your little sister to a lifetime with *him*." She jerks her head toward Ares, her dislike as clear as the crystalline waters off the Fisan coast.

Kaia's sharp, frightened inhale yanks out my heart and sends it spiraling into the pit of my stomach. I should have been nicer to Piers, or at least tried to get along. If I had, Kaia wouldn't be paying the price right now.

"No." My palm up, I reach out to Ares, beseeching. "Please."

The God of War looks Kaia over, assessing her. Kaia pales even more under his scrutiny and inches closer to Griffin.

Griffin's eyes flare with panic, and he angles his body to better shield his sister. Piers's face mirrors Griffin's horrified expression. Stepping toward her, Piers reaches for Kaia, his hand still covered in his own blood.

"No!" Kaia avoids him with a slippery twist, sliding between Griffin and me. In her colorless face, her own eyes blaze with fear and hurt. Still a pace away, Piers pulls up short, looking like he's been kicked in the heart.

Everyone stops where they are. My eyes dart around. No weapons are drawn. No one is shouting. It looks like we're standing around for a friendly chat when that couldn't be farther from the truth. Betrayal and heartache reign here.

I wrap my arm around Kaia's waist, laying claim to her in any way I can. "Thanos. I mean, Ares. You can't take her. Please don't take her." He's one of the only people I've ever pleaded with, mostly for inconsequential things. A child's whims. Other times, I asked him to not retaliate against someone who'd hurt me, although he never offered to punish my mother, who hurt me most of all. "Can't you just waive the rule? Not take someone this time?"

He finally lifts his gaze from Kaia, and the look he levels on me is somber to the core of his power-charged eyes.

My stomach sinking, I swallow all pride for my new family, for Kaia, and beg. "Please? For me?"

Griffin lays his hand on the back of my neck. He squeezes my nape, his arm sheltering Kaia between us. I grip her waist, grounding her to me. Kaia raises her chin and stares straight ahead.

"You think she can't handle war?" Ares asks. "Traveling the worlds with me, she would see many novel things."

Or she might die in her first battle and see nothing but blood.

I look again at Kaia. She has intelligence, courage, and a warrior's soul, and with a little training, likely a warrior's skills. She's long and lithe and strong. I've always thought Jocasta was a little softer and more prudent than Kaia, and yet Jocasta threw herself into the Agon Games and participated in a hostile takeover of the Tarvan throne. Jocasta acquitted herself more than well, with honor and bravery, surviving against all odds. I have no reason to think Kaia couldn't follow the same path as her older sister. In fact, I think she'd do it better.

"I think she can," I answer honestly. "But I don't want her to."

Ares's solemn gaze returns to Kaia again. He cocks his head. "I think you're right."

My heart clenches hard, and I can't move. I can only stare in horror and disbelief. Did he just miss the part about my not wanting her to go to war and be lost to us forever? I *begged.*

A small bleat leaks from Kaia, like the cry of a frightened lamb. It's heartbreaking and fills me with dread.

Griffin moves so fast I can't stop him. One minute he's beside us both, and the next, he's right in front of Kaia. "Try to take her, and you'll have to go through me."

Oh Gods. He means that.

"No!" I shout just as Ares sends Griffin flying away from us with a simple swipe of his God-powerful hand. I run to him, dragging Kaia with me. Griffin gets up again quickly, reaching for his sword.

"No, don't!" I step into his path, trying to block him.

"You'll just make things worse." I've seen Thanos—
Ares—when he's threatened. He's never scared, and he
can be cruel.

Griffin slams his half-drawn blade back into its sheath.
His face thunderous, he stalks forward, forcing us both into
a stumbling retreat. "He can't have Kaia. I won't let him."

I let go of Kaia to hold up both hands. "He's not a man.
He's a God. You can't defy him without incurring the
wrath of Olympus, and you *can't* win."

Griffin glances down at me, his jaw hardening to marble.
His eyes are stark and as dark as the storm clouds brewing on the horizon. I see the exact moment he decides to
disregard my warning, and I push hard, putting my whole
weight against him.

I don't even slow him down. Even counting Little Bean,
we don't weigh half of what Griffin does.

Words tumble from my mouth. Anything to stop him.
"Your immunity to harmful magic doesn't extend to the
Gods. Remember how Selena—*Persephone*—yanked out
your life force to heal Carver? Now that mystery is solved,
and Ares could probably do the same. Or take *you*."

"Then so be it."

So be it? So be it! "He'll kill you!"

Griffin looks over my head rather than at me. "I can't
choose myself over Kaia. What kind of brother would I be?"

The kind like Piers? Fear scrapes down my spine. I
could lose Griffin. Oh Gods, I could.

Griffin lowers his voice. "Maybe a fight will satisfy him.
Besides, I'm…vital to whatever is going on with you."

"You're vital to *me*." My heart twists sharply. I'm not
sure Griffin's reasoning is sound. "But I'm here. Alive.
With an heir…"

A tiny muscle contracts under Griffin's eye.

Sudden tears spike my lashes just as Griffin looks down. He winces, clearly hating my pain. *Our* pain. He grips my upper arms, squeezing hard and looking at me with all the passion and devotion a woman could ever hope for. I wait for him to pull me into his arms. His eyes fill with longing.

He lifts me up and sets me out of his path. Gasping, I whirl around and see Griffin take the final few steps to confront Ares.

"Fight me for her," Griffin demands. "If I can't best you, then it's me you'll take."

My heart forgets to beat. Griffin's sword arm flexes and lifts. He slides his blade from its sheath and then shifts his weight into a fighting stance. He looks like a force of nature. To me, he is one. Strong and brave and an earthquake in my world. But Ares is a God. One of the twelve Olympians!

Ares leaves all his weapons in his belt. His arms swing loosely at his sides. "You did well," he tells Persephone, completely ignoring Griffin's challenge. "They're a good match."

She scoffs. "Of course they're a good match. But it would have been nice if one of you *males* had told me you'd finally decided to point him in Cat's direction. I thought she'd been kidnapped. Or run away."

I blink. I had been kidnapped. Griffin did it.

"She had to figure things out on her own. Couldn't have you influencing her," Ares responds with a shrug.

"Oh, no." Persephone's sarcastic mock sincerity rivals my own. "Only you can do that."

Ares preens, just to goad her, and Persephone looks like she's about to attack. Ribbons of power race in circles around her dark-blue irises, brightening them from within.

She glares at the other God, her eyes terrifying. "She

was impressionable when she was with you. Thank the *Goddesses* she had her sister to teach her compassion."

My pulse speeds up at the mention of Eleni. My dead sister. Not my unborn daughter. A tight, hard lump lodges in my throat, and I feel my blood drumming against it. Eleni taught me to love. And protect.

"Thank the *Gods* she had me to teach her how to survive," Ares shoots back.

He taught me to fight. And kill.

"Oh, I think her mother helped her with that." Persephone's tone turns biting. She looks at me, her eyes twin pools of radiant blue light. "Trial by fire."

"It forges a heart of iron," I whisper, echoing my words to Flynn when we argued about Jocasta taking part in the Agon Games.

She nods, her gaze still holding mine. "And sets it alight."

I inhale sharply. I'm not sure what that means, and I can't process riddles right now. My husband might get beaten and taken from me. And if not him, then Kaia. I can't think about anything else. I can't even think about that.

I reach for Griffin, but he shakes his head. "Stay back, Cat. They're your responsibility now."

Who? His family?

Of course, his family. There's far too much of goodbye in his expression, and suddenly I'm drowning in open air. Little Bean's life force bumps through me in protest, and I nearly whimper.

Griffin's eyes turn bleak with sorrow. "Take care of our baby."

I shake my head in useless denial, staring at him through a sheen of tears. *Griffin.* So fierce and loyal. So selfless. How dare he do this to us? How dare he not?

I swallow the acid flooding my throat, and it burns a

path straight to my aching heart. I don't know what to do. I've never felt so helpless in my life!

Ares turns his attention back to my husband but makes no move to engage Griffin in combat.

"Thanos, please!" I play on old, strong ties by using the name I've always called him. "Please, let it go. Just this once."

Ares shakes his head, his thick, golden-brown hair brushing the tops of his sun-bronzed shoulders. "It doesn't work that way, little monster. I don't make these rules. Even though I should," he mutters as an afterthought, throwing a truculent look toward Olympus in the north.

Selena snorts. I mean Persephone. No one is who they're supposed to be!

Ares's expression remains one of mild curiosity while Griffin tenses for the fight of his life. My eyes jump back and forth between them. Something feels off. Well, nothing about this could ever feel *right*, but there's an odd gap, a strange discrepancy between our stark fear and heartbreak and the Gods' prickly banter and cutting jibes. Someone I love is doomed, and neither of them seems to care!

"I haven't fought a human in centuries," Ares muses with some interest.

"You fought me," I say. And knocked me senseless more than once. Usually by accident.

"I *trained* you," he counters, glancing at me. "That's different."

His eyes suddenly narrow, and he looks around. "Someone's coming."

Persephone nods, apparently sensing the same thing. I peer in every direction but see only the dark clouds rolling in.

"Decision time." Ares swings the full, power-heavy force of his gaze back on Kaia. "She's ripe for training."

Kaia shudders from head to toe. Her chin is high, though, and no tears wet her lashes.

Griffin looks at me, his eyes filled with a lifetime of words I'll never get to hear. He leaves me with the most important. "I love you."

It feels as though the ground drops out from under me. A terrible ache explodes in my chest, cutting off my breath as the only man I'll ever love turns back to the God of War.

"If you won't fight me for her," Griffin says, "then just take me inst—"

"There *is* another solution," Persephone cuts in coolly.

My heart nearly shatters with relief. I knew Selena wouldn't let me down. She wouldn't!

"Of course there is." Piers's voice hollows with pain. Looking at Ares, he pulls his shoulders back and swallows hard. "Take me instead."

CHAPTER 5

I STARE IN DISBELIEF. SURPRISE AND RELIEF MAKE THE GROUND roll beneath my feet, and I sway toward Griffin. I didn't expect that from Piers, hadn't considered it, and frankly didn't even know it was possible for the summoner to be taken. Unfortunately, now I can't hate him nearly as much. It's the best solution. The *only* solution. It's also bloody annoying when the root of the problem becomes the martyr.

Kaia lets out the sob I expect she's been holding back for a while now. Just one, and it's over quickly, but it racks her entire body. Then she pulls herself together and shakes her head, glaring at Piers like he just *now* did something truly wrong.

"No. *No.*" Her refusal is absolute, and my mouth opens in shock. *Kaia would sacrifice herself for Piers? For a traitor?*

Persephone steps closer to her. Despite the enigma she's always been and a certain aloofness in the core of her nature, the Goddess's instinct is to nurture and protect. "Hush," she says, laying a soothing hand on Kaia's arm. "It's for the best."

"Piers hates war," Kaia blurts out. "He'll do anything to avoid it. It's only loyalty to Griffin that made him fight or recruit soldiers in the first place."

Loyalty to Griffin? I barely contain the unsavory interjection burning on my tongue. As it is, I can't help the scathing look I throw at Piers. Did he think things were just fine before Griffin took over Sinta and started this Power Bid? With cruel, selfish, unpredictable Alphas, and royal soldiers doing as they pleased? *Sure, burn my home, steal my stuff, abuse my son or daughter.* How could Piers possibly have been happier with *that*? Or was he too wrapped up in his books and scrolls to realize what life was really like?

Piers looks at his sister, his expression deadened by resignation. "Don't argue, Kaia. It'll be all right."

"No, no, he can't go." Kaia glances around wildly, as if there's some other solution out there just waiting to be found, one we haven't seen yet. It's obvious that her fierce loyalty shapes everything about her, every decision she makes. Just like Griffin.

"Piers brought this upon himself," Persephone points out. "You are not to blame, nor should you be punished for his mistake."

"But that's it!" Kaia cries. "It was a mistake. Surely he can undo it. Something can be done!"

Ares shakes his head. Both he and Persephone look at Piers with assessing expressions, and suddenly I know: Griffin, Kaia, and I were never in danger.

The breath leaves my lungs in a great gust. "It was always him, wasn't it?" That discrepancy I felt makes sense now. It's why Persephone and Ares could taunt each other and stand around squabbling while I nearly had a heart attack and was scared out of my mind. "Why let us suffer? You made Griffin choose. You made Kaia think she was doomed!"

Ares frowns at my tone. "She was 'doomed,' as you call it—unless Piers did what he needed to do."

"But if you could just take him, then why didn't you?"

"Because he needed to learn a lesson," Ares answers flatly.

"And he hoped that Piers would sacrifice himself—with sufficient motivation. Ares always was a gambler."

We all startle at the new voice. Well, we humans do. I whirl, an echo of power still bouncing in my ears, even though the words were softly spoken.

I recognize the approaching Goddess immediately. When I can tear my eyes off her, they jump to Griffin. My husband recognizes her, too. His gaze is rapt, his full mouth slightly parted, his attention utterly absorbed. There was no earth-shattering entrance, no dropping from the sky, but she walks toward us with sure strides, confident and tall. Her grace is athletic, her bearing exactly what it should be for a primordial being immersed in both knowledge and war.

Sculptors throughout the ages have really gotten her likeness right, although no inanimate slab of marble could ever truly do her justice. She's everything I expect and more—the long, straight nose, the intelligent eyes, the tight, reddish-brown curls framing her oval face. She wears her warrior's helmet, with its proud crest, and carries her spear and shield.

I stare in undisguised awe. She's not beautiful, but she's breathtaking and bold.

Ares's voice tightens with annoyance. "We're handling this, Athena."

She slides a chilling look toward the God of War. "I'm sure you are. In your usual fashion."

"He's actually been surprisingly tolerable so far," Persephone says. "I'm sure it won't last."

Athena arches one dark eyebrow. "Persephone." She greets the other Goddess with cool neutrality.

"Athena." Persephone uses the same tone to greet her back. Not friendly. Not unfriendly. It's hard to tell where they stand.

Athena turns to us, and I can't help the explosion of

nerves that erupts in my belly. Griffin must be feeling the same thing, only a hundred times stronger. This is *his* Goddess, the one he worships above all others. He was attached enough to her—or to the idea of her—to haul a marble statue all the way north to Castle Sinta from his own tribal lands in the south and then place it in the main courtyard at the castle entrance. He and his soldiers kiss their fingertips and then touch them to her sandaled feet each time they pass the statue, leaving her toes polished and smooth by their daily devotion.

"Catalia Fisa. You are surprisingly entertaining." Athena smiles, not exactly warmly, but I'm not sure the Goddess does warmth. "One never knows if you'll live or die."

Lovely.

"And you…" Her eyes land on Griffin. They're large and an odd chestnut color, brown with hints of red and gold. The power in them is immense. She looks him up and down in a rather proprietary manner I don't like at all, as if she has some claim to him.

Griffin flushes under her blatant perusal, and a hot stab of jealousy pierces my chest.

Athena nods, seeming to approve of what she sees. "You are just how we planned."

Griffin finally blinks. "Planned?"

I frown. *Good question.*

"Oh, yes. We had a long talk with the Fates." Athena keeps looking at Griffin, a secret sort of smile spreading across her face. She leans in, something conspiratorial in her suddenly hush-hush manner. "Some things shouldn't be left entirely up to chance. The new Origin needed a partner she couldn't intimidate, dominate, or accidentally kill." Athena straightens again and then shrugs strong, almost masculine shoulders, her expression still animated by subtle delight. "Otherwise, she'd have walked all over you."

Griffin's face goes abruptly blank. He looks shaken.

Oh, no, no, no, no, no. I don't like this at all, even though it actually makes a lot of sense. Griffin has given me everything—a family, a kingdom, leadership, his heart, his body. I was the *one thing* that was his. *Made* for him. *Meant* for him. Or that's what he's always believed. Now Athena is saying that even this—*us*—was all about *me*?

No wonder Griffin has lost his awe-struck expression. He's not actually looking at anyone anymore. Not at me. Not at Athena. He doesn't say a word.

"What are you doing here?" Ares demands.

Athena takes another moment to gaze intently at Griffin, as if trying to deconstruct him with her eyes. Then she turns to Ares so quickly that her spear whistles through the air. Ares watches the weapon with a hint of suspicion, widening his stance. Athena eyes him with bored antipathy.

"I figured you'd muck something up and need my help. As it turns out, you only nearly broke the Origin's heart and sent her baby into hysterics, made her husband choose between staying with his wife and child and sealing a death sentence for his youngest sister, and scared a little girl half out of her wits." With a sharp downward thrust, Athena plants the blunt end of her spear eight inches into the ground, cracking the hard earth in every direction. She slowly claps, wearing irony like a crown. "Well done."

Ares's strong, scarred face mottles with rage. Persephone looks peeved as well, having clearly been included in Athena's scathing reprimand.

Kaia steps out from Griffin's shadow. "I'm not a little girl." There's a tremor in her voice, but it doesn't sound like fear. It rings like a bold and fiery fusion of emotion and ferocity.

Athena's head swivels smoothly on her long neck, reminding me of the owl I thought was her, or at least her emissary, outside the Chaos Wizard's house by the Frozen Lake. Her odd eye color, much like a raptor's, heightens the impression.

"My, my, you're a feisty one." A small smile plays around the corners of Athena's mouth, and her suddenly amused expression is both reassuring and utterly frightening at the same time. "You might have done well under Ares's command."

"I wasn't going to throw her into any wars," Ares grumbles, although he's looking at Kaia like he almost regrets it. I'm not sure I can blame him. Kaia's words are the anvil, her spirit the fire. She's only fifteen, and she's already in the forge that hammers out legends and heroes. "I was going to give her to Aphrodite as a handmaiden. She would have been fine, living a long, comfortable life with countless males falling in adoration at her feet."

Kaia's eyes brighten with obvious interest. She's naturally curious, experiencing all sorts of new feelings, and as far as I know, she's never been kissed. Her sharp, imaginative mind is taking her on a wild ride right now. In all honesty, mine is, too.

Griffin tenses beside me, and he was already impossibly rigid to begin with. Leave it to my insanely overprotective, traditional husband to appear more appalled at the idea of his sister ending up in some sort of Olympian love-court than on the battlefield. If the alarmed, almost panicked look on his face is any indication, he's probably picturing Kaia right now laughing drunkenly with Aphrodite while virile demigods take turns lapping wine from her navel. That's what I'm seeing, anyway.

I nudge him, and he blinks.

"If you were just going to give Kaia to Aphrodite, then you might as well give Piers to me," Athena reasons.

It's my turn to blink. *What? Why?*

"Good question," Persephone mutters, as if I'd just said that out loud.

I glance at her sharply, my eyes narrowing. "You *are* reading my mind! Oh my Gods, do you do that all the time?"

I turn to Ares in horror. "And you?" Heat blasts through me. I'm not often embarrassed, but right now, there's cause. No one should know even half of what went on in my head between the ages of twelve and fifteen, and especially not him.

Persephone scoffs. "Goodness, no. We were always in our muted forms around you, which blocks out a great deal of knowledge and puts us all at a disadvantage. When we were with you, we didn't know what was happening on Olympus, in the Underworld, with our enemies, with allies… But at least toning himself down meant that big brute never accidentally killed you." She jerks her head toward Ares, who glowers in response.

"It takes concentrated effort to read a mind when we're in human form. I did it with you, at first, to try to get to know you faster. But your thoughts were always so dark and violent that I mostly stopped. After a while, that faded somewhat, but then there was just too much sarcasm to bear."

I snort, the knot in my chest starting to untangle loop by loop. She's still Selena. She'll still tease me, and love me, give me frustrating half-answers, and tell me when I'm wrong. Right then, I realize I haven't lost her.

She smiles. She's definitely reading my mind.

"*Oikogeneia*," Persephone says warmly, using the old language.

The ancient word for family doesn't send a potent

shock through me like the first time she used it, claiming me as her own. That bond has already been forged, and the magic in it was so intense I should have guessed there was more to her than a powerful Magoi woman running a circus. There was a Goddess, and real family, because in a roundabout way and about a hundred generations apart, she's my aunt.

"Back to the question at hand." Ares examines Athena, traces of wariness and reserve creeping into his voice. "Why do you want Piers?"

"We're all in agreement—for once." Athena rolls her eyes, showing a frightening amount of white, and then gestures vaguely toward Griffin and me. "We need to keep these two together so they can get on with what they're supposed to do. Kaia should stay here, but Piers can go. Let me take him to Attica. I have scientists running amok with sensitive information." She shrugs, as if it matters, but not all that much. "He might be of use."

Scientists? Does she mean alchemists?

Persephone cocks her head, studying the other Goddess's face. "You're worried," she finally says.

Athena tenses, if the slight stiffening of her rather prominent jaw counts as tensing. "They may have forgotten all about worshipping me and lost their magic when they did, but Attica is still my world."

Ares grins all of a sudden, looking almost devious with excitement. "They do have interesting weapons there."

Athena turns a glare on him that would frost icicles. "I'll thank you not to stir things up. *Again.* And you would like anything capable of mass destruction," she adds bitterly.

"Mass destruction?" I ask. "Like Galen Tarva?"

All three Gods laugh at me. *Laugh!* At least they're finding common ground.

"So, can I have him?" Athena's tone goes back to neutral, almost bored, but she's not fooling me anymore. I doubt she's fooling anyone else, either. If she's here, and she asked for Piers, she wants him.

I glance at Piers. He looks totally defeated, and I get the impression he doesn't really care what happens to him after this.

"You'll owe me," Ares says.

Athena's brown irises flare with hints of power-infused red and gold. Then her eyes narrow to aggravated slits. "Owe you what?" she asks.

"An audience with your father. Zeus hasn't heard me out in decades." Ares turns to me and winks. "He put me in charge of you as a punishment. Olympian idiot. That was the most fun I'd had in an age."

I can't help smiling, even though it's weak. He was the best part of my life growing up, the only good part—him and Eleni. "Punishment for what?" I ask.

"For causing and prolonging conflict in Atlantis," Persephone answers for him. "Poseidon still hates you, by the way."

Ares looks perfectly all right with that. "He's not so fond of you either after you poked him with his own trident the other day."

Uh-oh. That was because of me.

Persephone shrugs. "He was moving too slowly."

"Or you're too attached."

Persephone snorts. "We're all too attached. Don't even pretend that you're not. You're even more revoltingly sentimental than I am." She nods toward his hand. "You still wear her hair around your wrist."

My heart slamming in my chest, I look more closely at the thick, dark cord around Ares's wrist. I'd hardly noticed it, thinking it was some sort of braided rope bracelet, but it's not. I know exactly what it is now.

I was ten, small but fierce. He'd bested me on the training field—as always—but I kept fighting with a broken arm, cuts and bruises, and one eye swollen shut.

Thanos dodged every knife I threw at him, got behind me, grabbed my hair in his big fist, and then started dragging me toward the castle with a frustrated curse. But I wouldn't stop. I kept hissing, spitting, and twisting like a slippery little snake, landing blows and shouting that I wasn't done yet. I was never done, because I was so determined to beat him one day.

"Enough, little monster. Time to find the healer, or you'll be weak for days."

And that would have left me vulnerable to my brothers. To Mother.

I still wouldn't listen. If I fought hard enough, I was sure I could finally win. He held on to my hair and pulled until my eyes watered. I wasn't getting anywhere with my thrashing and yanking, so I drew the last knife I had in my belt and cut off my hair above his grip. The second I could, I spun around and plunged the dagger into his thigh with a bloodcurdling scream of triumph.

Thanos had looked at me then, with my long hair still clutched in his fist, like I'd just become an entirely different creature. One he liked even better. It was the first and only time I ever drew his blood.

Staring at his bracelet now, I lift my hand and touch my head, memory's ghost still flitting through my mind. The morning of that training session, my hair had started out longer than it is today. The day had ended with a bushy tangle of barely chin-length curls.

The following morning, Mother had slapped me and

said I looked like a boy. Father, a nonentity in my life, hadn't recognized me for days. Thanos had given me a rust-colored scarf to cover the mess I'd made. He'd patted his thigh where I'd stuck him with my knife and told me he'd dyed the cloth in his own blood.

Remembering his pride in me that day, I get the most horrifying urge to cry. "You kept me alive all these years."

Ares shrugs. "I was nowhere about after you left Castle Fisa. The others made sure of that."

"No, you were here." I press my hand to my chest. His training was never about hurting me—or my trying to hurt him back. It was about skill, yes, but also about perseverance, about finding inner strength, both mental and physical, when the wells of each seemed not just dried up but completely drained and destroyed. His often-brutal methods taught me that giving up is never an option. A true warrior fights through pain. Through anything. Through everything.

"You're not dead until you're on the far side of the Styx," I murmur. It's what he always said. And I know that better than anyone for having nearly been there. Until you've paid the ferryman and taken his boat, there's always one more swing, one more kick, one more bite if it comes to that. That lesson never left me. Or failed me.

The urge to cry gets worse. "I owe you my life."

Athena huffs, half rolling her eyes again. "Let's not exaggerate. Now"—she rubs her hands together—"terms."

I glance at Piers again, still reeling from seeing Ares wearing my braided hair around his wrist. Not even the mention of terms appears to interest Piers, though. He's staring at Kaia, but his expression looks dull and unfocused.

Griffin watches his brother as well. Anger burns brightly in Griffin's eyes, stoked hotter by terrible hurt. I slip my hand into his, squeezing gently. He doesn't look at me, but after a moment, he grips my hand back so hard it aches.

I return my focus to the Olympians because looking at Griffin is breaking my heart. Piers's betrayal must have shattered him on a deep level. Now, perhaps even worse, he's about to lose his brother forever before he has time to even try to understand or forgive.

Ares glares at Piers. "He has to pay for what he tried to do to my little monster."

"She has a name," Persephone snaps out impatiently.

"I know," Ares snaps back. "It's Little Monster."

"No, it's Catal—"

"Not important," I interrupt. "What do you mean by terms?" I ask Athena.

The look Athena levels on me is so icy I get chills. She jerks her spear from the ground and then flips it in her hand, pointing it straight at me. For a terrifying second, I think she's going to run me through.

Her eyes narrow. "You're just like Artemis said. Irreverent in the extreme."

I swallow. I guess I overstepped. Or she's not used to me. Probably both.

Athena thumps her spear against her shield, startling everyone. Apparently, that's her way of opening negotiations. Better than skewering me, at least.

"He'll be fluent in the first ten languages he hears," she announces.

Good Gods! How many do they have?

"Hundreds. Attica's big," Athena answers, as if I'd spoken out loud.

Goose bumps flare down my arms. I don't want the Gods in my head. I don't want *anyone* in my head.

Persephone scowls. "His brain will explode."

"And that's not even a punishment. That's a reward," Ares grumbles. "He craves knowledge."

"He has to be useful," Athena points out, her tone a clear indication that she thinks we're all a torch short of being bright. "Six languages, then."

Ares glowers at her, crossing his arms. "Three."

Athena flashes her teeth. It's not a smile. "Fine. But no fewer or there's practically no point."

Ares takes his time considering. "Done. As long as he remembers everything about his life here—especially today. That will be punishment for years to come."

I look back and forth between the Olympians and Piers. On the one hand, Piers *should* be tearing himself up inside. On the other, believing he feels intense remorse confuses my own feelings. It's so much easier to just despise someone.

Athena tilts her head, studying Piers. She eventually agrees to Ares's stipulation. "Just not at first," she adds. "He'll need to adjust without any of that in the way."

"Then when?" Ares asks.

"Something will trigger his memories. When the time is right."

"What?" the God demands.

"I'll decide on the way," Athena replies through tightly gritted teeth.

A muscle jumps in Ares's cheek, but then he nods. Athena's answer seemed pretty vague to me, but apparently it's good enough for him.

Athena nods back before thumping her spear across her shield again, closing negotiations, I guess.

"Time to say goodbye." Athena's voice comes to us from out of thin air because she disappears before suddenly reappearing again right next to Piers, his upper arm already gripped in her large hand. Piers doesn't even react, while Griffin, Kaia, and I all startle in surprise. In fact, Piers doesn't look at her or seem to care about Athena or her negotiations at all. He just keeps staring at Griffin and Kaia like he's dead inside.

An ache tugs at my chest, and something inside of me shifts. Despite my best efforts to hold on to an everlasting, Olympian grudge, my hatred decides to swallow itself whole.

Griffin still holds my hand. I have my husband and an unshakable faith in our bond. I have a baby growing inside me. I have our friends and family. We have two realms and a populace swelling behind us on a wave of hope that I will keep alive for them, no matter what, even if it kills me, because the people of Thalyria *need* Elpis. After generations of oppression and living in fear, we have it within us, and within our grasp, to overcome the evils of this world and to not only survive, but to finally thrive.

Realization spreads through me, both stunning and frightening in its proportions.

Oh Gods. I don't just represent Elpis. I *am* Elpis—the personification and spirit of hope.

The knowledge hits me like a God Bolt, nailing me to the spot. Responsibility is a heavy mantle, and my shoulders nearly break under its sudden weight.

Persephone slides me a satisfied look, nodding once. Ares nods, too. They're telling me I'm right. Elpis isn't just an abstract concept or an ideology to follow; it's me. Flesh and blood *me*. I'm an idea in human form.

Fast and jumbled and dizzying, thoughts crash through my head like a storm. I don't have the luxury of denial anymore. I have to integrate and accept a different reality, a new paradigm that completely alters my view of myself and the world around me, and I have to do it *now*.

I force slow, even breaths. It seems fitting that this huge part of me would have come from Pandora's Box, dragged through all the darkness and violence known to man and beast and God alike, yet I would somehow be forged from the one intangible substance that remains steadfast and unbreakable through even the worst pain, suffering, evil, and plight. *Hope*.

Tears sting my eyes. Piers has nothing. No one. Not even Elpis.

"No! Make him forget!" I don't know if anyone listens to me. I only know that the Gods have their own set of rules, and morals, and as far as I know, little capacity for compassion, and even less for forgiveness.

Piers jerks, seeming to finally wake up. He looks at me like he's seeing me for the first time, and the sight of me hurts his eyes. Motionless at my side, Griffin is a shadow of his usual vibrant self. Kaia steps forward, leaking a sob, her hands outstretched to the brother she's about to lose forever. I start to follow her—I'm not sure why—but Griffin tightens his grip on my hand, stopping me. A heartbeat later, he grabs Kaia with his free hand and pulls her back.

Griffin moves away from Piers, taking us both with him. It's not just a step back; it's a message that opens a giant emotional abyss between Piers and us.

His eyes meet Griffin's, and Piers flinches. Then he and Athena are gone.

CHAPTER 6

THE TWO REMAINING GODS DISAPPEAR INTO THE ETHER SHORTLY after, and Griffin, Kaia, and I ride back to Castle Tarva in total silence, leading Piers's big roan horse behind us. I don't know where Griffin's thoughts are leading him, but I hope they're far from mine. Even after everything that's happened, and the Elpis stunner I still can't quite wrap my head around, all I can think about is how his attraction and devotion to me are somehow not his choice. If the Gods hadn't intervened, would he have looked at me twice? Would I still have been his first, his *only* choice?

Somehow, when Griffin would insist, low in my ear with a rasp in his voice, that I was made for him, I found that alluring, shiver-inducing, and safe. I reveled in it as much as I reveled in the feel of his big, sword-roughened hands skating up my bare ribs, and I started to crave those words like I craved his possessive touch.

Hearing that, in essence, he was made for *me* makes me feel like rocks are churning in my stomach. If the Gods had never given him his immunity to harmful magic with our common future in mind, an alteration that eventually brought him to Castle Sinta and then to me on that fateful day at the circus fair, would his heart and soul have carried him toward someone else?

With my thoughts still spinning in useless circles, we eventually sneak back into Castle Tarva—not an easy feat with so many people camped out around the royal residence. My feet drag, and exhaustion weighs me down, both

physical and mental. All I want to do is stagger up to our
room and then sit down on something that's not a horse, but
Griffin has to tell the others what happened, and for better
or worse, I'm part of this family now and can't avoid the
painful parts.

We go to the great room first, finding Flynn, Kato, and
Carver playing a game of cards. Jocasta sits near them,
sewing, but Ianthe sits alone. She stares into the fire, not
moving at all. Bellanca and her younger sister Lystra, the
two Tarvan ex-princesses we appear to have kept along
with the castle, are nowhere to be found.

Jocasta's joy at seeing Kaia again quickly turns into
tears and then into the far-off, vacant look of the emotionally overcome. Carver shuts down completely and
goes for the wine before Griffin is even done relaying
the day's unhappy events. Prior to his near-death in the
arena and watching his lost love wave him away from the
Underworld rather than welcome him with open arms, I'd
never seen Carver reach for a glass of wine, not even at a
meal when his cup was always full. Now, he reaches for a
drink far too often—and not only at mealtimes—and stares
at people without seeing them at all.

Carver tilts the earthenware jug directly to his lips, and
my heart aches even more. Griffin watches, too, and looks
helpless. Maybe even afraid.

Guilt is a thousand daggers hitting me all at once.
Without me in their lives, none of this would have happened. Carver would be laughing and joking instead of
drinking his weight in wine. Piers would still be at home
in the library, shuffling through scrolls, muttering about
ancient history, and getting ink stains on his hands. Kaia
and Griffin would never have been in danger today. No one
would have lost a brother. Or a son.

Oh Gods. Nerissa and Anatole. Egeria. There are still parents to devastate. Another sister as well. We'll have to go to them. Or send a message home. What do you write in that kind of letter? How is that even done?

I swallow past the tightness in my throat, watching Flynn and Kato quietly rage. The rest of Beta Team. *My* team. They weren't particularly close to Piers, and their anger rather than grief reassures me that perhaps I'm not entirely to blame. Piers made his own decisions, after all. No one forced him to dig up ancient scrolls or to use a series of words no one should even remember now, let alone utter out loud. And no one forced him to sacrifice himself in the end, either.

Bleary-eyed, Jocasta watches Flynn pace back and forth across the room, his boots clomping. He's agile and fast, but Flynn has never had a light stride.

"Stop." Her voice is no more than a tear-thick whisper, but the big auburn-haired warrior halts mid-step. He sets his foot down quietly this time and then turns to her.

"I need air," Jocasta says, looking right at him.

Without a word, Flynn goes to her. Jocasta takes his offered arm, and he leads her from the room. As far as I know, that was the easiest interaction they've had in years.

Kaia, who's no dummy, looks straight at Kato, the man she secretly adores. Never one to ignore a lady in distress, Kato offers her his arm, and she takes it. I think she's grown even taller since we've been away. Her dark head already reaches his chin, and she angles it toward him as they leave the room in the opposite direction from Jocasta and Flynn.

Watching them go, I can't help a small frown. I hope Griffin never catches on to his fifteen-year-old sister's obsession with his Adonis-like comrade in arms. For that matter, I hope Kato never catches on. He'd be forced to break Kaia's young heart, and he's far too soft on the inside to ever want to do that.

Ianthe is the only one who hasn't said anything so far. As opposed to me, my younger sister doesn't shift restlessly in her seat or try in vain to offer comforting words. She sits silently and observes. Ianthe never knew Piers, and I only reconnected with her recently myself. Underneath her rather stiff reserve, though, I wonder how fierce the storm is. As usual, her green eyes are shadowed, like she's wondering where she fits in here—or if she fits in at all.

"Ianthe," I call softly. "How good are you with a sword?"

She turns to me, her quiet strength an almost visible force around her. Or maybe a brittle barrier. "Better than you are."

She would know. She saw me in the Agon Games. "Jocasta and Kaia will need distracting, and they like to train. They've been doing it for a while now. I've taught them to handle knives, but they've only just begun with swords."

Ianthe nods. "It's always helpful to hit things."

Despite years of separation, my sister and I are strikingly alike. "So we understand each other?"

She stands. "I'll plan a schedule for the next week. They'll be too bruised, dirty, and exhausted to think."

"Thank you."

Ianthe nods. She leaves, and I close my eyes, still seeing her in my head. She's me—younger and with different magic—but still so similar in so many ways that I don't know if our likeness warms me in a peculiar, panging sort of way or scares the ever-living magic out of me. Even I know I'm reckless and extreme, and I think she's even more so.

The others are gone now, and Carver is slumped against

the wall, sitting on the hard marble floor. He has one knee up with a hand on it. The other hand is wrapped loosely around the neck of the earthenware jug at his side. He's more interested in his wine than in any useless platitude I could try to give.

I sigh. I've had it for the day, maybe for a few days, and a bath is calling to me, loud and strong.

I glance at Griffin. He's standing by my chair, looking dark and brooding. I hold out my hand to him, and for the first time ever, I wonder if he'll take it.

He doesn't reach for me, and a spasm contracts my whole chest. But then he turns just a little more in my direction, and his eyes change, brightening. He takes my outstretched hand and lifts it, pressing my knuckles to his lips.

"You must be tired," he says, still holding my hand. "And you haven't eaten much today."

I let out a slow breath. Griffin's hand warms mine, making me realize just how cold with worry I'd been.

"I'm not hungry. But I do want to wash and lie down," I say.

Griffin nods, helping me up. To my everlasting humiliation, I lumber to my feet with a groan. Not long ago, I was walking through fire, riding snakes, and climbing a Cyclops. Today, I suppose I proved I can still move fast when I really want to. Otherwise, it feels like I keep doubling my body weight every time I sit down.

"Gods, Little Bean. You weigh a ton," I murmur, stretching my aching back. She must already take after her father—big and solid.

Griffin's mouth quirks up, the small smile bringing some familiar and welcome lightness back into his otherwise drawn features. "I'm assuming I'm not Little Bean in this conversation."

I snort, taking a shuffling step. My body seems to loosen up once I start moving again—thank the Gods. "You're Big Bean. Look at you… You're huge."

"Not as big as Ares. Your *Thanos*," he mutters, an undercurrent of jealousy in his growling tone. It's neither unexpected nor entirely unwarranted. I did jump into the God's arms.

"He's too big," I answer truthfully. "You're just right."

Griffin is big and strong enough to protect me, should I need his help. He's big enough to make me feel feminine. And big enough to overpower me in ways I know I'll enjoy, since I also know I can trust him. He's a very large and powerful man by human standards, but he's not Olympian-sized, and I wouldn't want him to be.

Gripping my hand, Griffin leads me from the great room and then turns us toward the stairs.

"Why Little Bean?" he asks, using his free hand to snag a torch from a sconce on the wall.

I shrug. "It just came to me. Don't you think she's the size of a bean? A really heavy but tiny little bean?"

He smiles more fully this time, and some of the weight lifts from me. Or maybe that's Little Bean shifting around again.

"You're a bean." He squeezes my hand, and I feel even lighter. My heart seems buoyant after being so weighed down. It's definitely Griffin making me float.

Well, not exactly float, but I do manage to pick up my feet.

"We're a bean family," I announce.

He chuckles. "That sounds distinguished. No wonder we have so many followers."

"Absolutely," I agree with a nod. "Thalyrians are smart. We're also not prone to random massacres, which probably helps."

"Indeed."

I glance at him, arching my eyebrows. "*Indeed?* Is that scary warlord talk?"

He narrows his eyes on me, but something in the deep gray suddenly dances in the torchlight. "Indeed," he repeats.

I laugh, and it feels like years of tension slide off my shoulders.

"Your belly is hardly rounded," Griffin says, peering at the area in question. His eyes linger, and then he lets go of my hand to lightly draw his fingers over my lower stomach. "I didn't think you'd feel her so soon."

"Me either." I eye my stomach, seeing nothing unusual. I expected to be increasingly aware of her life force. I didn't expect the physical effects her apparent distress had on me today. "But I can't say I'm surprised that she's a special little powerhouse."

Griffin grunts. I guess he agrees.

"Where in the Gods damn bloody Underworld have you two been?" A flame-haired Harpy erupts from a darkened side passage, storming into our path.

I jump, even though it's just Bellanca Tarva arriving with the explosive energy of someone about my age but *not* pregnant.

"Gods! You nearly gave me a heart attack." I scowl at her. Ever since that three-headed monster leaped out at me in the ice caves, dark corridors make me nervous. To be fair, they made me nervous before that, but now it's even worse.

Griffin instinctively draws me closer to his side, even placing me a little behind him. He doesn't quite trust Bellanca yet, although I think he should.

Bellanca's hands fly to her hips. "What's wrong with everyone here?" she demands, seeming genuinely worried.

And spitting mad. Her wild red hair starts to spark, sending hot little flames sizzling down the curls. She bats at them, putting the Fire Magic out. "Everyone's crying. I can't find a courtyard where Lystra and I can walk in peace. I thought you'd gone off and gotten yourself killed! You, too," she adds, glowering at Griffin.

Bellanca's bald-faced disregard for the proprieties of rank rivals my own, but underneath her prickles and bluster, I think she truly cares, whether she wants to or not. Since her prophetess sister died to protect me and used her last breath to command her younger sisters to guard my unborn child with their lives, Bellanca has attached herself to me like an annoying and highly combustible leech. It was harder to sneak past her vigilance this morning than past the crowd outside the castle. I have a feeling her loyalty, once given, is an unshakable force. I can't seem to shake her, anyway.

Lystra, the youngest recently dethroned Tarvan royal, has mostly been hiding in her room. Or staring at Kato, but all females over the age of ten do that.

"It was a family thing," I answer with a worn-out sigh.

Bellanca's brow clears of the tight little wrinkles that were marring her forehead. Her stance relaxes, and she nods. For a person who grew up in an abomination of a household much like mine, the word *family*, said in the way I just said it, explains a lot.

"Well, don't go running off anymore." She huffs, clearly still cross with us. "At least not without me."

I pinch the bridge of my nose, rubbing a little. I feel the start of a headache coming on. "Who's in charge here?" I ask pointedly.

Bellanca's bright-red eyebrows slam together like crossing swords, two fiery slashes across her fair-skinned face. "Oh, that's nice! Just remind me of how you stole my realm and possibly my birthright."

"I will," I say. "And I'll remind you of how you helped me."

She pales, making her freckles stand out, and I want to kick myself. I just meant that she'd helped us. She chose our side over her power-hungry, cold-hearted, murderous brother's. I didn't mean to remind her of how she wrapped her flaming hands around Galen Tarva's thick neck and burned her own flesh and blood into a pile of ash.

Not that she did that for me. She did it because Galen had killed her beloved, sight-addled sister, Appoline. Appoline, who took Galen's knife in her chest for me. For Little Bean.

Gods, I'm an idiot. I see Bellanca's throat move on a hard swallow and feel even worse.

"Thank you." I reach out and grip her wrist. Emotional conversations aren't easy for me, and I don't know her well. "Thank you…for worrying about me."

She snorts, rolling blue-green eyes that remind me of Ares's unusual eye color but without the gleam of unbridled Olympian power in them. Bellanca blows a smoldering lock of hair out of her face. Her magic has been running amok since the takeover battle. The woman needs to learn some control. Then again, so do I.

"I wasn't worried. I don't even like you." Breaking my hold on her, Bellanca whirls and stomps off, moving into the family room we just vacated.

Griffin's face scrunches up. He bows his head, and his shoulders start to shake.

Uh-oh. He's finally cracking. Piers. Me. The baby. It's all too much.

I lean over and peer into his face only to realize that… *he's laughing?*

"What are you doing?" I demand.

"First Ianthe. Now her." He straightens and jerks his thumb over his shoulder in the direction of the great room, still quietly laughing. "I'm accumulating women just like you."

I scowl, and he tries to stop smiling. It doesn't work.

"What's that supposed to mean?" I demand hotly.

He puts a large, very warm hand on the small of my back and tries to sweep me toward the stairs. When I resist, he keeps pushing, propelling me along.

"It means I'm the luckiest man alive." He drops a kiss onto the top of my head as I reach for the ornate, gilded railing. "And all together, we'll be invincible," he murmurs against my hair.

Heat and pleasure radiate through me, warming my heart. Because Griffin is loyal to me, he immediately loved Ianthe like a sister. She also earned her place with us within seconds of our first encounter, leaping fearlessly to our defense, even though it meant defying a man who'd terrified and abused her. Bellanca earned her place that day as well, but she's harder to digest.

"Are you coming around to Bellanca?" I ask, starting to climb the steps.

Griffin follows. "She has certain qualities."

I turn, one eyebrow raised. "Like powerful Fire Magic?"

He humphs. "And a temper to match."

A muffled thump comes from the great room behind us, followed by a low, masculine grunt.

"Get up, you stupid drunk," Bellanca snaps. "Wine never helped anyone do anything but piss."

The sharp clatter of pottery smashing against stone reaches our ears. Griffin and I look at each other and cringe. Carver roars a curse. Bellanca screeches, loud and high-pitched. There's the sound of a scuffle.

Carver bellows in pain. "You burned me, you crazy Harpy!"

"Well, don't touch me! You burned yourself!"

"Control your hair!" Carver shouts. "Or I'll cut it all off!"

"Don't you dare come near me with that sword!" Bellanca shrieks back.

Griffin and I gape at each other. Then we take off as one, racing up the rest of the steps.

They're adults. They can sort themselves out—hopefully without killing one another in the process.

CHAPTER 7

A LIGHT MEAL IN MY STOMACH AND FRESH FROM A MUCH-NEEDED bath, I kick off my sandals as I walk across the bedroom toward Griffin. I lay my hands on his shoulders and squeeze once, tentatively. When he doesn't pull away, I start to massage the tense muscles in his upper back.

His hair is still damp from his own bath, and the gleaming black strands curl softly around his neck and ears. He sits on a simple stool in front of the writing desk in our room—the one we've adopted in Castle Tarva—probably having left the larger, more comfortable chair for me. There are discarded drafts of letters all around him.

"I sent it," he says, not looking at me. There are splotches of dried ink on both his hands. He can't seem to take his eyes off the rejected scrolls.

I smooth my fingers up into his hair and try to work some of the tension out of his nape and the back of his head. After I ate, or rather forced myself to swallow a few bites, I saw him release the dove. I continued on to the bathhouse, the weight in my chest so heavy I thought I might sink. He'd wanted to write and send the message alone, and Griffin doesn't shirk his responsibilities, no matter how hard or devastating they might be.

The smiles we managed to share earlier in the evening seem a hundred years gone, replaced by a bleakness in both of us that I don't know how to dispel.

I press my thumbs into the thick muscles near the top of his spine and work them in slow circles before sweeping them gradually up his neck again. "They wouldn't have wanted you to delay."

He lifts both hands to his face and scrubs, his fingers rasping over the day's worth of stubble. "I should have told them in person."

"The dove will get there faster."

"I have to go home," he says dully. "I have to face my parents."

My stomach churns with guilt. "They're with Egeria. We know Sinta is safe with them, and in good hands. And they're safe in Castle Sinta, with the realm at peace and the Ipotane protecting the border. I don't think we should leave Tarva City for now. It's too soon, and nothing is really established here."

Griffin leans into my massage, groaning softly. I press harder as I move down his back, working the muscles around and below his shoulder blades. Knots roll under my fingers. Some give. Others don't, stubbornly staying rock-hard and balled with tension.

"The Ipotane are protecting a border that no longer exists," he says. "We need to find Lycheron and try to convince him to patrol the Fisan border instead. We also need to get the bulk of our army here. The soldiers are useless in Sinta when we're in Tarva, and war is to the east."

"So first to Castle Sinta and then to Lycheron?" I ask.

Griffin grunts what appears to be a *yes*.

Unfortunately, there's a good chance that won't be as easy as it sounds. "Lycheron will probably try to get out of the bargain if we change it."

"That's what I'm afraid of," Griffin says with a sigh.

"And what about Tarva?" I ask. "We won't be gone long, but we'll need Beta Team's help to bring that many soldiers back. And Lycheron responds to force. It can only be a good thing to show up with our most trusted men and an entire army behind us. Things aren't unstable here, but I can't help thinking that all of us leaving at once might not be a good idea."

"So we don't all go," Griffin says. "We'll leave Jocasta and Kaia here as our presence in Tarva. Jocasta is always asking for more responsibility, and I think we've all been underestimating Kaia, despite her youth. They've both shown me recently that they can handle more than I ever thought they could. Taking them back to Castle Sinta now would be a...disservice to them at this point. And frankly not fair."

What a good idea. I barely have to think about it. Trusting Jocasta and Kaia implicitly helps. "I agree with everything you just said."

"They can set projects into motion, similar to the improvements we've been implementing in Sinta. They'll protect our interests here in Tarva and work on opening up the border to the west. We'll leave Lystra with them. She can either make herself useful or stay out of their way. Either way, with no magic, I don't think Lystra is a threat to them."

No. Griffin's sisters are far more fierce.

I slide my fingers over his broad shoulders again, and Griffin reaches up, pulling my hands down. He tugs until my upper body is flush against his back.

"What do you think?" he asks, his voice low, quiet, and full of weary gravel that speaks of the heartache and emotion of the day.

"I think you're a genius," I say, propping my chin on the top of his head and draping my arms more comfortably across his chest.

He squeezes our clasped hands. "Ianthe stays with us."

"Yes, definitely." There was never any question in my mind. "What about Bellanca?" I ask.

He inhales deeply before letting out a gusty breath. "I don't think you could get rid of her if you tried."

I laugh a little, my exhale stirring his hair. "You really want to go home?" I ask.

He nods. "Don't you?"

I try to straighten away from him, but Griffin holds on to my hands.

"Cat?"

I swallow so hard before answering that he probably feels my throat move against the back of his head. "It's daunting to think about facing your parents when I'm the reason for their loss."

Griffin, who was just starting to relax, goes noticeably rigid again. He lets go of my hands and then looks at me over his shoulder. "Nothing that happened today was your fault."

"I was never nice to Piers. I never even tried."

A shadow settles over Griffin's features, darkening his expression. "He was never nice to *you*. *He* never even tried!"

The anger in Griffin's voice takes me aback. That's not just a shadow in his eyes; that's fury. Intense and blazing.

"That may be true," I concede, "but he was also right about everything. I took Cassandra from him without even asking. I've put you, Carver, and Jocasta into dangerous situations again and again. And we're not stopping now. It's not over yet, and who knows what will happen. Today. Tomorrow. There's still my mother to deal with. And Fisa. You may be the hand helping to guide this sword, but everyone—you, the Gods—you've all made it perfectly clear that I'm the tip of the blade. I'm going to have to start swinging now, and people will get cut. That's war, and life, and there's no way around it. Piers was scared for his family. He was completely justified in his worry. And in his anger toward me."

Griffin swivels fully around and stares at me in disbelief. "So you have a conversation. You express your opinion, your opposition," he growls. "You withdraw your support. You go live as a Gods damn bloody hermit if you want to. You *do not* try to banish your brother's wife!"

I drop my gaze. "Your wife?"

He stands. "Yes, my *wife*. What kind of question is that?"

I glance back up, finding outrage and incomprehension on his face. "Do you... Do you think you would have loved me if the Gods hadn't meddled?"

Griffin stares at me.

"I mean... I just—"

"I know what you mean," he cuts in harshly.

My heart suddenly hammers in my chest. "You've told me you never really wanted anyone else—in a permanent way, at least—and then when you saw me, you knew I was the one. The one you wanted to claim, like you'd been waiting for me." I curl my bare toes into the thick sheepskin rug, looking down again. "But it sounds like they made it that way, made *you* that way, made it inevitable. What if they forced—"

Griffin grabs my shoulders in a hard grip. I gasp, jerking my head back up.

He loosens his hold. "We're not puppets, Cat. I have a mind of my own."

"But they push. They shove. They suggest." And Gods, don't I know it. They've been doing it all my life.

"They don't control my thoughts. They have no sway over my heart."

"But what if they do?" I whisper, raising my hands to his chest. I don't touch him, though. I curl my fingers into fists and then let my hands drop again. "We don't know."

Griffin gives me a gentle shake, urging me to look him in the eyes. "Then I don't care. It is what it is. You are the missing part of me, and I am *never* giving you up."

His truth burns through me. Heat thickens my throat, and tears prick at my eyes. Ever since Little Bean was conceived, I have the most aggravating propensity to cry. "But they changed you for me."

"They gave me a gift that's kept me alive. That got me Sinta and brought me to you." He lightly squeezes my shoulders. "And it's a good thing I'm indestructible where magic is concerned, because when you get excited, you light up the room like a storm."

I bite my lower lip. I want to smile. I still feel like crying.

Griffin sweeps his hands down my arms. His skin is rough, his touch gentle. "Don't doubt us, Cat. Don't doubt me."

I take a shaky breath. "I don't. I just... I'm..." I stop, at a loss.

Griffin lifts his eyebrows. "Inarticulate at the moment?"

Scowling, I thwack him in the chest.

"Overwrought?" he supplies, his mouth quirking up.

I thwack him again.

"Highly emotional?"

Thwack. Thwack.

"Apparently weak, because none of that hurt at all."

I give him the evil eye—a grumpy one.

Griffin smirks. It's that confident, smug look I've come to know and love. "You need a man you can't dominate? Someone you can't overpower? Even with magic?" His eyes suddenly gleam silver in the lamplight, and a little flutter twirls through my middle.

I nod. And what a good idea that was. I'd have no interest in a man I could intimidate.

Griffin moves fast. One minute, I'm standing there. The

next, I'm flying through the air. My back hits the bed, and before I even finish a bounce, Griffin's hands slam down on either side of my head. He's right above me—looming, caging, heavy, hot—and the way he looks down at me is both intensely dark and incredibly delicious.

A thrill darts through me. He still wants me.

His eyes glittering, Griffin pushes his knee between my thighs, spreading them. His strong arms bend, bringing his face closer to mine. The wall of sheer masculine power above me is intoxicating and sets my senses alight.

His breath whispers across my parted lips. "Can Little Bean handle rough?"

Excitement shoots like an arrow straight to the bull's-eye between my legs. I wet my lips, nodding. "She's sleeping. She's strong." And there's nothing Griffin would ever do that would hurt her, or me.

"Good."

One word, softly spoken but with a wealth of promise behind it, makes my whole body clench with need. His mouth nearly touching mine, Griffin holds himself above me, not moving. I wait, tension building inside me until I crave his touch, his kiss, or any contact at all, like an insane thirst. I start to throb with impatience. My pulse turns into a liquid beat where I want him most.

Charged air vibrates between us. His body is so tempting and close.

"Come to me." I move, trying to bring the apex of my thighs into contact with his thick, hard leg. His eyes narrow to shimmering gray slits, and then he rears up and flips me over in a tumbling rush.

I gasp in surprise. I can't wait to see what he'll do next.

He gathers up my dress and then flips it up my back. Cool air rushes over me, but all I feel is heat. Grinning like an idiot, I squirm and try to push up on my hands and knees.

"Don't move." Griffin's command is a warm, husky caress.

I wiggle anyway, flashing certain parts of my anatomy, and he lets out a hoarse groan. His hands land on my bare hips with enough force to sting. I almost wish he'd do it again, but then he hauls me to my knees, so I'm sitting upright. With rough tugs, he pulls my dress up and over my head and then throws it to the floor.

Griffin's arms come around me from behind. He palms my breasts, squeezing, and then drops his mouth to the curve of my neck. I tilt my head, and his shadow-rough jaw drags across my shoulder, sending a wash of goose bumps down my spine. His kisses are hot and openmouthed, sometimes scraping. He rubs his thumbs over my nipples, teasing. My stomach tightens, and my breathing turns ragged and loud.

"These are changing," he rasps, cupping both breasts and lifting. A sound of masculine approval hums in his throat. "They're rounder. Fuller. Heavier than before."

And even more sensitive. He rolls my nipples, tugging lightly, and my head falls back against his chest. Desire burns through me. The need sparking in my veins grows into towering flames. "Griffin…"

"*Agapi mou?*"

"I'm ready," I moan.

He chuckles, the sound like mulled wine swirling through my body. He makes my head spin.

"You're impatient," he says. "I like it."

"I want you." Desperately. Greedily. Forever.

He pinches my nipples hard, and I groan as the pleasure-pain sensation streaks straight to my throbbing sex.

"Touch me," I beg. "Touch me where I ache the most."

Griffin slides one hand down my abdomen. He stops just short of my curls, leaving me quivering with need. Anticipation sends lightning arcing through my body and then exploding across my skin. The room brightens, then dims.

Griffin pulls me more firmly against him, a deep rumble resonating in his chest when our bodies press together. But he's still dressed, and I want him naked. Now.

"Too many clothes." He feels amazing, but skin-on-skin would be so much better.

He nips my neck just beneath my thundering pulse. "I'm in charge here."

I press backward into his erection, and he draws in a sharp breath. I think I'm a little bit in charge here, too.

Moving his lower body out of my reach, he licks my nape. I shiver. Heat pools in my belly, and everything down low starts to pulse, desperate for the same sort of kiss. One of Griffin's hands still toys with my breast. The other lifts from my lower abdomen, and I instantly miss his searing touch.

Without warning, his hand comes down on my mound with a quick, hard slap. My hips jerk. My mouth opens on a loud gasp, and a rush of heat floods my core.

"Good?" His gravelly question whispers across my cheek.

I nod, his stubble lightly chafing the shell of my ear. Nerves throb under his hand. Reaching back, I grip his thighs with both hands and hold on.

He grinds his wide palm over me in a slow circle. Then he slaps again, swift and sudden and almost as unexpected as before. Pleasure flares between my legs, so powerful I jolt. Griffin curves his hand around me, holding me steady.

I shudder with need, feeling his heart thud like a battering ram against my back.

"You're flooding my fingers." He presses on the sensitive nub of nerves, maintaining steady but motionless pressure. "So hot and wet."

"Claim me." I move my hips, rubbing mindlessly against his hand. "Claim me all over again."

Griffin slides a finger inside me and pumps it in a frustratingly slow rhythm. I'm so slick, he adds another. Blindly, I start dragging at his pants, pulling them down. With a low curse, he shifts back, lifting his hands from me just long enough to undress. Then he grips me under my arms and moves me farther up the bed.

The look I throw him over my shoulder says I'm ready for anything.

The look he throws back says he knows.

Getting behind me again, he lifts my arms so I'm leaning forward and gripping the headboard. Then he's inside me, and I'm desperate for every inch of him. My back bows, and I moan, my pulse pounding in quick, eager beats. Griffin wraps his arms around me and slowly thrusts deep.

I'm so ready for him that he pumps his hips more roughly, setting an electrifying pace from the start. I hold on to the headboard so hard my knuckles turn white, gasping each breath, alive with sensation, drowning in emotion. Griffin grips me to him, each hammering thrust sending stronger and stronger tremors through me until I know I'm about to burst. My core muscles tighten around him. I throw back my head, a shout rising in my throat.

"Not yet," Griffin growls. He stops moving. I pant, my whole body in a state of sweetly agonizing suspension. He leans over my back, his hot skin on mine. In my ear, he rasps, "I claim you, Catalia Eileithyia Thalyria."

I take a shallow breath. Not Fisa. Not Sinta. Not Tarva. *Thalyria*.

"I claim you for my very own. With my blood. With my bone. With my heart. With my soul. You are mine. Forever. In this world, and in the next."

I shake from the force of his vow. It winds around me, spins through me, sinks into the woven threads of my life just like Griffin sinks into me—once, again, harder— sealing his promise with his own pulsing seed and pushing me straight over the edge along with him. The tight ball of tension deep inside me abruptly shatters, and I go reeling toward release.

Boneless, my hands aching from gripping the head- board, I drag in a shuddering breath. The crisp night air is sharp on my tongue. Sliding out of me, Griffin gently pulls me back and against his chest. Flexing my fingers, I settle limply against his body, my legs curled beneath me. He presses a kiss to my temple, his warm exhale feather- ing across my forehead. Emotion swells inside me, and hot pressure crawls up my throat.

Doing my best not to cry, I turn, curl my fingers into Griffin's hair, and then pull his head down to mine. Our mouths meet in an undemanding way, but when I touch my tongue to the seam of his lips, he parts them, offering a deeper kiss. The embrace quickly heats up, and soon our bodies are as tangled as our tongues. I straddle him, desire coiling through me again.

I grip his jaw with both hands and hold his face to mine, our lips still brushing and his breath feeding my lungs. Our eyes meet.

"I claim *you*, Griffin Thalyria." I remember every word he spoke to me. I'll remember them until I cease to exist. "I claim you for my very own. With my blood. With my bone.

With my heart. With my soul. You are mine. Forever. In this world, and in the next."

His eyes squeeze shut. He clutches me to him and buries his face in my hair. His hands splay over my back, holding me from neck to waist.

"I live for you," he says into the curve of my neck. "I love you."

Tears flood my eyes, and I wrap my arms around him, holding him tight. After a moment, we tip over with Griffin on top. I cradle his hips between my thighs, and he slides into me again, slowly this time. He makes love to me, his hands in my hair and his lips on mine. Braced on his forearms and rocking gently, he kisses me like he needs me in order to survive.

Tension and pleasure build, break, and then whip through me again. Griffin shudders above me, stiffening and then relaxing in turn. He rolls onto his back, taking me with him, and then murmurs the words that were forming inside me, expanding in my chest, but still smoky and without discernible form.

He tells me that we're one. That together, we're stronger, better, and something different than what we were before.

With lazy fingertips, I stroke his collarbone, my head on his shoulder. And as I drift off to sleep, half draped across my husband's warm, strong body, I decide that the Gods can say whatever they want. I wasn't made for Griffin, and he wasn't made for me. We were made for each other.

CHAPTER 8

NEARLY A WEEK LATER, I WAKE FROM A DECENT SLEEP—something that's rare for everyone these days. Lying on my side, I open my eyes. Griffin is facing me. He's still sleeping, but as if he senses me watching him, his lids slowly slide open to reveal storm-gray eyes framed by thick black lashes.

I reach out and lightly trace the bridge of his nose. "Good morning."

"Good morning," he rumbles back in a sleep-thick rasp.

Sighing, I start to get up, but he hooks his arm around my waist and drags me back. There's nothing sleepy or lazy about how fast he moves, or how hard he pulls, and I land flush against his solid chest with an unqueenly "*Oomph*."

"Where do you think you're going?" Griffin's leg pushes between mine, his crisp hair tickling the insides of my thighs. He slides a warm hand up my naked back and then cradles my head in his palm.

I wrap the hand that's not pinned between us around his shoulder, wiggle closer, and then inhale deeply against his neck. He smells so good to me, like man and mine. I want to lick him. Kiss him. Maybe bite.

I nuzzle the underside of his scruffy jaw, feeling his already impressive erection grow even harder against my lower belly. Griffin groans softly, shifting against me, and desire sparks inside me like flint on steel.

But it's late. I already woke up once and ignored the light—and all the things we need to do today.

Reluctantly, I stop nestling into Griffin's big, tempting body and tilt my head back to look at him. "It's time to get up. We're leaving this morning."

His eyes turn shadowed, and he grips me just a little tighter. The tensing of his muscles only lasts an instant. Even quicker is the pain that flashes across his features. He banishes it, exiling it to the place where he's been keeping the hurt of Piers's betrayal ruthlessly boxed up. Except when absolutely necessary, he hasn't spoken his brother's name out loud once.

"No one said we had to leave at the crack of dawn," Griffin mutters. His arm relaxes around me, but he doesn't let go. His callused thumb draws a slow, arching pattern through the hair behind my ear, making me shiver.

Fighting temptation, I twist around and glance out the window. "Dawn cracked a while ago."

And six days have passed since Piers disappeared with Athena. Five days ago, we started preparing Jocasta and Kaia to hold down the proverbial fort. Two days after that, we heard back from Castle Sinta. Devastation. And worse—understanding. Anatole, Nerissa, and Egeria don't seem to blame me for the loss of Piers any more than Griffin or the others do.

"Why the sudden frown?" Griffin asks. He untangles his hand from my hair and then gently trails a fingertip along each of my lowered eyebrows. "Is Little Bean bothering you?"

I shake my head. "No. She's settled. I'm fine." She didn't even make me throw up yesterday. Maybe we're moving out of that phase and into the next, whatever that is. Backaches? Constantly looking for a chamber pot? Waddling?

My frown deepens. Surely not waddling? Not yet.

"Then what's wrong?"

"You," I answer honestly. "I'm worried you're repressing your feelings."

Griffin grunts. It's kind of a laugh, but kind of not. "That's your area of expertise. Or it used to be. I don't repress anything."

"You're not talking about Pier—"

Griffin rolls me onto my back and kisses me hungrily. He takes me off guard at first, but then I kiss him back with just as much eagerness and lift my knees, curving my legs around his hips. He slides into me with so little effort that it surprises us both. I bite my lip, taming a wicked smile.

Griffin's expression is all satisfied heat. He flashes me a pirate's grin before suddenly pumping up on his arms. He dips his head and catches my nipple in his mouth, pulling on it with hot, wet tugs. Closing my eyes, I arch up into him with a moan.

He starts moving inside me, so slowly at first that it's decadently sensual. His stubble grazes my skin as he scatters scorching kisses across my chest. Midnight hair teases the hollow of my throat, and I curve my hands around his head. Griffin shifts up. His lips capture mine, and he pushes deeper into me, rocking hard. A rope of pure pleasure pulls taut inside me, making my toes curl and my mind go blank.

All I can feel is him, and all I want is more. Wings beat in my chest, unfurling with near-violence. Griffin speeds up, winding me even tighter. Release quivers just out of reach and then hits like a sudden storm.

Griffin stills and then pulses deep within me. His groan is long and low. He leans his forehead against my shoulder, holding himself rigid for a moment before dropping like a stone.

I croak something incoherent, and Griffin rolls off me, landing heavily on his back. He gropes for his pillow with one hand, sliding it under his head. He snakes his other hand underneath me, circling my shoulders and tipping me onto my side. He pulls me tightly against him. I wriggle my head up onto his shoulder and then drape my leg across his thigh, smiling up at him. He smiles back and then closes his eyes.

I blink in surprise. "You can't go back to sleep."

"Yes, I can." To prove it, he settles his body more firmly into the mattress.

"But…there are things to do. Realms to run." A journey to undertake.

His free arm flops across his eyes, blocking out the light from the east-facing window.

I stare at him in shock, not seeing much more than his slightly parted lips and stubborn jaw. After a while, his breathing slows.

I watch him, not at all sleepy, a niggling sense of unease overtaking pleasure. I'm completely aware of the fact that he just distracted me with amazing sex, and I let him. His focused blast of activity on his sisters' behalf over the last few days, his ability to find a smile here and there, especially for me, and very intense lovemaking are only masking the truth.

Griffin isn't getting past what Piers tried to do to us, to me, to *him*. If there's one thing that proves it, it's that he's not the one pushing us to get out of bed today—or any day at all.

⑥

I leave Griffin asleep in our room and make my way down to breakfast, only to find that breakfast is over, and there's no food. In fact, the dining room is completely empty. My stomach rumbling, I poke around the still largely unfamiliar palace, walking the dim, torch-lined corridors down a level toward where the main kitchen should logically be. I quickly get lost in the labyrinthine underbelly of Castle Tarva and have to ask servants for the right way not once, not twice, but *three* times.

Stupid sense of direction. I wish I had one.

Thinking I finally smell food, or *something*, I find myself foiled again when I pull up short in the doorway of the cavernous kitchen. In the middle of the room, Flynn is leaning toward Jocasta, his massive hands braced on the solid wooden worktable between them. Loose and wild as usual, his auburn hair reflects the light from the fire blazing in the hearth. Across from him, Jocasta is tipped forward as well, her hands wrist-deep in some kind of stewed herbs from the smell of it. They're glaring at each other.

"You think I can't handle the responsibility?" She pulls a handful of dark, limp leaves from her bowl and starts vigorously ripping them up.

"I didn't say that. Don't put words in my mouth, Jo."

"Then say what you mean." Even from the shadows of the hallway, I see her blue eyes flash and her expression tighten with a mixture of annoyance and frustration.

Flynn pushes off from the table with a scowl. "I'm saying you don't have to do everything alone. Find an advisor you trust."

"How should I know who to trust?"

"Ask Cat to meet people with you. She'll know who's lying, and what their intentions are."

Jocasta shakes bits of damp herbs from her fingers, flicking them back into the bowl. When most of her concoction is where it should be again, she picks up an already stained cloth from the table and then wipes her hands clean. "Cat's leaving today."

"And that terrifies you."

Jocasta's head snaps back up, sending a blue-black curl swinging against her jaw. Flynn makes a hesitant, almost imperceptible move toward it, but before his intention can become clear, Jocasta impatiently shoves the loose lock behind her ear. "Why do you say that?"

His hand drops, curling into a slack fist. "Because everyone relies on Cat. When she's around, we all have this ridiculous sense of security, like no matter what's happening, or who's swinging a sword, or throwing fire, or whatever terrifying person or creature is coming at us, she'll fix it. She always does."

Oh. My stomach crashes to my feet. For once, I'm pretty sure the queasiness isn't due to Little Bean.

Is that how everyone sees me? Is that what I am to them? What they expect?

Then it hits me—again. Of course it is. I'm Elpis. Unbreakable. Unshakable. Possibly going to vomit...

I breathe again, forcing steeliness on myself like a warrior donning armor. But it's an act, a disguise. Inadequacy haunts me like a completely justified ghost.

"Kaia and I will muddle through" is Jocasta's only response.

"You don't have to 'muddle through,'" Flynn says. "Ask them to stay a few more days, and get yourselves some people to help you. People you can trust."

"If Griffin and Cat thought we needed help, they would have suggested it. They obviously have more confidence in me than you do."

Flynn's jaw hardens. "You're putting words in my mouth again."

"Am I?" Jocasta smiles vaguely and without humor. "I guess you talk to me so little, I've started to invent."

Flynn freezes, staring at her. Emotional conflict makes him shut down completely. With Jocasta, anyway. He'll get into a roaring good fight with me.

"Cat and Griffin—they listen to people. Take advice," he finally says in a low, almost toneless voice. "Cat was Griffin's advisor at first. In a way, she still is."

If you ask me, Griffin's the sage one, but Jocasta eventually nods, conceding the point. "I'll think about it," she says.

"Thank you." Flynn seems to relax. "Get yourself a guard as well," he adds.

"I can take care of myself."

"I could take care of you better," he mutters irritably.

Jocasta grips the edge of the table like it's the only thing keeping her upright. Or like she might heave the whole thing up and over in a fit of rage. One or the other. I can't tell. When Flynn realizes what he just said, or rather how it could be taken, he pales until his shock of bright-red hair is his only color.

"I mean…" He clears his throat, looking up, around, anywhere but at her. "I mean you'd be twice as safe with a warrior guarding you. Me. Or someone else."

Jocasta slowly uncurls her fingers from the table. "Someone else?"

Flynn frowns. "I'm leaving today. I won't be here. You fought well in the arena, but we were all there. That doesn't mean you're ready for this." He waves his hand in an all-encompassing gesture. "Everyday danger? The insidious kind? It doesn't always come at you with a sword and a snarl. You might not see it coming."

That vague smile is back on Jocasta's lips, the one that speaks of utter disappointment. "So that's what you want? Some man following me around day and night?

Sleeping outside my bedroom door? Taking walks with me? Guarding me in the bathhouse?"

Flynn doesn't answer. He's too busy grinding his molars to dust.

"Well, I won't do it," Jocasta says. "I'm in a fortified castle and don't plan on leaving it. There are plenty of guards, high walls, and beyond them, there's a constant, swelling crowd that seems to genuinely love us. I'm not in any danger."

Flynn scoffs. "There's always danger. And it's most dangerous when you don't expect it. You can't let your guard down, Jo, especially while we're away."

Jocasta pushes the soggy, herb-soaked cloth farther down the table, wiping up a spill. When there's nothing left to keep her busy, she finally looks up at Flynn.

"Don't worry about me. Worry about yourself." She shifts from foot to foot, looking uncomfortable. "I certainly do."

Flynn leans in, his hands braced on the table again. Their eyes meet. "You do?"

Jocasta swallows so hard I can see it from here. Softly, she says, "You know I do."

Flynn's gaze drops to her mouth. Jocasta's lips part, and her tongue darts out to wet them. He targets the movement with his eyes, tilting his head slightly and suddenly looking like a hungry and very focused predator. She sways toward the man she's loved for so long, slowly closing the distance across the worktable. Flynn doesn't back off for once, and I start to feel like the worst sort of thrill seeker, because my heart is pounding for them, and I can't look away.

Do it. Kiss her. Claim her. It's all she wants.

Flynn's head drops a slow inch. Jocasta tilts hers up.

This is finally happening!

Bellanca charges into the kitchen through a side door.

Flynn and Jocasta jump apart. I jump, too, my hand flying to my chest where my heart starts kicking like a deranged donkey. Everywhere Bellanca goes, she goes like a bloody tornado. A bloody *flaming* tornado.

"What in the Underworld is that awful smell?" Bellanca waves her hand in front of her nose, looking at Flynn and Jocasta like it's probably them. Then she storms over, peers into Jocasta's bowl, and scowls. "What's that?"

"It's *going to be* a sleeping draught," Jocasta says tersely.

Bellanca wrinkles her freckled nose. "Who for?"

"For me," Jocasta answers from between gritted teeth. She's usually friendly to Bellanca, or at least neutral, so I know her crossness comes from being interrupted before her first kiss *ever*, and that from the man she's been waiting for for years.

Bellanca huffs. "You can't be that stupid."

Flynn's brown eyes narrow. The look he turns on Bellanca is truly terrible, but she doesn't seem to notice.

Jocasta takes a slow breath, her expression suddenly such a careful mask of politeness that I have no doubt she's erupting underneath. "Excuse me?"

"Why would you want to sleep that heavily? Only an idiot would do that." Bellanca looks genuinely confused. As usual, she's oblivious to anyone's reaction to her... forthrightness.

"Do you suggest I sleep with one eye open?" Jocasta asks coolly. "Or possibly not at all?"

Bellanca reaches between them and grabs an apple that somehow escaped the splattering of herbal sludge. "Good idea." As she straightens, she knocks Jocasta's bowl over, giving it a hard enough shove to dump it on the floor. The earthenware vessel shatters into tiny pieces, hopelessly contaminating the concoction.

Jocasta's mouth drops open.

Bellanca winks. "Eyes open." She crunches into her apple as she moves backward in a tinkle of gold bangles and a froth of sky-blue skirts.

Flynn steps after her, his voice lowering in pitch. "Did you just threaten her?"

Bellanca stops halfway across the kitchen, looking increasingly surly. She dabs a fingertip to her lips, wiping off a drip. "I'm trying to protect her."

"Do you know something?" Flynn growls, stalking forward until they're only a pace apart.

Bellanca takes another bite and then shrugs. "I know lots of things."

"Like what?" Flynn demands.

"Like potions such as that one are better left alone."

Jocasta stiffens. "I know what I'm doing. I'm not likely to overdose."

Bellanca shakes her head. "That's not what I mean."

"Then what *do* you mean?" Flynn asks, menace still heavy in his voice.

"Good Gods!" Bellanca rolls her eyes. "I was just trying to help. I'm going to change and pack." She takes another bite and then throws her apple at Flynn, hitting him square in the forehead.

I slap my hand over my mouth, stifling a gasp. Laugh. Gasp-laugh. I can't believe she just did that!

Stone-faced, Flynn wipes apple juice from his brow. Jocasta stares in horror. Bellanca whirls on her heel and then stomps from the room, going out the same way she came in—fast and flaming.

As soon as the Tarvan woman is out of sight, I back away from the open door before dissolving into fits of quiet laughter. Soon after, I hear Flynn and Jocasta do the same.

(6)

Jocasta doesn't ask me to stay and help her find an advisor, so I don't offer. I don't want her to know I was eavesdropping, but more importantly, I want to show her that I have faith in her and her decisions. I won't rattle her confidence just before we leave by asking if she needs my help. Besides, I agree with her. As long as they stay within the castle grounds, I think she and Kaia are perfectly safe.

We've all gathered in the courtyard, those of us who are riding out today and those of us we're leaving behind. It shouldn't be a dangerous journey, or long, but goodbyes are always hard.

Behind me, I hear footsteps and the creak of leather and turn from watching Griffin and Carver give last-minute instructions to their sisters. Kato drops my saddle onto Panotii's back.

"I can do that," I say, reaching to help.

He brushes my hand away. "I know you can." He bends down to tighten the girth.

No one lets me lift anything anymore, but I don't argue about that. Straps, however, I can handle, but Kato's broad back is blocking my attempt to help, and there's not a Satyr's chance in Tartarus he'll move out of the way. He finishes, tugs the stirrups into place, and then jiggles everything to make sure it's secure.

I pat Panotii's shoulder, and his enormous ears twitch in my direction. His chestnut coat is shiny and smooth, even though I haven't had much energy to brush him. By the time I think about heading to the stables, I'm usually ready for a nap. Maybe Griffin groomed him for me.

Kato turns to me. The rain-charged wind lifts his blond

hair from his shoulders, sending it swirling around his head. Storm clouds rush across the sky, darkening his blue eyes and throwing the courtyard into shadow. I shiver.

"Are you cold?" he asks, a slight frown creasing his brow.

I shake my head but keep rubbing my arms anyway. "Little Bean is like a bonfire inside me. It's... I don't know. Something in the air." Or right here in the somber courtyard. It's the ache of leaving Jocasta and Kaia behind in an only *mostly* stable situation, and the dread of separating them from their brothers and from the men they love. Despite my apparently confidence-inducing presence, anything can happen. An infinite number of things can go wrong, and I might not be able to stop them. What if they never see each other again?

"We can wait out the storm," Kato says.

I'm not entirely certain he's referring to the weather, but I shake my head again and then force a smile. "It's blowing east. We're going west. We'll be fine."

Across the courtyard, Bellanca detaches herself from a teary Lystra and then goes to her already saddled horse. Actually, it's Piers's horse. Bellanca decided the gelding was better suited to the long journey ahead than her aging mare and simply appropriated him. The horse's roan coat clashes magnificently with her fiery hair. As usual, the red locks still spark here and there. Even in the damp wind and coiled into tight braids on the top of her head, she can't seem to put them out. I don't know how she sleeps at night without catching her bed on fire. Sitting up? Maybe she takes her own advice and doesn't sleep at all.

Recalling the scene in the kitchen this morning makes me think of Flynn's pressure-heavy words again.

"Do you think I'm some kind of invincible warrior?" I

blurt out, feeling pretty vincible at the moment. Half the time, I just want to curl up around Little Bean and protect her. And I keep staring off into space.

"What do you mean, invincible warrior?" Kato asks.

Before I can answer, his cloak billows open on the breeze, and I see that his leather armor is new. There's a golden phoenix etched into the tough boar's hide. The artistry is outstanding, and I can almost see the bird in motion, raising its proud head as it spreads its burning wings. It's an indomitable creature, one that will always rise from the ashes, renewed by fire.

My pulse speeds up. I think I have my answer in the message Kato chose to write across his chest.

"I'm not sure exactly," I say, my gaze still locked on the phoenix. "Do you feel like when I'm there, we'll always win? Like no one will get hurt?"

Kato's big hands settle on my shoulders, squeezing lightly. "We all get hurt, and you're no exception."

I glance down, worrying my bottom lip. The Agon Games weren't kind to Kato, Griffin, or me. They were even harder on Carver, who nearly lost his life.

"But what about the outcome?" I ask, looking back up. "The end result?"

His hands drop away after another encouraging squeeze. "I don't know if we're always going to win. I don't think even the Gods know that. But I know you, and I know the lengths you'll go to. I've seen what your body can endure. And how you'll go one step farther when you've already got nothing left to give. And then another. And then more. I gave up hope when we got separated in the ice caves, and I thought you'd died. I gave up hope again when you got destroyed by the Hydra and stopped breathing before our eyes."

He looks up and over my head, and I know the memory still pains him. Sometimes it still pains me—popping skin, breaking bones, tumbling sky. Fear.

"But you came back every time," Kato says. "Stronger. Less reckless. More powerful. Wiser than before."

"Wiser? Well, that wouldn't be hard."

"And do you know what I learned?" he asks, ignoring my self-mocking tone.

I shake my head, already maybe knowing, and kind of dreading his next words.

"To never give up hope."

The air suddenly feels too thick for my lungs. Or maybe it's just me who can't breathe. "Hope?"

Kato's cloak snaps behind him on the growing wind, leaving the phoenix exposed to me. "You told us about Elpis before the Games, before we named our team after her."

I swallow with difficulty. "Her? Elpis is an idea."

He shakes his head. "It's more than that. It's an idea with a woman's form. It's something to latch on to."

"It's all ancient history most people don't even know anymore."

"But you brought the idea back," Kato insists. "Brought *her* back—into hearts and minds. Back to Thalyria. And now everyone's speaking it at once. Calling it in the streets. Using it as a greeting. Chanting it at our gates." His eyes meet mine. Striking. Blue. Devoted. "Now… I don't know. You're Elpis to me."

So much churns inside me that I can't separate my thoughts from my emotions. I didn't tell anyone about my Elpis discovery, not even Griffin. It just felt like too much pressure. The weight of the world. But it seems as though Kato figured it out all on his own, probably long before I did. And Flynn did, too, without putting it into so many words. And there's no doubt in my mind that Griffin knows also, however he chooses to think of it. He's known longer than any of us.

But Kato is terrifying me. He's raising me too high. "What if I fail?"

Kato looks at me with such sincerity, such platonic affection, that my chest squeezes tight.

"You'll still be my light in the dark, Cat. Even if you fail."

I inhale sharply, fighting the tears that always seem so close to the surface lately. Answering him is impossible. If I do, emotion will overwhelm me.

Blinking rapidly, I look around. The courtyard is unusually quiet, despite our gathering here. Flynn stands near his horse, his auburn brows drawn low, trying without much success to keep his brooding gaze off of Jocasta. From the looks of it, Jocasta is glancing Flynn's way just as often while still trying to pay attention to Griffin and Carver as well. Next to her, Kaia keeps looking at us, but I know it's Kato she's watching.

Having said her brief goodbyes, Ianthe is already at the gate. The guards have cleared a path for us, the crowd is waiting for our passage with bated breath, and Ianthe looks more than ready to leave the castle that's been more or less her prison for the last several months. She's riding Galen Tarva's enormous black warhorse. He's far too big for her—even bigger than Griffin's Brown Horse—and bad-tempered and jumpy to boot, but Ianthe wouldn't ride any other. If my terrible suspicion about Galen's abuse is correct, she's taking control of what's between her legs. I fear it's symbolic, whether she realizes it or not.

Bellanca mounts the roan, settling lightly and expertly into her saddle. She slaps at her sparking hair again, going cross-eyed when an ember pops and then sizzles toward her nose.

I smile, and it feels good. I haven't smiled enough lately.

Bellanca fishes in her saddlebag and then jams a floppy hat onto her head, maybe to smother the fire. "Gods, are we going or what?"

Beside me, Kato chuckles as he nods toward Bellanca. "I like her."

"I do, too." I reach out and grab his wrist. "And thank you."

His eyebrows rise in question. "For what?"

"For being the brother I never had."

His face loses all trace of humor. We're not related, neither by blood nor by marriage, but that doesn't matter. My heart knows the truth.

Kato lifts his free hand and ruffles my hair. He pats my head, and I know what that means. It means he loves me, too.

CHAPTER 9

HOMECOMING IS BITTERSWEET AND DOESN'T LAST LONG. FOR A group of people who have never shown themselves to be cowardly in the least, we sure get out of Castle Sinta as fast as we can. Home somehow doesn't feel like home anymore when Anatole's leathery face is creased with loss and Nerissa's eyes are red-rimmed from crying.

The fact that we came back without two of their daughters doesn't help. Staying in Sinta any longer would be pointless anyway since they immediately begin to pack. Castle Tarva is about to get invaded—by parents—and we're the escort back.

Egeria, who's shortly going to find herself managing western Thalyria alone, holds herself together admirably, and my respect for her grows. She agrees with and adds to Griffin's and my suggestions, our many detailed conversations together reinforcing how competent and practical they both are, especially my husband. Hearing him lay out plans for integrating Sinta and Tarva makes me realize I'm like a foundation and a roof, important at the beginning and at the end. Griffin is the house in between.

As we all gather in the courtyard and prepare to depart Castle Sinta on the first day I haven't seen anyone crying—yet—I turn to Egeria and say, "I'm sorry we're leaving you alone."

She smiles like that's one of the nicest things I've ever said to her. The terrible fact is, it might be.

"Sinta has been peaceful for months now," she replies,

seeming wholly confident. "The Ipotane will hopefully block any Fisan threat soon, and there's still part of the army here."

A small part. The rest is leaving with us, moving east to join the forces we've already begun amassing in Tarva. But it wasn't her safety I was worried about.

"That's not what I meant. I hope you won't be too lonely." She's used to being surrounded by a large family. There'll be no one left.

Her dove-gray eyes soften. "I'm not alone. Lenore is here."

Lenore? I search my memory. "Jocasta's maid?"

Egeria blushes and ducks her head. "Not *just* Jocasta's maid."

Oh. Oh! My eyes widen. Probably not Jocasta's maid at all anymore. "That's wonderful," I say, almost voluntarily hugging her. The sudden impulse fades before I actually get my arms up, but Egeria takes matters into her own hands and gives me a hearty squeeze.

"Why are you so pale?" Nerissa asks me after Egeria lets me go. She moves closer and inspects my face like she's already concocting a recipe for a vile-tasting medicinal soup that'll not only cure my lack of color but probably put hair on my chest, too. "You have shadows under your eyes, and your lips are practically white. Are you sick? I have herbal tonics I could fetch before we leave."

Nerissa's tonics smell like mud, barn, and goat manure. There's no way I'm drinking that. My stomach roils, and not just because of the threat of Nerissa's medicine. Little Bean has proven to me more than once over the last several days that she is not, in fact, done making me throw up.

"I'm not sick," I answer. Although lately, it feels a lot like I am.

Egeria gasps. "You're pregnant!" Her expression lights up in a way I didn't know was possible, turning her into a beauty to almost rival her younger sisters.

I wasn't going to announce the news now, here, like this, but I nod, since Egeria has already guessed anyway and looks like she could suddenly dance in place. Beside her, Nerissa's face positively glows for the first time since we've been back. Grinning, Griffin's mother folds me into a soft, herb-scented embrace.

Her delighted voice is soft in my ear. "Thank you for giving me my first grandchild. You'll be a wonderful mother, Cat."

Nerissa rocks me a little in her enthusiasm, shifting my balance to and fro. I hold on to her, powerless to stop it. Actually, I don't want to.

My heart expands almost painfully in my chest. Coming from the woman who secretly made me want to crawl into her lap the first time I saw her, those heartfelt words mean a lot. They also make me feel achingly fragile inside. Will I make a good mother? I don't know how to handle a child. Half the time, I hardly know how to handle myself.

Off to the side, I hear Anatole gruffly congratulating Griffin and pounding him on the back. Griffin says something equally gruff in response, but all I keep thinking is that Nerissa said the one thing I needed to hear above all else. Now I just need to believe it myself.

I pull back from Nerissa's arms and catch both Bellanca and Ianthe staring at us from atop their horses. The twin disbelieving expressions on their faces are almost comical, but I don't laugh, because really, it's not at all funny. They already know I'm pregnant. It's the warm hug that's taken them so thoroughly aback. I understand their astonishment, but if anyone can teach them that parental affection is possible, it's Nerissa and Anatole. It might be a slow process. I'm still learning myself.

Already mounted, Carver ambles up alongside Bellanca and Ianthe. "Blink, ladies. Chins off the ground. Especially you, Bellanca. I can see halfway down your throat. I know it comes as a complete shock, but yes, Cat does know how to hug." He winks in my direction. "Almost."

I refrain from a rude hand gesture, because Nerissa would scold me. Kato and Flynn chuckle as they finish readying their horses.

Ianthe's green eyes brighten with humor, and I love her even more. *She's* unbreakable. Does Elpis get an Elpis? Or two? Because along with Griffin, I think she's mine.

In typical Bellanca fashion, the redhead lifts her switch and bashes Carver over the head with it. He yelps in surprise, and maybe some pain, and then glares at her like he's seriously considering knocking her off her horse. Or pulling her hair. Given half a chance, the two of them would brawl like urchins in an alley. Luckily, Carver still has some control over his physical impulses, despite consuming a truly worrisome amount of wine lately.

He opens his mouth, and I'm curious to hear what he'll say, but Nerissa beats him to the verbal punch with something I'm guessing will set Bellanca even more firmly on her ass.

"Bellanca!" Nerissa calls out sharply. "Is that how a young lady behaves?"

The Tarvan ex-princess's face goes stark white. Then bright red. "He's unbearable!"

"Men often are," Nerissa responds philosophically.

"But he's always needling me!"

"Rise above," Nerissa and I say at the same time. We turn to each other and laugh, and the sudden twinkle in

Nerissa's eyes goes a long way toward healing the guilt I feel over Piers's permanent exile.

Bellanca looks like she's been swallowed by a whirlpool and spit out in Atlantis with no idea which way is up or down. Her eyes are huge and confused. Her mouth still gapes. I think she has a lot to say, but for once, she's actually questioning the wisdom of blurting it all out.

The second Nerissa turns her attention away, Carver gives Bellanca an epic smirk. Bellanca's eyes narrow, zeroing in on the smug turn of his lips like she's perfectly capable—and willing—to rip his mouth right off his face with her bare hands. Carver stops smiling and gets out of reach.

I smother a laugh. I'm glad Bellanca is here. Carver doesn't seem to react to much of anything besides her anymore.

When everyone is mounted and ready to go, Griffin gravitates naturally to my side. Panotii and Brown Horse lead the procession out of the castle and through the crowded, colorful streets of Sinta City. Bellanca, Ianthe, Nerissa, and Anatole follow us, trailed by a good portion of Griffin's Sintan army. Beta Team accompanies the soldiers, a large unit under each of their commands.

I wave to the cheering crowd almost as often as Griffin does. The people of Sinta City love us. Griffin because he's theirs. Me because I chose them.

But the attention is still something I can't get used to, don't really want, and am not sure I truly deserve. Relief feeds my lungs like fresh air when our slow parade finally exits the city and winds its way toward the sloping olive groves. Unfortunately, the respite is short-lived.

Griffin leans his dark head toward mine. "Next stop—Lycheron."

My shoulders slump, and I whine like a baby. "Do we have to?"

He chuckles. "At least there are no Ice Plains to cross this time."

No. Only half of Sinta. We'd wanted to confront Lycheron looking our strongest, with our soldiers behind us, so luck had been on our side when we didn't see the disturbingly virile Ipotane Alpha on our way to collect the army. A group of the warrior creature's sentries and their Nymphs—I'm still not sure how *that* works—stopped us instead. We asked them to find Lycheron so that we could speak to him on our way back.

"Do you really think you can get him to switch to guarding the border between Tarva and Fisa without making you go through a whole new challenge?" I ask. Lycheron will only bargain male Alpha to male Alpha. The first challenge involved riddles, forfeits, and Artemis—all of which I could do without.

"I can try." Griffin's gray eyes glitter from beneath his dark lashes as he turns to me, the mix of humor and determination in them making my breath catch. Man. Warlord. Husband. King. I love every part of him.

"I'm going to stitch that onto a banner for you," I tell him. "I'll turn it into your official motto."

The corners of his mouth kick up, and his expression brightens with surprise. "You can sew?"

"Nope." I grin. "But I can try."

Lycheron. *Good Gods.* He's still as potent as a creature can get. Half horse. Half man. And the man half is…

I'd swallow, but my mouth has gone dry.

…something to look at.

Frankly, the horse half isn't bad, either. Sleek. Black. Muscled. Huge. Everything—*huge.*

We're midway between Sinta City and Tarva City, meeting in the grasslands before they gradually turn into the hills and forests of the north. Beta Team flanks us with the army. Griffin's parents remain with Carver, hanging back with the troops, but Bellanca stays close to us, as does Ianthe. The Ipotane make our horses nervous, so we dismount and approach on foot. After squeezing my hand, Griffin steps a little in front of us, knowing that Lycheron will only negotiate with him.

Next to me, Ianthe stares in utter fascination at the Ipotane Alpha. What worries me, though, is how Lycheron is staring back. His focus is only partially on Griffin. His equine ears twitch, and his massive man-shoulders keep angling our way, as if he can't help leaning toward Ianthe. He sniffed me on the Ice Plains, like he was drawing in my essence and my magic, like he was tasting and learning them. Now he's sniffing my sister—repeatedly—and his tawny eyes turn hooded. Muscles quiver down his long horse back, and Ianthe's lips part on a softly shuddered breath. Her color rises.

The Ipotane Alpha watches her, his eyes focused and fierce, and something in the pit of my stomach starts to feel all wrong. Not because Lycheron is a magical creature. He's wholly male, and even I have a hard time not staring at his chiseled chest, sculpted arms, and decadently handsome face. It's because I *feel* the tension snapping between them—both of them—and the awful churning inside me springs from thinking I know exactly what the Ipotane will demand in return for his continued help.

Lycheron reluctantly shifts his attention to Griffin again. He tosses his head, sending ebony hair rippling down his back. "Our agreement was to guard your insignificant border for no longer than six months. If you don't need us here any longer, we'll return to the Ice Plains."

"I still want you to guard my border for the time remaining," Griffin says. "But as I've just explained, my border has moved a week's ride to the east."

Lycheron scoffs. "A week for you. For me, three days at the most."

My jaw nearly comes unhinged. *The Ipotane can cross all of Tarva in just three days?*

"Three days, then," Griffin says. "It's still my border. The deal should stand."

"It shouldn't. And it doesn't. You specified the border between Sinta and Tarva. Here I am. If this border no longer exists, I have no reason to guard it. And I certainly have no cause or reason to patrol the border with Fisa."

"You're reneging on our agreement," Griffin says, seething.

Lycheron stamps a hoof hard against the ground. "Our deal involved Sinta and Tarva. By your own decree, those two realms no longer exist. It's just Thalyria, no border, free movement, and my herd is trooping up and down the middle of it."

"I still have a border that needs guarding," Griffin grates out.

"Then you should have worded the deal differently." Lycheron's tone is cool, flat, and final. I can tell he's not done, though. He's too interested in Ianthe for that.

Griffin's nostrils flare on a calming breath. He needs more than one. "Then I offer you a new challenge."

Lycheron's honey-brown eyes gleam with genuine interest, but then his expression hardens again, and he visibly squashes the temptation. "No. I've seen how the Gods favor you. It's vexing, to say the least."

Bollocks. I thought the Ipotane couldn't resist a challenge. Apparently they can—when they think they won't win.

"We won't call a God," Griffin says quickly. "Especially not here."

Lycheron shakes his head. "They're always watching you two."

Always? Ack! I hope not.

"Offer me something else," Lycheron says, looking straight at Ianthe.

No. No. No!

"I have nothing to give that you'd want." Steel edges every word of Griffin's answer.

"I want her." Lycheron nods in our direction.

Griffin lunges for me, grabs my arm, and then shoves me behind him. From his angle, he must not have realized who Lycheron was really staring at.

"Not me," I squeak, clutching the back of his tunic.

Griffin twists around, his eyebrows slamming down. "What do you mean, not you?" From the completely baffled look on his also livid face, I think he can't conceive of Lycheron wanting someone other than me.

I tilt my head to the side, grinding out, "It's Ianthe he wants."

Griffin's eyes flick to my sister.

Lycheron takes another long breath, filling his lungs with the air around Ianthe until his impressive chest expands, clearly—and sensually—savoring whatever scent or magic he draws into his huge body along with the deep inhale. Ianthe noticeably shivers.

Griffin's enraged stare must hit Lycheron like a thunderclap. "You can't have her, either."

I glare daggers at the Ipotane Alpha. *Damn right, he can't!*

Lycheron swishes his tail, whipping his muscled hindquarters with it. "Then you're right, you have nothing I want."

Apparently, I don't make the cut anymore. Not that I'm complaining.

Lycheron smirks, this time at me. "Little Origin, your scent has changed." He inhales again, and it's like a warm fist wraps itself around my insides and gently tugs.

This time, *I* shiver. *How does he do that?*

Little Bean's life force reacts with a hearty thump and wiggle. *She felt it, too!*

"Ah, I see," the Ipotane says.

My hand instantly covers my belly. I don't want him seeing anything in there.

Down there.

Anywhere!

Lycheron shrugs. "No wonder you lost your appeal."

I gape at him, offended. I can't help it. Griffin looks like he's about to explode. Bellanca snorts a laugh, and I whip my head in her direction. The look on my face shuts her up fast. Ianthe is quiet.

"So that's it?" Griffin growls in anger. "That's what your word is worth?"

Lycheron bares his teeth. An amber glow pulses to life in the depths of his eyes, and deep-rooted anxiety jumps to full and sudden attention inside me. It comes straight from that place where survival instincts live, and right now, they're telling me to run.

Raw power laces the air with enough magic that it chafes my skin, and I can almost taste it. But wanting to turn tail and actually doing it are two very different things, and together, Griffin and I stand our ground. It helps knowing that while Lycheron may be terrifying when he chooses to be, there's no way in the Underworld he would risk the Gods' wrath by harming us.

Ianthe and Bellanca don't budge, either. Everyone else

might be too far away to realize how frightening Lycheron is, and I doubt Beta Team will tell them. That would be counterproductive to keeping our soldiers here.

"My word is worth my weight in gold, and my weight is significant," Lycheron snarls. "A bargain was struck. The wording was precise. The consequences are yours."

I hate to even think it, but unfortunately, he's right. I squeeze Griffin's arm, trying to convey that. We don't have a leg—and definitely not a hoof—to stand on. We naively hoped that Lycheron would give us the entire six months he promised, despite the specific terms of the bargain. But the fact is, we *did* specify the location of the border, and that's our fault.

"Reconsider." Lycheron looks at Ianthe again. His voice turns almost ominously deep. "You know what I want."

A flush crawls up Griffin's neck as his blood heats. His denial, while remaining purely verbal, borders on violent. "I don't bargain away my family's free will. Ianthe is *not* for sale."

Ianthe inhales sharply. I can practically hear her heart pounding from here, and mine sinks like a ship. Griffin has no idea what he's just done. He defended her, called her family, and put her well-being above his own ambition and needs. I'd bet my magic that no one has ever done anything like that for Ianthe before. If she's anything like me, and I'm pretty sure she is, his fierce denial to use her for his own gain just won him her undying loyalty. And we already know she's radically and terrifyingly self-sacrificing when it comes to us.

"No, Ianthe—"

Ianthe lifts her chin and speaks over me. "I'll go."

"No! I just got you back!" She's my Elpis. My other Elpis. I need her. She can't just *go*. Doesn't she want to stay with me?

"I'll go," Ianthe repeats with even more force, looking first at me and then at Griffin. "You need this. You both do. We have to protect the rest of Thalyria from Mother. With the Ipotane at the border, she won't try to get past. *You* can invade, not her. *You* can attack without fearing what's coming at your back." She shrugs shoulders that are slight, almost too thin, but so incredibly strong. "Besides, he can't be any worse than Galen Tarva. And it's only six months, not forever."

"But you don't know what he wants from you!" My voice comes out too high and shockingly loud. I bite my lip almost hard enough to draw blood.

"I know what he wants." Griffin's tone is a curtain of doom. My husband is incredibly angry right now.

Ianthe scoffs, understanding immediately. "That's not possible."

"Have you seen the Nymphs?" I hiss.

She slowly pales to a shade I don't like at all. Then her spine stiffens, and a blank, detached look changes her face entirely. "Like I said, he can't be any worse than Galen Tarva."

My knees nearly buckle. I can hardly breathe. She just confirmed my worst fears, and I can't help seeing in my mind how frightening and horrible it must have been. It makes me sick inside, the thought of that meaty brute on top of her, holding her down, and my little sister screaming and kicking and struggling underneath.

Mother sent her there. To be used. Abused. Ianthe could have fought him off with her Water Magic, but there's no doubt in my mind that Galen Tarva made her believe the consequences of that kind of resistance would have been even worse. For herself, and for others. A man like him would have no problem hanging the safety of his entire household over Ianthe's head—Bellanca, Lystra, gentle, addled Appoline. Everyone.

My voice shakes with rage, and I look hard enough at Ianthe that she finally looks back. "You are not an object to be used. We do not barter with your body."

"Stop speaking before I get angry." Lycheron's low voice swells with the warning rumble of a thousand pounding hooves.

I look at the Ipotane Alpha, and fear ices me over. *He wasn't angry before?* I guess not, because now his very presence hollows my chest and coats my stomach in acid. His eyes glow a violent amber, and I shudder, almost shaking in my boots. I don't know how he does this to me. Even Griffin looks cowed. Bellanca takes a step back, her magic sparking. Distance is no longer a sufficient buffer, and I feel more than see the hundreds of people behind us backing away, cringing, cowering. I want to do the same. Only Ianthe is still standing tall.

"I do not force myself on females. Goddess, creature, or human," Lycheron says.

"You've been with a Goddess?" Ianthe asks.

I turn, gawking at her. *That's* what she's worried about?

My head whips back toward the Ipotane leader. "Swear to me," I demand, knowing I'll detect any falsehood in his words, and that he'll be magically bound by the vow. "Swear to me that you won't touch Ianthe in a sexual way. If she goes with you, you will not touch her."

"Ianthe." Lycheron savors my sister's name on his tongue like a spicy mulled wine, dragging it out long enough to uncover all the nuances that make it both zesty and sweet. His power-charged eyes fade back to a warm, only slightly luminous brown, their heated concentration solely on my sister. His gaze is so focused that it's almost an ocular touch. "I swear to *Ianthe* that I will not touch her in any way she does not wish."

Ianthe flushes deeply. Her lips part. Her breathing accelerates. She nods once, her green eyes huge, and Lycheron's skin shudders over his taut muscles, absorbing the jolt of his unbreakable vow.

My heart starts pounding even harder than before. He swore to Ianthe, cutting me out of the loop. But there was no lie in his words when Lycheron said he doesn't force himself on females. He swore only to touch her in ways she doesn't object to. She… *Oh my Gods.* Ianthe might actually be safe with him. Safer than with us! We're heading for Fisa. For war. For Mother.

All of a sudden, I feel much better about this.

Griffin takes a deep breath that lifts his chest. Then his head bows, and his hands fall to his hips. For a moment, he looks defeated. When he looks up again, to Ianthe, he says, "I should thank you, but I really wish you'd just take it all back."

She breaks eye contact with Lycheron to look at him. "Take care of Talia." Her voice wavers at the end when she really sees Griffin's face and understands his sincerity—he *does* wish she would take it all back. "…Brother," she adds hesitantly, as if it's a new word she's trying out for the first time, one she only just learned the meaning of and isn't quite sure how to fit into her reality yet.

It breaks my heart, and the way my chest contracts crushes my heart even more. From Griffin's tortured expression, I know he understands the gift Ianthe just offered with a single word—trust. And letting her leave with this volatile, otherworldly male now pains him even more. Upset doesn't even begin to describe him. He's outwardly calm and quiet now, but I know the emotion that boils underneath.

Ianthe looks away, but not before I see the sheen in her eyes. We're her family now, the one she's probably secretly dreamed of since the day Eleni died, and in my selfish grief, I left her behind. Ianthe was nine. Alone. Unprotected. No Thanos. No Eleni. No me. Her magic was still so far from being mature that I didn't even know she would turn into a powerful Water Mage. Being the youngest among us probably spared her life but not much else. She's seventeen now, all innocence irrevocably lost.

I take a sour breath that tastes like my own failures and lay my hand on Griffin's arm. Already tensely coiled, his muscles tighten even more under my fingers. Ianthe isn't only a new sister to him, a female relation only two scant years older than Kaia. I think he also sees her as me, the young me he didn't know yet and wasn't there to defend and protect. I can feel him practically shaking under my hand with the need to shield Ianthe now from the things that have already happened to both of us. But it's too late. We're Fisan royals. We were born without shelter in the middle of a raging storm. We were wrecked and laid bare by a person we should have been able to trust, in a place most people consider safe. Mother. Home.

I grip Griffin's arm, maybe to keep from reaching for my sister myself. Ianthe is an adult. This is her choice, and we need to respect it.

Lycheron steps closer to Ianthe, carnality in his every look and move. "And now you'll swear something to me, my fragile little dove."

Ianthe cocks her head back to meet the Ipotane Alpha's penetrating gaze. Her voice gently rasps. "What?"

"Yes, Alpha," he rectifies, watching her carefully.

The slightly dazed look on Ianthe's face vanishes, and she snorts.

Lycheron grins, a slow, predatory smile that probably makes every female within ten miles flush. I know I do.

He doesn't insist, but he insists on something else. Lowering his voice, he leans in closer to tell her what he wants. "The only male or beast you'll ride for the next six months is me." It's impossible to miss the possessive—and baldly sexual—undercurrent in Lycheron's words.

Her back straight, her chin high, and not shaking in the least, Ianthe studies Lycheron, letting his words sink in. Looking at her, I see densely compressed spirit. Vitality, magic, courage, love—when she detonates, she'll rattle the world.

"I swear it," Ianthe finally says. "For the next six months, I'll ride only you."

She tenses as her vow crashes into her bones and blood. Her bright-green eyes dilate, and then she blinks. Satisfied, Lycheron holds out his large hand. Ianthe places her much smaller one in his. In the next instant, she's on his back, her legs wrapped tightly around his huge frame and her hands gripping his bare shoulders for balance. She gasps.

Lycheron's ocher eyes flare with heat, burning bright amber for a quick but alarming moment. Then, to Griffin he says, "You need not worry about the Fisan border. In three days, I'll have it covered and impenetrable from the east."

Without another word to us, he wheels and charges off, leaving a pounding of hoofbeats in the air along with a thundering call to his herd to make haste across the realm.

My heart in my throat, I lunge after my sister. "Ianthe!" I scream.

She doesn't turn, her long, dark hair snapping on the wind and her lithe form fading fast. Maybe she doesn't hear. Or maybe she doesn't want to look back.

I stare until she fades from sight. After eight years apart, she's gone again with only the clothes on her back, and we didn't even say goodbye.

CHAPTER 10

NOT LONG AFTER WE RETURN TO TARVA CITY, I KNOW IT'S TIME
to see a hermit about a potion. And not just any hermit.
The hermit of Frostfire, a powerful witch known for her
unparalleled concoctions. We're going to war. Mother is a
monstrosity of magic, hugely powerful and totally unscru-
pulous. I have significant power of my own, but it's unreliable. The fight with Piers showed me once again just how
fickle my lightning is. The magic is there. Now it just needs
to work when I ask it to and stop being so Gods damn
dangerously unpredictable.

The more we discuss the idea of going to Frostfire, the
more Little Bean's energy seems to jolt and jerk inside me.
I can only assume she's protesting a plan that involves my
traveling to the Ice Plains north of Fisa and drinking a vile
potion to unlock my magic. To be honest, it doesn't tempt
me much, either. But what choice do I have? Magic wins
wars. Magic is the only thing that can intimidate Mother.

Unfortunately, we can't spare anyone from their current posts, Griffin categorically refuses to let me go alone,
and I categorically refuse to take Bellanca. I don't know
all that much about the hermit of Frostfire outside of her
legendary potion-making abilities, but if anyone can make
a hermit shut the door in your face and lock it ten times
over, it's Bellanca Tarva. There's no way I'll risk being
turned away because Bellanca does something too loud,
flaming, or abrasive.

Which leaves Griffin and me. Beta Team, and especially

Carver, can take over his responsibilities to the army, but we can't trust just anyone with a secret mission to shore up my magic. Soldiers will help us invade Fisa, but my lightning is what we really need in order to face my mother.

Of course, we get constant arguments from the people we're leaving behind.

"You don't need *me* here," Bellanca insists, glancing around our impressive new army encampment on the outskirts of Kitros.

"We do," I say. "You'll help with organizing, recruiting, and training. The army is Beta Team's main responsibility now."

"Alpha Team," Bellanca corrects, although she looks pleased that I included her in the group.

I shrug. It'll always be Beta Team to me.

"You and Griffin are our main responsibility," Kato argues.

Griffin shakes his head. "We need you here. Too many people are arriving daily."

The ranks keep swelling with new soldiers, both Sintan and Tarvan. Even a few Fisans are starting to trickle in. Thalyrians.

"Then take some other people. Good, trained soldiers," Flynn urges.

Griffin and I both continue to balk at the idea.

"I really don't want anyone to know about this," I say. We haven't even brought Anatole, Nerissa, Jocasta, and Kaia into the loop, even though we visit them regularly. They're at Castle Tarva, spearheading civilian projects and working in tandem with Egeria to bring Sinta's new benefits east into our expanded territory.

Griffin agrees with me. "If word gets out that Cat's magic is unreliable, it could rattle the army, and even undermine confidence in our rule."

"Or Mother could hear of it," I add. "The last thing we want is her getting wind of our destination."

There are general grunts of agreement. Bellanca sparks a little brighter, too.

"I should be going with you," Carver says, staring broodingly at nothing at all.

That would be ideal, but that's not possible anymore. Just one more thing we can lay at Piers's feet. If Piers had chosen to support us, he would have headed all martial operations during any absence of Griffin's. Now that responsibility falls to Carver, which means he can't come with us.

Out of the corner of my eye, I watch the dark-haired swordsman, my brother by marriage and by choice. Carver has the kind of quick wit, razor-sharp smile, fighting talent, and teasing manner that make people want to stand out in his eyes and shine. Unfortunately, Carver's eyes also have an increasingly hard and unpredictable edge to them that makes those same people wonder what in the Underworld he's really thinking. If you don't know him already, it's getting harder to tell if he's joking with you or about to run you through. Not surprisingly, the new recruits are nervous around him, and nobody wants a bunch of jumpy men and women with weapons.

Which is just another reason that neither Flynn nor Kato can come with us. Flynn is a solid, unflappable presence for the troops to look up to, and Kato has a gift for inspiring ease and camaraderie, something we sorely need when faced with integrating two forces that recently saw each other as enemies and still aren't quite sure how to interact.

Bellanca can just be Bellanca. If anything, the troops will be reassured that we have intense Fire Magic on our side.

Not having a better option, Griffin and I choose a day

to leave, get ready, and then strike out on our own for the first time ever.

It feels strange to set out on a journey without our usual group, and its newest member almost refused to stay behind. Bellanca's determination is admirable, if exasperating. She trailed us for an hour until I ultimately told her about Griffin's magic rope, pulled it from his saddlebag, and then threatened to turn around and tie her to Carver until we got back. I wouldn't actually do it, but she's not the one who can detect lies.

Snarling, sparking, and spitting mad, the red-haired ex-princess cursed us both for idiots, wheeled her horse around, and then went back on her own. Threatening her with Carver worked like a charm.

Finally alone on the road, I don't know if we made the right decision or not.

Apparently, Griffin doesn't, either. He glances at me from under lowered brows, concern etching small lines around his mouth. "Maybe we should have let Bellanca come, or taken Kato or Flynn after all. I'm not sure it's wise to be out here on our own."

His thoughts echo mine, and the fact that we're so in tune warms me. That we both wonder if we made a mistake is less heartening.

I know what he's thinking, because I'm thinking it, too. I have no combat magic stored up, my lightning comes and goes in unpredictable explosions I have no control over, and half the time these days, I'm dragging physically, either tired or sick.

Griffin tugs gently on Brown Horse's reins, taking the road forking to the right. Panotii takes his cues from Brown Horse and follows. It's the road to Fisa. There should be warning signs. *Continue at your own peril. Danger. Are you* sure *this is the road you want? This way lies Andromeda, the Great and Terrible. TURN BACK!*

"What choice did we have?" I ask. "This potion could change everything. Having lightning I can control could stop an entire army in its tracks. It could stop Mother."

Griffin looks pensive. "I know. I just hate going alone."

I reach over and squeeze his forearm. "Carver's head seems to be screwed on backward lately, but we can't deprive him of his rightful place or take away something he's actually very good at. And with the army growing so fast, we need Kato and Flynn where they are, helping Carver."

"And you think Bellanca will scare off the hermit." It's not exactly a question, but Griffin doesn't seem entirely convinced.

"Partially." I bite my lip. "I also think she's a good influence on Carver."

Griffin looks at me, his eyes cool and hard under the overcast sky. A chill caterpillars down my back at his flinty expression, even though I know his lack of warmth isn't directed at me. He's worried about his brother. "How so?"

"She's the only one who tells him the truth about himself anymore."

Griffin turns back to the road. I think we both know it's time to intervene with Carver. But Griffin isn't acting like his usual self, either. Since that day with Piers, I've seen him avoid things he never would have before.

"Doing this means crossing into Fisa alone and unprotected," he eventually says. "And going back onto the Ice Plains."

"We're not alone or unprotected. We have each other," I argue. "And you know we can't bring anyone new into this, not when the basic usefulness of my magic is in question. The information is too sensitive to trust anyone with it.

Gods, we couldn't even trust—" *Piers*. Even unspoken, it's like I shout the name out loud.

Stealing a look at Griffin, I see that his face has taken on the blankness of emotional denial while still managing to seethe with anger. His expression more or less defiantly screams *I'm fine, perfectly fine, and don't you dare tell me that I'm not, because I bloody well am!*

Frowning, I face forward again. "Right now, Beta Team is more useful to us where they are, and the Ice Plains don't scare me anymore."

"But Fisa does." It's a statement. No question necessary.

But he's not exactly right. "It's not Fisa that scares me. It's just land, filled with people who will probably welcome us. It's Mother who petrifies me."

Griffin grunts, his countenance darkening even further.

As always when I think or talk about Mother, anxiety takes root in my belly, growing like a rotten but deeply entrenched vine. I've been conditioned—like a dog. Mother equals fear. Fear equals cold sweats and nausea.

It's too bad. Little Bean gave me the morning off from the fun of vomiting, and I was actually feeling pretty good.

Absently, I run a hand over my belly. Little Bean seems to have been lulled into a stupor by Panotii's even gait. She's not doing acrobatics with her zippy little life force or tossing the contents of my stomach around. Maybe I'm finally done with the morning sickness, and now I'll just start getting big.

I shift in my leather armor. It does feel unusually tight. I glance down. *Do I need to loosen the side buckles?*

To Griffin's delight, my breasts have already received the expansion message—loud and clear. Right now, I'm almost back to looking like I did when he first saw me, before all the running around and almost dying. It's nice to have a shape again. Although pretty soon, I'll likely have more shape than I can easily manage.

"Do you know what terrifies me the most?" I ask. *And by that, I'm not including giving birth or having to figure out motherhood, because those pretty much top the list— with one exception.*

Griffin shakes his head.

"Mother has no reason to keep me alive anymore."

He scowls, looking like he just swallowed a mouthful of rocks. "There's your Kingmaker Magic," he reluctantly points out.

Thinking about how she used me to discover truths, I stare off into the distance, unseeing, the memory of my unwilling participation in the misery of many jostling me like an army of cold, dead feet. The memories of the consequences of noncompliance aren't pleasant, either.

I quietly scoff. "I would never let her use me like that again."

"You were a child," Griffin says, as if youth exonerates all.

"So? I don't think that's much of an excuse. I never have, and actual age didn't matter when you grew up in Castle Fisa. None of us stayed children, not even when we were small. Survival trumped innocence."

"Children aren't meant to understand everything, to sort through the moral pathways. They can't."

"In my case, blissful naivety didn't last long. In fact, I don't remember ever having it."

"You stopped betraying people to your mother, despite her wiles and…incentives. Despite her violence and abuse. You protected lives at your own peril."

I snort. He's giving me more credit than he should.

Griffin levels his hard look on me. "Self-blame is useless

at this point. It's unfair to yourself, and to the people who love you. I talk in circles, and you don't listen."

My mouth drops open on a huff of breath. *Well then.*

"Ares was with you. *Bouncing you on his knee.*" His tone turns testy. Testy and jealous. "Why didn't *he* protect you?" Griffin demands.

I study the horizon again, not wanting to face the hostility and accusation in Griffin's expression.

"He did," I eventually say. "And he taught me to protect myself. But remember, he was in human form and not as powerful, all-knowing, or invulnerable as he otherwise would have been. The Gods' goal was apparently to get me to where I am today, whatever the cost." *Eleni*, my mind provides, and my heart spasms as if still fresh from the loss. "I guess to be what I am today, I had to take my knocks."

"Take your knocks?" Griffin echoes, incredulous. "Andromeda nearly beat you to death. Repeatedly. Where was *Ares* during that?"

"I don't know." I glance down. "He always came to get me after, he and Eleni. They'd bring me to the healer."

Almost every time I refused to betray someone's inner thoughts to Mother, I got beaten, sometimes to the point of needing a Death Mark. Healers leave those thin, silvery scars when they have no other way to save a person other than to split their flesh from elbow to shoulder and then enchant their blood. It's incredibly painful—if you're still conscious.

Conversations like this one always make my husband look like he's ready to beat something to a bloody pulp— preferably my mother. I doubt I'd object, and I'm not sure what kind of a person that makes me. Probably not a good one.

"She threatened. A lot. And carried through on her

threats spectacularly for the most part." I shake my head. "But she also bribed and cajoled me. There were times when I just…didn't fight. I told her what she wanted to know. She's a horrible person, but I'm not blameless, Griffin. Some things *are* my fault. Like relying too much on Eleni and loving my sister more than anyone else. *I* turned her into a target for Mother's obsessive life lessons and vindictive wrath."

"Stop." Griffin's voice drops an entire octave and comes to me through his tightly clenched teeth. "Is this what you want to teach Little Bean? To never forgive herself? What good does that do anyone? You tear yourself apart for things you had no control over."

"I did have control. My mouth. My words. My life!"

His expression darkens like a storm rolling in, one that's inevitable. The first crack of thunder is always the one that rattles me the most. "*Your life?* You think you're a coward and to blame because you didn't throw it away? Because sometimes you compromised what you knew was right in order to survive?"

While his voice rumbles deeply, remaining ominously low, I nearly shout. "When have you ever compromised?" Griffin is pretty close to perfect. Just. Right. Fair. Bloody infuriating!

"My morals?" He snorts. "Plenty of times. Every time I took a boy to war that I knew was lying about being over sixteen years old and then sent him onto the battlefield to fight and die just like anyone else. Every time I dealt a killing blow instead of a debilitating one just to be sure I wouldn't have to fight the same person twice. Every time I went to a willing and hopeful woman I had no real interest in just to satisfy my own baser needs."

I blink. The image slaps me hard. It looks like Daphne.

"Every time I look at you and want to grab you and hide

you away, keep you safe and mine. Not everyone's. Not Thalyria's. Mine!" He lets out a sudden bellow of frustration, and I stare, wide-eyed. Panotii's ears twitch. Brown Horse doesn't even blink. Little Bean wakes up with a bang.

His voice quiets again, but I can tell his emotions are still raging inside. Griffin never seems to get angry—except at me. "What happened to Eleni is *not* your fault. Neither was Galen Tarva threatening your mother with his power, or your mother deciding to turn you into a bargaining chip to keep him away."

"Well, that deal is more than off since Galen is dead. Mother doesn't need me now." Which brings me back to my original point. "I'm not an asset to her anymore; I'm only a threat. I haven't let her use my abilities for her own gain in years, and there's no Galen Tarva to hold off anymore with promises of delivering the Kingmaker to him for his own personal use. She'll try to kill me the first chance she gets."

I could swear Griffin almost flinches. He stares straight ahead, a muscle flexing in his jaw.

We ride in silence for a long time after that, both of us lost in our own thoughts.

Eventually, he mutters, "This witch had better know what she's doing."

"Oh, she does. Or at least that's what everyone says, including Ares back when he was Thanos. She's amazing with potions and stuff."

Griffin glances over, arching a dark brow. "And stuff?"

Is that humor I see returning to his eyes? Or at least normalcy? "That's what I said," I answer stiffly, faking offense.

"Make sure you add that to your queenly decrees," he teases. *"I hereby declare that the people of Thalyria shall be safe from royally sanctioned thieving raids, outrageous taxing, random massacres, and stuff."*

I mash my lips together, refusing to give him the satisfaction of a smile. "Maybe I'll let you write the decrees."

Griffin nods. "Wise choice."

"Pfffffff."

He smiles, giving me the satisfaction I just stubbornly refused him, but we always knew he was the mature one.

"Why Frostfire?" Griffin asks. "It's an odd name."

"From what I'm told, it's because there's both frost and fire." I shrug. "I guess we'll see when we get there."

"And when will that be?"

"Not soon enough." I drop my reins, lift my arms, and stretch. My lower back is already hurting. "After we cross the border at the Chaos Wizard's house, it's at least another two days to the northeast." And that's if my appalling sense of direction doesn't get us lost along the way.

"Are you planning to say hello?" he asks.

"To the Chaos Wizard?" I shoot him a horrified look. "Are you kidding me? Do *you* want a snake jumping down your throat? Because I'm pretty sure I'm incompatible still."

Thank you, Little Bean.

⚜

Frostfire. *Three and a half* days northeast of the Fisan border. It would have been less if I hadn't steered us wrong. But who can tell where east is on a cloudy day? And no one ever said not to take *that* fork in the road. Seriously. You'd think there'd be some kind of warning when there's a Manticore lair ahead. Then again, they devour their prey whole, leaving no sign of their victims—not a bone, not a scrap of clothing, not a bloody tooth. Luckily, Griffin and I can throw knives faster than the Manticore can throw poison spikes from its tail. And Panotii is damn speedy when he wants to be.

Magic nips at my skin. My blood pulses eagerly, wanting to snatch up all the power that washes over me with a slightly smarting caress. The magic in the air at Frostfire leaves a sweet-and-sour taste on my tongue, both corrosive and tempting. I'm not sure it's something I can take, though. It may be too intangible for that. Besides, the euphoria episode in Velos taught me not to steal spells or magic I haven't identified. Whatever is around here is enticing, but there's also something dark in the underbelly of it, and I'm pretty sure I don't want it.

"Finally." Squinting toward the hermit's house, Griffin blows on his chilled hands. He draws his Eternal Fires of the Underworld cloak more firmly around his broad shoulders. Jocasta stitched up the tear the Hydra made in the back of it, and the flaming threads glow gently on the inside.

I'm wearing mine, too, but it's completely dark. Little Bean keeps me excessively warm.

"Anxious for a hot meal?" I ask, eyeing the curling wisps of grayish-white smoke rising from the hermit's chimney. The air as we leave the thick evergreen forest behind us smells deliciously woodsy, like burning logs, crisp, frosty ground, and moldering leaves.

"There's no guarantee of that," Griffin says, although he does look hopeful.

"No. We could be attacked, welcomed, ignored... I have no idea." All I know is that the power here is staggering—and not exactly comfortable. "The magic here feels strange."

"How so?" Griffin asks, turning to me.

"Like it's not something I could—or should—take."

He frowns at that. Since my lightning is hit-and-miss—mostly miss—magic theft is my best defense at the moment, and neither of us likes what I just said.

"When you take and use someone else's magic, you heal from whatever wound they inflict on you, but they don't heal from the magic you throw back at them. Why is that?"

I offer him a cheeky smile I'm not really feeling deep down. "Because Poseidon wanted me to be able to play with the big fish."

Griffin grunts. But however I might spin it, we both know that's true. The gifts my God Father gave me weren't haphazard in the least, but carefully selected for the best chance of bringing me to where I am now—smack in the middle of a Power Bid that could reunite the realms.

That's the idea anyway.

We point our horses toward the hermit's house. The large, wooden structure sits at the top of a substantial clearing on the slope of a mountainside. The meadow between us and the house is still green, despite the chilly weather, and the grass is cropped short, so it must be used for grazing. I don't see any animals right now, but there is a barn. The tree line continues sparsely for about half a mile above the slant-roofed dwelling, and beyond that, the first of the snow and granite peaks of the southern Deskathis tower above this place, growing taller and wilder as they stretch northward toward Olympus.

We rein in partway across the meadow. The ground is soggy here, and there's a bubbling and probably frigid mountain spring that feeds a ribbon-like stream leading back into the woods. The modest, partially open-faced barn houses sheep and goats, who seem to have decided that inside is better than outside today. I wonder why. The sun is shining, even though it's cool. Buckets and rusty tools hang from the rough-hewn outer walls, along with a pair of old lanterns that look like they haven't been lit in years. The place strikes me as having an oddly abandoned, lonely feel, despite the livestock looking in good health and the chimney smoke flavoring the rich autumn air.

I shiver, although not from cold. Maybe this feeling that grates on me like a bad itch is exactly what a hermit looks for. Objectively, the setting is calm and beautiful, but the Gods know I could never live up here all by myself. The solitude would eat me alive.

Dismounting, I glance toward the pine forest we just left, with its dense, frosty carpet of fallen needles and continuous shadows. The warmth of day hasn't fought its way through—and probably can't—but it's still far more appealing than what I think is on our right.

My heart beating a little faster than normal, I turn and face what must be the unique Thalyrian phenomenon that gives Frostfire its name. Running along the edge of the meadow and directly abutting the far side of the house, there's what appears to be a sheer cliff. We can't see down into it from here, but the precipice supposedly drops off into an almost bottomless volcanic pit—although I'm pretty sure it's more than that.

Nervous heat billows up through me—a lot like a scorching blast from what I've been told is at the bottom of the ancient caldera: Hephaestus's forge, the smith God's fiery domain.

Griffin leads Brown Horse into an empty enclosure, and I follow him in with Panotii, relieved to turn my back on the yawning gap between us and the summits to the northeast. We don't loosen the horses' girths at all, since both Griffin and I are currently fervently and wholeheartedly worshipping the cult of *you never know, so be ready to run for your life.*

Little Bean has changed my outlook on a lot of things, my own safety being the primary one. I don't consider caution to be cowardice. I never have. It was just never my way before. Lately, to Griffin's unending satisfaction, I'm considerably less prone to running headlong into danger.

"I get the frost part," Griffin says, taking my elbow and guiding me. He must think I need help walking in a straight line up a hill toward a house. I don't object. His strong hand is too blissfully cool on my heated skin for me to want to pull away. "But why fire?" he asks.

I lift my nose and sniff. "Smell the air."

He inhales deeply just as a breeze swirls up over the precipice. His nose wrinkles. "Sulfur?"

"That cliff over there... It goes *waaay* down."

"*Waaay* down?"

I nod, skirting a small animal hole in the ground. "Apparently, that crater is Hephaestus's forge, where he crafts the weapons of the Gods. Also, Thanos once told me that Hades stokes his furnaces with the magma from the deepest depths of the Frostfire pit, and I assume he knows what he's talking about, Thanos being Ares and all."

Just then, whatever is far below belches up steam and a wave of heat, surprising us both. Maybe Hephaestus is working on something down there.

"Humph." Griffin's hand tightens on my arm.

I roll my eyes. "I'm not going to fall in, you know. The cliff is all the way over there."

He loosens his hold. Sort of.

I glance up at him, trying to tame my sudden smile. Domineering and overprotective doesn't even begin to describe my husband. There's also deliciously jealous, but that's another subject altogether. The black stubble framing his mouth makes his full lips look impossibly kissable. It's been hours since they were last on mine. And I love to kiss the hawkish curve of his nose. So strong and masculine. I adore that nose. And the rest of him. His powerful body. Muscle. Sinew. Bone.

I gaze up at him, nearly sighing. "I love you."

Griffin stops dead in his tracks and glares down at me. "That's it. We're leaving."

I blink. "What? Why?"

"You think something terrible is going to happen."

"No, I don't." I frown. "I don't think so."

His eyes narrow, wariness hardening his expression. "You do."

"What are you talking about?"

He scowls at me.

"Well, something terrible *could* happen," I concede. "But that's always true, no matter where or when. Tomorrow, I could trip over my own feet and break my neck for all I know."

Judging by the look on Griffin's face, I don't think that helped.

"You only say you love me or you're sorry when you're scared or almost dead. You're not almost dead, so what's scaring you?" he demands.

"I say I love you all the time!"

"When we're in bed. When I'm so deep inside you that you can't feel anything but me. Not when we're about to knock on a stranger's door. What's scaring you?" he demands again.

I huff. "At the moment? The way your jaw is popping like it's alive."

Griffin crosses his arms. "I want honesty. Right now."

"*Right now*, Your Imperialness?"

His nostrils flare. His hard look is spectacular.

I'm not intimidated. It makes me hot. Then again, so does just about everything at the moment, but not in the same way.

"If you must know, the magic around here is a little intense and…disturbing, but it's not scaring me. Not really. It's probably just something coming from whatever is down there in that God Pit," I say, waving toward the cliff. "I'm a shade nervous. That's all."

His eyes stay flinty and unconvinced. "That's all? That's not generally cause for a heartfelt declaration, at least not from you."

I toss my hands in the air. "Fine. I take it back. I looked at you, found you incredibly desirable, and my body got all hot and tingly. I blame Little Bean for an excess of sentimentality and…and…urges!"

Griffin stares at me. Then his mouth splits into a grin that makes me all kinds of angry. He reaches for me again, his grasp lighter this time.

"Incredibly desirable?" Looking smug, he threads his fingers through mine.

Scowling, I poke him in the chest with my free hand. "Well, you do have that whole overbearing warlord thing going on. Plus, plenty of muscles in all the right places, some good ideas, and, you know, a really big sword."

A laugh cracks out of Griffin, and my heart swoops like an off-balance bird. He's rarely free with humor these days, or maybe there's just not enough of it in our lives anymore. The happy flutter that wings through my chest takes any lingering irritation away with it.

Gah! Talk about mood changes!

Griffin captures my other hand and then pulls me in

to him until I'm standing between his legs. "I love you, too, Cat."

He kisses me, his mouth pressing softly against mine. Warmth rolls straight from his lips to my toes, which curl in my boots.

"Tell me again," he coaxes.

I shake my head, our noses brushing.

"Say it," he demands against my mouth.

"I don't think so."

"Last chance," he warns, gently nipping at my lower lip.

"Big sword."

Chuckling, Griffin swats my bottom. "There's more where that came from."

I look up at him through my lashes. "I sure hope so."

He grins. "I think you just managed coy."

"Good Gods! Has the Underworld frozen over?"

"Next, Centaurs will fly." He brushes his lips over mine again, not lingering, and when he lifts his head, his black hair ruffling on the faintly sulfurous wind, the teasing gleam is already absent from his eyes. "You're sure there's nothing else?"

"Nothing besides Little Bean wreaking havoc on my moods?" I shake my head. "But I wanted you before. I want you always."

He lifts his hand and brushes his thumb across my lips. Then his fingers fall away, trailing lightly down my arm until I shiver.

"You're the air I breathe," he says without a trace of humor in his voice.

My whole chest clenches hard, squeezing a tight, almost painful beat from my heart. "I admire you," I reply. "I need you. I love you with all my heart."

Griffin offers me a different kind of smile this time,

small, lopsided, gentle, and so entirely genuine. It fades almost immediately, though, and he straightens to his full, imposing height, abruptly pinning me with his warlord stare. "If you feel anything off here, we leave, with or without the potion we came for. You've got great instincts, Cat. Trust your gut."

I nod. I will. I always do.

"And trust *me*," he adds, everything about him turning urgent all of a sudden. "Don't trust anyone but me. Ever."

"You don't mean that. What about Flynn and Kato? Carver? He's your broth—"

"My *brother* betrayed me. He tried to rip you from me!"

I freeze, taken aback by the burst of rage in his voice. After weeks of granite features and near-silence on the subject, it looks like Griffin is about to erupt. It's fitting, since we're at Frostfire, and there's a volcano under our feet. Like the hot center of the world, a person can only stew and boil and brood for so long before the fire comes surging up.

"That wasn't Carver," I say, unsure of how to tread these turbulent waters with which I'm largely unfamiliar. My family's solution to squabbles is murder. Not exactly an example to live by. "That was Piers."

Griffin's jaw hardens to stone. "If Piers could do it, anyone can. And Carver… He's not the same anymore. He's…"

"He's my friend, which Piers never was. He's also sad, and maybe a little angry, because we have what he doesn't. What he wants. That's his right, Griffin. We can't change that. And it doesn't mean he'll betray us."

Griffin glances away from me, his face screwing up. "The closer you and I get, the more distance Carver puts between us. Looking back, I realize it started happening almost from the beginning. Then, after the Games and seeing Konstantina in the Underworld, he just caved in on himself. I never know what he's thinking anymore."

"He's thinking about how the woman he loved chose someone else and then died. He can never win her back. It's too late, and that's eating him up inside. He could live with it until he started being faced with *us* every day, and our happiness. That's hard for him. It has to be."

"It's changed him. He's sullen. And drinking again."

Again? I don't like the sound of that. "Lately, you haven't exactly been a stranger to dark moods, either. And that's *your* right. We all change. I certainly have. Look at me, I'm almost responsible. Give Carver time. He'll come around."

"I can't predict what he'll do." Griffin's eyes turn even more troubled. "I'm not sure you're safe."

"With Carver?" I stare at him in shock. "Are you kidding me?"

Griffin grunts, and I'm not sure what that means. What I do know is that he's looking for betrayal where there is none, where I know down to the very marrow of my bones that there never will be. Carver would die for me, and he would kill himself before he ever hurt me. He would do the same for Griffin, for any of his family, for Kato or Flynn. But Griffin trusted a core group of people with his life, with me, with *everything*, and one of them kicked a hole straight through his heart. A person doesn't just get over that, not even someone as balanced and confident as Griffin.

"Piers didn't think he was betraying you. In his mind, he was protecting you. Protecting his fam—"

"Don't." Griffin cuts me off, his glare ice-cold. "Don't defend him. He's dead to me."

I bite my lip to stop from saying anything else. Right now, the finality in Griffin's words is flat-out undeniable. Their veracity snaps inside me like a barb-tipped whip, almost as painful as a lie igniting a fire in my bones. With Griffin, a hard truth always sets off the flip side of my Kingmaker Magic. He's only ever lied to me once, and that was just to prove the truth—that he was in love with me.

"Fine." For now. "Just be careful not to convict Carver of crimes that aren't his." And for Griffin's sake, I hope he'll find a measure of peace with his memories of Piers, because that's all he'll ever have.

He nods once, but his eyes are flatter than I've ever seen them. I wish I could say something to help him, to heal him, but I don't believe there are any words that can stitch up a tear in a person's soul. Only time can do that, and the hope that it will eventually get better.

Oh my Gods. More things suddenly make sense to me than ever before. Hope extends from suffering. Elpis is the hand that reaches out to the torn.

I grab Griffin's forearm, squeezing hard. Maybe I can do something. Maybe I'm meant to.

He looks at my hand, then at me, and we stare at each other.

"You're the best man I know, and the only man I want." I tighten my grip. "You're the father of the future of this world. You're a torch, not the dark. I look at you, and all I see is fire and light."

Slowly, some of the distance fades from his eyes. "You're the light, *agapi mou.* You glow, and you don't even know it."

"If I glow, it's because you lit me up."

He shakes his head. "It's because you forgive."

"Me? Forgive? I can hold a grudge like an Olympian. I'm practically an expert."

A wry smile just barely lifts his mouth. "You forgive everyone except yourself."

I press my lips flat, not answering. His words are kindly meant, but they feel like lead on my chest, weighty and full of pressure. Like the future. Elpis. Thalyria. Motherhood. I don't think I'm ready for any of it. I'm not sure I'm qualified at all.

I'm saved from having to respond when the cabin door creaks open, the squeal of wood and hinges loud even from across the meadow. I let my hand drop from Griffin's arm, and we turn as one.

A severely stooped woman looks out from the shadowed entrance of her house. She's old, wizened, *powerful*. A sudden chill bursts over the back of my neck. I wasn't sure what we'd find here, and she's at the same time everything a hermit should be and not at all what I expected. But potion making is a nasty, slippery, dark skill, usually practiced by people who are nasty, slippery, and dark. To be honest, I think she'll fit the mold.

I take a deep breath and steel myself to deal with the kind of Magoi that are better left alone. It's time to meet the hermit witch of Frostfire.

CHAPTER 11

HER BRIGHT-GREEN EYES, MUCH LIKE MINE, STAND OUT EVEN from a distance. That's not unusual in the north of Fisa, or among powerful Magoi, but her eyes seem disturbingly vivid and intense for an old crone.

"Only the most temerarious of travelers come this way." She opens her door farther and takes a lumbering step out onto the front stoop. "Most are afraid of the pit."

She talks softly, pitching her words low. Shrugging off my initial unease, I move forward in order to hear her better.

"The pit's way over there." I nod toward the gaping hole on our right, a small but paranoid part of me wondering if she might have just threatened us. Probably not. I could take her down with one kick, and she's way too frail to push Griffin around.

Magic, though, is a different matter. Hopefully hers is limited to potion mixing.

Griffin's hand flexes on my lower back. Being the diplomatic one, he says, "We apologize for disturbing you. We know you like your privacy."

The hermit narrows her eyes. "And yet you came anyway. You want something from me."

It's not a question, and the statement is directed at me. *Of course I do.* We wouldn't be on a frosty mountainside next to the deepest crack in Thalyria otherwise.

Griffin and I stop near the opening in a stone wall that seems to be acting as a de facto gate. Flat slabs of granite form a pathway leading the rest of the way to the house.

"I've heard you make powerful potions," I say. "Potions for unlocking magic."

The witch looks me up and down. Her concentrated, almost hostile gaze penetrates me on a deep level, scraping as it goes. "Has your magic locked up, then?" she asks.

"It comes and goes," I answer with a small shrug that's a lot more casual than I feel. "It's unpredictable."

"*All* your magic?"

I shake my head. "Just the new magic."

The witch laughs. It's a cagey chuckle that sends a shiver tracking down my spine.

I ignore the icy prickle. Besides feeling some aggression from her, I can't pinpoint what's making my hackles rise. She's probably testy because she's a hermit, and we just interrupted her all-important alone time. She hasn't told us to get lost, though, and I don't feel I can justify turning back, even if a part of me almost wants to.

"No one has new magic. There's only magic you don't know how to use." Turning, she swings her door wide open and then shuffles back inside, fading into the shadows of the entryway.

"Don't just stand there," she calls irritably from somewhere inside. "Come in. But leave your weapons at the wall. I don't want them in my house."

I don't move. Or disarm. "What do you think?" I ask Griffin.

He shrugs.

I make a face. "That's helpful."

"You tell me," he says.

"She's creepy."

He frowns. "And?"

"And I don't know," I admit. Speckled, stooped, and wrinkled certainly aren't grounds for turning tail. Neither are power-filled green eyes. We're here *because* her magic is strong. "I guess we should go in and see."

He nods. It doesn't sit well with either of us, but we disarm and leave our weapons in a pile behind the stone wall. We leave our cloaks there as well since the day has warmed up nicely, and we likely won't need them inside.

Griffin enters the house first, scanning the interior before allowing me out from behind him. We both had to duck to avoid the lintel, and that's saying something for me. The witch made it under easily, her entire upper body being almost horizontal.

Inside, the house opens up into a large, rectangular living space with a rather surprising vaulted ceiling a good two stories high. The wood is a pleasant shade of light brown, and colorful, upside-down bouquets of wildflowers and bunches of drying herbs decorate the lower parts of the walls. The air is fragrant and warm, carrying a slight medicinal tang along with the stronger scent of something delicious-smelling simmering over the fire.

Three closed doors line the north side of the room. They're probably bedchambers and storage, since that part of the house is carved directly into the mountainside and therefore bound to be windowless. The main room is bright and unexpectedly welcoming, with comfortable-looking furniture and thick rugs scattered around. There are two enormous windows, one to the east and another to the south. The glass is barely wavy, the kind that costs a royal's ransom, telling me that the witch either sells her potions for a mighty fortune or someone gave her a very precious gift.

The hermit's lush, green meadow spreads out to the south, gently sloping toward the barn. A light wind ripples the grass in waves and teases the dark pine boughs at the edge of the woods. There's nothing at all beyond the other window, except for the not-too-distant snowy pinnacles of the nearest Deskathi peaks.

My stomach dips nervously, and I know without having to go anywhere near it that the east window directly overlooks the pit.

I inwardly shudder. I could never live this close to that yawning crack. I'd be afraid my house would fall in.

The crone drifts toward the fireplace, motioning for us to follow, and I turn my back on the towering, east-facing window with relief. The kitchen is set apart from the living area by a large, liberally scarred hardwood table surrounded by four solid-looking high-backed chairs.

I cock my head to one side, taking it all in. *Four chairs? You'd think she'd only need one, being a hermit and all.*

Then again, people come here for her potions, traveling great distances and probably paying dearly for them. The least she can do is give them a place to sit.

Catching my lower lip between my teeth, I crane my neck for a look at what's bubbling in her pot. *And maybe something to eat?*

The hermit takes a long wooden spoon from the table and then stirs what must be her dinner for a solid week. Her slow mixing sets loose even more of the mouth-watering meat and herbs aroma of whatever is stewing over the fire, and my stomach rumbles—long, low, and loud.

She slants me an unnerving, bright-green look before moving her slightly contemptuous gaze over to Griffin. "Does your man not feed you?" she asks.

I sense Griffin bristling beside me, as if his shoulders grow a foot in width.

"Of course he feeds me. More importantly, I feed myself." Sort of. I can pick berries. And maybe catch a fish. I can definitely start a fire. Sometimes.

I glance at Griffin, and he looks back at me with a defi-
nite hint of *Liar, liar, tunic on fire* in his eyes.

I shrug. I guess that's why we're a team. I'm Elpis. He
cooks.

The witch makes a small noise in the back of her throat.
"Feed yourself," she mutters, turning back to her pot and
shaking her head as though I just said some kind of absurdity.

I glare at her hump as she goes back to stirring the contents of her cauldron. I don't have much of a choice; the
lump on her back is higher than her head.

"You obviously feed yourself," I point out.

She stirs more vigorously, making her long black shawl
swish and bob around her ankles. "Only if there's no one
to do it for me."

Well, I guess that settles the question about visitors. Not
only do they come, they cook.

Good Gods, I hope she's not expecting me *to produce
something edible.* The only time I was ever truly alone in
my life, I nearly starved.

Damn it! Maybe we should have brought Bellanca after
all.

Scratch that. There's no way an ex-princess can cook
any better than I can, even with all that fire.

"You're not a very hermity hermit, are you?" I ask.

The crone, who's apparently redefining the word *hermit*
here in Frostfire, ignores that and pulls two wooden bowls
from a nook in the wall. She ladles healthy portions of her
stew into them both and then plunks them down on the
table along with spoons, earthenware cups, and a jug of
water. "Sit. Eat."

I look at Griffin. He shrugs and then sits down and tries
a bite. He doesn't gag or turn into a Satyr or anything, so
I do the same.

I groan. It's hearty and good, and the meat is so tender, it must have been cooking for days.

The witch nods, seeming satisfied. "Tell me about your magic." She doesn't sit with us or eat any of the stew herself but rather takes down a small pot from one of the pegs on the kitchen wall. She sets it on the table and then pours a measure of water into it from the deep bucket by the hearth.

I shift a little nervously in my seat, toying with my meal. The extent of my magic isn't the kind of thing I tell just anybody—or really anyone at all. But we came all this way for a reason. I don't particularly like the old hag, but she hasn't threatened us, she can cook, and it would be pretty stupid to back out now.

Reluctance still nearly blocks the words in my throat. "I have ichor in my veins."

She straightens. A bit. There's not much she can do about her hunchback state. It's more that she lifts her head, and her wrinkled lips purse in my direction.

"A child of the Gods. There aren't many left in Thalyria." Her eyes pierce me again, and I don't like it. I'm not sure why. If I could figure out what's bothering me about her, I could probably move past it. As it is, she makes my knife hand twitch.

I nod. "A few millennia removed, but yes, that's the basic idea."

"Whose line?" she asks, her already creased brow furrowing into even deeper grooves.

"Zeus," I answer.

Without looking away from me, she dips her hand into her pocket and then throws a handful of something leafy and brown into the small pot. She stirs, and an overly sweet, cloying scent mixes with the other kitchen smells, quickly overpowering even the strong aroma of the stew. It takes a concentrated effort not to recoil and wrinkle my nose.

"And?" she presses.

How does she know there's an and*?* Grudgingly, I cough up the rest. "Titan. I don't know her name."

"Then you are descended from the Origin." It's not a question. It's also the only option for anyone who knows their history, which she clearly does.

I nod. Flowing through my veins, I hold the legacy of the old Gods and the new. The trouble is, I'm broken.

"Ichor makes you strong. Stronger than most. Stronger than even the most powerful Fisan Magoi." The witch takes a short, thick, dark-brown stick from a cupboard along with a small metal grater and then scrapes some wood shavings into her potion. The ingredient could be anything from willow bark to callitris. I'm good at recognizing magic-based potions. Organic—not so much.

"And your power stems not just from any God, but from the king of Gods himself."

I look up from the now-bubbling potion, puzzled. Why would that matter? Ichor is ichor. *Right?*

Whatever the hermit is concocting pops loudly, startling me. Something rises up from the bottom of her potion, foaming, and then the whole thing turns a disgusting yellowish-brown color. Creeping veins of black appear, marbling the surface like growing spider legs. They spread out, oozing toward the edges of the pot.

Repulsed, I nearly shudder. The visual is as awful as the smell.

She picks through some jars on her shelves, pulls out a new ingredient, and then drops a fuzzy white flower onto the surface of the brew. I wish I'd paid more attention to my organics and herbalist tutors. *Asteraceae?*

The black streaks pounce on it, smothering the flower. The poor bloom shrivels and then sinks, sucked under. The black goes down, too, curling in on itself and then dropping to chase the flower.

I swallow the increasing need to gag. That was unpleasant.

The ever-thickening potion starts to froth and hiss.

"You should have no trouble using all sorts of magic with your heritage," the witch says. "Endless possibilities race beneath your skin."

"Endless possibilities?" I ask. "Aren't we limited to our birthrights? And to oracular gifts?"

"Most are." She looks at me like I need an intelligence-creating potion rather than a magic-unlocking one. "Are you like most?"

I shrug. *Well, when you put it that way...*

"What can the Gods do?" she asks.

Warily, I answer, "Pretty much anything."

She stares at me, partly disgusted, partly expectant. Definitely like I just answered my own question. It's the kind of look Mother used to give me, and I don't like it any more now than I did then.

"I'm not a God. Far from it." If I could do anything I wanted, I would have definitely avoided a few key moments in my past, like near-death by Hydra, for one.

"Shortsighted," the hermit mutters, going back to her potion. "No vision."

"Excuse me?" I say, stiffening. What does she know about me? About anything?

She shakes her head, stirring.

"Look. All I really want is the thunderbolt. It comes and goes. I can't seem to control it, which means I can't count on it when I need to. That's what the potion is for, right? To make the magic flow?"

She turns back to me, her power-lit, light-green eyes disturbing. I'm suddenly glad I don't see myself in a mirror very often. I don't know how Griffin can stand it.

Looking down, I push a chunk of meat to the back of my bowl. It gets caught in a tangle of orange and white root vegetables. I'm not hungry anymore, and as I meet the witch's piercing gaze again, the nasty feeling in the pit of my stomach grows.

"Born with the thunderbolt. Only the Origin was gifted so." She scoffs, and her bitter tone strikes me as excessive. Honestly, I'm not just uncomfortable anymore. I'm confused.

Wariness and true unease unfurl where there was only caution before. "I wasn't born with it," I say slowly, definitely not adding that I'm the new Origin of Thalyria. "It's only manifested recently."

Her gnarled and spotted hand is steady as she reaches into the deep pocket of her shawl and then pulls out another powder, this time contained in a small vial. She uncorks it and sprinkles the entire contents into her potion pot. The mixture foams again, stinking so much that I grimace.

Holy Gods, how am I ever going to drink that?

Stirring briskly, she says, "No one gets new magic. Not unless it's an oracular gift."

Well, it wasn't. Not this time. Does that mean I've always had it? Why didn't I ever feel it before I met—

Oh. Pieces of my own personal puzzle click into place. Griffin. He's changed everything in my life, changed me. Has our being together somehow unlocked power that was already inside me, just waiting to come out? The ichor? The lightning? He's certainly upped my will to survive. And protect. And *feel*. Has the magic been there all along, but I needed Griffin to help bring it out in me?

I turn to him. Griffin watches me. He watches the witch. Like me, he's hardly touched his stew.

Unfortunately, we still have the same problem we had before. Even if Griffin has helped make the magic surface within me, it still doesn't work like it should.

I track the path of the hermit's spoon through the now-lumpy sludge of her potion. I don't want to drink it. I want to leave. That's my gut feeling, but a big part of me wonders if it's instinct telling me to go, or my stomach protesting the idea of swallowing something so vile.

"You want immense power in your hands." The witch sets the spoon aside and then looks at me.

"I already have immense power," I reply. "Now I want it to be reliable."

She keeps looking at me, and I look back. I have no idea why we're having a staring contest, but at least I'm good at it. Eventually, she turns back to her brew and utters a series of words in the old language—none of which I recognize—directly over the pot. Finally, with an odd hiss, she adds a carefully measured pinch of something granular and mauve.

Amethyst? It's a balancing stone, enhancing intuition and mental powers of all kinds while also limiting their destructive nature. That would make sense for the kind of potion I need, especially when the magic in question is explosive, to say the least.

The coarse grains sink one by one, dragging the hissing top foam down with them. The potion suddenly goes still. All bubbling stops.

Griffin places his hand over mine and gives my fingers a light squeeze. "Can you help us, or not?"

"Us?" The witch's head jerks up from studying her concoction. "I wasn't aware the magic concerned you."

"Everything about Cat concerns me," Griffin answers, his expression as stony as the Deskathi peaks.

Unfazed, the old woman turns to her herb corner, takes three vermillion berries I can't identify from a glass jar, crushes them, and then adds them to her mixture. "Cat," she mutters under her breath, stirring again. "How pedestrian."

A chill slides down my spine, landing like a block of ice inside me. My hair tries to stand straight up, and my scalp tingles all over. She sounds just like someone I know. And hate.

"That potion is for me, right?" I eye the revolting con-coction. What if I *should* drink it? What if it works?

"Of course." She pours it into a cup. The transfer makes it smoke. "But I expect payment first."

"We brought gold," Griffin says.

Her upper lip curls in contempt. "I have no need for gold."

"I can hunt for you," he offers. "Bring back a stag or a boar. Cure it, and it'll last you the winter through."

She shakes her head. "I don't need food."

Her words pluck at my already tightly strung nerves, making them play an off-key note in my head. Everyone needs gold or food. They're the most important commodi-ties. They buy her comfortable-looking furniture and per-fect windows and keep her belly full. What old woman living alone in a remote area turns down an offer of food?

"Weapons?" I ask, frowning. I don't want to, but I could give up my blades—if that's what she really wants.

She shakes her head again, her green eyes scraping mine.

I have a jeweled crown I'd easily give her, but it's not here. The emerald and gold ring Griffin gave me the night of the realm dinner winks on my finger, but there's no way I'm handing it over. I won't give up my ice shard necklace, either. Or my wedding band. Not in this lifetime, or in the next.

I pull a three-tiered string of fat Fisan pearls from my pocket. I've been carrying it around for weeks.

"I have this." My heart not happy about it, I hold out Ianthe's circlet. She gave it to me to hold when she went off for a bath and forgot to get it back. That was the evening before we met up with Lycheron on the Sintan border.

More quickly than I thought she could move, the hermit snatches the royal heirloom from my hand. Her eyes shine as she runs the lustrous pearls through her fingers, making them softly click.

"This will do." She tucks the pearls into a drawer under her herb table, quickly hiding the circlet away. She hands me the cup.

Potions are universally disgusting. The smell hits me fully the second it's in my hands, and I almost choke. My eyes start to water. My gag reflex preps for battle, and I try to calm it by swallowing the sharp bite of acid in the back of my throat.

"Will it work?" I ask in a rough, unenthusiastic croak.

"It will do what it's supposed to do."

Well, that's cryptic. "Unlock my magic?" I ask, fishing for a precise answer. "Make it so I can control my lighting?"

She shrugs and doesn't elaborate, almost like she knows I'm a walking lie detector. With a thump, I set down the cup.

She pushes it toward me, right under my face, and noxious vapors sting my nose again. "The potency won't last long. Tarry, and it will take longer and be more painful to reach the desired outcome."

I don't detect any lies in her words, but something about them makes me sure that she's twirling around the truth.

"What will take longer?" I ask.

"The effects."

"What effects?"

"The effects inherent to the potion I just mixed for you."

I lean back in my chair, putting some much-needed distance between myself and the mysterious concoction. Is the witch just tight-lipped and surly, as old-as-dirt hermits probably tend to be? Or is she performing an expert bob and weave with traitorous words?

"*Specifically*, what will this potion do to me?" I demand.

She thumps her wizened hand down on the table, making the cup rattle and the potion fizz. "I made the brew. You paid me. This transaction is complete. Drink it, or get out of my house."

Griffin stands and holds out his hand to me. "Let's go."

I glance over. "But—"

"But nothing," he says. "You don't want to drink it, so don't. Trust your gut, Cat."

The hermit turns an irate glare on Griffin. "Stay out of this, Hoi Polloi." There's a heavy punch of power in her voice. *Compulsion?* It's not directed at me, so it's hard to tell. It won't have any effect on Griffin anyway, but there are never more than a handful of people alive who can compel another human being, like Mother and I can. The hermit witch just entered an entirely new category in my mind—almost certainly an Olympian one.

His features tight, Griffin doesn't respond to what was clearly meant as an insult. I'm not as polite.

"Give me back my pearls, witch."

She glowers at me. "Those aren't yours." She pushes the cup toward me again. "This is."

Conflicted still and hating it, I look at the brew once more. I need that lightning.

"What's in it?" I ask. I don't want to miss a once-in-a-lifetime opportunity. The hermit of Frostfire is famous for making potent concoctions *that work*.

"Things that will free your magic from your body."

Again, no lie. But the crone is definitely spinning her words, and I want to know why.

I stare at the cup. This won't be the first potion I've drunk. What if I'm being absurdly paranoid? I used to think obsessive suspicion was a good thing—a survival tool—but now I'm not so sure. Trusting people has brought me more happiness than my constant wariness and paranoia ever did.

And I need the full force of my magic. To defend my people. To defend myself. To unite Thalyria. The witch's brew could be invaluable. What's one nauseating drink compared to the lives I could save? To what we could gain if I can finally trust my magic to work? Enemies would tremble before the mighty thunderbolt, the weapon of Zeus himself. Surrender without bloodshed and war.

The potion bubbles and reeks under my nose, and all I can think about is how Galen Tarva threatened my mother with his unparalleled Elemental Magic. He made her dance to his tune for years, and nobody but them even knew about it. *I* could do that. I could show her my power and make her kneel before me. I could offer Mother her life in exchange for Fisa, and she'd take the deal because she wouldn't have a choice.

My fingers tingle, warming to the idea. I reach out and slowly close my hand around the earthenware cup. It's hot.

Griffin tenses by my side, and I turn to look at him. He shakes his head. He doesn't want me to do this.

My grip loosens. He's right. I don't need the potion. I never have.

A certainty I've rarely felt wells up from somewhere deep inside me, spreading like a fast-moving tide. It fills me up, buoys me. I already have the most potent concoction around—Griffin and me together.

"I'll unlock my magic on my own. Griffin is all I need." I swipe the cup to the floor, and it shatters, its thick contents bubbling between the hermit's feet and mine.

The hermit glares at me through a curtain of foul-smelling smoke. The way her head moves, the turn of her chin, *her eyes…*

I stumble back, my gasp barely making it into my lungs. The confidence I was just floating on crashes like a ship into solid rock.

"We need to leave." I'm suddenly terrified but not entirely willing to accept why.

Griffin sweeps his chair back, but I stay rooted to the spot.

"You always make things so difficult." Cruel, cold voice. Green eyes, so similar to mine. "You never did know what was best."

Dread erupts in me and rams savagely outward through my chest. My heart beats so hard I can't breathe.

I reel back into Griffin as the hag straightens, growing in a swirl of magic-hued green. The transition is turbulent. Horrifying. In mere seconds, the woman sheds the appearance of the hunchbacked hermit witch of Frostfire and turns into my worst nightmare. Mother.

CHAPTER 12

I SHOULD HAVE KNOWN. HOW DID I NOT KNOW?

Terror grips me, and I freeze just long enough for Mother to strike hard. Her hand whips out and cracks across my face, jerking my head to the side. A stinging burn explodes across my cheek, and I hiss in a sharp breath.

Griffin lunges for her, but his hands swipe through a cloud of dark-brown dust and green magic. Mother disappeared. *Disintegrated.*

Everything swirls back together in the blink of an eye, re-forming in the shape of a huge bird. Not a bird—a Harpy. It has Mother's head and torso. The rest is all talons and feathers. She bats powerful wings and rises toward the vaulted ceiling, out of our reach in two flaps.

I gape up at her, my face on fire from the brutal slap.

Metamorphosis! I didn't know she could do that. I didn't know *anyone* could do that.

Why can't I do that?

"A Harpy. That's fitting." Griffin gets firmly in front of me.

Mother's snide words come back to me. *Endless possibilities. Shortsighted. No vision.*

Maybe I *can* do that. What's holding me back?

She sneers down at us from above, and suddenly I know. Morality holds me back, something that Mother lacks entirely. Ironically, it's what makes me both the weaker and the stronger of us two.

I raise my hand to my still-blazing cheek. "The potion

would have set my magic free from my body?" Utterly true. My magic would have floated off into the ether, because I'd have been dead! "You were going to poison me," I say, appalled.

"The most expeditious option, given the circumstances." Her Harpy voice is sharper, more grating, like a bird of prey's strident call. "Victory to the swift."

Another of her childhood lessons. It rings in my ears. Strikes like a blade.

"Poison is for cowards," I spit back. She might remember saying that a few times, too.

Her emerald eyes narrow on me as she squawks a shrill command. I look warily around, wondering what atrocity will happen next. The answer is a flock of enormous crows shattering the south window with a thundering crash. The front ones drop dead, leaving their blood on the broken glass. The followers flood into the room in a raucous, cawing, black-winged turmoil. They're unnaturally big—Ice Plains crows. Piercing eyes, razor-sharp beaks, feathers a dense blue-black. There are at least a dozen of them, circling, diving, taking up all the air and space. They shriek and scratch and bat their wings, driving Griffin and me back.

A bird the size of a dog dives at Griffin, knocking him back a step as he raises his arms to protect his head. I spin out of Griffin's way, jump in front of him, and then grab the bird's tail feathers, yanking hard just as Griffin bats the creature away. I end up with two long feathers in each hand and Griffin with a gash near his ear. A trickle of blood creeps down his jawline.

Oh Gods. We're both unarmed, and my magic is totally unreliable. And now Mother knows it—right from my own mouth. I'm stupid, so bloody stupid, and I brought Griffin here, straight into her trap.

I flip the feathers in my hands and grip them down low, ready to use the stiff ends as weapons if I can.

"How did you know?" I demand, tilting my head back to watch Mother hover near the ceiling, her big wings brushing the beams. "We told almost no one where we were going."

Peals of harsh laughter burst from the crows. Mother laughs, too, and the room fills with the sound of flapping wings, cawing, and hate. "I have spies everywhere. On the ground. In the air. *Inside* of you."

My eyes widen in shock. *Little Bean.*

A vortex opens up in my middle, hollowing me out. Dark and violent, it churns with fear and wrath, and my heart sinks straight into it, imploding along with my lungs and breath.

I thought I knew rage and terror before? That was nothing. This is hot and horrible and consuming. Blood roars in my ears. My chest burns and squeezes tight while magic blasts through my veins. The sudden surge of power bounces inside me like a painful echo, not finding its way out. The ricochet shakes me hard, and I lurch, not knowing if I'm about to collapse violently inward or shatter outward into a million broken pieces.

Steadying myself on the edge of the table, I stare at Mother. I've killed people and sometimes felt satisfaction at the result. But I've never wanted to *murder* before, to kill savagely, paint myself in blood, and scream while I do it.

Mother cocks her head just like a bird would, as if assessing the best way to pounce on a worm. "Children. So innocent. No defense against the invasion of the mind. And yours… So new, and yet already so aware. So ripe for molding."

The black hole inside me expands. Little Bean, not even really showing but already thinking. *Knowing.*

No wonder her energy felt so disrupted while we were making our plans to come to Frostfire. She was scared. Confused. Maybe in pain. She was being used as a conduit for information!

An agonized shout builds in my throat, but no sound comes out. I swore this woman wouldn't touch my baby. Even if I didn't voice it as a magical vow, I swore it to myself. To Griffin. To Little Bean. And I failed. I've already failed.

Mother looks so disgustingly proud of herself. She one-upped me at the expense of my unborn daughter, and now she gets to share her victory with us and grind my face into my own heartbreak and failure.

I cross my hands over my belly, a crow's feather still clutched tightly in each fist.

"Cat! Let's go!" Griffin's voice barely penetrates.

Slowly, I turn to him. *Does he really think she'll let us leave?*

A huge crow slams into me from the side. I stagger but hardly feel it. Out of the corner of my eye, I see another one coming to bomb me, but I don't care. I don't respond at all.

Moving like a powerful wind, Griffin catches the bird before it hits me, snaps its neck with a sharp twist, and then hurls the limp body toward the monstrosity that is my mother.

"Stay away from my family!" he roars, white-faced with rage.

"Stay away from my family!" she parrots. Her crows caw with mocking laughter. "I'm trembling in my feathers."

Howling in fury, Griffin grabs the empty potion pot and long wooden spoon from the table. He becomes a maelstrom of muscle and movement. I blink, and five of the crows are already dead on the floor.

Flying herself even higher, Mother utters a sharp command. Her minions converge on me, diving as one. I lift my arms and strike out wildly. I see Griffin whirl back to me, but then I can't see anything at all, my vision cut off by a violent tumult of beaks and claws and wings.

Crows grab my arms, and I cry out. Sharp nails dig into me from wrists to shoulders, piercing my skin and scraping bone. My mouth pops open on a gasp. Then I'm off my feet and flying toward the vaulted ceiling, leaving my stomach on the floor.

"Griffin!" I cry.

He charges after me, but Mother swoops down and latches her talons into my hair, jerking hard on my scalp. I shoot upward with a hiss of pain.

Griffin jumps and just barely misses catching my foot. He climbs onto a chair to get higher, but then magic suddenly explodes below. Bright-green arcs skim my boots and singe my toes. They swirl around Griffin and scrape at his clothes. The room trembles, and then every last piece of furniture abruptly starts flying around.

He staggers and falls from his perch. He springs back up only to have to duck a zooming lamp. It smashes behind him, shattering. Oil coats the floor. Mother's telekinetic magic sends the flint and iron from the hearthside crashing into the same spot with a shower of sparks. Fire ignites, slithering the length of the stain.

Griffin leaps out of the way. Rugs, other lamps, broken furniture, and decorations all join the destruction, tumbling through the growing flames and catching fire. The magic has no effect on Griffin himself, but it upends everything else. Mother focuses her attack, making burning things crash into him. Griffin struggles through the wreckage while I can't do anything but watch from above in horror and shock.

Finally gathering my wits, I try to steal the magic from Mother, hoping to use it to deflect things away from Griffin. It nips at my skin, chafing and heating as it sinks into me. But the power seems to change character inside me, and what pours back out when I try to use it is nothing but a harmless green glow. Mother keeps launching the entire house at Griffin, and I can't stop her at all!

She hovers near the roof's angled peak, batting her enormous wings to stay in place. I hang there, my arms dripping blood and my scalp on fire while the contents of the hermit's home shatter, fly, burn, and slam into Griffin, burying him alive. I scream for him, and he fights his way out of the flaming debris only to get covered again. He bellows for me over and over, pure, crazed anguish ripping my name from his throat.

I swallow hard. I need to focus before the fire gets any worse. I need to fight.

Taking a deep breath, I reach down into my well of power, concentrating hard on what I know should be there. Smoke fills my lungs, but magic jolts in my veins. Lightning sizzles under my skin. My left side does nothing, but a current of white-hot power coils down my right arm. Triumph swells inside me, and I will the magic to explode into a mighty blast of Olympian power that'll incinerate the crows right off me.

The lightning fizzles at my fingertips, weak and puny and worthless. *No!*

I scream in frustration.

The birds gripping my right arm caw angrily, smoking and stinking, but they don't let go. Mother shakes me hard, and for a blood-chilling moment, I think she'll snap my neck. Pain darts deep into my scalp, making my eyes water.

"Zeus!" I call out to the only God who wields the

lightning bolt. The magic comes from him. The least he could do is make it work!

But no lightning appears, and no booming voice answers my plea for help. Flames lick up the walls, orange and red fingers climbing higher with every second. Smoke rises and billows around my head. I twist, kicking out at the birds, and hooked claws dig farther into my skin and bones. I gasp.

Below me, Griffin breaks free once more, erupting like a volcano from under a cage of fiery wreckage. He's bloody, scraped, and covered in soot. With a desperate sort of energy, he starts tossing things out of his way. His clothing is charred and torn. There are raw burns all over his exposed skin. He looks wild and fevered and, for the first time in my eyes, utterly destructible.

"Griffin!" I shout. "Run!" Mother can't kill him with magic, but she can bring the burning house down on him.

He jumps for me again, and his fingertips brush my boot. I strain downward, stretching myself. If he can catch my foot, he'll pull me down. There's no way Mother and the crows can hold both our weight.

Griffin crouches down low and then springs up, trying again. While he's in the air, stretched out and vulnerable, Mother uses her magic to sweep up a half-destroyed table and send it spinning into his ribs. He falls backward with a harsh grunt, breaking through a smoldering chair. The wood shatters, showering him with sparks. He hits the floor flat-out on his back and doesn't move.

Fear twists my stomach into a hard knot. "Griffin!" He's not invulnerable. He seems like it. He usually acts like it. But he's not, and right now, he's scaring me to death! "Get up!"

Fire glows all around him, closing in. My heart beats furiously. Lightning sparks—then fizzles. *Useless!*

"Griffin!"

He stirs, rolling over, but then Mother's green cyclone starts burying him under the destroyed and blackened contents of the room again.

My frantic pulse drums in my neck. My arms and scalp throb to the same hammering beat. "Get up!" I shout, my voice hoarse from yelling and smoke. "Get out of the house!"

Cursing my trapped position, I watch, praying to the Gods that Griffin will listen. The pile shudders as he starts to break free, and I exhale in relief. He finally rises, staggers, and then grimaces, clutching his right side. He doesn't look good, but he's up. He's conscious. He's breathing. And that's enough.

And I have *got* to do something! Where is the warrior who took down Piers like a ghost on the wind? Where is the woman who climbed a Cyclops and threw Poseidon's trident into its eye? And where is the Gods damn soothsayer who sometimes dreams of grave danger *before* it happens? A warning would have been nice!

Snarling, I close my eyes and dive headfirst into that place where my magic lives, pulling with all my might. Lightning pops from my hands with a loud crack, startling everyone. Thunder booms in my ears, and the crows closest to each hand drop dead, freeing my wrists. I fall a few feet with a shout.

Bouncing and swaying, I try desperately to break free before new birds can swoop in to help carry my weight. Too soon, though, more crows dig their claws into my hands and wrists, hauling me back up. Mother's talons scrape like burning sticks across my scalp, and I grit my teeth in pain, a roar building in my chest.

"I'm coming!" Griffin's ragged yell reaches me through a haze of agony and smoke. There's no way he can jump high enough to grab my foot now, not after that broken table rammed into his ribs. He looks around, his eyes frantic.

Limping, he gets behind the heavy kitchen table—the only thing down there that's still intact. He starts shoving it through the wreckage. If he can get it under me, he can climb on top. He'll be able to reach me then with only a small jump.

But the fire… Two walls of the house are completely ablaze. Pretty soon, the door will be cut off, and we'll be trapped.

"Griffin!" I shout, wincing from the heat. "Get out!"

"Griffin! Get out!" Mother mimics in her grating bird's voice.

He ignores us both, his burned and soot-covered face a mask of concentration and pain.

My arms feel like they're being ripped apart and pulled off, and the way I'm hanging makes it hard to breathe. The heat from the fire is nearly unbearable, the smoke blinding. I blink blood and sweat from my eyes. Griffin's hair is plastered to his neck and temples. Groaning, he digs in and pushes the massive table along. My chest aches for him.

His feet suddenly slip out from under him, and he crashes to his knees. I suck in a sharp breath, choking on it. He stands up again, bracing himself against the edge of the table. A final, herculean effort gets the huge slab of wood underneath me. His breathing labored, Griffin starts to climb on top.

Mother squawks a command, and the crows and she fly me just out of range.

"Very entertaining, watching him work for nothing." She caws along with her crows, laughing.

Griffin slams his fist down on the table. He glares up at her from his crouch, his eyes feral and his face covered in burns and blood.

"No more lightning? What a disappointing show," Mother criticizes. "Where's that ichor now? You never understood anything about magic. Want it. Cultivate it. Have it!"

That sounds just like compulsion. *Is that how she does it?* Her magic only seems to grow.

"There's no one left like us. The perfect mix of Titan and Olympian. And yet you're useless!" She shakes me, pulling my hair until I cry out.

"There's Ianthe," I growl back at her. And my younger brothers, but I know little about them.

"Elementals are tied down. Earth. Air. Water. Fire. They're linked to something's essential nature, bound by its limitations. They don't conceive with the mind."

"Conceive of atrocities?"

"Conceive of whatever."

Why is she telling me this? She's always fancied herself my teacher as well as my tormenter, but why share knowledge at this point? Because she's sure I'm about to die?

"If that's true, then why aren't you spewing lighting?" I bite out.

Her bird-shriek laugh tells me how stupid she thinks I am. "Lightning is Elemental Magic. The fifth element. Supposed to be Zeus's alone."

"But I'm no—"

"You are!" She spits the words out like a curse. "You're both. You have everything."

Does she mean... "I have more than you?" I ask, stunned.

Mother doesn't answer, and the truth hits me like one of her backhands across the face. Magic. The mind. I've always known they were connected, but not to the extent Mother is implying. If she's right, that means that if I can conceive of it, I can *do* it.

The problem is, I've never been able to conceive of beating Mother. In my mind, she always wins.

But this time, there's Griffin. This time, I have Little Bean to protect.

Gathering my strength and doing my best to breathe through the pain, I swing my legs up and try to kick the enormous crows off me. They flap and caw, and I bob wildly, my arms and scalp pulsing in agony.

"Cat!" Griffin shouts my name over the bellowing fire. He moves the table, chasing us across the room. He's almost underneath me again.

I thrash and yank, frenzied to break free, even if it means ripping my hair out. I can't stand Mother touching me; she's so polluted. I need to get her away from my baby, and I'll fall all the way to the floor and break both legs if I have to.

Mother curls her talons inward, tightening her hold on me. The sound that erupts from my mouth is raw and inhuman.

"I'm here!" Griffin leaps for me just as the crows yank, Mother leading the way with my head. His hand closes on thin air, and I yelp as we race toward the towering, east-facing window.

Instinct takes over. I haul my knees up to protect my middle and duck my head, screaming as Mother lets go of my hair, and I blast through the hermit's window with only the crows to hold me up.

Fear and pain storm through me so hard that for a split second everything goes blank. Then I feel each stinging cut from every jagged piece of shattered glass as momentum and the huge birds send me flying out over the pit.

"No!" Griffin roars.

"Griffin!" I scream in terror.

Mother caws a harsh call of triumph from inside the house.

I twist and look over my shoulder, blood in my eyes and my heart in my throat.

Griffin stands like a colossus on the table in the middle of the burning house, his legs braced apart, his hands reaching for me, and his eyes wrecked. Our petrified gazes lock for the space of a broken heartbeat before the injured and dying birds retract their claws, and I drop.

CHAPTER 13

HOT AIR PUNCHES INTO ME FROM BELOW, BUT PANIC ICES ME over inside. My heart hammers fast against my ribs. I can't see the bottom of the pit. It's so deep it narrows and then fades into darkness except for a distant red-orange glow.

"Help!" I scream my terror toward Olympus as I plummet to the center of the world, aiming it at Ares and Persephone, at Poseidon, Hades, and Zeus. But no one came earlier, while Mother was kicking our asses and burning the house down around us. Where are they? Are they all so busy that no one can show up for *this*?

Fear rushes through me like the sulfurous wind. Heat slams into me hard, increasing along with the fiery glow. I turn my head to the side, squinting. The air flaps so brutally against my face that my eyes dry out, and I struggle for breath.

This can't be the end. Of Griffin and me. Of Little Bean—who hasn't even lived.

My heart feels like it cracks wide open in my chest, and I yell savagely, refusing to believe it's over. I'm alive, and until I hit lava, sink into it, burn, and drown, I will *fight*. And I will get those bloody Olympian Gods to fight along with me.

"Thanos!" I scream.

The popping sound and blinding light hardly even startle me. I knew he'd come. Deep down, I knew.

"I recommend up, not down," Ares says, grabbing my upper arms. We slow to a halt, hovering high above the churning magma that's hot enough even here to burn my toes.

"Up," I echo dumbly. Seeing him, having his huge, reassuring hands on me, feeling him hold me up... It's like taking a battering ram to an already weakened dam, and I nearly burst into messy tears. But I don't have time for that. No one has time for that.

My stomach lurches violently. "We have to get back to Griffin. He's fighting her alone!"

"So spread your wings, little monster." Ares lets go of me and disappears.

My shriek gets snatched away by the pounding wind. *The bastard dropped me!* "Thanos!"

He explodes into existence again, huge and glowering. His power-filled, seafoam eyes roil with irritation. He makes no move to catch me this time, and I grab for him. He twists and keeps just out of reach as we fall together. I try to plunge through the air, frantically reaching for him, but these are currents I can't swim. I only dip and flail.

"Thanos! Help me!" I cry, the heat nearly choking off my words before they can form.

"Help yourself," he shoots back.

"How?" I shout into the racing wind.

"Spread your wings," he repeats, growling now.

"I don't have wings!" It's bright now. And viciously hot. The buffeting updraft bakes my dried blood right into my skin.

"Haven't you felt them? In here?" He pops me hard in the chest, driving the air from my lungs. I list backward, trying to suck down a breath and seeing a dizzying slice of clear, blue sky high above me.

Thanos grabs the front of my tunic and tilts me upright again. When he lets go, I lunge for him, but he neatly evades.

Wings? In my chest? Yes, I've felt them, but only when Griffin is with me, making me feel other things. They're not there otherwise, and they're definitely not there now. "They're *in* my chest, not out!"

Ares's face darkens. "Then get them out!"

"I don't know how!"

"Push!" he shouts. "Push with all your might."

He's nearly as frightening as the lava bubbling below, so I do as he says. I push, and I have a lot of might.

"Nothing's happening!" Only panic spasms across my chest.

"You're not trying!" he bellows.

It's too hot. I can't concentrate, and everything hurts. My hair burns my cheeks. My eyes feel scorched. "Thanos!" I beg.

Glaring at me, he rams the flat of his hand into my chest again. A bright light pulses from his palm, and I could swear my heart stops beating. My whole body goes rigid, my back bowing hard. Then pain rips through my shoulder blades, and I throw my head back with a scream. Wings unfurl behind me, catching the wind.

"Now fly," Ares commands, shadow and light splashing across his scarred features. Sweat beads his brow. The center of the world roars and groans just below, casting us both in a red-hot glow.

Still reeling in shock, I start flapping my arms. My torn skin pulls and burns.

"Your wings," he snaps, ruthlessly batting my injured arms down and sending me careening off balance.

Instinct rears up and helps me to beat my new wings. Somehow, I start to rise instead of fall. Stabilizing, I glance behind me. White feathers quiver on hot currents of air. The wings are strange and broad and almost as tall as I am.

I hazard a look down into the boiling pit, seeing great, popping orange bubbles letting off steam and heat. My eyes burn just from looking at it. The forge of the Gods, indeed.

"Concentrate!" Ares barks.

My head snaps back up, and I beat hard on the scorching air. I give a bigger push with my wings and shoot upward in a dizzying rush.

Flying is foreign, amazing, and strange. The whoosh of air around me is almost as exhilarating as the surge of relief inside me. Still, as we move farther from the ungodly heat, three thoughts play over and over again in my head: burning house, Mother, Griffin.

Adrenaline pumps through my veins, pounding along with my wings. "Thank you!" I shout to Ares. "How can I ever thank you?"

Floating seamlessly by my side, he shoots me an odd look. "Don't thank me. Thank Nike."

What? Now really isn't the time to be cryptic.

Frowning, I veer toward him by accident and then manage a wobbly rectification—*up* being key. "I have no idea what you're talking about!"

Ares looks at me like I'm unhinged. "You're the ultimate child of the Gods. Unique in all the worlds. There's no one else like you."

My eyes widen, although I'm not entirely surprised. Still, to hear it with my own ears... Straight from a God...

My mouth goes even drier. "No pressure there," I say.

"Olympus was fracturing. You know we fight like cats and dogs. The competition, the betrayals, the games. Thalyria has always been the glue that binds us, the one place where we all have a stake, the best of all our worlds. Or it used to be," he adds with a bitterness that startles me. "You carry Zeus's blood because he's your ancestor, but there are others who chose to help alter the path of Thalyria through you."

Others? Like Nike?

Sulfurous air stings my tongue, and I snap shut my wide-open mouth. "You *made* me?" I blurt out, incredulous.

He scoffs. "Your mother and father made you."

I draw back as if slapped. I don't like that any better, all considering.

"You look like them," he says. "That's the outside. Inside, you're all ours."

If it weren't so damn hot in this hole, a chill would probably be ripping down my spine right now. "Ours like who?" Why can't the Gods just say what they mean? Tell you who they really are? Be *clear* for once?

"Like Nike," he growls in answer, clearly losing patience with me.

Nike. I turn my head to look at Ares again, careful to keep a steady upward path this time. Nike is a Goddess synonymous with strength, speed, and triumph. One of Athena's closest companions. The idea of being partially shaped by Nike slowly starts to sink in—and I *like* it.

"Are you saying the Winged Goddess of Victory put her blood in me, and now I can fly?"

"You could always fly," he snaps. "You just repressed it, like everything else."

Shock ripples through me. "Why didn't you tell me?"

Before he can answer, a sudden gust of cool wind pushes heavily downward on us from above, and flying gets infinitely harder. I spread out my arms, trying to steady myself. We're almost to the top.

I shoot a glare at Ares, my pulse pounding hard. "Knowing I could fly would have been helpful when I was falling over a cliff. Or two!"

"You weren't ready. You weren't ready for a lot of things until recently."

Frustrated and desperate to get to Griffin, I beat my

wings harder and practically shout, "What does that mean?"

"It means you weren't balanced enough for that much power, and deep down, you knew it. You had no grounding force and no confidence in your own humanity."

And then I met Griffin. My grounding force. He didn't coax me from my shell; he dragged me, but every second that he was doing it, he also made me believe that I was good, worthwhile, and capable. He showed me how strong we could be together.

"I've always been an Elemental." I speak out loud for my own benefit, to finally believe it. "Who could fly."

Ares grabs me, stopping me just before I reach the top. Our eyes connect, and my breath cuts off. I've never seen him look so serious, and we've been through some serious stuff.

"You've been so scared of what you might be able to do that you never stopped to actually figure out what you *can* do. You've buried every bit of power you possibly could since you were six years old and made that one mistake with Ianthe. Your compulsion nearly killed her, and you've punished yourself daily by locking up your own magic and being terrified of it. Anything you're unsure of or don't understand? You bury it so deep it can't hurt anyone—or help. The Gods have favored you. Zeus offered you power like none other and gave you his own thunderbolt. You have a job to do here, but you keep throwing away the tools."

"I didn't throw anything away!" I wrench in his hold, but he doesn't let go of me. "I didn't even know I had them! And you could have helped me! Taught me! I could have saved lives!"

I could have saved Eleni! A sharp inhale tangles in my throat.

He shakes his head, reading my thoughts. "You were too weak by then. Andromeda had been battering you both in that arena for days."

"Which would never have happened if I'd had *any* idea of what I could do." My words are rough and accusing. And they should be.

If only I'd known Griffin then. He would never have just stood by and watched those dreadful days in the arena play out. The Gods may have gifted me with magic, but Griffin is the one who has truly helped me. His support and love gave me the courage to open those locked doors, even just a little, and to believe in my own decency and humanity enough to let my repressed magic peek out.

Ares releases one of my arms and then pops me again with the flat of his hand, this time right in the center of my forehead. My vision momentarily goes dark. "He brought stability to your chaotic heart. Helped you to believe in your own goodness. In your fated path. But free will, little monster. You have to know *yourself*."

I scowl. "Because everyone just wakes up one day and thinks *Hey, I'll bet I can fly and shoot lightning from my hands. Let's do it!*"

Ares's face turns terrifying. "I may love you like my own, but you are not exempt from my wrath."

I swallow the rest of the angry words boiling in my mouth. I believe him.

Slowly, he unlocks his hand from around my arm and then nods in the direction of up.

Heat rises from the magma-filled pit below. Chilled air races down from the snow-capped peaks above. The two collide and try to toss me around like a leaf in a storm, but I'm steadier now, inside and out. I beat my wings and shoot upward toward the open sky.

With a shout, I fly out of the chasm north of the burning house and then gulp down a less sulfurous breath. The air is thick and dark with smoke, though, and doesn't taste much better. I tilt, swooping around and scanning the meadow for signs of Griffin.

There!

I squint against the acrid burn of rising smoke and see Griffin stumbling across the grass. He staggers toward the cliff, damaged and unsteady on his feet, but my heart still sings in relief. I need him. Griffin helps me to see things differently. To see *myself* differently. Courage and strength were already there, but the most fundamental part was lacking: belief in myself. Through the mirror of his eyes, I finally saw someone worth knowing and fighting for. By his side, there's no more hiding or walking in the shadow of my potential. Griffin won't stand for that, and I find that lately, neither can I.

As I fly toward him from the side, Griffin falls to his knees near the edge of the pit and lets out a bloodcurdling howl. It chills me to the very marrow of my bones. His cry still echoing off the mountains, he reaches up and fists both hands in his hair. He pulls, rocking hard.

Fear sends goose bumps crashing over me in a wave. He's too close to the edge, desperate and devastated, and I'm suddenly terrified he's going to try to follow me over the cliff. I might be able to fly, but I can't carry him out.

A hot ache bursts beneath my breast. "Griffin!"

His dark head jerks up. He turns toward the sound of my voice, and his eyes widen, standing out in his blood-streaked and sooty face.

Tears burn my eyes. I close in on him, wobbling as I try to slow down.

His expression goes from stark and hollow to pure shock. He jumps up, reeling back from the cliff. "Cat?"

"Yes!" I cry, holding back the sob of the century.

A glassy sheen coats Griffin's eyes as I crash down nearly on top of him, my legs jarring hard when my feet hit the ground. The sob flies from me, and I pitch forward. Griffin meets me halfway. Our bodies collide, the shock of him vibrating through me. Heat. Muscle. Bone. We're both too injured to slam into each other this way, but neither of us cares. I throw my arms around his neck and hold on.

As if his legs can't hold him up any longer, he sinks down, dragging me down with him. We both end up on our knees, and Griffin clutches me so tightly that my ribs ache. I find his face with my hands and grip his jaw hard. We kiss, a frantic crushing and melding of lips. I taste sweat and blood, mine and his, and he groans against my mouth. It's not a sound of desire. It's the sound of just barely not breaking.

"I thought you were dead. I was sure you... And I couldn't..." His breath hitches, and he shudders. Seeing his lashes spike with moisture nearly breaks my heart.

My own breathing is far from steady, and my throat is thick with tears, but I need to say something that will take the fear out of his eyes—and the horrible, misplaced guilt from his voice.

I look at him straight on, knowing he'll never look away. "You think I'm that easy to kill?"

He makes a strangled sound, and I know he recognizes the exact same words I used at the circus fair the night we first met. He swallows and keeps staring at me, but he doesn't look quite so heartbreakingly terrified anymore.

"I remember when you said that. That's the moment I fell in love with you." Taking my face in his hands, Griffin brushes his thumb across my lower lip. "You and your smart mouth."

My heart swells, and my mouth tingles under his touch. I kiss his thumb.

Griffin curves his hands around my head and pulls me in to him, tucking me against his chest. For a moment, we both stop, needing to feel skin and heartbeats and breath.

"I won't leave you," I say almost savagely, clutching the back of his ruined tunic. Griffin is smart, kind, fair, strong, broad, bruised, and *mine*. I am never letting him go, and he's never getting rid of me. We have a life to live. Together.

He draws back, looking down at me. "I know, *agapi mou*. But I thought you'd been taken." His eyes flick over my feathers, and nervous heat rises in my belly. It fans out, spreading toward my neck and face.

I sprouted wings. *Helpful? Yes. Attractive? Debatable...*

Still kneeling and wrapped in Griffin's arms, I glance over my shoulder and try to extend my wings. They folded back down at some point after I landed without my really even thinking about it. One side snaps out, impressive. The other ignores me completely. *Great*. Nothing is ever easy.

I urge the extended one to relax again, and it folds down against my back, brushing the ground.

"Do they hurt?" Griffin asks.

I shake my head. "No, except for when they first popped out. But I hope you like wings. Now that they're here, I have no idea how to put them back inside me again. Or if I even can."

His brow furrowing, Griffin smooths one hand over my feathers. They're surprisingly sensitive, and a little shiver cascades down my spine.

Gruffly, he says, "You could grow horns for all I care. I love you. All of you. Inside and out."

I take a deep breath. "Good to know." In fact, it warms my heart immensely. "Because depending on which

Gods added their ichor to my veins, which apparently a bunch of them did, I could end up with pointy ears or a beard someday."

Griffin grunts, processing that, I guess.

"Speaking of Gods…" I look around, but the God of War is nowhere to be found. "Ares helped me out of the pit. He got the wings out of me. I'm part Nike—or something like that."

Griffin grunts again—more processing, I think—and then murmurs, "Winged Victory."

I frown, not feeling very victorious. Alive, though, and that's what matters.

"Maybe Ares contributed something to my blood, too." That would explain a lot.

Griffin doesn't look okay with that. In fact, he looks downright pained.

"My affable nature?" I ask, trying to lighten his scowl. "My peacekeeping skills?"

Not even a smile. It's too soon to joke.

"Is Little Bean all right?" Griffin's eyes drop to my middle.

Glancing down, I smooth my hands over my lower belly. "Snug as a bug on a sheepskin rug." I can sense her powerful life force inside me and feel her steady heartbeat. It's faster than mine.

"Good Gods!" Mother's voice slices through me like a knife made of ice. "I'm not even surprised. You land on your feet wherever you go."

Griffin and I jump apart and scramble to our feet. Griffin throws out his arm, pushing me behind him. Shock roots me to the spot. There'd been no sign of Mother when I flew over the meadow and the house. I'd thought she was gone!

But now she's within striking distance, one of my

knives in her left hand and my sword in her right. She probably wanted Griffin's, but it's too heavy for her to wield. Ianthe's pearls circle her head, holding back her loose hair. She's dressed in her own clothes now and looking like herself again, although I hesitate to call that human.

"Nice robes," I say, coming alongside Griffin. She's wearing all black, and I'm sure it's for the sheer intimidation factor.

"They're for your funeral," she answers.

I curl my mouth into a cool smile, forcing myself to show no fear. But the truth is, she *does* scare me. She scares the ever-living magic out of me.

"Or yours," Griffin snarls.

Mother laughs that off, and I barely suppress a shudder.

"Wings." She looks me up and down with distaste. "How hideous."

I notch my chin up. She's not fooling me. I see the envy in her eyes, turning them even greener. And I feel her lie punch through me, hot and pounding. "Jealous?"

She snorts. "Chances are, you don't know how to use them."

Truth. Unfortunately. "I figured out up versus down."

Her tone cutting, she says, "Mediocrity suits you. It's a good thing, since that's all you've ever striven for."

"And sheer evilness makes you special," I answer in kind.

She smiles. Of course that doesn't insult her.

I may have more raw power than she does, but I have no skill, and Mother knows it. So far, I've survived on luck, help, and accident alone, and today was no exception.

"Why did you ever even try to teach me about magic?" I ask, knowing that much of my ineptitude comes from refusing to listen to a word she said. I was so focused on not using my magic like she did that I ended up not using it at all. "So that I could be your spy in Galen Tarva's court?"

"It was in my best interest for you to survive there. With proximity, you could have controlled him."

"I'll never alter minds, not even someone like Galen's. A person's free will isn't a toy to play around with."

She scoffs. "You have no ambition. You don't deserve any crown, let alone mine."

If ambition means terrorizing people for fun, then she's right.

"Cruelty isn't ambition," Griffin says with utter conviction. "Setting limits on great power takes more strength than you'll ever have."

My heart skips a beat. Maybe two. *My Gods.* Griffin just put into words what it seems I've been subconsciously doing my entire life. But unlike Ares, he doesn't think I've thrown away my tools. He thinks I'm strong.

Mother's eyes flick to Griffin. "Don't speak in my presence, Hoi Polloi." She holds up my sword, making a show of inspecting it. "Is this Thanatos? The sword you named in my honor?"

"Not in your honor," I answer. "In warning."

"Of my impending death?" Her laughter is like a metal rake scraping deep furrows into my confidence. "I could hand you this blade right now. You'll never do it. You don't have it in you, and that's why you're a fool and a disappointment. All that power in a useless, cowardly package. You're the one I should have handed over to Otis instead of Eleni."

Rage explodes in me, coloring my vision black. "Don't talk about Eleni. Don't even say her name. You don't have the right."

"You're a failure."

"Why? Because I don't look forward to adding matricide to my list of family kills?" Sarcasm masks the knot around my heart, but the pressure inside me makes it hard to speak.

"Cat's never disappointed me a day in her life," Griffin says flatly, and the fact that no lie burns through me tells me that his capacity to forgive and forget is huge.

Mother freezes. For a moment, she looks taken aback. "Give it time. You haven't known her long."

"He knows me better than you do," I snap.

"He doesn't know the darkness in your heart." Her expression hardens again. "He doesn't know how you're made."

Well, I do. I know exactly how I'm made. More or less. On the inside, I belong to the Gods.

As if to reward my acceptance of my birthright, and maybe even my destiny, a surge of power wells up from deep inside me, and lightning webs down my arms. The Elemental Magic explodes from my fingertips, charring the ground at my feet.

I lift my magic-bright hands and aim them at Mother. "You're the one who doesn't know how I'm made."

Mother spins to the side, and my bolt hits the whirling material of her gown, punching a smoldering hole through it. She turns on me, livid, and I feel her try to push a fierce mental command straight into my brain.

It strikes me like an ice pick, cold and sharp. I gasp. Pressure and pain cut me off from my magic, and it takes all my strength to fight off her silent attack. My lightning sputters and dies like a guttering torch, but I shove her so fast from my mind that she reels back.

She shakes her head, feeling the backlash of her failed compulsion. Then, sneering, she says, "You're not entirely useless. You did take care of the Tarvan royals for me, although I can't imagine how."

Her tone and expression are everything they need to be

in order to make me doubt. In Castle Tarva, it was Ianthe and Bellanca, Griffin and Flynn. Cerberus. I hardly did anything besides rattle my tail and run my mouth. *Not entirely useless* pretty much sums it up.

Mother points the gleaming tip of my own sword at me. "And now, with a little help from Thanatos, Thalyria will be mine."

"Never." Griffin steps in front of me again.

Mother lunges with a quick jab. Griffin shoves me back hard while evading the blade himself. Mother swings again, keeping him dodging as her left hand toys with my knife. I watch her fingers adjust, tighten. She's going to throw.

Before I can warn Griffin, Little Bean does something that twists my insides. Her energy explodes with something that feels a lot like fright. Definitely distress. It stops my heart dead, and I know, just *know*, that Mother is trying to get to her again. She's battering her mind, and Little Bean is fighting back.

My lower abdomen goes rock-hard, and my hands fly to cover it. A pained breath hisses between my teeth.

Griffin turns back to me, alarm written all over his face.

"No!" I shout, dread hurtling through me.

He whips back around in time to see Mother release the dagger. He twists in front of me and doesn't make a sound when the knife sinks deep into his middle, but I gasp in fright.

My horrified gaze snaps back to Mother. I'm wholly unsurprised that she used Little Bean as a distraction. What I can't believe is that I didn't see it coming. Her throwing aim has always been average—thank the Gods—but she sneers in satisfaction anyway, flashing Thanatos in her other hand.

"The next one's for you, *Talia mou*."

The mocking endearment is like one of her stinging slaps across my face. My wings snap out in response, and her eyes widen in surprise. I hide my own surprise behind a heated glare as I grab Griffin's arm and try to pull him behind me. His face has washed of all color.

Locking his jaw, he growls, "Stay behind me."

"Stay behind *me*," I growl back.

He looks at me like I'm insane, like he would never use me as his shield. I step around him before he can react. Maybe I am insane. I have no combat magic, and my lightning is a sham. But double standards don't work with me, especially from the man I love.

There's a deafening crack of timber from above, and the hermit's house falls in on itself with a ferocious upheaval of fire and smoke, likely burying the real witch inside—already good and dead, I'm sure. Mother doesn't leave loose ends.

Sparks roar upward from the collapsed structure, turning the sky red, orange, and black.

"Apocalyptic," I say. "A fitting backdrop for you, Mother."

Her eyes narrow. "Certainly your end of days."

"How do you figure?" I ask.

"I'm the one holding the sword."

I smile, and it's vicious. I've kept this secret from her for years.

I turn invisible, and Mother gapes in shock. *Ha!*

I dart forward. All it takes is one sharp punch right above her elbow, and she drops the sword with a gasp. I kick it back toward Griffin. Before scrambling away, I reach out and wrench Ianthe's circlet from Mother's head, taking some of her hair along with it.

Mother grabs her head, her face contorting in rage and confusion. "That's mine!"

I backpedal and reappear out of hitting distance. "Then why did Ianthe have it?"

"She took it, the little wretch."

"Why do you want it?"

Mother eyes the circlet, her mouth flattening into a line. "Where's Ianthe?" she asks.

"Somewhere safe." *I hope.* "Out of your reach." *Definitely.*

"There's nowhere out of my reach."

Another smile shapes my mouth into something I'm glad I can't see. But I *would* like to see Mother try to confront Lycheron. Maybe get a hoof in the face.

"I'm keeping this." I back away another step, and Griffin comes up beside me with Thanatos in his hand. I try not to think about the knife in his gut.

"As you like." Her tone goes back to cool and detached, but her eyes say otherwise.

I grip the pearls, dying to know what's so special about them. But getting Griffin to running water so I can heal him is more important.

I look at Mother. Can we end this here? Now? No war. No army. No innocent deaths to regret. She must have used a lot of magical energy on steering the crows, the Harpy metamorphosis, and tossing everything around. And she just wasted more power on a failed attempt at compulsion. She might not have another truly dangerous trick up that black sleeve of hers—at least not until she can rest. That kind of magic doesn't just take power; it takes a deep well of it, and hers might be mostly dried up.

And yet she's standing here, unarmed. Is she really that confident? Or is she bluffing? Is this another one of her mind games, and just by asking myself all these damn questions, I'm already losing?

Her eyes dart to the circlet in my hand, and then it hits me. She doesn't want to leave without it.

"This amplifies magic, doesn't it?" I clutch the pearls harder in my fist. "It's spelled to channel more power. That's why you want it."

Her lip curls. "Don't be stupid. My power is already huge."

I spread my hands a little, waving the trinket she wants. "Then why are you still here?"

"To watch your Hoi Polloi husband bleed to death." She smiles. "The longer I keep you busy, the weaker he gets."

My stomach drops hard. I can help Griffin, even with my limited healing skills, but I need to get him to the stream and act soon.

I fold back my wings and reach out for my sword. We're out of time, and I won't ask Griffin to kill for me, even though I know he would. He gives me Thanatos without a word, his expression strained. The hilt is warm from his hand and seems to hum against my palm with a song to sing me, or a ballad to tell. I wish I knew how the story ended, but only silence travels up my arm.

Compulsion scrapes through my mind again. Pressure, pain, and then a deep-seated desire to turn the sword on myself.

I push back hard, jarring a flinch out of Mother. There's no sound between us, only the common thought of her trying to break me like she did once before, that dark moment when I lost all sense of myself. Eleni did, too, but she paid the heavier price.

Mother bores deeper, and I grind my teeth with effort. It turns out she wasn't bluffing. She has plenty of power left.

Gasping, I raise my hand to my searing head, still clutching Ianthe's pearls. The pressure and pain disappear instantly. I drop my hand, confused, and they come roaring back.

The pearls! They don't amplify magic; they block it!

I crown myself with Ianthe's perfect gift, and Mother's lips pull back in a snarl.

"I get it now. And this time around, I can break *you*." I cock my head to the side, looking her up and down. "Maybe I should."

Thanks to Ianthe, I'm protected now from mental attacks, and for the first time ever, I see uncertainty flicker in Mother's eyes. It doesn't bring me nearly the satisfaction I thought it would.

"Do it then," she taunts, even stepping closer in challenge.

My whole body locks up tight. *Gods, I'm tempted.* But in the end, I say, "I'm not a monster like you are. I won't take away anyone's free will."

Her bright-green eyes seem to shutter. "Take first, or everything will be taken from you."

I shake my head at her. What kind of warped philosophy is that? It's like her "Love nothing, and no one can hurt you." It's a total perversion of natural sentiment. How did she get this way? Why didn't she try to change?

"Don't waste your time trying to impart your twisted wisdom." I raise my sword and get ready to exercise free will. "Any last words?" I ask her.

The look she levels at me is scathing. "You're the embodiment of my every mistake."

Well then. I guess I shouldn't have asked.

I lift my chin. "It's a shame you never tried to see how a real family acts. You might have liked it."

Maybe I just imagine the small flinch from Mother. Either way, it makes me hesitate as I step forward with Thanatos in my hand, and Mother starts to laugh. The sound makes my belly churn like it did when I was a child.

"I knew it," she says. "I didn't even bother to run."

Holding out his hand, Griffin grinds out, "Give me the sword, Cat."

I shake my head and then force my shoulders back and down. They keep curling up around my ears.

I can do this. I should have done it already. Minutes ago. Years before.

Steeling myself, I leap forward and swing in a hard arc.

CHAPTER 14

MOTHER'S EYES WIDEN. SHE DIDN'T THINK I'D DO IT. HONESTLY, I wasn't sure I would.

She jerks back enough to get thoroughly out of my reach, and I scowl. I must not have tried very hard.

"Cat…" Griffin growls. "It's now or never."

"I can do it!"

"You don't have to!" he says. "I'm here. I'm here for you."

And while I stand there, refusing to give up my sword but indecisive and stupidly torn, no matter what I just said, Mother runs away. She heads up the hill toward the burning house, getting a dozen paces from me before I even move.

Finally, I stalk after her, Thanatos a far too heavy weight in my hand for such a small sword.

She stops and turns, a splash of darkness against the bright-orange blaze. "You never could stand the heat." Using her telekinetic magic, she picks up a flaming plank and then hurls it at me.

I duck, cursing. *How could I have done this? Failed again?*

Mother rains down wreckage on us from above. A smoldering board hits me in the shoulder, and I stagger, the bone jarred straight into numbness. Another one sails over my head, and I turn. Griffin dodges it, grimacing and holding his stomach. My heart lurches, and I reach for him, but something crashes down between us, showering us with sparks.

Before she can launch more fiery debris down the hill, Griffin rips the knife from his abdomen and then throws it at Mother. It lands in her shoulder instead of her heart, knocked off course by the telekinetic magic whirling all around her.

Her mouth drops open in shock. So does mine. Her magic crashes to the ground, the green cyclone disappearing and leaving everything abruptly quiet. The wound isn't fatal, but it did stop her. For now.

And now there's only Thanatos—and I have the sword.

Griffin beckons to me. "Give me the sword."

I shake my head, tightening my grip on the hilt.

His eyes flick over the blade. "She's not your responsibility alone. Her death won't haunt my conscience."

Like it'll haunt mine?

I don't move, and Griffin takes the weapon from my hand. Even injured, he's much stronger than I am, and Thanatos slips from my grasp.

I open my mouth but say nothing. I stand there, frozen. Little Bean's energy stirs, a tiny flutter that feels like a pat, and I wrap my arms around my middle, silent and watching as Griffin prowls forward to do my dirty work for me, one hand armed with my sword and the other trying to hold his blood in.

Something huge suddenly crashes in the forest. I whip my head around to look. Our corralled horses snort sharply at the beat of heavy hooves, and then a monster explodes from the woods.

I take a reflexive step back, my pulse surging hard. It's the biggest horse I've ever seen. The equine fiend races across the meadow, its enormous strides shaking and devouring the ground. It skids to a halt near Mother and then rears, reaching terrifying heights. Its long mane snaps on the fire-hot wind, and its wild red eyes stand out like malevolent flames in a jet-black face. The beast tosses its head, staring straight at me. It looks like it can taste my fear and wants to drink it down.

Griffin turns back to me. "What is *that*?"

A creature straight from nightmares. It bares sharp teeth, and visceral fear punches me in the gut.

"One of the Mares of Thrace," I answer, trying to keep the tremor from my voice. Aetos killed one on the Ice Plains years ago, and my friend wears the gigantic, pure-black pelt as a trophy cloak. Three are left. "They eat humans. Only the most powerful Magoi have ever managed to control them. Only one has ever been killed."

"Hungry, darling?" Mother speaks to the horse, but she looks at Griffin. Her face twists in triumph. "I wonder if Hoi Polloi tastes like inferior meat."

I snap out of my shock. *Good Gods, if there was ever a time for my lightning to work.* I pull hard on the threads of magic inside me and…nothing. *Gods damn it!*

The mare paws the ground, getting ready to charge. I start to sprint. If that monster wants to eat Griffin, it'll have to go through me.

A deafening pop and a ground-shaking boom nearly send me crashing to my knees. Ares steps in front of me, his huge, weapon-decked frame a solid barrier between the mare and me. Persephone glides in from the right to protect Griffin, only a curved knife in her belt. She leaves it there.

I swing a wide-eyed gaze back and forth between the two Gods. "*Now?*" I ask, both irate and incredibly relieved.

Persephone turns to me, asking coolly, "Did you expect us sooner?"

At this point, I'm not sure I expected them at all. "You need to heal Griffin."

Her eyes move up and down my body, taking me in. "And you, too."

I look down at myself. I'm a mess. But Griffin is worse.

"What's this?" Mother's shrill question comes from where she's still occupying the high ground with her terrifying beast.

The God of War stalks forward, and I see her eyes focus on Ares, get stuck, and then sharpen. She recognizes Thanos. Bigger. Scarier. More powerful. But still Thanos.

Quick comprehension has never been a problem for Mother. Driving the mare with her mind, she commands the creature to get down low on its front legs and then jumps on top of the horse with the help of her uninjured arm. The mare rises, and with only a thought, Mother and the monster race away from the meadow so fast they become a dark streak in the air. I blink, and she's gone.

I missed my chance.

Persephone slides me a sidelong glance, one perfect eyebrow raised, questioning—and patently judging.

Less subtle, Ares whirls on me. "What was that? Did I teach you *nothing*? You froze!"

No, I think I chose. But I keep making the wrong choice.

"What happened to the woman who *survives*!" Ares bellows, livid.

"She survived," Griffin snaps, dragging himself toward me. At this point, I'm pretty sure it's sheer stubbornness keeping him upright.

"Not by much," Ares fumes. "And no thanks to herself."

It's true, all true, but right now, my only concern is Griffin.

Hurrying to him, I take some of his weight against my side and lead him to Persephone. She runs a critical eye over us both but then takes out her knife and splits Griffin's tunic up the middle, baring first his bloody midriff and then pushing his shirt off entirely. The gash looks deep, but it's not very wide. Even Griffin can't survive on determination alone, so the blade must not have hit anything too vital. There's a deep-purple bruise spreading up his side from where the table struck his ribs. I don't bother cataloging cuts and burns. They're everywhere.

"This is deep. And there are two cracked ribs. You might want to sit," Persephone tells him.

"Then you'd have to sit, too," Griffin says.

She looks up from his injuries, frowning. "So?"

"A Goddess shouldn't kneel in front of a human," he replies stiffly.

She stares at him, unblinking. "Are you making the rules now? Should I inform Zeus?"

Griffin's cheeks color, the splash of heat painfully obvious in his otherwise bloodless face.

"Sit," Persephone orders, "or I'll make Ares hold you down."

Ares scoffs. "You won't *make* Ares do anything."

"You think I can't?" Frost laces her magic-heavy words.

My stomach clenches, anxiety gripping it like a fist. It turns me inside out to see them fight.

Ares squares his shoulders, always ready for a confrontation. His eyes race with Olympian power and light. "You, your irritating husband, and that fleabag Cerberus all together might ha—"

"Stop arguing." I cut through their pointless taunting, my voice like a barbed knife. "Griffin, sit."

Ares turns to me, crossing his arms. "Oh, there you are. I thought you'd left Thalyria. Maybe went on holiday. Or took a nap."

My eyes narrow. "Is this a game to you? You're the God

of War. Why are you even helping people who are trying
to bring peace?"

Ares smiles. It's genuine, heart-stopping, and completely frightening. "Peace might be on the horizon, but in
the meantime, you're giving me a damn good fight." His
smile fades into an expression of pure disgust. "Except for
today. Today was pitiful."

I nod. I can only agree.

"Besides, there are always Attica and Atlantis for more
wars. Thalyria has seen enough. The magic is too strong
here to continue like this. Someone's bound to destroy
the world."

Someone like Mother? Or someone like me?

Ares manages to chastise my inner thoughts with a
single look.

I glower back. I can think what I want. If he doesn't like
it, he can stop listening in.

Griffin grunts and then draws in a sharp breath when
Persephone lays her hands on his stomach. She releases
more magic, and he tenses so much his back bows. I grimace along with him. Healing is a painful process, often
much more so than the original wound.

Hating his pain and knowing it's my fault since he
was protecting me, I drop down behind him and put my
hands on his shoulders, helping to brace his weight and
steady him against the onslaught of magic. He leans in
to me, throwing his head back and looking up at the sky
in silent agony.

Persephone draws her hands back, flexing her fingers
discreetly. Griffin breathes deeply and then more shal-
lowly again when she goes back to healing him. She works
quickly, sinking huge amounts of magic into him. I feel her
power pricking hard at my skin as it smooths out Griffin's,

knitting his flesh, erasing bruises, and mending bones. The accelerated process must hurt like a hundred burning knife wounds, but it'll be over fast. Griffin clenches his jaw, his face bone-white.

Then it's done, and Persephone lifts her hands from him. The tense, tightly bunched muscles in Griffin's shoulders relax. Still holding on to him, I lean forward and kiss the slope of his neck, breathing him in.

"Thank you for jumping in front of a knife for me," I murmur.

A grunt is his only answer, but he reaches up and grabs one of my hands. He pulls it to his mouth and kisses my palm, then holds on, keeping me curved around him.

Persephone stands. After a deep inhale, Griffin rises as well, pulling me up with him. I look him over. He's still a sooty, bloody mess, but those stains are only war paint now.

"You'll be sore." Persephone inspects her healing work with a slight frown. "Eat well and rest."

Griffin and I look around, and I can tell we're both skeptical. The house is a burned-out ruin. We have only light traveling food.

The Goddess shrugs. "Sleep in the barn. Kill a goat. I don't think you'll have any trouble making a fire."

I glance at the collapsed house. There'll be smoldering embers for days.

Griffin nods to her. "Thank you."

She waves a dismissive hand. Healing Griffin probably took very little out of her, but I'm still grateful and say so as well.

Persephone reaches out to me, and her hands begin to feather over my skin, light and careful. I'm covered in lacerations, puncture wounds, burns, and scrapes, and no matter how gentle she is, healing still *hurts*. Everywhere she touches, I ache and sting even worse than I did before, and every time I wince, hiss, or gasp, the groove between her bright-blue eyes deepens into a harder frown.

I see Selena in her as she works—the thick blonde braid, the graceful way she moves, the fathomless eyes and perfect features. Physically, Persephone is only a little different from the woman I've known and loved. She's taller, more powerful, and more otherworldly in a way I never imagined, but those differences seem huge and daunting now that I know who—and *what*—she really is.

A pang hits me square in the chest. I miss her.

I'm still her.

The words arrive directly in my head, and I scowl. *What does it take to have a private thought around here?*

And you're definitely still Cat.

There's more wry humor than real scolding in her silent words as she steps back from me, her movements almost liquid in their shimmering fluidity. I follow her with my eyes, still somehow surprised by her innate power and light. She's mesmerizing.

Nearly entranced, I absently whisper the fear that's been festering under my now-healed wounds. "What if I can't do this?" Mother tried to kill me. I *didn't* kill her. I'd thought we were finally going to settle this, but the pattern just repeats itself. I can't seem to break it.

Before Persephone can even begin to answer, Ares bursts out with an aggravated sound. His eyebrows slam down.

"I thought I raised a fighter." His tone is sharp. It certainly cuts *me*.

Persephone snorts. "Raised?"

"No one else was doing it!" he snaps.

"If anyone raised her, it was her sister," Persephone snaps back. "And then me."

Anger seems to gather around Ares, weighing down the air. "Where were you? Where were any of you for the first *fifteen* years?"

"It wasn't my turn!" Persephone seems to grow along with her ire, and something terrifying and dangerous flashes in her eyes. "I had to stay away. The others forced me to. The Fates made the plan, and Zeus approved it."

I sense an epic, ground-shaking God fight coming on, and I'm not letting them do that—at least not without me.

"Why didn't either of *you* just kill her?" I ask, suddenly furious as well. "Mother was right there. So were you. It could have been over. Alpha Fisa—gone!"

Persephone swings her gaze back to me, her expression abruptly cooling. "Is that really my role?" She sweeps a hand toward Ares. "Or even his?"

I glare at them both. "Should it really be *mine*?"

I see deep affection warring with the frustration in her eyes. She doesn't answer.

Is that a yes? A no? She doesn't know?

"Everything is for a reason," Ares says cryptically.

"Oh, that's helpful!" Little Bean picks that moment to feel like a tumbling bubble in my lower abdomen. Smart girl. She obviously agrees.

I growl. It's loud. The air suddenly vibrates with power again, but this time, it's mine.

Some of the most terrible moments of my life flash through my mind, and my heart starts to race. Griffin knocked down and unmoving in the middle of a maelstrom of magic and fire. Birds throwing me into a volcanic pit. Eleni—dead in the sand.

My rage grows like a storm inside me, around me. The wind begins to howl. "Give me your reasons then. Because from where I'm standing, they don't look very compelling."

CHAPTER 15

"Everything is for a reason," Persephone agrees. Unlike Ares, I can tell she's tamping down the power in her voice and all around her, maybe trying to limit her agitation. Or mine. "Everything is laid out like a map."

"I can't follow a map!" I never could.

"You don't have to follow it. Just know that there are multiple roads. You alone choose the ones you take. Some lead to the same destination via different pathways. Others lead to similar or dissimilar outcomes, depending on where you turn."

I shake my head. She's talking, but all I hear is noise. "Why can't I make my lightning work? How do I get rid of these wings? I can't protect my baby!"

And there it is. The crushing root of my fear. The reason I'm terrified like never before.

I stumble back, bumping into Griffin.

Ares moves toward us, angling his head in concern and making a gruff sound I remember from my childhood. The low hum hurtles me back to a time when I still had my sister, when I was sure I'd fight harder than anyone, save the people I love, and die on my feet. It was a time when Thanos was my only God, even though I thought he was human, just like me.

All of my earliest memories include him. Eleni and I hiding behind him, because he's as big as a house. Thanos spending hours in the nursery, watching over us and scaring off our older brothers when they took their cruelty beyond the usual harassment. Crying in his arms before I understood how to control my tears—a skill I've obviously forgotten lately. This scarred, hardened, giant-of-a-man lifting me up off the blood-slicked floor after Mother beat me and then holding my hand through the hard bite of healing, Eleni always on my other side. I threw up on him more than once, usually when I was at the final threshold of pain. Thanos put my first knife in my hand, curled my small fingers around it with his enormous ones, and then showed me how to use it.

My eyes snap up to meet those of the God of War. Persephone is wrong about who raised me. Eleni was my best friend. But Thanos was everything else.

Ares and I stare at each other. He knows exactly what I'm thinking, and how my emotions are raging inside me right now. His wide-set eyes soften, but that just makes it worse.

"You could have stopped it!" I lunge forward and pound on Ares's chest, anger, hurt, and bitterness making me rash. "You could have stopped it all!"

Griffin wraps his arms around me and drags me back. I shout, still striking out as he plants me on my feet and holds on to me.

Ares's expression shows just enough of the temper he has boiling beneath the surface to make me straighten up and pause. *But doesn't he understand?* I saved *no one*. Eleni died right next to me, and I was too weak to even get up. I've dragged Griffin through vats of blood—his own *and* mine—and put him through so much. And Little Bean... Mother was in her head! What lies did she feed my baby? What horrors did she expose her to? Will they stay with her, even though she's so tiny right now?

Persephone spreads her hands in a calming gesture. "Zeus didn't create humans so we could play with them like dolls, moving them here and there and filling their mouths with our own words. You're not marionettes, and you don't dance when we pull strings."

"So what in the name of the Gods *are* you doing?" I ask, still too seething to let this go.

"Setting things into motion," she answers. "Helping—when really necessary."

"You mean when it suits you!" My heartbeat echoes in the hollow space beneath my ribs, the place that should have been filled with siblings and family and home, but they were ripped out, one by one, or else I never had them at all. Slowly, that empty space has been filling up with people I love, but what's to stop them from being torn from me now? "Where were you when I needed you the most?"

A shadow flits through Persephone's eyes. Ares's expression tightens just before his seafoam gaze drops to the ground.

My voice lowers, trembling. "If anyone should have been chosen, protected, it was my *sister*."

Persephone reaches out and gently grips my face with both hands. Magic thumps from her palms. It should sting my cheeks, but it just feels cool and gallingly numbing. "Stop, Cat. You need to move on. Eleni served her purpose."

I gasp. If she'd struck me with a hundred whips, her words couldn't have cut me deeper, or scathed me more. I jerk my face out of her hands and lurch back into Griffin. "So you *killed* her?"

"We did nothing of the sort." Persephone's hands fall slowly back to her sides. "Your mother and brother did that."

That may be true, but… I turn accusing eyes on Ares. "You were there. You let it happen."

Real sorrow clouds his rugged features, the kind that's unmistakable and true. "Would you be where you are right now if Eleni had lived? Her death influenced the road you took on the Fates' map. It brought you to Sinta. To Persephone. To him." He nods toward Griffin. "It got you to Poseidon's Oracle. It got you away from your mother. It brought you to where you needed to be."

Unbelievable! "You can't rationalize her death like that! My life's not worth hers. And I could have gone to Sinta with her. We could have gone together!"

Persephone shakes her head. "Eleni had a destiny, just like you. She knew it, and she fulfilled it. She chose the road she needed to, and she took it without regret. Her life was worth a great deal, and she knew that, too. She knew how much it was worth to *you*."

I gulp back more angry words. Persephone—my Selena—has always mixed empathy with hard truths in a way that makes them impossible to escape or ignore. She's right. Eleni must have known what her death would do to me. Did she also know it would get me out of Fisa? To Selena? To Griffin?

Eleni had her secrets, just like we all do. I have oracular dreams. They're infrequent, and usually apply only to the near future, but what if Eleni had visions, too? What if she saw much farther than I ever have?

I reel in shock, remembering. She once told me the entire world was mine.

My Gods. She knew.

"I felt her loss, too." Ares's simple words neither heal nor cut, but like Persephone's, they make me listen again when I don't want to hear. "I was with her for fifteen years, just like you."

His truth hits me deep in my magic with the usual burn, and a sudden image of us all together invades my mind, both wonderful and heartbreaking. And utterly simple—as the best things are. We were outside in the springtime, away from the castle, and Eleni was practicing with her flaming birds since her Fire Magic had finally started to mature. They were still wobbly, half formed, and slow to react, but Thanos let her chase him around the field with them, running, dodging, and acting like he was scared. We knew he wasn't, and it made us laugh. We never laughed much otherwise.

Persephone moves forward and takes my hand. Magic sparks, and I hate it because I know she's using her healing power to calm me down. I want to stay angry. Devastated. Eleni deserves it. She deserves my loyalty.

"I don't need your tricks." I pull out of her reach again, refusing to lessen the fury in my heart. It's been my companion for so long that I'm not sure how to function without it.

Persephone steps back, glancing briefly at Griffin. "No, I suppose you don't."

Is that hurt in her voice?

Feeling guilt now along with everything else, I reach up, take Ianthe's circlet from my head, and then wrap it around the front of my belt, right over where I think Little Bean is. Mother won't reach her again with compulsion. No one will.

"We thought she'd inherit her father's immunity to harmful magic, but apparently she hasn't," Persephone says. "Or maybe it simply hasn't matured yet."

"I'll let you know," I say bitterly. "If she lives long enough. Maybe I can even keep her alive past seventeen."

The Goddess's mouth turns down before she speaks again. "You're too adept at focusing on the negative. Think about what Eleni gave you. She taught you goodness, compassion, laughter, and love. You were sorely in need of her influence, because I doubt your *Thanos* was teaching you any of that."

"You're wrong," I shoot back. "He did." He also taught me to fight to win, to see even when there's blood in my eyes, to overcome the worst kinds of pain, and to never give up. Lessons that served me well—until today. Today was an epic example of all things not to do.

"Nevertheless, she was your light in the dark," Persephone insists. "And she kept that spark of hope inside you alive, no matter what you went through."

"Were put through…" Ares mutters.

I look back and forth between them, trying to understand, maybe even trying to accept what they're saying instead of just railing against it. "So why take her from me? Why take my light? Wasn't there some other path?" I'm desperate for a reason, anything to justify my loss. Maybe I'm even desperate for something to take the blame off my shoulders for something I always believed was my fault.

"*Elpis*, my dear, damaged Cat." Suddenly, Persephone is Selena again, having reduced her physical body and Olympian radiance back to human proportions. She takes both my hands in hers and squeezes hard. There's no nip of magic, and I don't protest. I'm still angry, confused, and hurt, but I'm also stupid and needy enough to crave her maternal touch.

"Elpis?" I ask.

Persephone nods. "Could you have ever truly understood the primal, raw hope you carry inside you, that you give to others now, without having experienced suffering first? Without nearly unbearable loss and pain to overcome? How can you gauge joy without knowing despair? It's the journey, Cat. The outcome. Certainly, you were special from the start, but you weren't born with the inner

strength of a thousand men or the wisdom to rule a kingdom. You're building them, minute by minute, as you live
each wonderful or terrible day of your life."

A chill ripples over me. A wave of warmth chases it
away. Her words resonate on a deep level, but I'm still
not ready to let go of my resentment. Clearly, I'm not that
strong yet, or that wise. "You let her die so I'd have suffering to overcome?"

"We didn't intervene to save her," Ares says gravely.
"And her death saddened us greatly."

Heat builds behind my eyes. "You should have chosen
her. Why would anyone want me to rule Thalyria when
Eleni could have done it? She was kinder. Brighter. More
responsible. Gods..." I shake my head. "She was everyone's light, not just mine."

"You're wrong." Ares looks at me, his eyes flat with
pressure. "You're everything she was, and stronger still.
Your light shines just as brightly, but to see it, you had to
come out of her shadow first."

I inhale sharply and then flex my hands, forcing away
the urge to make them pay with my fists for what happened
to my sister, these two who were supposed to protect me.

None of this is even remotely fair, especially to Eleni,
but could they be right? Did her death somehow trigger
light inside me instead of the darkness I've always thought?
Is that where it comes from? Is that—

"Elpis." Griffin unknowingly finishes my thought. He
looks down at me, his eyes shining, his expression veering
toward awestruck. "It's not just an idea. It's *you*."

Persephone nods. "More or less. She's *grown* into
Elpis—with your help."

"You mean..." I frown. I don't know what she means.
"It wasn't in me from the start?"

"Hope is always there in everyone, to be crushed or nurtured, held close or abandoned. Elpis is the ancient, original spark from which all hope springs, and she only seeks out and attaches herself to the selfless warrior, the one who fights not for herself, but for others."

My mouth opens. Closes. I have nothing to say.

"Ares taught you to fight, but you adapted that to your own moral code. Your guilt is enormous each time you've killed in self-defense, but you feel no particular remorse when you do whatever it takes, no matter how violent and extreme, to defend someone else."

I snort, the sound raw. "I guess Elpis isn't any smarter than I am. We're sure to get each other killed. Or ourselves, since we're apparently the same thing now."

Ares's blue-green eyes blaze with sudden inner brightness, and a shiver tracks down my arms, leaving the hair raised. When he speaks, though, his voice holds more gruff affection than anger.

"No one does everything alone, little monster. Not even the Gods. We have our wives or husbands, our lovers, our allies, our offspring. You had Eleni, but she wasn't the person you needed for this part of your journey. When we put the weight of this world on your shoulders, we never expected you to heft it alone."

My mind skips over the "weight of this world" thing like a rough bump in the road—something to fix later. "So you made Griffin for me." Pressure bears down on my chest, the heaviness coming from a feeling of unease I can't seem to get rid of, despite Griffin's assurances. "The man the Origin couldn't intimidate, dominate, or accidentally kill." Those were Athena's exact words. I'll bet Griffin remembers them, too.

Ares folds his massive arms over his chest and looks

sideways at Persephone. She's more than a full head shorter than he is and not vibrating with magic now that she's in her human form, although she's still stunning, powerful, and otherworldly in her own way. She nods, indicating that he should go on.

Good Gods, they're sharing.

"We knew you'd be headstrong," he says.

Griffin snorts. I guess that's putting it mildly.

"And powerful," Ares continues. "And we knew what gifts you'd be likely to earn, and need, if you were to fulfill your destiny. The idea of a partner was formed. Like you, he's physically a mix of his parents. His mind is his own. His loyalty, inner strength, and calm are both a product of his experiences and inherent to his nature, and a good match for your loyalty, inner strength, and…"

"Not calm," I supply, narrowing my eyes.

"Exactly." Ares nods. "But we decided on a vital improvement before we set everything into motion. The Goddesses came together and Aphrodite had a stroke of genius," he says proudly. "Just like she never wanted a male she could control, she knew someone as strong as you were destined to be would never fall for a man you could overpower."

My cheeks start to heat. In some situations, I definitely want Griffin to be the dominant one.

Persephone looks first at Griffin and then back at me. "But putting you in that vulnerable position also meant giving you someone you could trust."

Of course I trust Griffin. More than anyone else.

"You *chose* me for Cat." Griffin's voice vibrates with something very close to anger. "You *changed* me for her."

My stomach suddenly feels off-kilter. I didn't like this the first time we heard it, and I like it even less now. Griffin's expression remains mostly neutral, but the mask looks close to cracking and revealing something dark and irate underneath.

Nerves build inside me, and words pour out before I can stop them. "I'm so sorry, Griffin. They forced this on you. You didn't ask for any of this. For me…"

His eyes shift to me, hard as rocks.

"Griffin was selected before you were born based on his own potential merits," Persephone explains, "and then enhanced to fit the future Origin's needs."

Griffin's mouth twists in fury, and a horrible, sinking feeling carves through me, hollowing me out. The same fear I felt the day Piers betrayed us comes roaring back, this time doubly gut-wrenching because Griffin isn't fooling himself anymore. I can see it in his face. His anger is terrible to behold.

He's given me everything—command of Beta Team, the crown, his body, his devotion. His child. He's loved me unconditionally, despite my many faults, because he convinced himself that *I* was made for *him*, not the other way around. If that illusion somehow hadn't fully shattered before, it has now. Persephone just crushed it and threw it to the four winds.

I stop breathing at the angry flush spreading across Griffin's face.

"You waited *this* long to bring me to her?" His voice turns low and livid. "Why all this wasted time? I could have been healing her broken heart, protecting her, giving her a family! Do you have any idea how unsatisfying my life was without her? Without my missing piece?"

Stunned, I watch him rage.

"And you…" He turns to me, his eyes shockingly bright.

Goose bumps wash over me in a wave.

"If you still doubt me—doubt *us*—then clearly, I have

things to prove." The promise in his eyes is unmistakable. And scorching. "Because I swear to the Gods, you'll never doubt me again."

Pain laces his incensed words, and guilt slams into me like a hard punch.

Why did I doubt him? "What is *wrong* with me?"

It's only when Griffin answers that I realize I spoke out loud. "You still don't trust yourself, and that makes you incapable of trusting anyone else."

CHAPTER 16

"I TRUST YOU!" I CRY, STUNG. NO, WORSE—*HURT*.

"Insofar as you're capable," Griffin answers stiffly.

My jaw drops. I want to say something, but nothing comes out. *Is he right? He's usually right.*

"You're wrong!" *Damn it!* I slap my hand over my mouth.

Both Olympians abruptly disappear, apparently leaving us alone to fight. The magic that gets sucked from the air, vanishing along with them, is staggering. I didn't realize how much it weighed on me until it was gone.

"You want to know why your magic doesn't work?" Griffin asks.

I lift my chin, knowing I'm not going to like whatever he's about to say, and that it'll hit me straight in the heart. "Why, then?"

His eyes flash with gray fire. He doesn't even try to contain his emotions, and Griffin without his usual calm in place is a formidable sight.

"It doesn't work because you don't trust yourself. Because you think it's going to backfire. Because you're so sure you're going to hurt someone you want to protect!"

"Oh, and that's never happened!" The sudden spike of adrenaline in my blood sets my heart to pounding. "The fire in the woods? Flynn under the arena? I burned a hole through his leg with a lightning bolt!"

Griffin reaches out and grips my upper arms, squeezing just enough to keep me still. "I am not Eleni. Little Bean is not Eleni. None of us are Eleni!" he thunders. "And what your mother did to her wasn't your fault!"

My already hammering heart goes into overdrive. My throat tightens, closing over. Suddenly, I'm burning up and freezing cold, and the whoosh of blood in my ears is deafening. Pounding. It's all I can hear. Weight seems to press down on me, crushing me from the sides, squeezing me all over. I don't know if I'm going to pass out or throw up, but everything blurs, and I can only see one thing: Little Bean *is* Eleni. She'll just have black hair.

Black hair. Blood. Seventeen years old. A knife in her heart. Dead.

Panic beats through me in dark waves. There's no air.

Griffin's expression goes from fuming to anxious. "Cat?"

My chest squeezes painfully as I wrap my arms around my middle, caving in on myself and searching out Little Bean's spark. She's still there. And she'll be here—until the day she's not.

"I can't protect her." My pulse pounds too hard, too loud, too fast. My breath saws in and out. "I can't protect her. She'll die. She'll die. She'll die, and I can't protect her."

"You can," Griffin says, holding me fast.

I clamp my eyes shut and shake my head.

"I'm sorry." Griffin pulls me close. "I'm sorry I yelled at you."

I shudder against him, leaning in, and his hand curves around the back of my head.

"Shhh. Nothing will happen to our baby. I swear it."

"Don't make…promises…you can't…keep," I gasp out against his chest.

"I swear it," he repeats, gripping me firmly.

I shake my head again. For the first time ever, I don't

believe him, even though no lie burns through me. I can't, and not even the sternness in his voice, the strength of his embrace, or the solidity of his body will make me.

But his steadfastness and gentle hands do eventually help me to stop shaking and to breathe again. Griffin breathes with me, cradling my head and stroking my back. The sharp, wild panic from before starts to recede, leaving me raw and aching and oddly detached.

Or maybe not detached. Maybe this is just the other side of the overwhelming dread, the side where I can finally think and function again. It feels as though I've run through an entire night, scared and hurting, but then dawn broke and gave me a second wind. Daylight and Griffin don't quell all my fears, but they help, just like they always have.

He holds me, and I hold him back. We stay like that for a long time, quiet.

"I'm tired," I eventually say, the horrors of the day catching up with me, physically and emotionally.

"I know."

"I love you."

He kisses the top of my head. "I know."

"You don't have to know everything," I mutter.

He pulls away enough to look at me. "I don't know everything, but I know what this is. I've seen it happen, even to the best, most seasoned warriors. Sometimes there's an obvious reason for it, and sometimes it's just a scent or a sound, but it triggers something that no one can control. Panic does awful things to the mind and body, Cat. You're strong, but you're still human. The future is scaring the magic out of you—possibly literally. And Little Bean is a huge change—for you, *in* you—and you love her so much already that it's paralyzing you."

Paralyzing me. I can't protect anyone that way, or even live long enough for Little Bean to take her first breath.

Griffin gently clasps my face in his hands. "You're constantly fighting yourself. You're your own worst enemy, Cat. You have to refocus."

I'm pretty sure Mother is my worst enemy, but... "Refocus?" I ask.

"You don't fight her like you fight any other threat. You need to stop thinking of her as your mother. She's never been that. She's been your adversary since the day you were born. Fight her like you did Galen Tarva, your brothers, or the other teams in the Agon Games. You give everyone their chance at mercy. If they opt out, they get crushed. *Crush* her, Cat. Crush her for both of us. For all three of us," he says, "and for whatever else our future holds."

His words conjure an image of a whole castle full of little dark heads. Home. Family. I want that. I want it so much it hurts.

I tuck the vision away, keeping it safe for now. "But how? My lightning doesn't work, at least not consistently, and Mother seems to know every trick I don't."

"You're stronger than she is. Inside and out."

"But I hesitate with her when I don't with anyone else, and I can't seem to stop." The *one more chance* syndrome I've developed where Mother is concerned is going to get me killed—get all of us killed—if I don't find a cure for it soon.

"You also have something she'll never have—me, Little Bean, our friends and family. Reasons to *live*."

Those heartwarming reasons bring a sudden prick of tears to my eyes. Stepping back from him, I smile a little wryly. "When did you get so wise?"

Griffin looks down at me, his face perfectly serious. "The day I decided you were the most important thing in my life, and always will be."

I huff a small breath. "Very smooth." *Okay, I'm thrilled.*

He winks. "I know."

"The Gods are gone." I look around, just to make sure they haven't come back. "I still had questions."

"Like what?" Griffin asks.

"Like how to get rid of these wings. And how to make sure my lightning will work when I need it to."

Griffin takes my hand and starts leading me toward the barn. The sky is darkening, and not only because of the smoke from the still-burning house. "I'm pretty sure they'll be around," he says. "You can ask them later."

"I want to know now."

He turns to me as we walk, his dark brows lifting. "Right now?"

"Yes, now!"

He nods. "I see what you're doing. You're giving me practice for when Little Bean turns two."

My mouth falls open. I pinch his side. "That was completely uncalled for."

He slides out of my grip. "So was the pinch."

I give him the evil eye. Actually, I give him two. "So, Your Arrogant-I-Know-Everythingness, how do *you* think I get rid of the wings?"

Griffin's gaze roams over me in a way that makes my heart start to race. His voice gains a husky resonance. "I like the wings."

I feel myself flush. "Fine. Great. But I'd like to control their sliding in and out."

Heat sparks in his eyes. "Sliding in and out?"

I press my lips together to keep from smiling, but warmth

spreads through me, and my blush deepens. "Griffin!" He's incorrigible. Insatiable. *Thank the Gods.* "This is serious."

He instantly puts on his warlord face and answers earnestly. "I think the wings are like the lightning. Both come straight from your Olympian blood, but while the lightning is magic, the wings are inherent to the framework of your body. Theoretically, you should be able to control the in and out of both—the lightning with your will and your mind, and the wings with your muscles and bones, almost like raising an arm or reaching out."

"Theoretically?"

"Yes, although the lightning has proved temperamental so far. The wings might, too. But then again, so have you."

I snort. Loudly.

His hand smacks down on my bottom, and he hauls me up against him. My front collides with his bare chest, and I grip his shoulders, reveling in the heat of his skin.

"The warlord face is an act, isn't it? You have other things on your mind." I know I'm starting to.

"Warlord face?"

I nod. "The scowly, serious one."

He grunts, and then his mouth descends on mine. I kiss him back, deep and hard, desperate to get closer still. When we pull apart, our breathing is ragged, and Griffin's eyes gleam with want.

"Keep kissing me like that, and we won't make it to the barn," he says thickly.

"I don't need a barn. I need you." We came so close to losing each other today. I need to feel him, touch him, to know that he's okay.

"Cat." He leans his forehead against mine, his quick breaths fanning my lips. His eyes close but then pop open again almost instantly, looking haunted.

He swallows. "I can't stop seeing you crash through that window. Fall…" His hands fist in the back of my tunic, gripping hard. "I forbid you to die. Or to ever scare me like that again. Do you understand me?" he demands, his voice so low I barely hear the tremor in it.

I shiver, but I shake my head. "I'll do my best, but I can't promise you that. You know I can't."

"I put you in danger. I forced you out of hiding. I brought you to this." His expression turns pained. "You were safe before you met me."

"No." He shouldn't believe that. "I was never safe. But I was never happy, either."

"But you could be safe." Those haunted eyes turn frantic, and I think the downswing of all that fear and adrenaline is hitting him now and pushing him into shaky territory. He held it together to keep me from falling apart, but there's only so much a person can take.

"Griffin—"

He slices his head back and forth, cutting me off. "We'll stop. We'll stop here." His eyes dart from side to side, although I doubt he means *here* here. "Your mother won't live forever. We'll wait her out. I'll keep you safe. You and Little Bean. I swear it, Cat. That's all that mat—"

"Stop." I put my finger over his lips, quieting his agitated words. "We don't have a choice. Not anymore."

"We do. You. Me. Castle Sinta. We'll put as much distance as possible and two realms' worth of soldiers between Fisa and us."

"You mean all those soldiers we recruited on the hope for a safer kingdom for everyone? Who believed in us? Who came to us of their own free will? Use them as a buffer for our own safety and not even try to deliver on our promise?"

He flinches away from me, his jaw clenching hard.

"What happened to *refocus*?" I ask. "To *crush her*? Maybe I can, and maybe I can't. I don't know, but I'm willing to try. I can't forget about all the people who have rallied to us. Who chant 'Elpis' at our gate. Who are waiting for us to change their lives. Suddenly, it's 'to the Underworld with them'?" I shake my head. "That's not you. I know it's not."

A long moment of silence goes by while he simply looks at me. Finally, in an utter monotone, Griffin says, "You matter more to me."

My Kingmaker Magic doesn't ignite. He means every word.

"Thalyria matters, too," I say gently. "And that's okay."

His mouth flattens, and the arms he still has wrapped around me harden from tension he can't seem to govern. "Thalyria may matter, but I choose you. I will always choose you."

I look up into his eyes, emotion clogging my throat. "You can choose me. That's your right. I'll choose Thalyria—for both of us."

He curses and then grinds out, "It's not worth it. It's not worth your life."

"I used to think that, too. But then I met a warlord who took over a realm because he didn't like the way it was run. People there are happy now. Settled. Prosperous. More so than in centuries."

His eyes narrow. Yes, I'm playing dirty, but that's the only way I know how, even if it means catching him in his own idealistic net.

"If no one fights for a better world, there *is* no better world. We've started this now, Griffin. You can't go halfway and then stop."

"I can if it means losing you."

"I'm not the same person I was last summer. You opened my eyes. You spent weeks convincing me to see the bigger picture, the greater good, and I can't just close them now because that's convenient for me, or us, or because we might get hurt."

"Might?" he growls.

"You saw something in me. You saw the light when all I saw was the dark. You made me believe there was more to me than the blood I've shed, the sister I lost, or the realm I abandoned. You broke through the...*dread* in me and filled the emptiness inside me with hope. Elpis," I say. "I'm Elpis because of you. Because of *us*, together. I can't turn my back on that, and you can't ask me to. It's too powerful, too much a part of me now. I can't change that. And I don't want to."

Griffin's eyes flick down and then back up again, his pain and love laid bare across his features. His throat moves on a hard swallow. "I'm afraid of losing you. Or leaving you too soon. I don't want you to have to fight alone."

A spasm arrows through my chest. "I understand what you're feeling. I feel it every day, too. Am I scared? Yes. Do I know if we'll succeed?" I shake my head. "But not trying... That would be worse than ignoring the gift of Elpis. That would be betraying it, and betraying everyone who's placed their faith in me."

A war of emotions crosses Griffin's face. I reach up and lay my hand on his cheek, and he leans in to me, even though his jaw stays rigid. Standing together, I tell him what's in my heart.

"When I close my eyes, I don't see my death. I see people looking at me with a spark of hope just starting to burn in their gazes, hope that springs from me. It's mine to either snuff out or ignite into the kind of fire that reshapes the world. I see you right next to me, looking at me like you did during those days when we were tied together with a rope, and I had no idea what to think, or do, or whether I should help you. You knew then, for both of us, and I grew to trust you. I know now, and I need you to trust *me* this time. I don't know how to finish what we started, but if we stop here, I let the darkness back in. Into me. Into everyone. And it'll consume me with guilt."

His face twists from the conflict inside him. "I can't lose you. Our baby…"

"Then fight alongside me. Fight for Little Bean's future. Help me be strong."

Abruptly, he pulls back from me, shaking his head. "I didn't understand before, no matter what you said, or what happened with those creatures your mother was driving. I see her for what she is now. We're better off in Sinta."

"Of course we're better off in Sinta. But I'm not giving up, and neither are you. That's not you, Griffin. Mother is cruel, soulless, and horrifically violent. Now you've seen. Now you know. You just need time to adjust after your first physical encounter with her."

"Adjust?" His eyes flare. "Adjust to the idea of you in a pool of your own blood?"

I snort softly. "It wouldn't be the first time."

Griffin's face goes blank for a split second before flushing darkly.

Uh-oh. My stomach flips over. *Wrong thing to say.*

His eyes rake over me, over my bloody clothing. Then he reaches out, grips the neck of my tunic with both hands, and pulls hard in opposite directions, ripping it clean in half. The torn garment hangs from my shoulders, fluttering on a cool breeze that feathers over my skin and makes me shiver.

Griffin undresses me, his eyes as steely and focused as the rest of him. My belt hits the ground, and my pants drop to my ankles, pooling around my boots in what I'm sure is a very attractive manner. Griffin steps back, glaring at my mostly naked body.

I stare back. I'm not sure what this stripping is about, or what he needs to do, but I'm going to let him figure it out.

"Still blood everywhere," he mutters. He dips down and then lifts me up, slinging me over his shoulder. His arm clamps around the back of my knees.

I grip his hips and push off to keep from bouncing against his back when he starts walking. His free hand rips my boots from my feet, and my pants slide the rest of the way off. We leave a trail of clothing across the meadow.

"Griffin?"

"I'll never *adjust* to the idea of you dying. To the Underworld with the greater good. The idealist who tied you up with a magic rope to keep Sinta in good hands? Gone," he says flatly. "You and Little Bean—that's all that matters. And Alpha Fisa beat us today."

"Beat us? We're both still here. She had to run away!"

"She ran away because two Gods showed up! And I'm only alive because she's insanely arrogant. After you went through the window, she knocked me on the head with something. I don't know what. She probably thought I was unconscious and would burn with the house, but I was only stunned. She was too busy searching for Ianthe's pearls to pay attention to me anymore. She stormed out once she'd found them."

My eyes widen. *Thank the Gods for Griffin's hard head!*

"I thought she'd gone, but she must have been watching and then came back to finish us off when it turned out we weren't dead." He works my tunic off my back, ripping it free from around my wings. "I'm not trusting your life to anyone. No army. No team. No *God*. We can't count on anyone. Not anymore."

Oh no. "Is this about Piers?"

"This is about *you*!" he snarls.

"No, it's about *you*!" I snarl back, twisting to try to look at him. "If I gave up and crawled under a rock every time someone betrayed me, I'd have turned into a grub by now."

Damn Piers! And damn his shortsighted stupidity. Didn't he know his brother at all? Betrayal from someone he loves is clearly the one thing with which Griffin cannot cope. That, and the thought of losing me. No wonder those two things collided in an epic explosion when Griffin found out the extent of my omissions during our early time together. I broke his trust by not telling him the truth, and loyalty is the air he breathes.

But when Piers betrayed Griffin and tried to get rid of me, the explosion never happened. It was implosion instead.

"Castle Sinta, or here?" Griffin demands, crossing the sloping field with purposeful strides. "Your choice. I'll build you a Gods damn bloody house right here and never leave."

"I'll run away."

"Then it's a good thing I have a magic rope."

"Griffin!" He's not being rational. I start trying to get loose, and his free hand lands on my bare bottom with a smack.

I growl as we pass in front of the pasture holding our horses. Panotii lifts his head and flicks his ears, nickering at me. Brown Horse ignores my flopping around in favor of the grass.

Griffin suddenly bends down and plops me into the spring-fed stream with a splash. I gasp, ice-cold water

shocking me as it rushes over my lower half. I instinctively
curl up, and my reaction must have some kind of retracting
effect on my wings because they shrink with a rustling of
feathers. There's a quick slice of pain, like a shallow cut,
and then they disappear into my back. I think.

I turn, trying to look over my shoulder. "What's there?"
I ask. I can't really see.

Griffin leans over me and looks. "Nothing. Not even a
scar."

I don't feel the wings anymore. Not a tickle of feathers.
Not a flutter in my chest. Nothing.

He kneels in front of me, uncaring that he's still partially
dressed and getting soaked. He bunches up a handful of my
destroyed tunic, wets it, and then presses the frigid linen
against my chest. The cold stalls the breath in my lungs.

A deep groove settling between his eyebrows, Griffin
starts washing the dried blood off my healed skin. Stream
water sluices around my arms and middle as I lean back
to brace myself, almost shivering. If this is what Griffin
needs, I'll give it to him. I needed a bath anyway. Blood to
wash off. Mother to erase.

The icy water is refreshing and restorative once I get
used to it. I watch my husband carefully. Griffin doesn't
look at my face. He looks everywhere else and washes me
with such determination that my heart aches. His big hands
are all over my body, but there's nothing sensual about
it. He's efficient. Single-minded. Top half. Middle. Legs.
Wingless back. Face. He still doesn't meet my eyes.

When he's finished, he rocks back on his heels, seeming
immune to the cold, and stares down at his hands.

I reach out and touch his chest. His skin is hot, feverish.
Or maybe it's just my hand that's cold. Goose bumps sweep
over his torso. I shift up onto my knees, take the cloth from

him, and then start to gently wash him. He stares down at his slack hands where they rest against his thighs, not stopping me. Not helping me. Not saying anything at all.

"Griffin?"

After a while, he grunts.

"It's okay to lose control every now and then. I certainly do."

His head stays bowed. "I'm supposed to be the steady one."

"You are the steady one. But you're human, too."

Silence. Then, "I thought you were dead." The bleakness in his voice cuts straight through me. He's still staring at his hands, almost as if they were the very weapons used against me.

He finally looks up, regret shattering his expression. "You thought you failed Little Bean today?" He shakes his head. "I failed you both. I couldn't protect you. I promised you I would. I promised you so many times, and you believed me."

"No," I tell him softly. "You believed it, but I never did."

My heart breaks at how devastated he looks. My name is a whisper that barely crosses his lips. His eyes glass over.

Mine do, too, and as I wrap my arms around him, I tell him what I've always understood and believed. "From the moment I let you in, I always knew we'd be protecting each other."

CHAPTER 17

"So…" I shiver. I've had it with sitting in the icy stream. Enough is enough, even for me. "Mother. Big fight. Gods. I fell apart. You fell apart." I huff a dry laugh. "What a day."

Griffin nods, his eyes still haunted.

"Are you still considering giving up?" I ask.

"I'm debating," he answers.

"Don't waste your time. I won't let you."

He frowns.

"You put me in charge, remember? Crown? Head? Me?" I pat the top of my head.

A small grunt escapes him.

"So what's next?" *So much for being in charge.*

Griffin must see the humor in that, too, because his expression turns slightly less somber. Then, with a gusty exhale, he stands, pulling me up with him. He sweeps his hands down my chilled arms, warming my pebbled skin.

"You're cold," he says in surprise.

"We're knee-deep in freezing water, it's autumn on a mountainside, and the sun just dipped behind the trees."

"I thought you were immune to the cold."

"Not entirely, although Little Bean does her best to keep me warm." I glance at my belly. "Maybe she'll have Fire Magic," I say, patting where her little life beat is a constant spark inside me. "Auntie Bella can show you how all that fire stuff works."

Auntie Bella? Where did *that* come from? And Bellanca Tarva is hardly the epitome of control.

Little Bean's energy tumbles under my fingers like she agrees, although I don't know with which part. Her power branches out inside me, reassuring me. I don't know how Hoi Polloi mothers can stand not knowing what's going on in there, at least on some level. At this point, they probably wouldn't feel much of anything, and maybe even think the occasional flutter low in their belly was just digestion—or rather, *indigestion*.

For my part, I'm so increasingly aware of the budding magic in Little Bean's blood that it's almost as though I can talk to her. I know when she sleeps. I know when she wakes up. I know she's interested every time Griffin puts his warm hand over her or speaks close enough for her to hear. I know she likes riding Panotii, especially at a trot, because the bouncier the better, it seems. And I know she's completely tuned into me as well, thumping me with her life force when I'm nervous and relaxing when I'm not.

We could communicate even more, I know. Mother obviously did.

I immediately trample the thought. Little Bean doesn't need me in her head, even if it's only to tell her that I love her. She already knows that. She needs me around her, protecting her, simply being her mother.

"Auntie Bella?" Griffin looks like that's going to take some serious getting used to. I completely agree.

He dips and picks me up. Funny how he does that. He knows I can walk.

"Aren't you cold?" I ask, looping my arms around his neck.

"Freezing. My balls are about to fall off."

I laugh. Then scowl. "That's not funny."

"For either of us," he mutters.

He strides uphill but bypasses the barn, heading toward

the smoldering house instead. At the outer wall he puts me down and picks up our discarded gear. Luckily, everything was far enough from the house to be safe from the flames. He throws my cloak around my shoulders, pulling it closed. The magical threads heat, and I groan like I just took a bite out of a freshly baked spice cake.

"That good?" Griffin asks, a smile tugging at his mouth.

"Better," I answer, reveling in the warmth.

He puts his own cloak on, takes my hand, and then leads me back across the meadow. His grip is firm, as if a part of him is still afraid of letting me go.

He gathers up my pants, boots, and belt, although he only gives me the latter. I buckle it low on my waist inside my cloak so that the pearls sit right in front of Little Bean again.

"Ianthe knew what that did," Griffin says, glancing at the pearls. "That's why she didn't get the circlet back from you. She wanted you to have it."

I nod, a pang bumping hard against my ribs. *Selfless Ianthe.* She gave me her best protection against Mother. I don't think my heart can take another sister turning herself into a shield for me, or sacrificing her life for mine.

Griffin steers us into the barn. It's warm from the animals. It smells like them, too. A pungent mix of beast, hay, must, and manure. He takes flint to steel and lights two of the lanterns that are hanging on the wall, handing one to me. I hold out the light, careful of where I'm stepping in my bare feet, but the straw is fresh cut, relatively clean, and not too prickly. Mother must have eliminated the real hermit only shortly before we got here. The farm is in good shape. Dinner was still bubbling over the fire. Without that wrong turn I took, I wonder if we could have saved the witch of Frostfire.

We climb a ladder to a loft filled with sacks of grain,

drying hay, and a huge supply of fragrant medicinal herbs that significantly dampens the odor of goat.

"Your mother won't come back?" Griffin asks, suddenly looking tense again.

I shake my head. "Two Gods showed up, and they weren't on her side. She's long gone. She's adept at many things, and one of them is living to fight another day. She'll need to get her shoulder healed. Plus, did you see how fast that mare was moving? She's probably halfway to Castle Fisa by now."

Griffin nods, but concern lingers in his eyes. Not about Mother coming back today, I think, but about the future, and whatever new nightmare our next encounter with her might bring.

He leaves me upstairs in the barn to warm up and then comes back with our saddlebags after seeing to the horses. As soon as he reappears, he tosses a pair of wooly socks at me.

I catch them but then set them down beside me. "My feet aren't cold."

"How is that possible?" he asks, not even trying to repress a shiver. His lips are dark, like they're tinged with blue.

It's possible because I've been all tucked up under my cloak for a good twenty minutes when I probably should have been helping Griffin with the horses and getting him out of his wet clothes.

"Eternal Fires of the Underworld. Come." I hold out my hand. "I'll warm you up."

Heat flares in his eyes. Smiling, I pat the hay next to me, feeling even warmer myself.

Griffin sits, propping his cloak-covered back against the wide, rough-hewn planks of the deeply shadowed loft. I get in front of him and pull off his boots. It's hard work, considering they're soaked through. I set them aside to dry and then peel his pants down his legs—hard work as well, but definitely worth it when I get the visual confirmation that his balls have in no way, shape, or form fallen off.

I lay his pants out to dry next to his boots and then kneel between his legs, making sure my smoldering cloak covers his bare and frozen feet. The garment does little to hide my nakedness, and Griffin's concentrated gaze heats me up so much that the fiery cloth dims.

Leaning forward, I sweep my hands up his thighs. His skin is damp and cold, his powerful muscles are taut, and his short, dark hair is coarse against my palms. I dip my head and kiss the first hard ridge of his abdomen. His midriff tenses. My breasts sway under me as I move, brushing his growing erection. He groans, the sound hoarse with need, and then curls his hand around the back of my neck. His fingers are like ice.

I slide down, kissing the next ridge and tracing the hills and hollows of his torso with my tongue. My lips never leave his skin, and my breath swirls between us as I lick the indent next to his hip. Humming softly at how good he tastes—like cold, fresh water and crisp mountain air—I brush a slow, hot kiss all the way to his hard length and then take him into my mouth.

Griffin's head thumps the wall behind him. His hand tightens on my nape.

I suck with my mouth and stroke with my hand. I want to warm him up. I want him to forget his fear.

Griffin gathers my hair into his fist, holding it back. He says my name, his voice rasping and rough. "You're so Gods damn beautiful. My amazing wife."

My heart swells with love. I need more of him. Always

and urgently. Irrevocably. I sink down on him, taking him deep into my mouth.

His hips flex, his body naturally meeting my rhythm. His breathing shortens to harsh pants. When I sense his muscles tightening, I look up, licking my lips. He groans, his eyes like molten silver. From the hot, intense look on his face, I think he's going to drag me up to straddle him, get inside me, and then help me to ride him fast and hard.

Instead, he carefully turns me and then lays me on my back. He takes his time, his hands gentle but his expression everything that's predatory and fierce. His heated look roams over me from my head to my toes—every curve, every dip, every naked inch.

Anticipation mounts in the wake of his scorching gaze. He's the wolf here, and I'm definitely ready for him to pounce. Gods, I even hope he bites.

"I'm going to savor you. My mouth is watering. There's not a single part of you that I won't taste."

True to his words, Griffin lifts my right calf and starts at my foot, trailing his mouth over my toes, the arch, and then kissing the inside of my ankle. I shiver. Who knew that feet could be so sensitive?

Little bolts of pleasure race up my leg, and I catch my lower lip between my teeth, moving my hips to try to relieve some of the pressure gathering in my core. His hands, his tongue, his lips… They're everywhere. The back of my knee, my inner thigh, the curve of my hip, the dip of my waist. He's tender. Focused. Thorough. Slowly devouring me.

By the time Griffin centers his mouth over my throbbing sex, the tension in my body is already explosive. Gripping his hair, I whisper his name, my exhale shaky with desire. I need him to press down on me. I want him to drive me over the edge.

He softly blows, and I stop breathing.

"What you feel right now?" He moves back down and then starts all over again with the other leg. "It's what I feel every time I look at you."

I gasp when he flicks his tongue along my instep. "Then I don't know how you can function."

He chuckles, the sound thick with passion. He takes almost more time than I can stand to move back up my body, but it's the sweetest kind of torture. Unrelenting, he drowns me in sensation.

When Griffin finally reaches the top of my legs again, I'm desperate for release. His hands splay over my hips, holding me steady, and his hot kisses are everywhere except for where I want them the most. I clutch his head, trying to center him. His eyes flick up, meeting mine. I tilt my hips in offering, and he finally gives me what I crave. A long, sinuous lick. A good hard suck.

I buck, and his hands tighten on my hips. The throbbing pulse between my legs beats hard, and I cry out. He gives me more of what I need until my head kicks back, my spine arches, and I climax on a ragged breath.

I feel Griffin's husky groan clear to the center of me. It's like a coil of heat deep in my core. He waits me out, watching my body settle and my breathing slow. Then he says, "Again."

His mouth lands on me for another blistering sweep of his tongue.

I gasp, arching away. "I can't."

"Again," he rasps out, merciless.

I settle beneath him once more and tangle my hands in his hair, alternately pulling him closer and pushing him away. Panting, I dig my heels into the straw, my legs going rigid with mounting tension. My head thrashes, and my pelvis comes up, riding his mouth. I shudder, already close to shattering again.

Griffin slides his hands up my body and then palms my breasts, squeezing. He finds my nipples and gives them a light pinch, but it's the sharp tug that pulls me over the edge. The explosion starts beneath his mouth and then streaks outward in perfect, pounding waves.

He coaxes every last ripple from my release. I moan, long and deep, and then go limp, my eyes half closed. I eventually remember to breathe.

Griffin moves up my body, stopping to nuzzle, kiss, and lick. Heat ignites inside me again, and I start to shift restlessly against him. I didn't think it was possible, but I still feel edgy with need. I want *Griffin*. Not just the climax he can bring.

Wrapping my legs around him, I meet his gaze. "I need you."

He kisses me deeply, taking my breath away. I grip his shoulders and frantically kiss him back.

Griffin lifts his head. "No. Slow."

I press up into him. "You don't like slow."

"I like everything with you." He slides his arms under me, one behind my back and the other angling up underneath me to cradle my head in the palm of his hand.

I reach down between us to guide him inside me. Griffin moves forward with a slow thrust, and I start to close my eyes.

His fingers tighten on my head. "Look at me."

I open my eyes again.

"Do you feel this heat?" He rocks once, filling me completely. "I burn for you."

My lips part on a soft gasp.

"Touch me, Cat."

I skim my hands over the hard muscles of his shoulders and then up his neck. Diving my fingers into his hair again, I grip the inky locks.

He looks down at me, his expression open and earnest. "I am caught. You caught me. Not the other way around. From the very first day. And from the very first day, I would have done anything for you—except let you go. I couldn't. Not when deep down, I knew we were meant to be like this. To love like this."

Without moving inside me, he dips his head and kisses me. It's slow but nothing like gentle. It's intense and fierce, burning and passionate.

"I was arrogant and high-handed," he says, lifting his head. "I took you from your home and from people you love. Sometimes, I wish I could say I'm sorry for that, but I'm not."

"I'm not, either," I tell him. "I still have them. But now I also have you."

"Always," he says fervently.

"Always," I echo in kind.

"My eyes are fully open, but I see only one thing."

"Griffin..." The threat of tears thickens my voice. My eyes blur, and I blink.

"Don't cry. Not now. I need you to listen to me."

The urgency in his voice makes my breath hitch. I banish the dampness from my eyes.

"I don't care if the Gods changed me for you. They changed you for Thalyria. The gifts. The Oracles. Your whole life. That doesn't alter how I feel about you. My love isn't conditional. We are who we are." He holds me close, surrounding me, speaking to me straight from his heart. "The first time I saw you, it was like a thunderclap hit me. My ears rang. My heart raced. I knew I would never be the same again. So what if they chose me for you? *Planned* me for you? Something like that can never be a path with only one direction. If they made me for you, Cat, then they made you for me, too."

I nod, but he grips my head, making me stop.

"No, don't just nod. *Believe* it. Believe *me*. I don't care who came first, why, or which God played a role in any of it. That thunderclap? It didn't come from them. It came from you, and me, and what was inevitable between us, even though I'm the arse who kidnapped you, and you're the spitfire who fought me for all she was worth. I love you. There is no place in my heart where you don't belong. Do you understand me, Cat?"

My chin trembles, and I press my lips together tightly. Finally, my voice wavering, I manage to ask, "Are you still expecting me not to cry?"

Griffin's grip relaxes on the back of my head, and he searches my eyes with a softening gaze. "You've changed so much."

I sniff. "I know. It's awful."

He chuckles. "It's not awful. You're finally living."

Is this what living feels like? Beautiful and painful all at once?

I swallow hard, and my tears ebb back down my throat. Hate is an easier emotion to deal with than love. Hate is cold, with a strong, hard shell. Love is burning, with a thousand fragile cracks that lead straight to your soul.

"My heart is on fire, Griffin. I don't know when it'll stop."

His expression seems to light from within. "It won't ever stop. I won't let it."

I nod, understanding better now. This isn't a bad thing, this living, loving, *feeling*. It's a gift. Just as Griffin was a gift to me, and I'm his gift as well.

"Thank you," I say, touching his cheek.

"For what?" he asks.

"For showing me that I can be loved unconditionally, and love wholly in return."

He smiles. It's small, crooked, and perfect, and I love him even more. How can joy make a person want to both laugh and weep?

"I was so stupid," I say. "I can't believe I ever fought you. Fought us."

"You had every right to fight me. I'm not perfect, and I don't always do what I should. You don't need to be perfect, either, Cat. You just need to be you."

I kiss him gently. "And together, we'll do our best."

Griffin nods. Holding me, he starts to move. We let our bodies speak for us, and I wrap myself around him and feel.

CHAPTER 18

THE ARMY GREW EXPONENTIALLY WHILE WE WERE AWAY.

"Where did all these people come from?" I ask, just barely keeping my eyes from popping out of my head.

"Everywhere," Flynn answers. "That whole group over there is from Fisa." He points to a far-off gathering of people and tents.

That many people came from Fisa? "How did they get past Lycheron and his minions?"

Kato chuckles. "Apparently, the Ipotane round them all up, bring them to Lycheron every few days, and then he does a sniff check, one by one. He reads their worth right from their scents, they say."

Huh. He sniffed me pretty hard. He sniffed Ianthe even harder. "That's disturbing."

"And useful," Flynn says. "They're good people, those Fisans. Brave."

"They'd have to be to face Lycheron," I murmur. "Have any of them seen Ianthe?"

Flynn nods, squinting and shading his eyes from the sun as he scans the sprawling encampment with an assessing but satisfied gaze. "She's fine, they've told us. Or she at least looks that way. But Lycheron doesn't let her out of his sight. She's on his back at all times, and they see that as a sign—a Fisan princess joining the fight. She's encouraging them to come to us, rallying people to your side."

"Some turn back," Kato says with a shrug. "They take one look at the Ipotane and then head back into Fisa."

Griffin grunts. "Good. If they're scared of being sniffed, the Gods only know how they'd react on the battlefield."

I nod. I've been in plenty of battles but not on an actual battlefield, with armies involved. I don't have to have been, though, to know he's right.

After greeting Kato and Flynn and gathering the most essential news, we all move toward the Fisans. Carver and Bellanca are apparently among them, and since we arrived without fanfare on the opposite side of the camp, they still don't know we're back. As we progress in their direction, I see Tarvans and Sintans mixing together in one big, spread-out group. They soon realize who we are, though, and stop what they're doing to watch us pass, seeming awestruck.

Griffin takes the sudden attention in stride, surveying his soldiers, his warlord face firmly in place. I do my best to shake off my nerves when I see the way people are looking at me—like I'm not even human, but something more. I manage a small smile. It's probably more of a toothy grimace, but it's better than nothing, and I turn it on all sides, not wanting to exclude anyone.

On the south side of the camp, Carver is deep in training with a new recruit, his focus undivided, even when everything in the Fisan area starts grinding to a halt.

"Zeus's bollocks! How many times do I have to tell you not to drop your guard?" Carver pulls up short, inches away from skewering the man he was just sparring with.

Stepping back, his opponent nods to us. Carver swings around, and the tip of his weapon drops to the ground. His whole body seems to relax. He wipes the sweat from his brow with the back of his hand and then sheathes his sword as he strides toward us.

"Took you long enough." There's a layer of tension in

his voice, his words both teasing and not. "Bellanca was threatening to go after you."

That doesn't surprise me in the least. And from the way Carver just said it, I think he was planning on leaving with her.

Carver's Fisan trainee stands there staring at us with eyes so wide I get the insane urge to look behind us, just in case there's something there. But no, he's watching *me*. He's probably in his mid- to late-twenties. He's broad-shouldered, good-looking, and lean, with unusually close-cropped sandy hair. I very much doubt he's used to holding a weapon because he lets his sword drop to the ground, unheeded.

"Kneel!" he suddenly calls out to his compatriots— maybe even to the whole army. "Kneel before the Queen and King of Thalyria!"

Hearing our intended titles ring out like that is a shock to my system, and my pulse leaps into action.

He kneels and then bows so low that his forehead touches the ground. The whole encampment goes incredibly silent. It's a big space with a lot of people, and yet there's not a whisper of sound.

And then every last soldier—Fisan, Tarvan, and Sintan—drops with a creaking of leather and the thud of knees on dirt.

Good Gods. Fire and ice shoot through me at the same time, and my poor heart just stops. It doesn't know how to react any more than I do.

Only Beta Team is still standing. I see Bellanca now that everyone else is down, still fire-bright, one hand on her hip, and packing enough attitude to make Olympus shudder.

Griffin looks to me to speak. I clear my throat.

"Rise!" I say, because this is just too weird. *Um...* "And continue!"

All these people are showing us deference. I'm pretty sure I need to add something good, something motivating.

Damn it! Nothing comes to mind.

The army slowly rises. No one dares disobey me, but nobody really moves, either.

"Good work here. We're impressed." Griffin nods all around. I nod, too, feeling wholly inadequate with my awkward smile and bobbing head.

"Carry on, soldiers!" Griffin's simple order in his commanding, brook-no-argument, I-conquered-realms voice fills the hole left by my silence and my utter lack of leadership skills. Thank the Gods we're a team.

It's like a spell breaks, and everyone breathes again, including me. No one really goes back to what they were doing before, though. They mostly keep watching us like we're riding a rainbow from inside a sparkling golden chariot drawn by Pegasus. *Gods, the pressure.* Griffin seems fine with it, but I feel like ants are crawling up and down the back of my neck.

Smiling, Griffin claps his brother on the back. "Carver."

Carver claps Griffin back, flashing us both a genuine smile—the first I've seen in what feels like months. His face is even leaner than before, like he's been training too hard and not eating enough, and his eyes are slightly bloodshot. He hasn't shaved in days, and his hair looks like it could use a thorough wash, but he still looks better than he did when we left.

Caught by impulse, I rock up on my toes and plant a kiss on his scruffy cheek.

Carver's eyebrows fly up, his gray eyes lighting in surprise. "I knew you'd wise up and choose the better brother one of these days."

I laugh. "You want to be the King?"

Grimacing, he scratches the back of his neck. "Hmm... Forget that. Griffin can have you."

Griffin snorts. Kato and Flynn chuckle, and it feels so good to have the group back together again that my cheeks start to hurt from smiling.

After catching up with Carver about the almost daily influx of Fisan volunteers, I'm ready to get out of the sun and rest, but I can't help noticing that the man Carver was sparring with is still looking at me. And not just looking. *Staring.* He's close enough to start making me uncomfortable. Not because I feel threatened—far from it—but because he gazes at me like I'm the sun, the stars, and the moon—maybe the whole damn sky. And that's even worse.

"My Queen." He addresses me directly when I really look back at him, his voice a rasping whisper. His hand trembles as he drags the sorriest-looking bunch of dried flowers I've ever seen out of his breast pocket and then holds them out to me.

Okaaaaay...

Stepping toward me, he says, "I prayed every day for your safe return."

Guilt sinks sharp claws into all my softest places, and it turns out there are plenty. I ran away. I left Fisa. I let him down, failed him for years—this person, and so many others.

The abysmal bouquet of small meadow flowers stays outstretched between us. His hand still quakes. His voice strengthens, though. "Your sister was kind and generous, but I always knew it would be you."

What? The blood washes from my head so fast I feel queasy. Is he another oracular soul? Someone who knew my fate before I did?

No. He's Hoi Polloi. Otherwise, I'd feel his magic.

Something about the way he's holding out the flowers and willing me to take them plucks at a memory. It only takes a second for it to punch me in the heart, and a long-ago day of hard-won freedom comes rushing back.

"You're the shepherd boy." The realization flies from me, taking my breath along with it.

He nods, his whole face lighting up. It's a handsome, strong face, with dark-brown eyes and a square jaw that seems even firmer and more angular without any of the usual longish, masculine hair to obscure it. He stands taller. Prouder. He's thrilled I remember him.

And why wouldn't he be? I am his Lost Princess. I am his Queen.

"We met on the hillside," he says. "My father was there."

I nod. I remember that day perfectly. I've dreamed about it multiple times. Eleni and I ran into him and his sheep. Literally. We barreled over a rise without knowing, or caring, what was on the other side, and we knocked over half the flock as well as the boy tending to the beasts. Fisan royals never showed mercy, and his father was terrified we'd kill them both on the spot just for being in the wrong place at the wrong time. My magic didn't work like that, although I could have done it in myriad other ways, even as a child, but Eleni could have easily ended them both with the simple conjuring of a flaming bird.

The thought never occurred to either of us. I gave the boy the flowers I'd picked earlier that day. They were already crushed and half wilted, but he'd looked so frightened, and I didn't want him to be scared. Eleni took her hair down and gave his father a jeweled clip that probably fed their village for years.

My heart races like water in a rushing stream—bubbling, tumbling, slightly out of control. "How did you know?" I ask, my voice surprisingly soft considering the torrent of emotion inside me. "How did you know it would be me?"

"Gamma Fisa had rounded edges," he answers, this shepherd turned soldier.

Gamma? That's right. We were still young. Eleni was Gamma Fisa, and I was Delta, fourth in line for the throne.

"You were as sharp as a blade." There's pride in his voice, like that was exactly the right thing for me to be—a weapon.

"That should have scared you." I *was* scary. Wild. Unpredictable. Often, I still am.

"It did. You were this force of nature. Packed with power. But then you held out these flowers, and you glared at me until I took them."

"Glaring isn't usually reassuring," I point out wryly.

He shakes his head. "You wanted me to feel better. To not be scared anymore. But you did it so fiercely, like you were ready to fight about it. I knew then. I knew you could protect us. I knew that you would."

My heart swells to painful proportions in my chest. "The sword and the shield," I murmur, reminded of something Griffin once said to me. Am I the blade *and* the shelter? Maybe Griffin is, too.

The man nods. I don't know his name. I never did. He sinks to his knees again, still holding out the dry and brittle flowers.

I sink down with him. "Keep them." I gently push his hand back toward his chest, careful of the old blooms. "Wear them into battle."

Tears flood his eyes. Mine flood, too. Quelling the tide is beyond me. I don't even want to.

"My Queen," he whispers after a hard swallow.

"My Fisan commander," I whisper back.

A heartbeat passes, and then his eyes widen. They're the deepest of browns, like good dirt to grow good things in.

"Cat..." Carver's voice holds a hint of warning. "He doesn't have any experience."

"Do any of the Fisans?" I ask, blinking rapidly so that I can see the crowd, all these dusty, tired people watching us with rapt attention. They look like farmers and tradesmen, people who have never held a weapon in their lives. They left their homes and families anyway. For Thalyria, but also for me. For the Queen on her knees.

I glance up at Carver, finding his lips pressed flat as he surveys the group of Fisans with a critical eye. When he doesn't answer, I take that as a no. Not a trained soldier among them.

"What's your name?" I ask the new commander of my Fisan ranks—under Griffin, me, Carver, and all of Beta Team, of course.

"Lukos."

I nod. That's a good, strong name. "Will you follow me?"

"I will," he answers without hesitation.

"Do you think we'll win?" I ask.

I'm smaller than he is by a head. The Fisan shepherd looks down at me as we face each other on our knees.

"You climbed a Cyclops and killed it with Poseidon's own trident. You can do anything."

My breath catches, and my bones burn. He believes that. Unequivocally. Magic whips through me, and I'm reminded of all the people I read at circus fairs over the years, asking them questions and my body reacting to their answers. Feeling truths used to be so rare. Now, more and more, I feel the ones that carry the fervor of powerful belief, and Lukos's conviction is stronger than any lie.

"Do you know what Elpis means?" I ask.

He nods again. "There's not a person here that doesn't know. And more will come."

More will come. To follow me. To die for me.

Steeling myself against that thought, I ask, "Do you know what I have in my heart?"

This time, he shakes his head, because how could he possibly know, when I'm only just figuring it out myself? In less than half a year, I've changed completely. Maybe I've finally become the person I was meant to be. The person I *want* to be.

"I have hope." Standing, I reach out and draw Lukos up with me, holding what I now see is a raw and sword-blistered hand in mine. "And I'll share it with the world."

Griffin quickly sets about organizing quarters for us in a more central location, so I go to Carver's nearby tent with him to catch up and rest. There's no question that Carver will remain in charge of the Fisans. Without a single swordsman or career soldier among them, they need the most guidance and training. Flynn and Kato will continue to supervise mixed groups of Sintans and Tarvans, which is the unity-promoting organization they'd already put into place while we were away. All three of them will again report to Griffin, who'll oversee everyone and everything.

"You don't have to stay at the camp," Carver says, letting his tent flap drop back down behind us to block out the bright splash of autumn sunlight. "You could live in Castle Tarva with the rest of the family."

Without Griffin? No thanks. Although I am the only one without a real job here. Unless being stared at and incubating Little Bean count. And inspiring troops with rousing speeches like "Rise and continue!"

"I'll stay here." I grimace. "Maybe babysit Bellanca."

Carver chuckles. Then his expression shuts down, darkening, as if he didn't mean to let himself laugh.

I glance around, frowning. Carver's tent is as disheveled as he is. I've never known him to be messy before, but he has to dig his only chair out from under a pile of disorganized weapons and other bits and things before I can even sit down on it. I'd wanted a better feel for the state Carver is really in, and judging by my surroundings, it's not good.

Parched, I search the tent for water. All I see is a jug of wine, the thought of which turns my stomach and doesn't tempt me in the least, even though my tongue is so dry it's sticking to the roof of my mouth.

Carver blows out a long, drawn-out breath. "Bellanca is…"

I glance back at him, waiting for him to continue. He slowly shakes his head, his hands on his narrow hips. He doesn't say anything else.

"Indescribable?" I supply.

He nods.

The Tarvan ex-princess is still with the Fisans. Although they're not her people, I think she might feel more comfortable with them because, contrary to the other, larger contingents, there are Magoi among them. Not many, but some. I could feel their power in the air, scraping at my skin, beckoning me. It felt mainly like Healing Magic, which makes sense. Healers have never been given their due in Fisa, or any say in whom they can help. Their discontent is well known.

There's also the distinct possibility that Bellanca's own people hate her. I doubt Bellanca herself did anything to

merit their loathing, but she was part of the family that terrified and terrorized them, although that was really Galen's
and Acantha's handiwork. But I never heard of the younger
royals doing anything to set themselves apart or to defy
their brother's authority. Not publicly, anyway. As for the
rest, only Bellanca knows.

It doesn't matter now, though. People will eventually
find out she killed Galen Tarva with her own two hands,
and they'll forgive her. They might even love her for it.

Well, maybe. She's a little hard to love.

Bellanca didn't bother greeting Griffin and me. She just
glared at us like it's a damn good thing we somehow managed to survive without her help. I think her standoffishness
is payback for driving her off the morning we left. There's
no way I'll ever tell her how close we came to never coming
back. She might not let us out of her sight again.

Just before Carver and I ducked inside his tent, Bellanca
threw up her hands in disgust at a young Magoi's flounder-
ing, bellowing out, "You call that fire? *This* is fire!" She
promptly went up in flames. She's probably still that way.

I wipe the sweat from my upper lip. Bellanca, Little
Bean, the frankly uncalled-for afternoon heat... There's
not a drop of moisture in the air. *It's the rainy season, for
the Gods' sakes!*

"Can I have some water?" I almost wish I were back at
Frostfire with its bubbling mountain stream and constant
breeze.

Then again, I could do without the gaping volcanic pit.
Just the thought of that seemingly bottomless hole makes
me shudder. At least the army encampment doesn't have
that. And it has Beta Team instead of a burned-out house.
Wherever they are is home.

I sigh. I'm not sure why.

Carver rummages around, finally coming up with a waterskin that he finds under a pile of tack. It's almost full. Knowing full well that Carver's horse may have been the last to drink from it, I take a few long swallows anyway and then hand it back to him. He sets it aside and then drinks from a different container, one that leaves a small bead of red liquid on his lip. He wipes it off with the back of his hand.

Watching him, my stomach churns with worry. I want to say something about his wine consumption, but I don't know if I should.

"That'll kill you." Decision made. Apparently.

Carver looks over sharply.

I get up, take the earthenware jug from him, and then sniff cautiously at its contents. The acrid punch makes my nose wrinkle. The wine inside is acidic and strong. Clearly, he doesn't care how it tastes. It's definitely not watered down.

I level a frank gaze at him. "The day you need to be clear-headed and sharp, you won't be."

He slowly reaches out and takes his wine from me. Putting the mouth of the jug to his lips, he tilts his head back, and I watch his throat work far too many times. To my shock, he must down half the contents of the container. When he lowers it, he wipes the back of his hand across his mouth again, his eyes glinting with something dark and challenging.

My eyes narrow in return. "Are you defying common sense? Or just me?"

Carver shrugs.

"Do you know what's worse than getting yourself killed?" I don't want his answer, and I don't wait for it. "Watching someone you love get killed because you're too drunk to stop it."

"I'm not drunk."

I cross my arms over my chest. "Yet."

"Ever." He looks at the jug in disgust. "This doesn't even work."

"Then throw it out."

He takes another sip. Purposefully. Obstinately.

"That's a crutch. Have you been crippled?" I ask. "Do your legs not work? Or is it just your brain?"

The look Carver throws me is part flinch, part snarl. "Back off, Cat!"

I unfold my arms and, without any real reflection, shift my balance, whip up my leg, and kick the jug. The piece of glazed crockery shatters in Carver's hand, and the remaining contents splash all over him. Maybe I didn't quite think that through. I kind of regret that it looks so much like blood. I've seen enough blood on Carver. And it'll stain. But I don't regret that the wine is gone. I'll never be sorry for that.

"Gods, Cat! What in the bloody Gods damn..." Carver throws the jagged neck of the container to the ground with a growl. "What is wrong with you?"

"What's wrong with *you*?" I shoot back. "Is the Carver I know tied up in a dungeon somewhere, and you're his idiotic twin brother that no one knew about? The one who makes bad choices and doesn't seem to care?"

He blinks.

"You have your family. And believe me when I tell you, you have a *good* one. You're going to be an uncle. You're the best swordsman in all of Thalyria. You have an entire army looking up to you, and especially a bunch of completely untrained Fisans salivating for your guidance and hanging on your every word. You have more than hundreds of thousands of other people will *ever* have, and you're turning your back on them. On yourself. On everyone!"

Carver moves toward me, prowling menace in his swift steps. I hold my ground, craning my neck to look at him. Although his face is leaner and his nose straighter, the similarities to Griffin are startling. The storm-gray eyes. The stubborn jaw. The way his expression flattens when he's feeling too much.

Carver lifts his hands as if to grab my shoulders, but then his fingers clench into fists and drop back to his sides. "I thought you of all people would understand."

"Understand what? Being an idiot?"

That seems to surprise him enough to add something new to his countenance. A trace of humor softens the stark lines of his face. "No." A wry smile just barely curves his lips. "Maybe."

"I am an expert idiot," I say. "I practice all the time."

Little Bean chooses that moment to agree—or maybe disagree. In any case, a strong ripple of chaotic baby magic rocks me hard. I hiss in a breath and grab my lower belly.

Carver turns whiter than a realm-walking spirit. "What is it?"

"Little Bean," I gasp out.

He spins on his heel. "I'll get Griffin."

I shoot out my hand and grab his arm. "There's no need to worry Griffin. I'm fine. She's strong. And…experimenting. She's done this before." And she likes to let me know when her uncles are being asses, but I don't add that. "I just need to sit."

Carver gets me back into the chair like his life depends upon it. My feet actually leave the ground for a moment, but he helps me to land softly enough. Once I'm seated again, he kneels in front of me, gripping my hands hard. He looks terrified, pale under the dust and sweat on his face. His hands even shake a little, probably from a rush of adrenaline. I almost want to laugh at his complete over-reaction, but it's just not funny in the end. It reminds me of something Jocasta once said about pedestals, glass cases, and sisters. Carver confronted the Hydra with a smirk on his face, but this makes him look like he's about to vomit.

"I'll get more water. Do you need food? A blanket?" He looks around, his eyes turning frantic when he realizes he has none of those things. "A hot bath? A cold bath?"

I shake my head. "A bath would be fabulous. But it can wait. Right now, I need you to talk to me."

Almost impossibly, his brow furrows even more. "About what?"

"About what's bothering you enough to turn you into a drunk."

He sits back on his heels without letting go of my hands, his expression turning wary again. "I'm not drunk."

He does seem relatively sober. His words aren't slurred. He's not wobbly. Beside his somewhat unkempt appearance and the two wine jugs in his tent, not including the one I just smashed, there's room for him to argue. Unfortunately for Carver, not drunk *right now* isn't a strong enough argument for me to leave him alone. What about tonight? Or tomorrow? What about when we're fighting for our lives?

"I know what it's like to lose someone," I say gently. "And to lose myself because of it."

He stares up at me, and the pain in his eyes is almost too much to bear. His mouth flattens as his throat works on a painful-looking swallow. A lump rises in mine. Then he lets go of me, his hands slipping from my lap as he starts to back away.

Before he can get too far, I reach out and push a lock of dark hair back from his forehead. It was hanging over his eye and clinging to his eyelashes, bouncing with every blink. I continue the movement, sliding my hand through his hair and smoothing it back, trying to comfort him. He needs it.

Carver stops moving. I do it again, and a shudder rattles through him. Then, in a movement of slow surrender, he gradually leans forward until his forehead rests upon my knees. Still on the ground in front of me, he breathes once, long and deep, and then sits more comfortably, turning his face so his head is in my lap.

My heart aching, I keep lightly stroking his hair. His eyes close. I don't say anything, letting him rest while I try to figure out the words that might help him.

When I do finally speak, I pitch my voice low and even, like I would if I were trying to keep a skittish animal from running away. "I thought I'd live a short life and die alone. Griffin was never in any of my plans. And certainly not Little Bean. I was so convinced my path would be a lonely one that I think I even ended up wanting that. It was safe, in a certain way. There was no one to endanger. And it was much easier than wanting what I thought I could never have. What I thought I didn't deserve after Eleni died."

Carver sinks more heavily into me, wrapping his arms around my legs. There's something so weary and needy in the way he seeks comfort that my heart breaks even more for him, and it was already pretty torn up.

My eyes sore with unshed tears, I trail my fingers through his hair, wishing I could take away his pain.

"Then what?" he murmurs.

"Then Griffin. You. Kato. Flynn. Your whole family." *Not Piers.* "Ianthe. Little Bean. If I'm being honest, even Bellanca."

Carver snorts, the quick puff of breath warm through the light linen of my pants.

I smile as much as I'm able to right now. "I like her. She has spirit and flair."

He snorts again, like that's a colossal understatement.

"You all lit a fire inside me. The good kind. The best kind. And now my heart is so full, it can be overwhelming." I brush Carver's nearly shoulder-length hair off his neck, smoothing the dark strands to one side. His neck is warm and tanned. Strong. His hair is straighter than Griffin's and feels slightly coarser, but maybe that's because it needs washing. "It hurts sometimes," I admit. "A lot."

Carver takes a deep breath. "I hurt all the time."

My eyes burn, and I beat back tears. Carver needs me to be strong.

A splash of sunlight brightens the tent, and I look up to see Griffin standing in the entrance, holding back the flap. His eyes widen, his expression turning anxious. His worry for Carver is palpable, and there's no doubt in my mind that he wants to come in and help in any way he can.

I give Griffin an almost imperceptible shake of my head. With his eyes closed and his head in my lap, Carver has put himself in my hands, if only for a moment. I feel as though we've struck a pact, and even Griffin isn't a part of it. I try to convey that with my eyes, hoping Griffin will understand.

Griffin hesitates for only a second, and then he steps silently back and lowers the tent flap again, leaving us alone.

I look back down at Carver, my hand still on his neck. "The more you hurt, the more capable you are of great emotion."

Gods, that sounded stupid and trite, even if it's true. I go back to stroking Carver's head. I don't have much experience with comforting people, but a gentle touch seems like an okay thing to do. It's better than meaningless words.

After a long silence, I try again, figuring I'll be better

at hard truths and tough love than at subtle insight or attempted finesse. "Instead of focusing all your passion on a woman who is gone from this world, why don't you look to the living instead?"

Tonelessly, he says, "I don't want anyone else."

I nod. I expected as much. "I don't claim to know much about what happened. Actually, I know next to nothing, but Jocasta said that Konstantina didn't choose you. Did she marry someone else?"

It takes Carver a while to answer, so long that I start to think he won't. His eyes stay closed, his long, thick lashes not quite covering the dark smudges peeking out from underneath them.

"A rich Magoi saw her," he finally says. "She was so beautiful. He wooed her away from me, promising everything I couldn't. Wealth, influence, children with magic. A different, softer kind of life. With him, she'd never get pushed around by royal soldiers again or taxed into near-poverty." He pauses and then almost so quietly I don't hear, he adds, "Nearly raped."

My stomach dives hard. "Did you save her?" I ask.

He nods. "Barely. That was the first man I killed. We were children. He was already on top of her and didn't see me coming."

I flinch at the thought of a young Carver being forced to cover himself in blood. "But I thought your father's army stopped that kind of treatment in most of the southwest."

"It did. It got better. Like I said, we were young."

Swallowing the ache in my throat, I smooth my fingers from his temple to the back of his skull and then down his neck, gently massaging. I lightly retrace the path again, never breaking contact. "If the Magoi was a Southerner, he probably actually had very limited magic. You're far richer now than any Sintan Magoi noble anyway. You're Griffin's brother, and part of the Royal House of Thalyria."

Carver sighs. "It doesn't matter what I have now. She's dead."

And a vindictive, petty part of me hopes that Konstantina is ruing her terrible choice from the Underworld. "Did she choose him for security only, or was there more?"

His shoulders lift in a small shrug. "I don't know. Once she made her choice, she wouldn't talk to me. Wouldn't explain. Wouldn't let me near her."

Probably because she was scared she'd change her mind, and she craved riches and refuge more than she craved Carver. At least in her head. Her heart might have been giving her some serious back talk, which made avoiding him her only option.

"Did you forgive her?" I ask. Carver has been living impaled on a double-edged sword. On one side—loss. On the other—deception and betrayal. Both cut deep. No wonder it's been slicing him up inside. The only mystery is how he kept it from everyone for so long. I had no idea, and everyone else seemed to think he was fine. Recovered. Before Griffin and I became a solid unit, I was convinced that Carver was an irrepressible flirt, always smiling, always ready for a laugh or a bawdy joke. Then the relationship Griffin and I developed must have reminded Carver of what he'd lost. It made him moody, but he was handling it. Then the Agon Games happened, the Underworld, and Konstantina.

He's quiet for a long time. He eventually opens his eyes, but only to stare at nothing at all.

Finally, in a voice weighed down by fatigue and emotion, he says, "I didn't have time to forgive her, or even to see her again. The Magoi took her away, to the city he lives in. I was so angry at first, and too full of pride to chase after her. She died in childbirth eight months after her wedding. The child lived. She didn't. Then I... For about a year, I acted a lot like this." He sweeps a hand out, vaguely indicating his jugs of wine and messy tent. "I thought the boy was mine. I finally decided to go and claim him."

My heart skips a beat, my hand hovering over Carver's hair. "But you had no right to a child born in wedlock. No authority in Thalyria would honor your claim."

"I didn't care. He was mine."

I bite my lip to keep from arguing more and lightly stroke his head again, my touch feather-soft. "What happened?" I ask when he doesn't go on.

"I got myself sober and cleaned up and went there, to that big house with guards, fancy gardens, fountains, and all the meaningless things Konstantina wanted more than she wanted me. It was huge and intimidating. They wouldn't let me in, so I waited. And watched." Carver's eyes close, and I'm sure he's seeing it all in his head again.

"And?" I prompt gently.

"And then I saw him. The boy was as fair and fat as his father, with bright, blue-green eyes. He wasn't mine."

I exhale slowly, both relieved and saddened. Knowing Carver, he wanted that piece of the woman he loved, that piece of them together.

"Do I forgive her?" He shakes his head against my legs. "No. I still love her. But I still hate her. It's tearing me apart."

I sit there in silence, my heart cracking wide open in my chest. I have nothing profound to say, nothing that will truly help him. My affection and my hand on his head are the best I can offer. He hugs my legs, his head in my lap, and I desperately want to share with him the hope I've found. But Elpis doesn't work that way. Only Carver can know when he reaches the other side of his suffering and is ready to live again.

"Wine won't help you," I eventually say.

Silence. And then, "I know."

"Can I take it away?"

He clears his throat. His arms tighten around my legs, but then he nods. "Give it to Bellanca."

I frown. "Why?"

"Because I avoid her at all costs."

An unexpected laugh cracks out of me. "She's *that* bad?"

Carver actually smiles. It's small, barely moving his mouth, but I still see it. "Maybe not. But when I want a drink tonight, I'll think twice about going to get it."

"And if you give in to the urge, she won't give it back." I know her well enough now to know that.

He chuckles, genuine humor rounding out the sound. "She'll do something to distract me. Lecture me for a while. Kick me a few times. Probably set me on fire."

"Then it's a good thing you won't be steeped in spirits," I say dryly. "You'd go up in a snap."

Carver straightens, dragging his face off my thighs. There are crease marks on his cheek and temple. His hair is completely flattened on one side and sticking straight up on the other where my fingers have been working through it. He's still as handsome as they come, strong, loyal, and funny. I can't understand Konstantina. How could she turn her back on a man like Carver? Did she regret it? Did she care that she was shattering him in the process?

I reach out and touch his whiskered cheek. "The people in your family love with everything they have. Look at your parents. At Griffin and me. You." I don't mention his sisters, even though their devotion is just as strong. The loves they're harboring and the people they're harboring

them for aren't any of Carver's business until they decide
it is. "But you made a mistake."

His eyes search mine, questioning. He doesn't draw
away from my hand.

"You didn't choose wisely. You gave your love to someone who wouldn't, or couldn't, give theirs fully back. Choose
better next time. It'll be worth it. It'll change everything."

He swallows. "You think there'll be a next time?"

I nod.

"How do you know?" He sounds curious when I
expected belligerence. Maybe, deep down, Carver hasn't
truly given up on love.

Lowering my hand, I look at him like he's one Centaur
short of a herd. "Soothsayer, remember? I *know* stuff."

A spark of the old, always-teasing Carver brightens
his face. "You're a fake. With a fake crystal ball and a
flashy sign."

My mouth pops open in protest. "I am *not* a fake! And
in this case, I'm not even just making things up."

Carver arches both brows, clearly skeptical. Standing,
he pulls me up with him. "I don't blame you for what happened to Piers," he suddenly says.

I freeze, something jolting in my chest. Carver has lost
a lover and a brother. I pray he gains from now on, rather
than loses more.

Carver kisses my forehead and then folds me into his
long arms. "If Piers had bothered to get to know you, he
would have loved you. He almost ruined a lot of lives
because he refused to see past his own nose. Whatever he's
doing in Attica, I hope the next time he gets involved in
something he doesn't understand, he does what you just
advised me to do—make a better choice."

CHAPTER 19

Volunteers arrive daily, mostly from Sinta and Tarva. Our army doubles in size, which gives Kato and Flynn plenty to contend with. Carver dedicates himself to the Fisans with the single-mindedness of someone who wants to forget everything else, and I hardly see Griffin because he's so busy overseeing it all. Everyone but me is exhausted. Even Bellanca finally dims to a soft glow from the sheer fatigue of trying to wring useful magic out of people who don't have very much.

My days consist of walking around, a crown on my head and Ianthe's pearls at my belt, waving, nodding encouragement, and trying to look regal—if dusty. Being seen and not getting into any trouble seem to be all anyone needs or wants of me at the moment, leaving me bored, increasingly restless, and privately grumpy.

But while the inaction grates on me, I know this is the time we need to take in order to get the army fully equipped and into fighting shape. And more importantly—into a cohesive unit. The already mixed Tarvans and Sintans come together fairly easily. They're mainly soldiers to begin with, or at least men and women with fighting experience. The Fisans mostly have no military background and some magic, setting them apart in all ways. And while I'm careful to spend equal time among the groups and to encourage them to mix together, my heart calls me toward the Fisans. Maybe they need me more. Or maybe I know what it's like to not fit in.

Little Bean is hardly showing, but she certainly isn't a secret anymore. I can barely move without dozens of people asking me if they should carry me on a litter, or bring me water, or go get the King. It's incredibly annoying. Do I look like my feet don't work? Do I look like I'm about to faint? Do I look like I need Griffin's help to take the last two steps to the bloody chair that's *always* waiting for me wherever I go?

By the end of each day, I'm growling to myself and ready to explode. But each day I sit, because that's what's expected of me, and I grind out a smile as I plant my bottom in the chair, because that's what's expected of me, too.

My knife hand starts to twitch more often, and the rest of me feels like it needs to take off at a run. Not to run away. Just to *move*. I'm trying to give the soldiers what they want, what seems to motivate them, but it's strange and hard to reconcile. The warrior princess inspired them. Rallied them. The pregnant Queen had better sit down and fan herself, or the world might end. It makes no sense. Then again, human emotion rarely does.

People definitely look at me differently than they ever have before. I think it's because of that very first day when we arrived at the army camp, and I humbled myself on my knees in front of a Fisan shepherd. Sure, I killed a Cyclops, but almost no one here actually saw that. Their first real impression of me came from watching a small woman dressed in regular clothing sedately ride into camp and then kneel in the dirt among her people, among Thalyrians. On my knees, I humanized myself in their eyes. In an instant, the legend got eclipsed by the person, while Griffin remains larger than life to them.

Was it a mistake? I don't know. I don't think so. I didn't do it on purpose, that's for sure. But I feel the difference everywhere around me—in looks, in whispers, in hearts and eyes. Before, these soldiers would have fought to please and impress me. Now, they'll fight to protect me. I think I know what's worth more.

And that's why I let myself get plunked down in this bloody chair, day in and day out. Because it makes these people happy to take care of me. Because it makes them feel like there's something they've already won—me. I'm theirs. I'm everyone's. I'm Elpis.

At least the training sessions and interactions are interesting to watch, and the daily improvements are impressive. I only wish I were more actively helping them to come about. But maybe that's not my role anymore. Maybe it never was.

Beta Team thankfully doesn't treat me like I'm in need of constant rest or assistance, but we only come together for the evening meal. Griffin and I have the nights, and thank the Gods he doesn't treat me any differently, either. He's still tender when the mood takes him, just like he's always been, but it's not any more often than it was before. I would miss our wildness if he changed. He knows I want both, the fast and the slow.

Just like I want to be the warrior princess as well as the expecting Queen.

CHAPTER 20

I'M GETTING ANTSY ENOUGH TO ALMOST BLUR THE LINES AND get involved in drills when Griffin proposes a training exercise and asks me to help oversee it. Something to do, thank the Gods. He wants to put a reduced number of soldiers—sixty men and women, but the best trained and most natural leaders we have—through the paces of a mock assault on a fortified city. He thinks it will help them to know roughly what to expect and to be better prepared to help organize and execute an attack on Fisa City, which we all know is the inevitable outcome.

He originally planned to have the war games play out in nearby Kitros, even though we all expressed concern over the possibility of the densely populated area housing spies that could report back to Mother about the state of our forces and our techniques. It's Bellanca who suddenly has a stroke of brilliance, suggesting that we use the ruined city of Sykouri instead. The exercise can be even more realistic there. We can use catapults and battering rams, and it won't matter in the least. The city is already vacant and wrecked.

Decided, we choose our players, gather materials, and then make our way to Sykouri, using the travel days to practice moving heavy equipment over rough roads and working together as a group. When we arrive, we set up a makeshift camp in the abandoned fields around the city and then pick our way up the debris-strewn main artery of the once-magnificent metropolis. On foot, we skirt fallen-down columns, tumbled archways, and crumbling buildings. Everyone is curious to see what's left of the city. The shattered bones of Sykouri are mostly blackened, burned by a long-ago inferno ordered by one of my ancestors during a Power Bid. He and his Magoi lackey, a Fisan named Phoibos, destroyed Sykouri with Phoibos's deadly fire, took the lives of most of its Tarvan inhabitants, and then pushed the Fisan border farther west to where it still stands today.

Nervous tension gripped my insides the moment we set foot in Fisa. But the Ipotane, only a day's ride from here, protect everything to the west, and we're nowhere near anything important or strategic to Mother. We're barely into Fisan territory, and we'll come and go so fast she'll never know we were here.

More than simple curiosity, our exploration of Sykouri is also reconnaissance. Griffin would never attack a city, even a ruined and ostensibly empty one, without making sure there was no one inside. It would be irresponsible to do so, especially with the increased number of Fisans, both refugees and volunteers, moving toward the nearby Tarvan border. We passed a whole group of asylum-seekers on our way here. Only yesterday, we saw the Ipotane rounding them up to take them to Lycheron for his sniff check. If any of them decide to volunteer for the army, they'll find Anatole taking names and barking out orders until our return. Beta Team, including Bellanca, is leading the practice attack.

The city is a mess. The destruction makes me shudder. My inquisitiveness turns into a sinking feeling as I take in the depressing evidence of what powerful magic and no conscience can do to a place. How it can rip lives from the world.

The deeper we move into Sykouri, the worse the feeling

gets. "Does anyone else feel sick?" I ask quietly, rubbing my arms. There's a tingle, almost like magic nipping at my skin, but other than Bellanca, our Magoi aren't powerful enough to disturb my senses.

Kato absently scratches the tattoo on his neck. "Something feels off."

Anxiety spikes in my blood. I'm pretty sure the Drakon Titos left some kind of magical mark on Kato besides the tattoo. If Kato has a bad feeling about this, I believe him.

My stomach starts to churn. *Was that movement amid the rubble?*

"Did you see that?" I discreetly tilt my head toward a burned-out building.

Griffin nods. "I saw."

"Refugees?" Flynn squints in the same direction. "They might not know if we're friend or foe."

A blade glints, peeking out from behind the scattered debris and catching the afternoon sunlight.

My pulse leaps. "That's not something a refugee would have."

Griffin curses under his breath.

I turn to Bellanca. "Why Sykouri? Why here? Did someone suggest it to you?"

Her eyes widen. "No. No one. I…" She frowns. "I can't remember. I had a headache."

My heart sinks like a stone. "It's a trap." I unsheathe my sword. "Mother drew us here. She used Bellanca to get us beyond the Ipotane."

"Compulsion?" Bellanca shakes her head. "But…"

"She can do it. She can get in your head and suggest things you never would have thought of. It comes with a bloody Gods damn headache," I grind out.

"Oh my Gods." Bellanca looks sick.

I lift my sword to get our squadron's attention. "Out! Everybody out!"

As if I were shouting to them, Fisan soldiers crawl out from behind crumbling walls and ruins. They don't waste any time and attack. Weapons clash. Our men and women fight back. Beta Team springs into action. Lukos joins us, helping to protect Bellanca as she becomes a weapon all by herself. He takes a hard hit but then pushes back. He's gained muscle weight from Carver's almost draconian training. He and Carver cover Bellanca as she throws fire at the oncoming Fisans. Carver is back to full speed and strength and looks rabid as he drives each new threat away from Bellanca. Flynn bellows. Kato swings his mace. Griffin and I fight back to back.

With Bellanca in full, flaming force, two of our Magoi, Elemental twins with wind, race over to blow her fire farther into the Fisan ranks. The enemy outnumbers us, and I can definitely feel their Magoi now—waiting, powerful, hiding all around us—but Bellanca is gloriously cutthroat and fierce. Fisans scream. Burn. Run away. With the twins' help, Bellanca starts clearing a path toward the gate.

As a group, we battle our way toward the crumbling portcullis. If we can get out of the city, we stand a better chance. In here, we're hemmed in, surrounded, and more Fisan soldiers keep surfacing. *Son of a Cyclops!* They're everywhere.

Sykouri should have been empty. It's been a ghost city for years. Mother's spies must have gotten wind of our planning a training exercise, and then she used compulsion to lure us here. Bellanca couldn't have known. Most people never experience the scraping pain of someone infiltrating their brain.

We're almost to the gate when I feel her—Mother and

her polluted magic pulling on the air. I kick out hard, getting rid of an oncoming attacker, swipe my dagger across the chest of another, and then whirl to face her, my sword glinting in the light of Bellanca's fire.

Mother is next to the exit. She looks at me, and then a great, green blast of telekinetic power rattles the keystone and finishes off the utter destruction of the huge arched gateway into Sykouri. Stones fall with a nightmarish thud, crashing down on top of the nearest combatants, ally and enemy alike, and cutting off our escape.

No! It only takes a second for the demolition to happen. Dust billows. Grit in my eyes. I recoil. I can almost smell the blood.

Horrified, I watch Mother climb atop the fallen keystone. The noise of battle, previously clanging all around us, dies as all eyes turn to her, Sintan, Tarvan, and Fisan. Lingering power makes her black robes billow around her. Her green eyes glint in the sun, and the remnants of her magic reflect off her crown of Fisan pearls. It's the Origin's crown, the symbol of absolute power as old as Thalyria itself.

Mother uses a fresh graveyard as her podium, and the look on her face tells me everything I already know: we're surrounded, outnumbered, and trapped in a ruin without a door.

I throw the knife in my hand straight at her. It veers to the side, right into the gauntleted hand of a Fisan Metal Mage.

Anger pounds through me. Trying again would be a waste of a blade.

"Less hesitation this time," Mother says, her tone mocking. "Is it because I almost had your husband eaten by a horse?"

I narrow my eyes. It's time to bluff like there's no tomorrow—because there might not be. If I can make my lightning work, I can still save the rest of our people. No Metal Mage or anyone else could stop me. I'll use Mother's own lesson against her. *Conceive. Believe.* Want it. Make it happen.

I reach into my well of power, searching for that elusive spark. "Surrender, and I'll let you live."

She chuckles, and her laughter makes the metal breastplate she's wearing over her dress move. Like her, the armor is ostentatious and hard. "You never were this funny as a child. It's almost a shame to end you. You've become so entertaining of late."

"You didn't find it entertaining when Ares and Persephone showed up and chased you off with your tail between your legs."

She arches dark eyebrows. The withering expression on her face turns my stomach, mostly because I know I can look exactly the same way. "But it was vastly entertaining to throw you into a volcanic pit."

I feel more than see Kato's sharp look and know his cobalt eyes are boring into the side of my face. Flynn makes a growling sound deep in his throat. I probably should have told them about that myself.

"It must have been a lot less funny for you when I flew back out," I say.

Her mouth pinches, and her body language screams disapproval. Mother never could stand it when I refused to enter into her mental games or managed to subvert her razor-edged questions.

"Which is why I've decided to concentrate less on the show and more on the result." Magic gathers around her. "Any last words?"

Throwing my own words back at me is a joke to her, I suppose. I start to move forward. There are people between us, and she'll go through them to get to me. Griffin, Flynn, and Kato follow my lead, flanking me.

I can't help looking at the fallen. The twins are there. They were leading us toward the gate, blowing fire to clear a pathway. Bellanca, Carver, and Lukos nearly knew the same fate.

The three of them draw toward us, condensing Beta Team into a line with our soldiers behind us. When there's nothing but empty space and crushed bodies between Mother and me, I look her up and down with disgust.

I have no Dragon's Breath left. I let out burning words instead. "I spit on you and everything you stand for."

No one moves. Nothing does. The collective stillness is the result of fear. Mother's soldiers fear her wrath. Our soldiers fear for us.

"I stand for me," Mother answers, something defiant in her tone.

Is that really what she wants? What *anyone* would want? That's the most unfulfilling and lonely life I can think of. "It's too bad you can't see beyond yourself. You're a dark hole, and the world is full of color."

Mother's expression seems to turn even more brittle as she stares at us. She looks at me, at Griffin. At Beta Team on either side of us.

Her chin lifts. She barks a command, and more Metal Mages pull hard on our weapons, making them shudder in our hands.

"Secure your weapons!" Griffin orders.

We've trained for this. Our people slam their swords and knives back into their sheaths. The blades still rattle. *Gods damn it!* We're surrounded by them—Metal Mages everywhere.

Weapons are no longer an option. We're down to fists

and what little magic we brought with us. I could steal a Metal Mage's power, but it wouldn't do us any good. I could grab a weapon, but one of them would just take it right back.

I search the air for something else, something more useful, but Bellanca's fire is the only other combat magic I sense. I ignore the few healers I feel, and from Frostfire, I already know that Mother's telekinetic magic isn't something I can use.

Turning inward, I probe myself hard, and the best I can say is that I feel my lightning lurking somewhere. It doesn't leap to the fore. In fact, it doesn't leap at all.

Mother smirks knowingly. "Still need that potion?"

Somehow, I smirk back. "I'm very effective with my bare hands."

"Ah, I taught you something, then? I did try, you know. If you hadn't been so poorly influenced by your sister, I'd have made something of you."

Poorly influenced? Fury boils inside me. My hair starts to rise. I recognize this feeling, this storm inside, and grab on to it. A current coils down my arm and snaps between my fingers. *Ha!*

I throw out my hand and let a bolt fly off my fingertips.

Mother ducks. "Touched a nerve, did I?"

Despite her flippancy, she sounds rattled. I'm sure she is. And when she's rattled, she—

Ah! Power punches my brain, and I gasp. I grab my head, just like everyone else except for Griffin. His eyes widen, and he reaches for me.

"Cat?"

I groan. It's excruciating. I almost rip the pearls from my belt and slap them over my forehead, but I can't do that. They're for Little Bean, protecting her from this. I grit my teeth, fighting back.

Mother batters me—batters everyone. Is this what she's capable of when her magic isn't already depleted? Or when she's not wielding it from a distance? The power is staggering. Her compulsion is a chisel pounding away at my brain, shaving off layers, each hit separating me from my will, separating me from who I want to be. I hear her over and over again in my head. She's telling me to kill. Kill everyone around me. Kill now. Kill until there's no one left.

Soldiers—hers, ours—turn on one another like animals. They have no hope of fighting off her horrific command.

Next to me, Flynn raises his ax, his face contorting with bloodlust and rage. The blade glints above me, and I stumble back, still clutching my hammering head.

Griffin slams into Flynn, knocking him down to protect me. The two men, fast friends since childhood and alike in size and skill, grapple with each other on the ground. Flynn rears up, still trying to attack me. Griffin's fist collides with Flynn's jaw. Flynn shakes off the blow and then changes target, sinking a brutal punch into Griffin's stomach. They beat on one another again and again and then drag each other down and roll. Griffin on top. Flynn on top. The world spinning out of control.

I shake my head, trying to dislodge the terrible pain and the even more terrible command to kill. My mind throbs, and the desperate struggle against the onslaught of violent urges makes vomit surge in my throat. I'm the only one still fighting her. Griffin is immune, and he and Flynn battle in the stones and dust. Carver and Bellanca battle each other. Flames. Blades. He strikes hard. She just barely dodges, screaming savagely, completely on fire. I don't see Lukos anymore. Where's Kato?

I spin, and blood sprays in my face. I jerk back, my vision pulsing like a fading heartbeat. But I can still see soldiers fall, cut down by comrades, friends, and family. Brothers and sisters who came to us together, who trusted us to lead them, rip at each other's throats, turned into vicious, mindless killers with no free will of their own.

A knife lands in my left shoulder. I grunt in pain and shock. Heat flares out from the wound. I recognize the blade. The Metal Mage must have thrown my own knife back at me. This is Fisan irony, otherwise known as vindictiveness. At least it always gets me my weapons back.

I pull it out and feel blood wash down my side. The sting in my shoulder is nothing compared to the agony in my head. If Mother didn't have everyone else to control, I think she would have already vanquished me. I don't know how much longer I can fight her.

Warring splotches of light and dark overwhelm my eyes, and I can't find her anymore in the chaos. I hear Griffin roar at Flynn to snap out of it. There are grunts and hard punches. There's Flynn snarling like a wild beast.

Where's Kato? I can't see!

I battle for control of my mind while fighting rages all around me. I don't have to see it to know what's out there—blood on hands, hate in hearts. Mindless and corrupted.

"*Give in!*" Mother's ruthless command hits me with the force of a thunderclap between my ears. It's shattering, invading, bleeding into all my edges and forcing me down the wrong path—the path I'll never want.

Crouching down, I wrap my head in my arms. Sykouri and I are one—razed, wrecked—and Mother's voice is the most terrible of Siren calls as it pummels me over and over. Pounding. Pounding. Pounding.

This has to end. The promise of no more pain seduces my imploding consciousness like a mirage in the desert. But that's just what it is—a lie. Every instinct tells me that

I have to fight for all I'm worth, fight for my life. I hammer at my head with the palms of my hands, trying to beat her pollution out. The darkness is too close. It's overtaking me, inside and out. My heart resists. It's too filled up with better things to flood with malice and hate.

I rock. I've been here before, and I lost myself. I lost myself to this terrifying pressure commanding me to betray myself and everyone I love. This is what Mother did to Eleni and me. She tore us apart. She made us fight like enemies, like mindless creatures in the dirt.

Not again! I explode upright, screaming. Even blinded by Mother's crushing magic, I see Eleni with perfect clarity in my head. It's her image that drives the shadows back. Like a ray of sunshine, her memory pierces the dark, and together, we eject Mother from my mind. In a way, my sister saves me again, and the reverse rip of power leaves me reeling as I come back to myself.

I blink, drawing my nearly fractured mind back together again. Some of the pieces feel like they don't quite fit. It's a struggle to make myself whole again, but I know that I can, and I know that I won. I can hardly believe it. This time, Eleni and I won.

Steadying myself, I look around at the utter devastation. Mayhem and bloodshed surround me. I may have won my battle, but I'm the only one. Everywhere else, the savagery is chaotic and loud, jarring and brutal.

Sickened, I search for Griffin. I need to know he's safe.

Blond hair and familiar features are the first things I see when I turn around. Kato's heavy arm slams into my chest from the side, knocking me to the ground. Stunned by the blow, devastated by its source, I expect his mace to swing down and crush my skull. Instead, it arcs around with a frightening metallic whistle and hits the crazed-looking man lunging at me with a dagger. The Sintan, one of our own—one of Kato's—flies back, one whole side of his face shattered and opened to the bone. Before he even hits the ground, there's no longer murder in his eyes. There's nothing at all.

Still flat on my back, I gape up at Kato. His snake tattoo is racing all over his head. It slithers across his forehead and then dives into his hair before circling back under his jaw, moving up his cheek, straight through his eye, and then across his forehead again.

"Titos is protecting you! Mother can't get into your head!"

Kato hardly acknowledges me, alert to the next threat. And that's when I realize exactly what I'm in the middle of.

Armies clashing. Me in the center of a raging storm. Bodies strewn around me.

And they're all Mother, just like I somehow knew they would be. They might not look like her, but they *are*. Every last one of them is an extension of her.

My eyes widen in shock. I knew it would come to this. I *knew*.

A strange mix of cold dread and detached calm washes over me as comprehension sinks in. Not a simple nightmare or embedded fear, then—one that wormed its way into my consciousness to plague my thoughts. This scene I thought I imagined was a vision of the future. After Griffin found out who I am and we fought, I closed my eyes, and I saw *this*. I saw Mother looking at me like I betrayed her, because in her eyes, I have. For the first time, I came out on top.

My gaze swings to Mother on her pedestal, tripping over Griffin and Flynn just long enough to know they're alive and still locked in combat. Mother's concentration is unwavering, but her furious eyes hold mine.

Watching her wield her destructive p
against the Gods for giving me foresight w.
anything clear. The vision didn't come to me in
like the other occasional times I've been touched by th
sight. I couldn't place it as real. As coming. As something
to avoid. What I saw wasn't anchored in a setting. Besides
Mother, I had no notion of the people involved.

My eyes jerk back to Kato. With tattoo Titos's help, he
must have stood guard over me, helping Griffin keep me
alive for however long my battle raged on the inside, for
those long moments when I couldn't see or hear anything
but Mother pounding away at my head.

Above me, Kato fights with the strength and skill of ten
men. He takes care of all threats, and I stop looking. I trust
him implicitly to watch my back while I make sense of
this—and figure out how to fight back.

But I can't block out the sounds of pain and rage and
death. There's an ache alive and blazing in my chest, a burn
that will never fade. If only I hadn't frozen up at Frostfire.
If only I'd killed Mother then. We wouldn't be here now.
Everyone here would have been safe.

I do my best to set aside those useless thoughts. Regret
is a part of life, and *if only* is a bottomless well where
wishes don't come true.

Closing my eyes for the briefest of moments, I force
down a steadying breath. I'm ready to fight now. I'm ready
to take my people back.

CHAPTER 21

I TWIST UPRIGHT AND SPIN TO MY KNEES, HEARTSICK AT THE circle of death around me. Crushed skulls. Mace-imploded chests. Most are ours, those unlucky enough to have been closest to me.

"Stay down," Kato barks. "You're injured."

But I'm already up. I look for Griffin again and startle when he appears next to me. There's a flash of black hair. A flash of auburn. Angry eyes and blood.

I jerk back into Kato just as Flynn's ax blade whistles past my ear. Griffin grabs the handle above Flynn's two-handed grip. Snarling, they wrestle for the weapon, both injured, limping, *mauled*.

Being in physical contact with Kato is like getting hit by a lightning bolt of pure Olympian power. Titos's magic jumps to me in a sudden rush, but I don't hold on to it. I use myself like a slingshot and send it straight at Mother without a second thought.

She cries out and drops to her knees on her stone perch. She shakes her head, looking dazed.

For a second, Flynn stops. Everyone does. Griffin rips the ax from Flynn's hands and flings it away.

Mother stands back up and her power strikes again, skipping over me like a flat stone on water. My defenses are shored up. Kato has Titos. Griffin is impervious. But Flynn bellows again. Scores of people do. The battle resumes, and those still standing fight like savages, many dropping their weapons to tear into each other with their bare hands.

Griffin and Flynn are just as feral. They're too evenly matched and clash relentlessly. Griffin gains the upper hand, but he won't kill his friend. Flynn is too skilled to be incapacitated easily, or fully, or even at all. They roll, growling and grunting, locked in a tangle, one trying to kill the other, and the other trying to keep them both alive.

Flynn lands a hard punch, and my gut clenches in fear. Griffin's face is mottled with bruises, his upper lip is split, and his nose is swelling. None of that worries me as much as the gash at his hairline. Blood slides down his face, blinding him.

Flynn looks better than Griffin but wilder. He's mindless, driven by violence and blind rage. In my heart, I know that Griffin could take Flynn down permanently if he wanted to. But he doesn't want to, and that's going to get him killed, because right now, Flynn's moral compass has been wiped out by the most immoral person alive. He's not suffering from any form of honor or rational thought. He's been utterly freed from the yoke of ethics. There's nothing to make him hesitate, and if I don't do something fast, Griffin will pay the price.

I whip around at the sound of Bellanca's distinctive scream—furious, pained, and unhinged. Carver roars in pain as well, his sword arm singed. Their differing strengths are the only things keeping them alive. Carver can't get his blade in close enough to kill her because Bellanca is utterly on fire and throwing off what must be a terrifying amount of heat. And Bellanca can't burn Carver to a crisp because his blade is keeping her just out of reach. They circle each other, waiting for the chance to pounce.

Around us, people rip into each other. There's no rhyme or reason. It's just kill, kill, kill. And the killing needs to stop.

"I know what to do!" I shout to Kato. Hopefully Griffin hears, too.

Counting on Griffin to keep Flynn busy on one side and Kato to guard me everywhere else, I inhale slowly to center myself and then pull magic from deep within, feeling the boost Titos's tattoo shot through me still sparking in my blood. I concentrate with every ounce of energy inside me and focus all my thoughts on one specific desire—I *will* gather the bright sparks of human minds all around me. I will take them from Mother, even if that means making them mine.

I shut my eyes and see them even better, brighter. They're beautiful, like stars in the night. Some flicker out, their light erased from existence even as I watch. Others, I still might save, but this day will torment them forever. This is the total loss of self a person never forgets or truly overcomes. This is where black marks on hearts come from, and where nightmares are born.

A big part of me rebels at the idea of latching on to human minds. A person's head is a sacred place, one of truth. It's our most private inner sanctum, where we're all alone with our good and bad thoughts, know our own deeds and desires, and our choices should only ever be our own. All my life, the invasion of the mind has been my point of demarcation, the one line I swore I'd never cross. I'm about to do it anyway. Is it an act of mercy? Survival? Maybe it's both. It doesn't matter anymore. I've made my choice.

Shoving long-standing fears aside, I pull on the minds around me. Lights gravitate toward me, but they don't come fast enough, or even all the way. Mother's hold is solid, and the brutal tug-of-war I initiate between us starts to feel like it could tear me apart.

She holds on to what she's claimed with iron strength. I

double my efforts, quaking from the sheer amount of magic required to try to steal away her prize. The lights begin to whirl, and my head spins along with them. The sounds of fighting fade until all I hear is the fast thumping of my own pulse.

I pull harder, my head starting to grind with pain. The pinpricks of light turn searing. I coax more magic up from the swirling well of power inside me, but my concentrated, powerful effort at compulsion doesn't work. I don't capture a single spark.

Kato hisses. The sound breaks my concentration, and I open my eyes, searching for him. My vision swims as my magic pulls my brain tight like a bowstring and then snaps back down into me with the painful backlash of unused power. I gasp, lurching. When I regain my balance, I see Griffin and Flynn still grappling and growling at each other. Closer to me, Kato is injured now. A deep slice in his shoulder paints his arm red.

Gods damn it! I haven't changed a thing.

A woman lies either unconscious or dead at his feet, joining our other attackers. The circle has grown since I closed my eyes and tried to wrest control of everyone from Mother. Kato switches his mace to his left hand, raises it, but then shifts his balance and uses his injured arm to land a knockout punch on the man charging us from the side. I recognize the assailant before he hits the ground, incapacitated. He's one of our Sintans. One of Griffin's from the start.

Nausea plagues me, and not only from my headache. We're fighting the people who flocked to us from the four corners of Thalyria. We're fighting Fisan soldiers, too. For efficiency's sake, it was everyone, or no one, so Mother simply took them all.

Magic bites the air near the ruined gateway, different from Mother's. Metal whistles. People scream. There are mostly Fisans over there, but Mother doesn't care. The point of this massacre isn't for her soldiers to best ours. The point is to leave no one standing—because that's how she gets to *me*.

I focus on my compulsion again, sliding my consciousness into a different place, one of magic and instinct. I reach for the sparks, trying to corral the jumble of minds, but they resist me. Mother's hold on them is rock-solid, absolute, and the longer she has them, the firmer her grasp seems to get.

"Cat!"

Kato's warning shout severs the bridge of magic I was building again and sends me crashing back into the battle. I whip a kick at the Fisan who got past Kato. He staggers but stays upright so I spin again, this time crouching down low. He falls when I sweep his feet out from under him. A quick lunge puts my hand at his throat, and I squeeze until his eyes roll back in his head and he goes limp, asleep for now.

"Cat..."

I whirl at Griffin's strangled call. He sounds desperate, his voice thin and hoarse. It does something to me on a visceral level, and every part of me sharpens like a blade, ready to fight.

Griffin and Flynn are facing off on their knees, their hands their only weapons now—and those are wrapped tightly around each other's necks. Both their faces are purple, airless, with veins popping out at their temples and their lips drawn back.

I spring up and race toward them, suddenly understanding what I'm doing wrong. I'm trying to do too much at once. I need to prioritize, and getting Flynn back is my absolute priority right now. One mind at a time is the answer, not everyone all at once.

I leap on Flynn, grab his bloody, bruised head in my hands, and concentrate all my magic into one pure blast. He's mine! And I am *not* giving him up!

He yells like he's being ripped apart. I scream. Mother screams. *Ha! Take that!*

Flynn releases Griffin and crashes to the side, taking me down with him. I scramble to my knees and pivot so I'm leaning over him, my hands now gripping his shoulders and my eyes frantically searching for signs of the Flynn I know and love. He stares at the sky, his brown eyes wide open but blank and unseeing.

Fear punches a hole through my ribs. He's not breathing. *What have I done?*

Flynn's broad chest rises on a loud gasp. *Thank the Gods!* I nearly sob out loud.

Alarm flashes across his face, and then absolute horror floods his expression. I feel his emotions even more strongly inside me. The confusion. The guilt. The panic and pain. I hold him tight in the cradle of my mind, careful not to give him any invasive direction, and then search out Carver in this unutterable mess. Like a snake weaving through long grass, my magic skirts everyone in between and then strikes at him with focused purpose, claiming him fast. Carver staggers, and I jump straight to Bellanca, not giving myself a second to rest because I know she'll kill him in the fleeting moment he's too shocked and confused to fight back.

"You're free," I whisper through magic, and space, and minds.

I feel every awful part of Carver's and Bellanca's distress and confusion as they go from fighting each other to defending one another, experiencing along with them their gut-wrenching regret. It's the lostness that batters me the hardest, the desperate internal screams of *How could I?* and *What happened?* and *I don't understand!*

Flynn's anguish is the worst. His guilt crushes me, his mind sinking into darkness and doubt. He looks at Griffin, at me, and I know he'd exchange his own life as penance for what he's unwittingly done.

Griffin wipes blood from his eyes and then holds out his hand to his friend.

Flynn swallows hard. His head jerks awkwardly from side to side as he watches the people around us turn on whatever neighbor is still standing and viciously attack. It's sickening, and in truth, he's seeing it for the first time.

"This is humanity reduced to Mother. You are not at fault." I offer him my hand as well.

Flynn's throat works again. He hesitates, unsure of himself. Then he grabs both our hands, and we heave him up, setting him back on his feet.

"Thank you, Cat." Flynn's voice is gruff. He won't meet Griffin's eyes.

Tension wraps around my heart. I'm not sure he should thank me for being in total control of him. If I told him to run himself through right now, he would.

"I got Carver and Bellanca, too," I say, pointing to them. "They're working together now. They're okay."

Kato nods. "Then it's time to gather the rest."

I nod back, still shrinking from the idea. Griffin and Flynn spread out, defending our sides while Kato remains my faithful inner shield. Turning toward my magic again, I search for and feel the sparks of dozens and dozens of minds all around us. Many blaze with bloodlust. Some flare with pain. Others flicker, slowly dimming. The fighting was so undisciplined that it might have ended up being more incapacitating than fatal in enough cases to give me hope—hope that with effective triage and some decent healers, we can save many of these men and women before it's too late.

Lukos comes into focus, still a bright and intact spark. I take him back next, and his bewilderment, sorrow, and shock flood me, stealing my breath and battering my heart.

From there, I jump from mind to mind, not knowing which side these people started out on and not caring. I only know that from now on, they're mine. It's easy once I start, like plucking cherries from a bowl. One more. One more. One more. Taking until I've consumed them all.

I crossed my final, really my *only* line, and I did what I swore I would never do. I overtook human minds and made them mine to control. I can't regret it, though. I don't regret it at all.

Mother makes an inhuman sound from her gory perch and tries to take my people back, her power wrenching hard through my mind.

The pain is fierce, and I whip around with a shout that somehow rocks the ruined city. Magic pulses from me like a shield, driving out her pollution and pain, and it's unlike anything I've ever seen before, or felt, or done. It's bright green, shimmering, and so clear that even the dust particles in the air come sharply into focus and then stop, hovering like tiny glittering specks in a vast emerald sea. Silence blankets the world, thick and absorbing. Nothing moves. No one breathes. Everything has been suspended. Everyone stops except for me.

Wings spring out from my shoulder blades, ripping through my tunic and punching holes in my leather armor. I gasp because it *hurts*. They grow and unfurl, huge behind me, rising like twin nightmares above my head. With the sun at my back, I see my shadow before me—beautiful, horrifying—and in that moment, I can pick out a single, golden thread in my blood, pulsing with ancient power.

The ichor in my veins snaps to life and tells me my own story. I am what frightens the untrue of heart, burns treachery from them, and demands divine justice. Nike may have contributed to my wings, but she's not the only one. I am daughter of the winged Furies. My veins run with their harsh blood. Throughout time and worlds, the infernal Goddesses have wielded the punishing whip of justice. Truth and vengeance have always been theirs.

Ruthlessness sweeps through me, dark and cold with purpose.

Kingmaker. Truthsayer. Settler of scores.

In the silent, green stillness of pure magic, I feel the tapestry of my life overlap my body, all the threads the Fates wove for me, all their twists and turns. The Furies both gifted and cursed me with the power to discern the real from the false. They formed me in their own images and then sent me forth to punish those who break sacred covenants, those who betray life's most valuable currency of trust.

"What's more important than loyalty?" Griffin's voice whispers through my mind.

"Made for me," my heart whispers back.

My lesson was a long time coming, this unveiling of the truth. I think I've learned it now, after wading through the swamp of my own distrust and lies. I've finally stepped onto dry ground and can see the future before me.

"Punish those who swear false oaths." New voices overlap in my mind, grating and dark, seductive and powerful, the voices of primordial beings that could boil my

blood and flay me alive. In fact, they already have—an experience I have a feeling was much harsher for me than for most.

I look at Mother. Just like everyone else, even Griffin, she's frozen in my flood of magic. And what I see is a parent whose children are pawns to her. And a queen whose subjects live in fear of her. Mother. Ruler. Her implicit pledges, the responsibilities that should have been anchored deep in her heart, mean nothing to her. Give birth but don't protect. Hold absolute power only to abuse it. She is the very embodiment of betrayal.

A burning sensation flares in my wings, and I look over my shoulder to see the white feathers turn jet-black. A brass-studded scourge appears in my hand, a gift from my partial makers in the Underworld. The whip is wooden-handled and long, an ancient and vicious-looking tool. Dozens of thin leather straps trail in the blood and dust of Sykouri. I lift the weapon and feel the weight and sway of the studs as they clank against one another in a terrible, melodious dance.

I swing the whip up and crack it once, testing it. The menacing snap is still ripe in the air when my magic crashes to the ground, disappearing back into the fabric of the world just as suddenly and mysteriously as it appeared. A final ripple sends everything shuddering back into motion, and I fill my lungs with air that tastes of sweat and blood. I let out the inhale on a battle cry worthy of my terrifying benefactors.

Lightning strikes above my head. Thunder roars in response. Ground-shaking power pulses from me, and the remains of Sykouri gasp their last breath. The ruins on either side of the main thoroughfare collapse, imploding with a long, low groan. Stone dust clouds the sky, momentarily blinding. When the storm settles, everything and everyone is silent.

Around me, the ancient city is leveled. Newly opened marble gleams in the sun. The white stone contrasts sharply with my black wings, which suddenly seem too dark.

Mother staggers to her feet, having fallen from her shattered pedestal. She stares at me in shock, her mouth ajar.

I stare back, my mind filled with Fisans, Tarvans, and Sintans. I have them all. Everyone but Mother. I don't want her.

"I took these people from you." I don't mean to sound any different, but my voice comes out powerful, layered, and deep, like an echo of thunder from the high peak of Mount Olympus. "And I give them back their free will."

I slam down barriers behind me in each and every one of them as I exit their minds as fast as I can, leaving them fortified with my own natural resistance to compulsion. The move is impulsive and totally instinctive, but also very difficult. It shreds my power down to the deepest, rawest layers. I give so many people a piece of myself that there's not much left when I'm done.

I hold very still, my spine straight and my shoulders back, not showing my loss of balance. "I just coated their minds with the armor of my magic. You cannot touch them ever again. No one can." Not her. Not me.

My voice is normal again, evidence—at least to me—of power lost. I don't let on. Mother sniffs out weakness like Cerberus sniffs out snakes.

At the same time, I can't entirely regret what I just did. Right now, parceling out my magic to protect the survivors feels more worthwhile to me than black wings and a whip. Darkness and vengeance chafe against Elpis in my heart. I'm not sure there's room for both.

Mother's face flushes with anger—and maybe

something else. Real worry. Her eyes dart from side to side, her hands clenching into fists.

The satisfaction of seeing Alpha Fisa scared is suddenly overcome by an intense throbbing in my shoulder. I forgot I'd been stabbed. Injury and magic fatigue start to plague me, but I'm not finished yet, and my reserves have never failed me.

I force the tremor from my hand and pull a knife from my belt. This fight isn't over, and maybe it's time to finally accept that Mother's name is written on my blade in blood.

CHAPTER 22

I DON'T HESITATE. UNFORTUNATELY, NEITHER DOES SHE. JUST before I release the blade, Mother morphs into the shorter form of a Harpy, and the knife sails over her head. She shoves off with a beat of powerful wings and flies away, abandoning her remaining soldiers and contingent of Metal Mages without a backward glance.

Cursing under my breath, I watch her go, a mix of disgust and relief churning in my gut. I would have done it this time. But I didn't. And I don't know which sickens me more.

I don't fly after her. Seeing to the welfare of the people right here in Sykouri holds more sway over me. Even though it galls me, dealing with Mother will have to wait.

No one resumes fighting. Everyone is too stunned. Or afraid. Or troubled. Or in awe. Mother's soldiers lay down their weapons, not interested in pursuing a battle for a leader who literally just took off on them and is definitely not coming back. Or maybe it's because of me. I'm bloody, winged, powerful. I wouldn't want to fight me, either.

Behind us, I hear a shout to search for the wounded. It's Lukos's voice. At least someone is taking control like they should.

I whirl to face Griffin. "What is *wrong* with me?"

Griffin frowns. "What are you talking about? You did it. You got everyone back."

I glare at him. Yes, there's some positive. But this was also a colossal failure. "*After* half of them died!"

"Not half." He sweeps a hand out. "Look around you. There are more injuries here than deaths."

I refuse to acknowledge the pride in his voice and flex my empty hands. The scourge is gone. I didn't use it. I chose healing instead, and the Furies took their ancient weapon back.

"Stop looking at me like I did something right," I snap. "Sometime, somewhere else, all this starts again. Gods *damn* it!"

Griffin shakes his head. He looks terrible. There's blood everywhere and a huge gash at his hairline. "No. She won't underestimate you again."

I scowl. "Great. So we'll lose faster next time."

Griffin looks like he's gearing up to argue again, so I turn away from him, really just wanting to stomp off and lick my wounds. I won't. There are more important things to do, like find my husband a healer.

I pull up short when I see the way Flynn and Kato are staring at me. Flynn is wide-eyed and has the strangest, bemused look on his beat-up face. As for Kato, all the strong, masculine lines of his features have softened, and he doesn't once take his blue eyes off me.

Suddenly self-conscious, I fold down my wings, trying to get them back inside me. They stay where they are— huge, heavy, and solid black. I bite my lip, tasting shattered rock and the sour residue of failure on it. I don't say anything, and neither do Flynn and Kato.

Carver and Bellanca limp closer, both of them barely intact. Carver's burn-reddened arm is slung tightly around Bellanca's blood-soaked waist, and I don't know if her pinched expression is because she's having to rely on Carver, or because she's in pain. Probably both. They stop just short of me, Carver supporting most of Bellanca's weight.

"You have wings!" Carver's expression is both dazed and awed. "And what was that magic?"

Probably for the first time in her life, Bellanca keeps her mouth shut and just looks at me. I half expect her to shrug Carver off, but she doesn't. It seems odd, considering they were just trying to kill each other—and clearly nearly succeeded. Turning homicidal against one's will must draw people together. Tomorrow they'll likely be bickering again. For now, survival trumps all.

"I don't know," I answer about the strange magic. "I think I put everyone but me into some sort of stasis." I leave it at that, because that's all I've got.

"It was like the whole world went dark," Carver says.

Huh. For me, it went green. But there was darkness on the inside. Enough to color my wings black.

Conflicted, I think about the Furies' blessing for bloody vengeance. I think about how I ignored it—ignored them. And now Mother's gone.

Today's bloodshed and loss will haunt me forever, but for now, I open my senses and search for healers in the overwhelming field of Metal Mages Mother left behind. I feel the strong, liquid tide of their power in more than one place and know that at least some of the healers survived.

Our soldiers haven't dared approach us, so I have to call out to the nearest ones. "Find me the healers!" To another group hovering not too far away, I shout, "Organize triage. Those who can wait, wait."

"What about theirs?" one of the Sintans calls back.

"There is no *theirs*," I answer in a tone that successfully conveys my loathing for that question. "I see no difference between dying Thalyrians."

He pales and nods. He and his comrades rush to do my bidding.

To drive home my point—unity and all—to a group of Fisans that didn't arrive with us, I say, "Put the injured on the left." I point to the pockets of shade created by the rubble. "The dead go on the right."

I don't bother to ask if they brought any healers with them. Mother thinks she's too omnipotent to ever need a healer for herself, and she doesn't care about anyone else.

Instead of moving like I asked them to, the Fisans look at me like I'm a ghost. They're a good decade older than I am, which means they might have known me as a child. A child in a cage. I've gone from a cage to wings. Is that fear in their eyes, or pity that I'll never be able to fly away and be free?

I give them a hard stare, and they vacate the vicinity within seconds. I know I must look like a monster. If I still had the brass-studded whip, it would definitely complete my *Don't mess with me, or I will annihilate you* look. Pent-up aggression seethes inside me, but my rage is directed inward. Maybe that's the difference between the monster that is Mother, and the monster that is me.

With only Beta Team within earshot again, I say fiercely, "I did everything wrong." I'm livid at myself, at my own irreversible choices. "I had the magic. I had a weapon. I could have ended her—ended all of this. Fifteen years ago, I could have stopped her. At Frostfire, I could have stopped her. Here, I could have stopped her, but I didn't! I *never* do!" I ball my hands into fists. I want to beat them down on myself. "Instead of ending it like I should have, I gave up the magic. I lost the bloody weapon!"

Griffin grips my shoulders, looking at me intently. "You did what you had to do, Cat. What you felt was right. You saved everyone you could."

"I sacrificed the win." I wrench from his grasp. "You know I did."

His eyes search mine, their steely strength battering my divided soul. "Would you do it again?" he finally asks.

I turn away. *And that's the damn hard question, isn't it?* I don't know.

For a few moments, I was a terrifying instrument of truth and vengeance. I saw the fear in Mother's eyes. But instead of wielding the whip of justice against her like the Furies clearly meant me to, I used all that power to erect barriers in everyone else's minds instead.

Why? Why did I do that?

"I should have ended it," I say, my mouth as dry as ash. "It was the obvious choice. The objective one."

Griffin doesn't agree or disagree, but his eyes hold no censure, when I know they should.

Next to me, Kato reaches out and lightly touches the arch of one of my dark wings, drawing his battle-roughened finger down the fluttering edge of a bold, black feather. "Maybe you make other choices because it's not your role to end it, Cat. Maybe that's someone else's job."

Not my role? His words make hopefulness and disbelief grapple inside me, both of them trying to gain the upper hand. Doubt wins out since the burden seems to fall squarely on my shoulders. And I've done a bang-up job so far with a resounding tally of fail, fail, fail.

Still, I can't help asking him, "Then what's mine?"

The smile that spreads across Kato's handsome face breaks my heart, and I don't even know what it means. He seems to light from within, so bright he's almost blinding.

"*Thea mou*," he whispers. *My Goddess.*

My breath catches, but I shake my head. "*Adelphe mou*," I whisper back. *My brother.*

Heartfelt words spoken in the old language always hold power, and I gasp as they squeeze my chest. Kato looks like he's been struck by a lightning bolt. Then his eyes flick to the side, and his expression changes entirely. He rams into me, sending us both crashing to the ground.

My injured shoulder jars painfully, and I cry out. Before I understand what's happening, I see the knife in his throat, feel his blood on me.

No! I rear up. Kato stays down. Blood spurts from his neck.

My mind refuses to believe what I'm seeing, but my heart instantly does. It shatters beat by beat. I press my hands around the blade. It's my knife, the one I threw at Mother before she flew away. A Metal Mage must have thrown it back at me, but Kato intervened.

Blood gushes between my fingers, running in hot rivers over my hands. *So much! Too fast!*

People shout for a healer. Griffin is there. There's noise and chaos all around me, but I only hear one thing—the wet clicking in Kato's throat as he desperately tries to breathe.

I shake, tears blinding me. A wound like this leaves no time, no time to make it right!

Kato's cobalt eyes dim, losing their wonderful light.

"Selena!" The scream rips from my throat, but even as I yell for her, I know it's too late. If she showed up right now, it would still be too late.

Every moment Kato and I have spent together is a kernel of warmth in my heart. I want a thousand more like that. He's deep in my soul. He makes me laugh. He never judged me. He kept me sane in the dark.

The others surround us, but Kato doesn't look away from my face. I don't think any force in the world could make him. The final pinpricks of light fade from his eyes, and I can't breathe at all.

"Stay with me!" I plead, grief wrenching my soul.

Griffin's hands curve around my shoulders, but somehow I don't feel them at all.

Kato's big frame settles. The last tension dissolves from it, and a shuddering breath rattles my aching chest. He shielded me with his own body. He traded his life for mine. It's Eleni all over again. It's too cruel. This can't be Fate.

I crack straight down the middle, and there's no way I'll ever fit back together again. Magic explodes from me, disjointed and out of control. It throws everyone else away from us as I drop forward onto Kato's chest and sob. He's still warm and pliant, still here, yet not. His life force begins to swirl around me, his warrior's soul heading for the golden path. It brushes my skin, and I could swear it whispers over me that he doesn't regret a thing—and that he'd do it all again.

I grip him harder. But *I* regret. I would change *everything*.

I can still feel him—with me, around me—and I want so badly to keep him that my magic condenses into an entirely new thing, so blindingly powerful that at first I don't even recognize it as coming from me. But then...

My head snaps up, and I take a startled breath. *This* is what Mother was talking about.

Conceive. Believe.

But it's immeasurably more than that. It's the reality that has always been written in my bones, but that I could never read. Ares tried to tell me at Frostfire. Even Artemis said it way back in the Ipotane vale. I *am* more a child of the Gods than I ever realized, than I ever dared to believe.

True understanding thuds into place like the building blocks of my own past, my now, and my tomorrow. I had all the pieces. I just didn't know how to put them together before now.

Mother wields magic so expertly because of our Olympian bloodline—and because she has no conscience to interfere with her desires. I have more than the ancient bloodline in my favor. I have actual parts. My outside is a combined shell of my human parents. My insides are a stew cooked up by the Gods—Elpis, Nike, the Furies, and who knows who else, with Zeus's own blood as the binding broth.

I can do anything I want, anything I put my mind to. Griffin knew it all along. Probably everyone did. Ares as good as told me I'm the idiot who second-guessed myself into near-total magic loss when I have the power of the Gods at my fingertips. The only thing ever stopping me has been *me*.

My magic storms around Kato and me. He's the brother of my heart. I will not lose him.

With Kato's unmoving chest beneath my hands and not even a twinge of regret in my conscience, I shed my second skin, the armor that wasn't so much protecting me as protecting everyone else from what I could become. That mantle falls away, and a cold, hard sort of determination takes its place. I gaze down at Kato's bloodless face. Stubble on his jaw. His blue eyes open. I'll make them see again.

"Stay with me." This time it's not a supplication. There's compulsion in it, strength of will. It's a command.

My power grows, raging within me, outside of me, everywhere. Lightning webs through shadows. I let the storm turn wild and use the first bolts to seek out the Metal Mages, not knowing which one of them threw the knife. With only a thought, I annihilate them all. Then I pull the storm back in, tightening it around us until Kato and I are cocooned in a cyclone of dense magic shot through with crackling bolts. My power weighs on my back and blocks his soul, keeping it with me until I can figure out how to bring him back. I *won't* let him go.

I pull the knife from Kato's neck and drop it on the ground. I can't heal him with that in there. But it's more than healing him, isn't it? I have to go beyond the realm of any magic I've ever known and do what only the Gods are capable of.

Large hands grip my shoulders and pull hard. Griffin yells my name, his voice frantic and hoarse, but I shake him off, the storm pounding out of me in gusts. Only Griffin can get through to us, but he can't stop me. No mortal can.

My power turns dark and deafening as I grip Kato tighter, trying to search out and understand the magic I'll need in order to give him back his pulse. I block everything else out, pushing the world away from me, pushing even Griffin back, far from my fractured heart. Somewhere in the infinite cosmos is the answer I seek. All magic begins to unfold for me, revealing its secrets one by one. I sift through the endless possibilities for the only thing I need or want. I'll find it. I swear to the Gods, I will.

But suddenly, an unstoppable force takes my lightning from me, ripping it from my control. The bolts change direction and then crash straight down, forming a blinding column of light that cuts Kato and me off and makes Griffin reel even farther back.

I cry out in pain and shock, knocked sideways across Kato's chest. A second surge of unimaginable power overcomes my storm completely and delivers a scorching blow to the air above my head. For a moment, everything is warped and white and blazing. Then a hot, heavy hand seems to press down on me, crushing. Crushing until I know I've done something terribly wrong.

A punishing blast of lightning turns the already charred

circle around Kato and me into a deep crater of boiling dirt
and stone. Heat cooks me where I lie, and I can't move a
muscle, paralyzed by the unending, catastrophic boom. If
the city weren't already flattened, the God Bolt would have
leveled it. The merciless strike deafens me, hollows me
out. No one is left standing. Not dead, I somehow know,
but knocked out. Limitless and vast, foreign and final, the
magic overloads my senses and without any words explains
to me just how puny and powerless I really am.

The cold determination I felt just moments ago burns
away as my helplessness to alter Kato's destiny sinks in.
This is a lesson in mortality, in humility, delivered by Zeus
himself. The message is brutally clear in the monstrous
amount of power still searing me through deep layers of
my skin: my human side is no small part of me, and I can't
seize from the Fates their ultimate control over the tapestry
of life and death.

My eyes burn from the heat. Bitter tears evaporate
before they can fall. Lying over Kato, I grip him to me,
trying to shield his body from the scorching, angry, roaring
power of Zeus. I hold on to him, because how can I ever
let go?

A sharp crack hits my ears. A flash blinds me. With a
sudden lurch, I drop face-first onto the battered cobbles of
the street. Gasping, I push back up and stare in horror at the
empty space beneath me.

I lost him. I lost Kato. He's gone!

Only the ancient and crushing magic remains. Suddenly,
that vanishes as well. Stillness replaces everything, a
shocking backlash to the raging storm. My ears can't
adjust. They throb for sound, but there's nothing to hear
except for the heavy pounding of my own broken heart.

I turn my head, and my eyes meet Griffin's. He's on

his knees, mouthing something to me from across the still-boiling circle around me. He lifts his hand, reaching for me, his lips moving frenetically, his face full of pleading and devastation and panicked fear.

I shake my head. I can't hear him. I don't understand a word.

My hair lifts straight up as a great force abruptly pulls at me like a breath sucking me in. I clutch the blood-slicked cobbles, suddenly sick with fright. My nails break, my grip slips, and my fingers pop off the stones. Screaming, I shoot upward, still reaching out and kicking as I go.

My desperate shout makes no noise. Griffin, Sykouri, then Fisa and all of Thalyria spiral away, tunneling to a point beyond my vision. A vast and quiet darkness inhales me, swallowing me whole. The stars and I whirl in an endless loop, their far-off flickers of light the same gold I saw reflected in the swirling depths of the Chaos Wizard's timeless eyes.

There's no breath. No light. No sound. I don't hear my heartbeat anymore, or feel anything at all. Somewhere in the ether, I close my eyes and go weightless, anchored only by the terrifying realization that I didn't just lose Kato today. I must have lost myself.

CHAPTER 23

I COME AWAKE TO SHADOWS. THAT'S ALL I SEE. AROUND ME. IN me. I still can't hear, and my head pounds like it's been kicked and kicked and kicked and will never recover. Not from this.

I look around, but I already know that Griffin isn't here. No one I love is, except for the tiny person I carry inside me.

I lower my hand to my belly, and for the first time ever from the outside, I feel Little Bean kick.

Her tiny life force flutters steadily as I stare blankly at a horizon of granite and cloud. I'm high up on a cliffside with a somber valley below. The cliff continues upward, sheer and soaring above my head, and my shelf of rock is small—no more than a few paces in any direction. There's no way off.

Well, there's down. But my wings seem to have disappeared again, and without them, down isn't much of an option. At least my shoulder is healed.

I can't be dead or else my daughter would be, too. And I've seen the steps a person takes to the Styx—a series of events that had nothing to do with this. The dreariness here reminds me of Asphodel, but there's neither the same sense of finality for what once was nor the implicit potential to move on to the next phase of existence. This feels stagnant and stale, like nothing ever alters in this place.

I fit right in with the bleak landscape, just another shadow along with the rest. I breathe and have a pulse, but there's no hunger or thirst. I doubt there ever will be.

This doesn't seem like a place for mundane, mortal needs. This seems like a place where scary things crawl out from under rocks.

Even that thought doesn't bother me. I'm numb except for the very real physical ache in my head. Numb even to Little Bean's tender stroke.

A cool, damp breeze sends my hair swirling around my head. It's shorter than I remember, and the ends look like they've been burned off. For some reason, there's only one dagger left in my belt. I slide it free, fist my hair in my other hand, and then shear it off at my nape. I open my hand, and the light wind takes the scorched ends away, sweeping them off into the deep, dark gap. I drop the dagger by my knee. It hits the stone shelf in total silence.

No sound. No needs. No emotion. Maybe the three go hand in hand.

I stare blankly ahead into a thick bank of clouds. Across the valley from me and on both sides, they drape the hills and craggy mountains like colorless garments and misshapen hats. Fog clings to rock, obscuring the closest peaks and even the cliffside right next to me. My shelf is open and clear, though, just like the valley below. There's a path right to me, cut through cloud. There's nothing natural about it, but I can't bring myself to care.

I sit and watch, although there's nothing to see. At some point, a swarm of small black birds swoops through my field of vision, breaking the monotony with the brisk fluttering of hundreds of wings. I don't startle at the unexpected sight, or wonder at the utter silence of it. Dulled inside and out, I watch the birds dive back down into the valley and out of sight.

Staring into the endless gray, I eventually debate letting feeling back in—if I even can. It's the only way for the rawness of loss to settle into me, like a stepping-stone. My existence is built on them. On these blocks of death. If I climb it, then I'm accepting losing Kato, like I eventually accepted that knife in Eleni's heart. I don't want to do that. Not when I could have brought him back. If Zeus hadn't stopped me, I *would* have brought Kato back.

But he did stop me. Zeus wrenched from me all that power I was finally ready to embrace. He took my wings. He brought me here. And now I'm a shadow, like everything else. Gray rock. Gray ground. Gray sky. Gray me.

It's better that way. To see in color would be too painful. To live in color would be a betrayal of those I couldn't save.

A lot of time must pass while I sit there on the side of the high cliff, my legs dangling over the ledge. It feels like a long stretch to have no needs, no desire to rest, or speak, or move. I don't try to explore my surroundings—not that there's much to see or anywhere to go—or to modify anything about my strange new circumstances. There's no sun that rises or sets, no changing of weather, no passing of days. It's neither too hot nor too cold. It just is, and that's the best anyone can say of me, or this place.

The monotony is soothing. It doesn't require thought. Or memory. It doesn't poke at dormant emotions like a child prodding a snake with a stick. Nothing uncoils and strikes without warning. Nothing makes me feel. The gray doesn't conjure the faces of those out of my reach, and it's better that way. There's almost peace.

The clouds remain as thick as ever, except for right in front of me. There's nothing to see, far less even than on the Plain of Asphodel. There are no despairing souls, no angry evildoers. There's no ferryman, no River Styx. There's no Kato to send off to a glorious afterlife.

A spasm bursts beneath my ribs. It seems I can still feel. It's awful. The spasm fades, replaced by gray.

I eventually lie down on my shelf of rock, looking out and letting my hand dangle over the edge. Hanging it over the side hides my wedding ring from me, because Griffin is starting to bump his way into nearly all my thoughts. He's stubborn, not leaving me alone. With my thumb, I spin the metal band round and round on my finger, my mind straying to the lone figure who was still conscious in Sykouri, his bloodstained hand outstretched to me, his grief-stricken eyes pleading, his mouth moving on frantic words I couldn't hear, trying to call me back from the brink of my own destruction.

Each blink solidifies the image, so I stop blinking. My eyes stay open, gritty and dry. I wish I could sleep. Sleep is the only real escape, especially from this thing inside me that keeps poking at that snake and trying to wake it up. Emotion stirs, bubbling inside, bubbling up. Closer and closer to the surface. If it boils over, it'll leave me in a place I'm desperate to avoid. I need to shut it down, shut myself down. But it's getting harder and harder, and sleep doesn't appear to be a requirement here—wherever *here* is.

As if that stray thought were a question, it conjures what might be an answer in the slow reveal of the landscape. It might take minutes. Hours. *Days?* I don't want to be interested, but I can't help watching and wondering as the blanket of clouds gradually evaporates, disappearing from the hills all around me, leaving them stark and bare. The bumps and cliffs and contours around the deep, dark valley slowly show themselves. Everything is still somber, just more grays upon grays, but for the first time, the air is clear, and I can see what's around me.

The final clouds dissipate like wafts of smoke that

might never have been, and I blink. I blink again. *That can't be right.*

I sit up. Across the sheer drop to my right, a man rolls a boulder up a steep hill. He's muscular and strong, his thighs and arms bulging from his work. He concentrates on his task, never once looking at me, or at anything else around him. His feet dig into the hillside, pushing, pushing harder, pushing up. After an endless stretch of labor, he's almost there, almost to the top he's worked so hard to reach. He's right across from me now, high above the valley floor. He wrestles the boulder onto the narrow summit of the daunting rise and then straightens, wiping his forearm across his brow.

The boulder tips over, flattens him with its first full rotation, and then crashes back down the hill. I gasp, my heart rate picking up for the first time since I got dumped here. Almost immediately, the squashed man re-forms into his previous shape. He stands again, loosening his shoulders and shaking out his huge, strong limbs.

I stare in shock. He looks…fine.

The boulder finishes its long, silent descent, traveling what looks like a well-worn path. My unnerved gaze swings back and forth between the man and the rock. *Did I just see what I thought I saw?*

He begins to walk back down the hill, his stride neither energetic nor dragging. My pulse thumps wildly. I know what's going to happen. I know that when he's behind that boulder again, he's going to get down low, brace his hands against the rough and ragged side, and then start to push all over again.

I scoot back from the edge of the ledge and track him with my eyes. Dread takes a sharp chisel to the stony numbness still encasing me, hammering out a solid crack.

That's Sisyphus. The ancient king was punished by Zeus himself for his egotistical behavior, underhanded cleverness, and chronic deceit.

Time feels like it has no relevance, but it must take him hours to perform his task again. I don't take my eyes off him. All the way down. Starting back up again. Roll. Step. Roll. Push. Slowly up the hill.

I swallow hard.

The harsh shriek of a bird of prey shatters the protracted silence I've been existing in. It's the first sound I've heard since the God Bolt hit Sykouri. The strident call pierces my eardrums like the tip of a lance, and I jerk my head around to the left.

A terrifying sight greets me. My eyes widen. Not far from me, but across a space of sheer rock too wide for me to possibly reach him, a huge male is strung up and brutally chained to the side of the cliff. His head hangs in defeat, his long, brown hair trailing into the tangled, curling mass of his beard. He doesn't fight at all when the giant eagle falls upon him and tears into his side, ripping out his liver and eating it in one bite. The bird's beady eyes flash over me. Gore and blood drip from its beak. It tucks its wings against its sides and then plummets back down into the valley, the arrow-fast dive taking it quickly out of sight.

The harsh tang of fear bursts across my tongue. My nostrils flare on too-fast breaths. The eagle's call reaches me once more from far away, mixing with the new sounds I hear all around me. There's nothing novel or distinct in the noises, just the muted whir and whump of a world that's not so stagnant after all. And all the while, the defeated colossus of a man just hangs there, his face contorted in pain, waiting for his body to regenerate.

Which it will. Because it always does.

Shaking all over, I get my feet under me and then scramble the few steps back toward the rock wall. The cool stone bumps my back and blocks any hope of further escape. My eyes jump to the right—endless, drudging boulder roll. Jump to the left—man pierced with a hole.

Oh my Gods.

The sickening scent of my neighbor's fresh blood and bile hits me with each new panicked inhale. My senses reignite, and the breeze that made no sound for so long now seems to carry the desolate sighs of a thousand miserable souls. I lean away from the gaping valley with all its shadows below and try to fuse with the sheer cliff face. The Gods only know what I'll see if I really look down.

I turn my frightened gaze back to the broken and bloody male sharing my bleak stretch of rock. Some legends say Prometheus escaped imprisonment with the other Titans after the War of Gods only to be punished later by Zeus on the mortal plane for stealing fire from Mount Olympus and giving it to the humans of the worlds. I guess the legends were wrong. His torment isn't being carried out on any mortal plane. He *is* far below the Underworld, in a place reserved for torture, eternal suffering, and endless pain. A hero to mankind but condemned by Zeus for his daring impertinence, Prometheus is in Tartarus. And so am I.

CHAPTER 24

A MAN POPS INTO THE EMPTY SPACE RIGHT NEXT TO ME, SCARING the magic out of me—and I was already on the verge of a pretty epic panic attack. Gaping up at him, I try to tilt my whole body away without really moving. I'm rooted to the spot, yet I want to run. Like a rabbit, my heart thumps out the fast and unsteady rhythm of fear against my ribs.

He's hard to look at full-on, and *man* isn't at all the right word for him. Male—yes—and of alarming and gigantic proportions. He's neither handsome nor ugly, neither old nor young. Long hair the color of dark smoke flows around his massive shoulders. His full beard is a shade lighter. He trains on me frightening, bronze-hued eyes with oddly large pupils, and all I can think is that he's power incarnate, that he's here for me, and that he's definitely not a friend.

I dart a glance to the left and see Prometheus looking over at us. I'd thought my neighbor was beyond caring what went on around him and his own pain, but his eyes are wide and filled with questions and life. Our gazes catch for only a heartbeat, and something squeezes in my chest that has nothing to do with my own fright. He's not defeated at all, which makes his daily plight a whole new twisted sort of beast.

The bronze-eyed male props his staff against the rock wall and crosses his arms over his muscular chest. He doesn't spare even a glance for the Titan chained to the cliff wall next to us. His fearsome, metallic gaze stays locked on me, and every instinct in me screams that that's a terrible place for his focus to be.

With nowhere to go, I can only stand there and watch the colossus that must be the King of Gods, my eyes hiccupping over him because he's just too frightening and stupefying to really look at. I swallow, but there's no banishing the lump of dread in my throat. I think I'm looking at Zeus. I think my life sentence is about to fall.

No, not life. That concept has no significance in this place. Eternal. Everything is eternal here.

He doesn't speak. He *looks* at me so fixedly it hurts. His smoky hair and beard give him an almost sage appearance, but it's violence that rolls off him in waves. His eyes bore into me like twin fires, boiling metal in a forge. They scrape me, peel off layers, burn. His blistering stare marks me for the miscreant I am.

Flinching away, I wait for some kind of horrible ax to fall. I can't help glancing at his staff. It's tall, the dark wood topped by a swirling opaque ball. A petrified vulture's claw holds the ball in place, the long, time-blackened talons curving up to cradle the orb. Staffs like that pack an incapacitating magical punch—and I have no idea how they work. I shudder.

"Come."

The God's voice thunders through me, resonating in my chest. I don't move, both frozen in place and confused. There's nowhere to go.

"It's time to go," he announces, looking me up and down with obvious annoyance.

Not taking my eyes off him, I brace myself against the cliff wall and do my best to stop shaking. "Go where?" My voice is the smallest it's ever been. *Oh Gods, please don't say it's somewhere worse than here.*

His frown and shaking head show me he thinks I'm an utter idiot. "I told Zeus he was putting too much stock in you."

I blink. I thought he was Zeus. And that I'd lost his favor.

"Go back," he supplies, huffing impatiently at my apparent inability to grasp simple concepts.

"Back?" I don't understand. There is no back from here.

"Would you rather stay?" he asks in exasperation.

I stare at him. I feel like we're speaking two different languages, and I may not understand either.

The God—because he's definitely that, even if he's not Zeus—leans down to my height, getting us more nose-to-nose than I want to be. I inch back, and he follows.

"Do you know where you are?" he asks.

I nod. I wish I didn't, but denial seems to have abandoned me completely.

"Then let me tell you about Tartarus, the land where you're not dead, but you end up wishing you were. It's either horrifically boring or horrifically painful." Without looking at Prometheus, he jerks his head toward my unfortunate neighbor. "Either way, it's worse than you can possibly imagine. I've been here forever, and an eternity on top of that—no hunger, no thirst, no war, no sex. *Nothing.* Then you showed up, huddling like a pathetic, dormant little ball on your cliffside when you're the *only one* with the means to get out of this place."

My jaw loosens. *What?*

"Zeus told me all about you. The Queen you should already be. The magic you should already have. He said you're my passage to the Underworld—*finally*—so you had better not ruin this for me."

"I…" I don't want to admit it, especially to this rage-filled mammoth, but… "I don't understand."

Scoffing impatiently, even though he hasn't explained anything, he finally waves a hand out over the valley. "Fly out of here. Open a tear in the sky with the lightning Zeus gave you, spread your wings, and you're free. Which is a lot better than I can say for anyone else on this abysmal plane," he mutters under his breath.

I glance over my shoulder, already knowing what I won't see there. "Zeus stripped me of my wings. He took control of my magic. I can't fly."

The huge male prowls forward, the magnitude of his presence forcing me away from the rock wall. "Fly off this cliff yourself, or I'll throw you over."

Anxiety shoots through me. But I also don't believe him. One thing is clear—he won't kill me if I'm his passage out. I detect no lie in his words, though. Maybe my Kingmaker Magic doesn't work in Tartarus. Or maybe it doesn't work on Gods.

I take another step away from him, moving toward Prometheus. I need space, and there is none.

"Tartarus is where you're alive but don't live. Do you want to live?" he asks, driving me toward the sheer drop.

I nod, wide-eyed. Of course I do. And not here. The numbness from before has been thoroughly shocked from my system, and a flood of emotions is battering me. One feeling stands out: leave this place. Leave this place now.

I glance down, the dizzying height suddenly making my gut clench. I'm on the edge of the ledge with nowhere left to go. I try to flex wings that aren't there. I don't feel them stirring. There's no now-familiar flutter in my chest. There's nothing at all.

The God growls. "If you're lucky here, you simply exist. If you're not, eternal punishment is your reality... *forever*. And believe me, young one, you have no idea what forever means."

He steps forward again, looming over me. My stomach

hollowing, I use my last inch, sending bits of shale careening off the shelf.

"Your baby will never grow, never be born, never live."

I swallow. Little Bean should live.

"Your husband will grow old and die and go to a place where you will never see him again. He'll wait. And despair."

My breath cuts off. *Griffin*.

A crafty smile lifts his lips. "Or maybe he'll grow tired of waiting for you and find comfort in the arms of another woman."

That potential outcome flashes before my eyes, heartbreaking. "I have no wings," I say, my voice like gravel.

"Do you know who I am?" He grabs my arms, and I gasp at the hot jolt of power that writhes through me like the living thing it is.

Not breathing, I shake my head. I have no idea. I don't want to know.

"I am Perses."

My eyes widen. The Titan God of Destruction. A primordial being even older than Zeus!

"And I'm supposed to make sure you finish what you started." And with that, the bastard lifts me up and throws me off the ledge.

𖠋

I shriek. Pounding air. Panic. *Oh my Gods!*

The valley floor is a long way down. It still rushes up to meet me. Fear for Little Bean slams into me. I need to fly. *Now!*

I strain, twist, scream, *roar*. No wings spring forth. I can't reach them. I don't know how!

Too late!

Terror gives way to blinding pain. Consciousness somehow remains apart and alert, even though every single part of me is broken. Splintered. Shattered. Splattered. No bones left. Blood everywhere. Little Bean—dead.

There's a mind-ripping push and pull, and I take shape again, forming in a backward rush. A tortured animal sound leaks from me as my body knits itself back together. I'm aware of every second of it. The fear. The suffering. Little Bean's life spark pulses again, and then what feels like the hand of a God grabs me and yanks me violently up. I fly through the air, still solidifying as I go. I end up intact and utterly petrified on the high-up shelf of rock.

I fall to my knees and vomit. There's not much in me, just saliva and dry heaves and my mind supplying the sharp memory of blistering pain and a vivid image of my own broken body.

I turn my head, gasping for breath. Granite and gray waver before me. I see triple, double, and then Prometheus comes into focus.

"*Fly*," he mouths to me, a deep crease between his heavy brows. There's no hole in his bloodstained side anymore.

Perses glares at me. "Are you ready to spread your wings, or do you want me to do *that* again?"

"I…" I shake my head, dazed. As soon as I can, I stagger to my feet, trying to banish the nightmare of Little Bean's and my deaths. I brace my hand against the cliff wall for balance and push and prod at where my magic should be. There's nothing. I feel emptied out and scraped clean.

My heart sinks. "I don't feel the wings."

Snarling, Perses grabs me and heaves me over the edge.

I scream. I scream all the way down. I hit the ground screaming. I scream when Little Bean leaves me, ripping my soul apart. I scream when she comes back, my heart wrecked from both pain and relief. I scream all the way up the sheer cliff again as my body glues itself back together with my own skin and marrow, bones and blood. I scream loudest of all when I rise on trembling legs to face Perses again and then strike out with a closed fist.

He weaves out of my reach. "I told you to fly, not punch."

He reaches for me again, and instinct kicks in. I run. He's bigger, stronger, and a lot faster. He's a bloody God, and there's nowhere to go!

I'm airborne before I can take two steps, and there's still no hint of my wings. Instead of screaming, this time I strain through my chest and shoulder blades for all I'm worth. I'm still pushing when I hit the ground and feel and see myself explode, still pushing when this horrible world pieces me back together again, and still pushing when it propels me straight back up to the feet of my Titan tormenter once more.

The next time I fall to the valley floor, I see an emaciated man desperately grabbing for a cluster of figs he'll never be able to reach. Focused on his eternally unattainable feast, he doesn't even look at me as I shatter right next to him and then keen like an injured beast.

I re-form and rise again, knowing I'll never feel hunger here like he does. That's not my punishment for trying to control things beyond my mandate. *This* is.

"Why won't you fly?" Perses thunders. His lips draw back to bare his teeth. His bronze eyes boil with power and anger as he lifts me up and gives me a dangerously hard shake.

"Why won't you teach me?" I thrash in his hot and biting grip. I kick out, landing solid hit after hit. He's going to throw me over the cliff again, and I fight with every bit of strength I have left. "Everyone just expects me to do it, but no one ever says how!"

"Because it's instinct! Just like any magic. You either have it, or you don't. There *is* no how!"

My other magic I could always feel. I knew where it was, coursing through my veins, pooling in my blood. I could reach for it, command it. I never could with either the wings or the lightning—the two things I need right now!

I pound at him with both feet. "You're not helping!"

"Maybe this will help." Perses launches me over the edge with a disgusted curse.

I'm not as scared this time. I separate myself from the fear and pain, letting my body break while I tuck my heart and mind into a separate place that can endure all this from afar. The fall won't kill Little Bean or me. I know that now. I don't even try for my wings, concentrating on numbing myself to the rest instead. I just want this new round of torture to be over. It's just physical pain. I've dealt with it all my life. Endure. Pass the limit. Surmount. *This is no different.*

"This *is* different," Perses grinds out, obviously reading my thoughts as he catches me on the granite shelf in his bruising hands. He pulls me right up to his livid face. "This can go on *forever.*"

Well, that does put a dark spin on things. I ram my head forward and crack him in the nose.

He tosses me over the cliff.

It goes on and on like that. I eventually lose track of everything—mainly of myself. I have no idea how many times I go down, and my mind stops grasping the fact that I come back up. I stop fighting Perses. I don't kick or claw. My existence turns into an endless, agonizing blur, with my only hope being to burrow as deeply as I can into that separate place inside of myself where I can hide. I'm only vaguely aware of anything else, like the hard and painful impact that marks the moment of my own repeated demolition, or Perses ranting and shouting and cursing me for a fool. The eagle comes and goes, its habitual shriek before it attacks a strange counterpoint to my new, internal silence. Every now and then, I hear Prometheus whisper to me to fly.

Fly? I haven't tried in what feels like years and a thousand deaths. If I even have wings anymore, they're beyond my reach.

"It's not working!" Perses shoves me hard, but this time, he doesn't push me over the edge. My wingless back bumps into the rock wall, and I slump against it, panting. I blink a few times, and some of the focus and feeling I'd forced aside return to me.

"You ride from life to death and back again, and you don't even care!"

I laugh, nurturing the hysterical edge. I can tell it enrages him. Perses's torture technique to try to get what he wants from me reminds me of Mother, and I wonder if I could be resisting him on purpose. Is defiance somehow ingrained in me? A previously learned behavioral pattern that I'll never break?

I cough up another laugh, just to see his face darken and twist. "Physical pain means *nothing* to me."

That's not exactly true, but it's close enough. There's a point when choosing not to care and actually not caring start to converge. I mentally removed myself further from every fall until I was experiencing the plummet, the shattering, and the reconstruction from an outsider's perspective. The Titan's plan didn't work. Finding my wings became entirely secondary to remaining an observer looking in on someone else's horrific fate. And so each stomach-lurching drop got easier. I knew what to expect, knew the damage wasn't permanent, knew Little Bean would be okay.

My breath hitches. *But* by Gods, *she'd better not be feeling any of this.*

That horrendous thought snaps me fully awake, popping the bubble I'd been protecting myself in. How dare the Gods do this to her? How did I ever once think they cared?

Motherhood's wrath fills me. It's a powerful force. "You're a pawn!" I yell out. "And you've chosen the method of a dupe. This will *never* work."

A chilling coldness replaces the fury on the Titan's face. Perses closes in on me until the ancient power inhabiting him scorches my skin, and his breath heats one whole side of my head. Each puff of air against my temple feels like a volcanic eruption—volatile, explosive, ready to burn me alive.

I shudder. His very approach spells agony on deep levels. There's no part of me that doesn't want to run.

Perses dips his head, and his dark-as-night whisper makes a terrifying promise in my ear. "Then I guess you've turned down the easy way."

CHAPTER 25

FEAR DETONATES INSIDE ME. *IF THAT WAS THE EASY WAY, THEN what could be the hard?*

"Do you have any idea how much time you've wasted?" Perses asks.

I shake my head, a quick, jerky movement made up of trauma and trembling nerves. I step back from him, gaining space to breathe without inhaling danger and anger and primordial magic with every lungful of air.

Perses slides me a viperous side-eyed look. "I do."

Oh Gods. Time means nothing here, but in Thalyria...

Anxiety hits me like a hammer, ratcheting up my pulse. "Why are you saying this?" My voice rasps from screaming. I sound like a badly butchered sheep that's been left to bleat and bleat and bleat.

"I'm saying this because after millennia of imprisonment, Zeus finally granted me a potential end to this mind-numbing forever. I could be fornicating. Eating my fill. I could be thumping goblets with great warriors in Elysium right now and watching the red wine slosh over my wrist like the blood of the enemies I've slain, *but I'm not*"—the Titan's tirade builds in pressure with every word, his face turning a raging scarlet—"because you won't find your backbone and fly out of here first!"

I flinch away from his fury. For my sake, I wish I could give the son of a Cyclops what he wants.

"The magic is gone! I'm telling you, it's not there anymore."

"Not gone," he snarls in contempt, "or we wouldn't be here."

"Zeus took it from me. I found my spine in Sykouri. I had lightning. I had wings. I was ready to use them both—for whatever means." I throw my hand out toward the gray landscape. Tremors rattle my fingers, and I snatch them into a fist. "Now I'm here—*with neither.*"

The God's mouth pinches hard. He looks at me with unimpressed eyes. "It's all or nothing with you, isn't it? There's no moderation."

I snort. *Moderation?* This from the being that just rewrote my definition of torture by repeatedly killing my child and me? All my near-deaths? Well, they weren't any fun, either, but *this*… This was life-and-death whiplash—and not just my own. Prolonged. Pitiless. Mind-breaking. Most of me wishes I was still on the outside looking in, because inside is just too wrecked to think.

Perses studies me with a sour look. "Too much humanity. Then not enough."

My eyes narrow. Something in his words pecks at me like Prometheus's eagle, a sharp jab straight to the gut. "Why do you say that? What do you mean?"

"Your balance is off. From what I hear, it's been off your entire short life. Repress. Explode. Repress. Explode. On endless repeat."

I inhale sharply. That sounds too right. I can't help wondering… If I had better control over myself, could I have saved Kato?

Pain and loss slice through my chest like a barbed saw. My heart clenches, and I throw up a wall in my mind to block out the sight of blue eyes without any light.

I swallow. Maybe with greater control, I would have known better than to try at all.

An awful smirk contorts Perses's face. "You think that's all you've lost?"

I stop breathing. All of me stops. *Oh Gods, Griffin.*

No. He was injured, but there's no way those wounds would have gotten the better of him. There were healers.

What in the Gods' names is Perses talking about?

My pulse starts to pound, panic hitting my veins like a shot of poison. He's trying to scare me. And it's working.

There's a hitch in my voice. "What do you mean?"

"Zeus sent you here because you overstepped. You wielded the power you were given for something only the Gods should control, and you did it without a hint of restraint. For his *favored one*, he apparently considered a temporary stay in Tartarus to be punishment enough." Perses spits out that revelation in a way that makes me feel like a spoiled child who should have gotten her backside paddled a thousand times over but never did. "But unlike everyone else in Tartarus, Zeus is giving you a second chance. Understand your magic. Finish what you started."

"Understand your magic?" I glare at him. "The magic I didn't even know about for years? That I've never *once* made work like it should? That *no one* will tell me how to use!"

Perses nods.

"Let me make sure I understand this. We're the only two in Tartarus who can get out of here, and *I'm* your second chance?" I laugh just like Mother would and revel in it for once. "That's unfortunate for you."

Bronze eyes bore into mine, humorless, pitiless, flat as coins. "I've waited millennia for this. You will not take it from me. Now wake up, before it's too late!"

He reaches out, and I dart to the side, expecting him to try to hurl me over the cliff again. He doesn't. Instead, he draws a symbol against the cliff wall in front of me, repeating the same archaic swoops and lines in a big square pattern until the invisible traces of power meet again in the place where he started.

I frown, watching him. I'm familiar with the magic. Thanos showed me those ancient figures when he tried to teach me some protective ward marks, but I never used *open*. I only ever tried *lock*, and since lock never worked like it should, the written counter-spell of *open* was moot.

Perses drops his hand from the wall, and the rock shudders, ripples, and then stabilizes again with a new view seeming to come from the inside. There are depth and color and sound. Like a window opening to another world, the square in the rock reveals a scene I recognize. It's the great room in Castle Tarva, the place where we gathered as a family—for what little time we spent there. But it's different, cozier, and filled with a din that's indistinct but that speaks of habitation, activity, and warmth.

The scene swoops in to focus on a man in a chair. The ledge seems to lurch beneath my feet, and my eyes fill with tears. Trembling, I step toward the rock wall, closer to the only man who'll ever make my heart both beat and stall.

"Do you have any idea how much time you've wasted?"

Perses's question comes back to haunt me. Nausea roils in my stomach.

Gray shoots liberally through Griffin's black hair, the silver threads more heavily concentrated at his temples. His face is thicker. Still handsome and strong, but lacking the sharp angles and hard planes of manhood's prime and the trials of war. The familiar lines on his face are deeper, like they've been cut more permanently into his skin. He looks wiser. Settled. Concentrated on his task.

"You think that's all you've lost?"

My heart drops straight through the gaping hole in my middle. I think I've lost a dozen years—or more.

Griffin is seated next to a small but crackling fire. His long legs are stretched out before him and crossed at the ankles. His familiar gray eyes diligently scan the parchment in his hands. He squints a little while reading, which he never used to do. There are more scrolls at his feet, not scattered around like I would no doubt leave them, but stacked tidily next to his chair and placed well away from the fire. When he finishes reading, he neatly rolls up the parchment in his hands, binds it, and then sets it down with the others.

He straightens and lifts his face. His expression lights up at once. *He sees me!*

I reach for him, and my fingertips bump against hard, cool rock.

"Griffin?" I whisper.

He smiles, warm and welcoming, loving, and my heart expands ten sizes in my chest. But then his eyes shift to follow a dark-haired boy who suddenly comes into view. He prances in front of Griffin, a hobbyhorse between his gangly legs and a wooden sword in his small hand.

The lump of emotion clogging my throat turns into something that starts to strangle me. That child is Griffin's. There's no way that he's not.

The hobbyhorse's head is made entirely of deftly woven hellipses grass. The long mane bounces and rustles as the boy makes battle sounds, waving his toy sword and preparing to charge.

A young girl springs into the scene from the side and jumps in front of Griffin, as if to protect him from an enemy. Griffin chuckles and encourages her as she deflects the boy's first blow with her own small sword.

In shock, I stumble back from the vision. The boy looks to be about seven years old and the girl a little younger than that. Her wild, wavy locks are a striking red.

I can't breathe. And I can't look away, even though my breaking heart is screaming at me to run from this.

She's a fierce little thing, and her second thrust with her wooden sword is a ferocious enough jab to put the boy on his guard in earnest. He jumps off the pretend horse, flings the toy aside, and then they both switch to more balanced stances. Laughing and goading each other under Griffin's watchful gaze, the children bang out a mock battle with fluid moves and actual skill. It's a fighting dance of play and trust.

I slam my eyes shut. When I open them again, the scene is still there. Utterly crushing. Entirely real.

Footsteps. A woman's lilting laugh. Sickness heaves through me, shooting acid up my throat. I know what I'll see next.

Knowing still doesn't prepare me for the swift and brutal kick in the gut when Bellanca strides into view, and Griffin's eyes light on her with all the passion, possession, and protection I only ever thought he'd bestow on me. Smiling, she drops into Griffin's lap like she has every right to be there, and his arms come around her waist like it's the most natural thing he could do.

My mouth goes as dry as salt. This can't be happening.

Except it already has. If the boy with the carefully handmade hobbyhorse is anything to judge by, it happened about eight years ago.

My vision wavers, darkening. There's no air, only a grinding weight on my chest. It presses down, crumbling my heart into dust.

Bellanca leans into Griffin, and he nuzzles her fiery curls.

The same satisfied, warmth-filled smile plays around both of their mouths as they watch the children play. *Their* children.

I try to swallow, but there's nothing to wash down my grief. There's not even a scream to drive it out, although I feel it building, silently flaying the inside of my throat.

I didn't come back. I hid from pain and stopped searching for my magic, and while Perses kept throwing me over the cliff and I found nothing to stop him, Griffin and Bellanca found each other. Found love. Griffin would have given me time, waited for me, searched for me. I *know* that. But then... There's always a point when people move on.

Scalding tears track down my cheeks. This is my fault.

A new nightmare crops up in the form of a third child who wanders into view. Another girl. She nestles into her mother's skirts, and Bellanca settles her hand on the girl's small head. Bellanca's free fingers start drawing affectionate, lazy strokes on the back of Griffin's neck, and my heart lurches in protest.

Bellanca is older as well, and no longer the sharp-edged, tight-strung, wild-looking woman I knew. Maturity and maternity have softened her, and her rounded hip is the perfect fit for Griffin's large palm. Her low-cut gown and full breasts draw his attention, and the barely banked heat I recognize in his roving gaze hollows me out inside.

They both look up, distracted at the same time by something new. Bellanca frees her hands only to have them filled back up again with the warm, wiggling weight of a baby.

The part of me that was still trying to somehow deal with this shuts down completely. The nurse backs away, leaving the small bundle in Bellanca's arms. The newcomer is delicate-boned, dark-haired, and clearly another girl, bearing a striking resemblance to what Kaia must have looked like at four or five months old. Bright-blue eyes lock onto her father's face, and the baby girl looks at Griffin like he's the center of her whole world.

Griffin's mouth splits into a wide grin, and he tickles her tummy, making the infant giggle. Then he lifts the little girl still standing by the chair onto the knee Bellanca and the baby aren't occupying and adjusts his embrace to cradle them all.

The already gray world around me darkens to near-black. A sob rips the air from my lungs, and I turn away, choking and trying not to lose my mind as my entire future shatters before me. I fall to my knees and then pitch forward onto all fours, my violent sobs turning into retching. Nothing comes out of me. *And why would it?* There are years of emptiness in my stomach. Hunger I didn't feel. Days I never spent.

I heave. I heave, and I can't breathe.

"You know what to do." Perses cuts through my heart-sickness with flat detachment. "Crack the sky with lightning. Fly through the fracture. Take him back."

Light-headed, I shake all over. "They're a family."

"You were a family."

"Were!" I hurl the word at him, my stomach still trying to turn itself inside out.

"Do you give up so easily? That's not what I heard. But then, you've disappointed me completely so far."

I force myself to breathe more evenly. To swallow. My throat slowly opens back up, and I look at the Titan towering above me, seeing him through a haze of pain and hate. I'll kill, I'll maim, I'll torture, and sometimes, I might not even care. But some things are sacred to me, whether I have them or not.

"Annihilating a family isn't a game to me." And family means everything to Griffin.

"You think he wouldn't choose you." A sly look goes hand in hand with the ancient God's wilting jab.

Sitting back on my heels, I wipe a shaking hand across my mouth. I can't stop my eyes from jumping back to the magic window. I don't want to watch Griffin being happy with someone else, but I also can't look away. My heart hurts with a fierceness I can hardly bear, but I also know deep down that there are worse things than this. Griffin could be dead. He could never have known fatherhood, or his children's love.

"No," I answer dully. "I think he would." But Griffin would never let his children go. They'd always be there, and so would Bellanca. Reminders. Competition. Not mine. Not *ours*. No one would ever be truly happy again.

Resignation settles over me, heavy and dark. Without me there to muddy the waters and force Griffin to tear himself in half, they can be a family forever—in this life, and in the next.

I look at the scene. I hate it, and my heart weeps for what should have been mine. I want Griffin for myself. I want him desperately, but I want him to be happy more.

Perses must read my thoughts, or simply my posture, because his power-deep eyes flare with sudden panic.

I lock my tear-sore gaze with that of the Titan God and chuckle. The sound is so black it's like midnight has invaded my soul. "I guess the hard way didn't work, either."

My physical pain didn't get him out of Tartarus. My emotional destruction didn't even get us off this cliff.

"Fly," Prometheus whispers from the side.

The eagle shrieks. My neighbor grunts in pain. I don't even turn my head. I stare at the beautiful yet horrible tableau painted with living strokes on the rock wall before me. It doesn't change. Time must pass, but they're still in the great room, still curled up in Griffin's chair.

"You wallow in self-pity when you could be taking your life back!" Perses spits out. "It's not too late!"

I gaze at my husband, his wife, and their children. "It was too late the moment you showed me this."

Perses growls like a savage beast. His primordial power ignites around him, flooding the air and biting my skin. The hand he flings toward the scene vibrates with anger. "Then I guess I can get rid of this."

"No!" I leap up, putting myself between the Titan and the rock wall. If I'm going to be here forever, I want at least this much of Griffin with me.

Perses stares me down, his ancient eyes swirling with malice. "You need this, too? We have eternity before us. Are you afraid I can't punish you enough?"

My raw and aching heart jerks in fear. He didn't get what he wanted from me, and now he's going to make me pay. "You son of a Cyclops," I hiss.

"Zeus doesn't come around here often. He'll forget about you and never know about all the fun we'll have together." His metal-bright eyes shift briefly to the great void over the edge of the ledge. When he looks back at me, his voice drops to a lethally soft level that sends ice sliding down my spine. "I can put you back together so slowly you'll beg for mercy before you even have a mouth."

My eyes widen. I want to scream in terror. I also want to rip off his face. "Bastard," I say through clenched teeth.

"Not technically," Perses answers.

"Technical isn't the point when calling someone a bastard!"

One smoky eyebrow lifts. "There's the fire I've heard about. Too bad you didn't find it before this happened." Perses nods to the scene again.

I look, and my throat closes up tight. Griffin and

Bellanca are in a shaded garden now. Her belly is huge and round with child. He leans down and murmurs something in her ear that makes her face light up with happiness and love. Then he sweeps her into his arms and kisses her just like he used to kiss me.

I stare, frozen in place. There are no tears now, only gritty, swollen eyes and lips pressed hard together to keep me from shouting out to people who will never hear me— lips that feel numb and bereft and betrayed.

"You're here. They're there." Perses shrugs his massive shoulders, the movement filled with tension and dislike. "You're not much of a fighter. I don't know why Zeus thought you could have finished what you started. It all stopped when you did."

The disgust in his voice is tangible, and I can almost taste it on the dreary air. But I couldn't care less what Perses thinks of me. What's the point of caring about anything anymore?

"You lost your favored soldier in the war, but you *gave up* everything else. Maybe it's for the best. You? You're not what anyone needs anymore. But look at them. They fit just right. They're perfect together, made for each other."

Perses's hateful words scrape through my mind like a sharp and rusty trowel digging for roots—the root of something important to me, something I know deep down and forever.

Made for each other?

A blast of heat bursts outward from my chest and nearly ruptures my heart.

No. No, they're not.

Griffin was made for *me*, predestined to be my partner in life, and death, and whatever else there could possibly be. He was handpicked by the ruling Pantheon and physically altered for *me*. Poseidon, Ares, Athena, and Persephone all told me as much. He's *my* husband. *Mine*.

The sudden, sure knowledge that Griffin would never betray me bubbles up through me like a last, lifesaving breath of air before I drown. New pieces fit into place like the rest of the jagged, rough-cut bricks that make up my shaky foundation. Artemis once said that Zeus has plans for me. I guess this is it, or at least part of it. My bloody bastard of a far-removed grandfather saw this coming from months, maybe even years, away. Or maybe he had it planned out with his rotten friends the Fates and all those other conniving Gods before I was even born.

I clench my hands into fists. I want to wring Zeus's despicable, unfeeling Olympian neck.

"You lost your favored soldier in the war..."

The battle was over, won, but Zeus still sacrificed Kato in order to show me what I was capable of. He delivered an epic slap-down in the form of a God Bolt and then dropped me in Tartarus to teach me my place. He sent Perses with a special blend of pain and heartache to try to channel me into a middle ground, and just leave it to an all-powerful Olympian weasel like Zeus to think that torment and anguish can lead to anything good or sane.

My gaze bores into the deceitful scene of Griffin and Bellanca. I see both red and black, my vision on dark fire. It also clears at last.

With the sure knowledge that Zeus is a scheming toad I'll never trust again, I howl and launch myself at the treacherous beast of an illusion Perses so heartlessly conjured against the cliff wall.

CHAPTER 26

HOPE AND WRATH IGNITE, SLAMMING TOGETHER LIKE TWO irreconcilables that somehow work as one. I roar in fury. My pulse thunders with the violence of a breaking storm, and I pound my palms against the scene, not even feeling the hard impact of rough stone. Power surges in my veins, awakening with the force of a cosmic blast.

I'm going to get out of here. I swear to the Gods, I will. But first, I'm going to erase the deceit that tore out my heart and threw it down a dark hole. I'm going to eradicate it with my bare hands, destroy it with the force of my own blows.

The shelf of rock rumbles beneath my feet. Fissures form in the cliffside, sending stones tumbling down the vertical slope. Prometheus groans, his chains rattling and his big body shaking to the rhythm of my rage.

The illusion shudders, and Perses grabs my arm to jerk me away from it. I swing around with preternatural speed and strength and punch him in the throat. The ichor-laced Olympian brew in my blood must be worth something, because just like that day I attacked Piers for his treachery, it's a brilliant hit. Fast. Instinctual. Precise. I strike Perses right where it counts, crushing his windpipe. The Titan's eyes pop wide open, and his face turns purple from pain and lack of breath. He stumbles back from me, clutching his neck.

He'll recover quickly enough—he's a bloody God, after all—but his brief incapacity will give me the time I need to rattle his spell.

I spin back around and pound on the wall again.

"Show me the truth!" Violence and savagery and total shock make me pummel the granite with all my strength. If there's one thing I should know, should *always* know, it's the Gods damn truth!

I should have suspected sooner, or not been so easily convinced. But this is the first time in my *entire existence* that anyone has succeeded in lying to me. Perses didn't just get away with a falsehood; he crushed me with one. He used the love of my life to do it. I can hardly breathe— like someone punched out *my* throat. The gut-awful, heart-wrenching feeling of the wool being pulled over my eyes is completely foreign to me. It's horrifying. Debasing. Blindsiding. I'll never lie again.

I don't know if my Kingmaker Magic doesn't work in Tartarus, or if it doesn't work on deities, and I don't care. I finally truly understand why Griffin went so crazy the day he found out I'd been dishonest with him for weeks. He had faith in me, believed in me, and I stomped all over his trust. I don't love or trust Perses, but his coldhearted, calculated deception cuts me to the quick. This level of deceit is unconscionable, for anyone, anywhere. Wrong. A thousand times wrong—for humans, creatures, or Gods.

"I want the truth!" I scream at the wall.

My palms split open on the sharp edges of the newly splintered rock, and my blood instantly changes the scene.

I gasp. It's Griffin. *My* Griffin. Finally—the truth.

Blood Magic. I've never understood it. Didn't want to. That was Mother's domain. I know it's an amplifier. I know powerful blood leaves a trace in the air. I know you can find people with it, but instead of someone finding me, this time, I've found my someone.

He's in Castle Tarva, but not in any warm or cozy family

room. He's in the bedroom we shared. There are no noises around. No fire. No scrolls. There's no gray in his hair, but his eyes are dull, and somehow, they do seem old. He looks haggard. And terribly bruised. The blows he and Flynn exchanged in Sykouri still mark his face with fading yellows and blues. The cut at the top of his forehead closed messily, obviously without any magical care. Raw and red, the fresh scar flashes angrily from beneath a disheveled fall of hair.

Relief sears my eyes, but I don't let the heat burn into tears. I don't want anything to blur my view of Griffin. I know the normal rate of healing, what time does to cuts and bruises and blows. I know that two to three weeks have passed, not half my life in years!

Perses suddenly flings past my shoulder a jug of water he got from only the Gods know where. The earthenware container cracks against the cliffside, its contents diluting my blood and erasing the symbols he drew on the wall.

"No! Come back!" I reach out, trying to hold on to Griffin, but he's already gone.

My heart breaks again, but not quite so hard. Turning, I swing hate-filled eyes on Perses. He'll pay for this.

"You deserve Tartarus." I advance on him, not caring that I'm half his size, not anywhere near as powerful, and not at all immortal. "You dare to pass judgment on my humanity when you have none? You're a cold-hearted monster. You should be the one chained up and getting your liver pecked out. Or starving. Or forever rolling that rock up the hill." I throw a hand toward Sisyphus. He's still at it. He always is.

Perses shrugs, like he didn't just attempt to carve me up and let my soul bleed out with grief.

"You think you're so clever, so above mankind, but you're not even smart enough to understand us lowly humans and our mortal hearts." I glance down at the great, somber valley I've seen the bottom of too many times and then laugh right in the Titan's face. The sound couldn't be more razor-sharp if my teeth were serrated to points. "You need me to find the spark—that buried ember of magic that will get us both out of here and make your dreams come true. But you drown me in pain. You show me everything I don't have to live for. You fling me from agony to loss."

I shake my head at this ancient God who hasn't roamed the worlds since the creation of human beings. The only people he knows are the ones who got stuck right here in Tartarus, just like him. Probably not the best slice of humanity from which to learn. Zeus supplied him with the essentials about me, but clearly that wasn't enough. How could it be, when I've just at long last understood something essential about myself?

The Elemental Magic I only recently learned was inside me and could never grasp how to use finally leaps to my bidding, ready and eager. It's all suddenly so clear. I'm not powerful just because of my heritage, or my innate magic, or my stubborn-as-a-donkey will. I'm powerful because there are people in my life who refused to let me be alone, even when I was so desperately convinced that I should be, even when I thought that solitude was what I both needed and deserved.

The steadfast weight of Griffin's devotion and optimism, of Beta Team's loyalty and friendship, of my new family's acceptance and love... All of it slowly bore down on the conflicted scales inside of me until they tipped, and Elpis climbed into the brighter cup. Now, in the endless gray twilight of Tartarus, that brighter side of the balance thunks down hard, once and for all. The magic I've needed isn't about fear. It's always been about hope.

Even without wings, I suddenly soar. "Listen carefully, you imbecilic, incompetent, worthless fool of a God, because I'm about to give you the secret to dealing with mankind. And you can tell Zeus when you see him next, since he obviously needs the reminder." I step toward Perses again, getting so close I burn from his primeval magic and heat. Currents of lightning snap and spiral a sizzling path through my blood, no longer dormant or hidden from me. I can have my husband. I can have a family. I can have my kingdom. I can have it all, because despite my flaws, I deserve happiness, and I'll do my very best to bring it to others as well.

"A crushed spark never ignites," I tell Perses. "That's not how you fan the flame."

I shoot out my hand and smack the Titan right in the sternum just as a lightning bolt rolls down my arm. It doesn't fracture the air, but it fractures Perses. The immediate crack of thunder shocks my eardrums and makes Prometheus let out a long, low moan. Through smoke and noise, I see the bloody, charred mess of what's left of the Titan's barrel chest as he flies backward off the ledge. I catch the look of utter agony on his face and don't feel a hint of remorse.

A deep, steadying breath anchors inside me my previously elusive power. I take control of the turbulent magic, learning it, taming it, and finally making it my own. The storm settles, but an underlying current of lightning still hums and purrs in my veins, branching out through every part of me and settling like a lazy cat in the sun into all the places where I know I can always find it again.

Grim satisfaction curves my mouth into a hard almost-smile Mother could be proud of. Then, with just a thought, I make the power ignite again and shoot another bolt straight out in front of me. The Elemental Magic only Zeus and I possess leaves a zigzagging path of light across the otherwise monochrome sky. It cuts through the gray and hangs there, waiting. It's my door.

Now I have to find my wings.

(6)

I don't think for a second that this is going to be easy. I don't feel even a tickle in my chest or a pinch in my shoulder blades, and that can't be good.

Not to motivate me—I'm pretty Gods damn motivated now—but because I can't stand the emptiness here for one more second while I try to figure this out, I use my own blood to draw the same archaic magic symbols that Perses used back on to the rock wall. I paint the four sides of the square, focus all my heart and mind on Griffin, and open a window back to him.

He hasn't moved, but the shadows in the bedroom have grown heavier. There are still no flaming candles. There's no fire burning in the hearth. He sits in a chair and stares out the open window, his face so bleak and filled with pain that I don't know if he's desperately hoping against all hope that I'll appear, or trying to come to grips with the fact that I won't. He's utterly still. Palpably devastated.

"I'm coming," I tell him, wiping my bloodstained hands on my pants and knowing full well that Griffin can't hear me. But by Gods, I am.

Wings. No human should have them, but I somehow do. *So where are they?*

I pace back and forth along the narrow rock ledge, thinking, *wishing*. I push out with my lungs. Spread my arms. Tense my back. There's no flutter in my chest. No tickling brush of wings against my ribs. There's absolutely nothing besides the cold lump of worry that starts to inhabit my breast. It grows with each passing, wingless moment, despite the latent heat now coursing through my veins from the Elemental Magic I've found at last.

Multiple elements. I understand now that it's not just lightning stirring my blood. The ground rumbling under my feet? Fissures snaking up walls, and storms brewing all around me? It was all there—air, earth, the thunderbolt—manifesting for the first times as those scales inside me tipped slowly out of the quagmire of my past, tipped slowly toward believing that I could have—that I *deserved*—a better life.

I nearly snort out loud. Funny to think that something as intangible as brightness outweighs muck and mud.

I turn on my heel and walk the length of the ledge again. Starting to balance my hopes against my fears revealed my magic to me. Finally understanding optimism brought the power to life.

I spin around, my frenetic strides devouring the small shelf of rock and forcing me to turn again after only a few steps. I clench my hands into fists. Too bad I didn't figure this out sooner. I could have given Galen Tarva the thrashing he deserved. I know without a doubt that I could crack open the ground right now and toss the broken rocks around on a gale. I could have helped Ianthe fight.

A sharp pain slices through me at the thought of my sister. Gods, I hope she's all right.

I whirl again, muttering a curse under my breath. It's infuriating to know that I've been both spoiled rotten and methodically crushed by the powers that reign. I can't even pretend to be surprised. No one ever said Olympians were logical. They're mercurial, vengeful, fickle—a Gods awful lot of all-powerful beings playing around with people and worlds because what else does one do with an eternity of existence?

That doesn't mean they don't care about outcomes. About individuals. About *me*—although I'm not entirely certain that's good fortune or bad. My life would have been very different without their interest, and likely a lot shorter. The Gods' actions are mysteries, their dealings and emotions unpredictable. They measure time in eons rather than in years and can set trials into motion with generations to spare.

What's less of a mystery to me now is Zeus. The King of Gods is a stinker, smellier than a round of goat cheese. Thalyria went to the dogs, so Grandpa Zeus set me up as the new Origin, the living, breathing equivalent of *Hey, let's try this!*

I scowl, whipping around again and pacing with energy at odds with the dull monotony of Tartarus. I guess I should never have expected so much from a deity with his own private, eternal torture chamber. He was bound to be lacking a heart.

Self-determination? Sure, with a few major tweaks and significant nudges along the way.

Healing? Here, have Griffin—a great force of stubbornness predestined just for you. Not only will he eventually succeed in making you hate yourself less, but he'll push you into that pesky destiny you've been trying so hard to avoid.

Bring Thalyria full circle? Why not? If we can. That's everyone's plan, after all—the Gods' and ours. Why not bask in a little peace and glory before whatever new path we establish opens up all avenues again?

I shake my head, stomping along the ledge. Endless cycles. Human choices. The Gods watching it all and manipulating outcomes. Because above all, we're entertainment to them, albeit entertainment they might become attached to.

Thalyria today. Attica, Atlantis, or even Tartarus tomorrow. *Who knows?*

I'm a pawn. Griffin is a pawn. Probably in what was a moment of curiosity for them, the Gods threw idealistic optimism and bleak-hearted cynicism together and waited to see what would happen next, which one of us would temper the other.

Are they surprised to find that Griffin's loyalty and steadfastness won out over my distrust and doubt? If they are, they're idiotic and, once again, don't understand the human heart. What every person longs for is a connection, whether they'll admit it or not. I'll bet even Mother does, deep down, somewhere in her most secret and lonely thoughts.

I stop and reach out but don't touch the image of Griffin, too afraid of disturbing the magic with my dried blood. I need to get back to him, to what we're meant to do. My speculation about the Gods and their motives is worthless if I'm stuck on a cliffside in Tartarus. In fact, my guesswork doesn't matter at all, because the Fates have already laid down their map. All that matters is what *I* do next. Which path *I* choose.

And I know exactly where I'm going, which means I need my wings back.

I watch Griffin through time and space and magic, mentally commanding my obstinate wings to spring free. I demand forcefully. I coax. I try using compulsion on myself, but apparently I can't control my own mind, at least not in that way. My heart and psyche converge, and I focus so intently on Griffin, yearning for him, that tears cloud my vision. Nothing I do works. Hours pass with no more success than before, and fear and anxiety at my lack of progress start to creep through me like a poisonous vine.

Apart from when the wings were shocked out of me by some Olympian force, I've only felt any evidence of them with Griffin—when something he did made me feel treasured, or needed, or loved. He's here with me now, in a sense, but it's not the same, and it doesn't give me whatever magical potion of emotion I need to set my wings to beating.

I worry my lower lip with nervous bites. I pace. I curse. Griffin sits like a dark statue in the night-blanketed room until dawn finally breathes pale colors across his face. He looks awful, like he hasn't slept in weeks.

I don't know what to do. Ares smacked me in the chest, and my wings popped out. I thump my own chest. Again. Harder. It doesn't work.

Not entirely sure it's a good idea, I point a lightning bolt at myself. I let fly, and the hot, bright flash of magic doesn't do anything to me, not even singe my grubby clothing.

Bollocks! Bollocks again!

I turn to Prometheus. The eagle will be coming soon, and the Titan is watching me with a sort of blank insistence that makes me wonder if he sees anything at all.

Our eyes meet from across the short distance of sheer cliff, and my heart turns over heavily in my chest. He's suffering. He's so close to me, but so completely unreachable as well.

"Fly," he whispers for the hundredth time.

I plant my hands on my hips. "Any ideas how?"

"Fly," he says with more intensity, his eyes wide and emphatic now.

Huh. He's as helpful as everyone else.

CHAPTER 27

FOUR AND A HALF THALYRIAN DAYS, TWO LIVERS, AND NO WINGS later, I make a shallow slice across my palm, dip a finger from my other hand into the gathering pool of blood, and then draw a second square of symbols onto the cliffside wall. When my *open* is complete, I think of Ianthe.

The magic is so easy with just a small trace of my blood. She appears before me instantly, and I exhale the restlessness I'd been harboring in my chest since the moment she left with Lycheron. I'd needed to see her, to be sure she was all right.

Her head is tipped forward for the moment, and her loose hair obscures my view of her face. She's in a dress unlike anything I've ever seen before, like she's wrapped in a fluffy, white cloud from the neck down. It's cinched at the waist with a ropelike sash, and to be honest, I'd want to live in a garment like that if I had one. Maybe it's Nymph gear, or something Lycheron picked up somewhere else. Magical creatures aren't bound to their world like humans are. Olympus is their universal hub, just like for the Gods.

It's well past dusk wherever she is on the Fisan border, and another day in Thalyria is crawling toward night. Unlike Griffin, who only sits in the dark, Ianthe moves from candle to candle, illuminating her tent. Her surroundings look comfortable, truly cozy and warm. I see a table and chairs, a bathing corner with a big brass tub it must have taken a few Ipotane to carry in there, a pile of books, and a chest for clothes.

Lycheron gains a few points in my book—and I *am* keeping score—because he obviously supplied Ianthe with whatever she needed after she left us with nothing but the clothes on her back, not even her protective pearls.

I touch them at my waist. Even here, I wear them to protect Little Bean from outside influences. No compulsion can get through them, no mind control or planted thoughts. Mother can't reach my baby. With any luck, the Gods can't, either.

In Ianthe's tent, the remnants of a one-person meal wait on a tray, ready to be taken out. Ianthe obviously ate alone, and I wonder where Lycheron is. He didn't look like he was planning on letting her out of his sight when he galloped off with her...*what? Two months ago now?*

Of that time, I've been in Tartarus far too long. The tangle of nerves in my abdomen draws ever tighter, and it isn't Little Bean doing something odd. She only kicked that once, and if I couldn't feel the steady hum of her life force inside me, I'd be terrified she was gone. She's just not growing here, not changing at all while I try to figure out how to get us both home.

Far from me and yet only a few feet away, Ianthe moves a painted screen of folding panels off to one side and then lights the candles near the previously concealed bed. It's not so much a bed as a large pallet of cushions and furs, the luxurious pile thick enough to be nicely raised off the rug-covered ground. It looks like something a weary body could sink into and not want to get out of for days. The bulky, warm weight of the golden fleece crowns off the bedding, sprawled haphazardly across the top.

The tawny, one-of-a-kind treasure reminds me so much of Kato that something painful roars across my chest. My heart screams, and it's all I can do not to scream along with it.

Blinking hard, I push past the tear in my soul and focus again on Ianthe instead, watching her as she continues to chase the shadows from her snug little corner of the world. When she finishes her tasks around the tent, she sets the candle she was using to light the others down on the table and then looks up, seemingly right at me.

I take in every detail of her face. The straight nose, the green eyes, the small but stubborn chin. I miss her. I lost her too soon and then found her too late. I fear our time will never come.

Ianthe isn't really looking at me, though. She has no idea I'm watching her. She must hear something, because she glances toward the tent's door just before Lycheron pushes his large, muscular frame through the heavy flap, his imposing presence instantly filling more than his fair share of space.

Stillness grips them both the moment their gazes lock. Neither of them seems to remember to breathe. A current passes between them that I don't have to see or feel to know is there. The raw strength of it reaches me even here. I swear a natural disaster could crack the world wide open under their feet right now, and they wouldn't even notice falling in. Nothing but the two of them exists.

I snap my jaw shut. It's epically apparent they've formed a deep attachment—far beyond mere interest or lust. I get the strangest impression of the two of them both settling and vibrating, like being in the same room together is as much a comfort as a thrill.

I see it in them, because it's so much like Griffin and me. They haven't touched. They haven't spoken. *But oh Gods, I think they're in love.*

Ianthe finally breathes. As if to steady herself, she curls her fingers around the edge of the table, gripping it hard.

"Did you find out anything?" The slight hitch in her voice hints at both eagerness and fear.

My heart speeds up, making me realize how starved I am for living noises, for words besides my own. Tartarus is a lonely place, each of us trapped and isolated in our own solitary punishment or labor. Besides grunting his thanks for food he hardly touches, Griffin doesn't speak. When he leaves the bedroom, he must talk—presumably, he still has two realms to run—but he always comes back, silent and brooding, and I can't seem to follow him anywhere else. The last conversation I had was with Perses. The Titan hasn't reappeared, although he's no longer a crumpled heap down on the valley floor. And Prometheus is the very antithesis of talkative. Ianthe's is the first much-needed and familiar voice I've heard.

After a slight hesitation, Lycheron answers her with a small shake of his head. "No, little dove. Nothing."

Shock stamps a startled look across Ianthe's face. Her eyes widen, and her lips part, forming a small, crestfallen oval. She makes no effort to hide her emotions. They're right there, written all over her features.

"But Talia can't just have disappeared. Someone must know *something*," she says.

Her disappointment has an obvious impact on Lycheron, as plain to see as Ianthe's own unguarded distress. His jaw hardens, and a visible twitch vibrates along his long equine back. He moves farther into the tent, his glossy black coat gleaming in the flickering candlelight. Fluid muscle ripples beneath his skin. The Ipotane Alpha exudes virility and strength like the sun radiates heat and light, all that masculine potency an inherent part of his very nature.

"If they do, they're not telling me," he answers, a sour note creeping in to embitter the deep timbre of his voice.

He ties the tent flap closed behind him, and then to my utter astonishment, he turns into a man. Not a horse-man, just a man. Well, not *just* a man. A naked, glorious, huge-in-every-possible-way man. It only takes a second, a blink of an eye, to make the seamless transition from brawny magical creature to jaw-dropping, powerful male.

My chin hits my chest. Ianthe doesn't seem surprised, but a flood of color still blazes across her cheeks. She lowers her gaze. I don't. My eyes are huge. I can't stop staring.

So that's how they do it. I'd wondered how those Nymphs could possibly manage, how anything could…fit.

I cock my head. Fitting might still take some work.

Lycheron reaches for a garment much like Ianthe's, only bigger, and inserts his thick arms into the sleeves. He ties the sash, covering his nakedness and leaving only a vee at his neck, his striking face and his long mane of black hair visible on top. Strong calves and attractive bare feet flash as he rounds the table to reach Ianthe. He steps toward her and then cups her jaw in his large hands, gently tilting her face back up.

Lycheron's thumbs brush a tender stroke over her cheek-bones, as if writing an apology right onto her skin. "I consulted Artemis in her icy labyrinth, but she wasn't talking. I went to the lake at the Phthian Gap, but that bastard Titos didn't even show up for me. I combed Sykouri a hundred times and then a hundred more trying to pick up her scent, but the God Bolt cooked everything within the walls. I don't know how anyone survived in there, even though they somehow did. I smell her going in, but there's no trace of her ever leaving again." Frowning, he delves his hands into Ianthe's thick, dark hair, holding the sides of her head. "I'm sorry, my love. I don't know where your sister is."

I startle at the importance of the endearment, even

though I *knew* just from watching them. Talk about taming the beast. It took Ianthe a matter of weeks to have Lycheron laid out at her feet.

Ianthe forces down a hard swallow. She tilts her head, leaning into his touch, and the vulnerability she's willing to show makes it pretty clear that she's laid out at his feet as well.

I look back and forth between them, trying to shift everything I knew about them into this new paradigm. The Lycheron I encountered those few times was sly and volatile and patently out for himself. I can scarcely reconcile the care and calm I'm seeing in him now.

Then again, while compassionate and ready to defend, the Ianthe I last saw was also a tight, brittle ball of rage and reserve—hardly the unguarded woman in the tent.

She lifts a hand between them and lightly touches the triangle of bronzed skin at the hollow of his neck. "I missed you. While you were gone. I..." She presses her lips together, flattening her mouth before speaking again. "I didn't sleep as well."

Lycheron's ocher eyes slide closed as he leans down and places a lingering kiss on her forehead. It's ardent. Not chaste, but not invasive or demanding, either.

Ianthe's hand slides down, opening the garment to the center of Lycheron's sculpted chest. Her fingers visibly tremble as she traces the hoof-shaped scar on his left pectoral. Lycheron straightens, holding very still.

Her eyes flick up, meeting his. "Will you make me forget?"

My chest implodes, collapsing into a hard knot. She's not talking about me. Well, maybe a little bit, but my disappearance isn't really what she wants to forget.

Lycheron knows it, too, and his eyes flare with amber

light. His glowing eyes are still frightening, but not to Ianthe. They burn with an *I will crush all your nightmares under my hooves and defend you with my body and my life* kind of light, two blazing infernos of absolute promise—and what woman doesn't want that?

Ianthe shivers, and Lycheron sweeps his hands down her arms, chasing away her chills.

She leans forward and presses a sweet kiss to the arching blemish imprinted onto his torso. It's a little awkward. A lot hesitant. Lycheron looks like he's in pain.

His voice drops to a quiet rasp. "If you want to stop, we stop. You're in control."

My heart shatters, my eyes burn, and just like that, Lycheron earns my eternal gratitude. Somewhere between Ianthe deciding to gallop off with him to ensure the Ipotane's menacing presence on the Fisan border and this moment now, she and Lycheron have become friends, and so much more. I didn't think it was possible, didn't imagine it, but Lycheron must have depths he chose to reveal—or found—only for her.

The expression on his face as he looks down at my sister—passion, protection, need, patience—it all combines to tell me that she's confided in him, trusted him with things that happened at the hands—and body—of Galen Tarva that she's hardly even hinted at to me, and that Lycheron was worthy of her trust. And that means that no matter his strange past behavior toward me or his dubious dealings with Griffin, for as long as Ianthe wants him in her life, he has a place with us.

Unfortunately, *life* may be a problematic term for them. Eternity rarely mixes well with mortality. There are things about it that simply don't work.

But Lycheron and Ianthe don't seem to care—at least not

right now. They're more interested in the kiss that begins heating up between them. It turns positively scorching.

Lycheron breaks the embrace to drag Ianthe's roaming hand over his heart. Breathing hard, he holds it there.

"Do you feel this?" His powerful rumble of a voice could never be soothing, and his eyes glow with a heated intensity that's not even close to being metaphorical. Everything about him screams *danger*, but Ianthe isn't threatened at all.

"I feel it," she answers huskily.

"It beats for you."

My breath catches. Ianthe molds herself to her surprising creature and seeks his mouth again with hers. I reach out and smear my blood across their images, wiping the scene from the rock. She's in good hands, safe, and whatever happens next is no one's business but their own.

I close my eyes, still seeing them. Ianthe and Lycheron are two beings that needed each other. As individuals they were one thing. Together they're something else. A new creation. Something *more*.

And that reminds me of the person I most need to get back to, of how in Griffin my jagged pieces found a safe place to become a whole. He shored up my foundation, but I've always been the mason of my own construction. I know the placement of every stone. I know that each building block has a flip side that's shown itself and will show itself again—light, dark, forgiving, vengeful, protective, violent. I know there are things I'll do, things I won't, and things I'll always struggle with. And in the perpetual gray of Tartarus, I take a deep breath and finally decide that that's okay.

CHAPTER 28

The sudden burn in my shoulder blades catches me off guard. The unexpected rip and pop and grow lasts mere seconds, but for the time it takes for my wings to spring free, it hurts like Cerberus is scraping poisonous fangs down my back.

The throbbing quickly fades. I glance over my shoulder, and my new wings reveal a regular pattern of white and black. White is the more dominant color, with only the tips of each feather steeped in shadow. The root is light. The periphery is tarnished. I look at them, and know that each individual feather is a reflection of me.

Deeply satisfied with the fitting new shading, I flex my wings. *Balance*. I have it now. Or at least I know what it looks and feels like. I understand how it functions inside me. Some days the scales will tip one way, some days the other, and as long as I don't lose sight of what's at my center, I can accept that, just as Griffin always has. I don't need to be perfect, or have all the answers. I just have to be me, and fair, and do my best for the people and place I love.

I kiss my fingertips and then press them against the still-open window to Griffin. As I drop my hand, I wipe the scene from the stone. I won't leave any part of him here when I go.

My lightning strike still marks a slashing door in front of me over the valley. The blaze intensifies, as if beckoning me, and my heart pulls me straight toward it. I take a step toward the edge of the ledge. I don't have any idea how this works, and I can't see anything beyond the bright tear in the air, but I know Thalyria is on the other side. I hope if I concentrate hard enough on Griffin, I'll go to him first.

Soon, though, because I'm not done here yet.

I turn to Prometheus. This is going to be tough.

"Fly," he whispers when our gazes connect. His eyes are bright and alive with something for the first time since the fog lifted and revealed the tortured Titan. It's happiness. Hope. Not for himself, but for me.

I smile, my own joy reaching out to meet his. "Not without you, my friend."

Two flaps of my wings take me across the space that's separated us all this time. I hover before him, the steady beat of my feathers fanning us both. Prometheus flinches away from me, pressing himself against the cliff. I understand—a winged creature coming at him usually spells pain and organ loss.

"Look at me." I keep my voice soft but firm.

Slowly, he turns his head, his eyes uncertain now.

"Do you know the world of Thalyria?"

He shakes his head, making me wonder where he roamed before he ended up in Tartarus. His story certainly spread. As did his gift of fire.

"Thalyria is my world. I want to take you there. Will you come with me?"

His eyes dart to one of the thick chains holding him tightly against the rock wall and then back to me again. I read the question there. His four limbs are shackled to the cliff.

"I'm going to melt the chains off you. It might hurt."

His stare is blank for a moment, but then he gives a quick nod, little more than a jerk of his bearded chin.

I glance at the air behind me, assuring myself that my vertical door home continues well down toward the valley floor. Once the Titan is loose, we won't be going up—or even out very far. Wings or no wings, with his weight, we'll drop.

Lowering myself, I say, "I'm going to start with this foot." I touch his bare ankle, finding the skin under his bindings so callused and tough that I wonder if he'll even feel the burn through the thousands of years of thick, hard skin he's built up. "Ready?"

I don't wait for his answer but call power to my finger-tips and try to control the surge of lightning as I grip the shackle with both hands and pull. The metal glows red-hot and grows malleable. I rip it apart, freeing Prometheus's foot. His skin does blister from the heat, and I'm sorry for it, but he doesn't say a word. As for me, I feel no pain or burn.

Gently, I guide his big foot onto the peg-like anchor fixing the chain to the cliff. "Put your weight here," I tell him.

Beating my wings to hover steadily, I free his other foot. Slowly, Prometheus bends his knee enough to balance his weight atop the chain's anchor without my help. I hear his bones creak as he moves, and then he groans. He's stand-ing for the first time in millennia. The angle on his arms shifts, and he groans louder still, probably as much in pain as relief. Like me, he doesn't appear to have changed from his original state in any way besides forming the calluses under his bindings. His body is strong and hard, beautifully sculpted and muscled—and likely as heavy as an ox. His mind, though... I have a feeling it's not nearly as intact.

A gentle push on the air brings me to eye level with his right wrist. I melt the shackle off, leaving more burns in exchange for his freedom. I press the now-dangling chain into Prometheus's trembling hand. "Hold this for balance. Don't let go."

I look him hard in the eyes, trying to get him to focus on me and maybe stop shaking. He's going to rattle us both off the cliff.

"I need your help," I say. "It's very important. Prometheus?"

He blinks, glances away from me to look at his giant hand gripping the chain, and then brings a steadier gaze back to my face.

"I don't think I can hold you up." Actually, I know I can't, but there's a difference between outright lying and not being abysmal. "*You* need to send us into that light. You see it, don't you?"

His eyes jerk to a spot beyond my shoulder and then shift down. He nods, another quick dip of his chin.

"After I free this hand, *you* grab me, and *you* push us off the cliff. You push us right into that light." The muscles in his legs are enough to make three times the leap I ever could. I just hope they're not too stiff to work. "I'll do my best to fly and guide us, but we're going to fall. You understand that, right?"

"Fly," he whispers, and my heart clenches so hard it stops.

I nod. "Yes. Fly." *Gods, I hope so, anyway.* "Flip us so that I'm on top."

He nods again, understanding that he needs to twist us in the air, or we'll end up performing an experiment in upside-down wing use that's sure to end poorly.

"What...about...on the...other side?" Prometheus asks haltingly.

Emotion rips through my chest and steals my breath. It's the first time he's said anything but *fly*, and to me, his rusty voice is sweeter than a song.

"I'm going to think really hard about arriving down

low," I answer. "And hope for the best." Because really, what else can I do?

His eyes search mine, and for the first time, I notice their color—a rich hazel that seems to mix every palette of the earth and sky. Back to a whisper, he says, "Thank you."

I smile, even though this huge, generous, damaged male tears me up inside. "Don't thank me yet. We still might fall to our deaths."

He frowns, and his hand twitches like he wants to release his grip on the chain and reach for me. He doesn't. "Don't say that, firebird. I would let go of you first."

And then I would fly. Oh Gods damn it, I'm going to cry. Prometheus—ever selfless, willing to sacrifice his eternity for the comfort of man.

I swallow, my throat thick. Well, his punishment is over. Today, I make sure his life begins again.

"Don't you dare let go," I say fiercely, my voice unsteady and low. "We'll make it out. Together."

He doesn't deny or confirm. He doesn't even give me that bumpy jerk of his chin.

"Ready?" I ask, taking hold of the final chain and letting my hands begin to heat. I don't wait for an answer any more than I did the first time. I melt the metal until I can pry it apart, and Prometheus grabs the loose chain, steadying himself.

We're not touching yet, but I see and feel him gathering himself before me, getting lower and winding up tight so that he can spring off his footholds in one sudden burst.

I take a deep breath. Here goes everything. "Go!" I shout.

With a roar, Prometheus lets go of the shackles that have bound him for lifetimes and throws his arms around my waist. At the same time, he uses his muscular legs to propel us outward and send us both flying out over the valley. He heaves his great weight to one side, and we spin in the air so that I'm on top.

"Umph!" My whole body goes vertical, with Prometheus dangling from his crushing grip. His colossal weight drags us both down fast, but he jumped far enough out that we're almost to the door. I beat my wings, straining fever-ishly, and somehow bring us closer to the fissure between Tartarus and Thalyria. Gritting my teeth, I flap hard and push. I'll get us there. I swear to the Gods, I will.

We plummet toward the bottom of the bright line in the sky, and I grip Prometheus's shoulders so hard I'll leave marks. There's no way I'm letting him go. I have more lightning, but every instinct in me screams that this first blast I shot into the gray is my one and only door. That power was a one-time deal—my reward. The gate will close behind me, and I won't have that ability anymore. If we fall too far, I can fly back up here, even from the valley floor, but I could never lift my passenger again. This is Prometheus's only chance.

But what about Sisyphus? And that starving man with his fruit? I feel a moment of panic that I can't take more people with me but then push it aside. I can't save every-one. But I'll save the one I can.

With a scream and a mighty flap of wings I feel all the way to my toes, I fly us the few more feet we need to tumble through the very base of the lightning door. We're both shouting now, the Titan's mammoth arms clamped around my waist, my wings stretched out and pounding hard. We hurtle down a long tunnel with blind-ing, white-hot walls. Through it all, I somehow manage to envision a lot of things. Griffin. The inner courtyard of Castle Tarva. Not being far above the ground. I even manage a big, fat, rude hand gesture directed right at

Zeus along with a *Ha!* and an *I took your prisoner, and I am* not *giving him back!*

And just when I'm at my most irreverent, an all-encompassing, bearded male fills the space around us. Deeply powerful eyes settle first on me and then on my hulking cargo. It's Zeus. This time, I'm sure of it. He nods to us, as if we did something right, not terrible. A similar male with a golden trident appears and mouths words I can't hear, looking satisfied and even happy. Another figure soon joins them, as if called to the gathering in this huge and distorted space between worlds. The newcomer is sleek, shadowed, and sinfully attractive—the Lord of the Underworld, I have no doubt.

Seeming pleased by the turn of events, Zeus, Poseidon, and Hades all nod to each other and then blink out of my awareness, leaving only the blinding flashes and branching crackles of the passageway around us.

But then a weightlessness grips us, arresting all motion. I draw in a sharp breath at the sudden change in velocity, and Prometheus tightens his hold on me, as if afraid we'll drift apart. All goes suddenly dark.

I blink, trying to adjust my sight. No, not just dark. Night. And there are torches all around us.

The weightlessness abruptly disappears, and we drop, falling straight into the heart of Thalyria.

CHAPTER 29

THERE'S HARDLY TIME TO GASP BEFORE WE LAND IN A BONE-jarring heap. Prometheus takes the brunt of the fall, and I come down on top of him. He doesn't breathe at all, both sides of him punched hard. I recover first and scramble off him, getting my weight off his chest. His first inhale wheezes in his throat. His second doesn't sound much better, but it goes deeper, expanding his lungs. He sits up with a grimace, and guards close in. About twenty blades aim for his throat.

"No!" I throw out my arms, shielding him. Getting to Prometheus means going through me. Everyone stops instantly.

But no one stops yelling. The yelling is deafening. It's pandemonium. Celebration. "Queen Catalia! Queen Catalia!" My ears ring with my own name, and the noise is an uproar I can hardly bear after the dullness of Tartarus.

I inch closer to Prometheus, letting his massive body buffer me from some of the overwhelming welcome. Maybe I'm shielding him as well. He doesn't look any more comfortable than I feel.

Kaia is the first of the family to race into the courtyard. I see her beyond Prometheus's big shoulder, her cloak barely tied together over her nightgown and her long hair streaming down her arms. I see her eyes widen as she stumbles to a stop. I see the moment she realizes through the dark and the racket and the happy roar that the man with me isn't the one she so desperately wants. I see her heart break all over again, and mine can't do anything but break along with it.

She looks away, hiding her tears.

"Kaia!" My voice rings out sharply—too sharply—but I need to shout to be heard. The din diminishes, and everyone waits for me to speak again.

Kaia turns back to me, blinking hard.

"I need your help."

At first, she stares blankly, as if she doesn't understand my words. But then she nods and moves forward again, the guards making way for her. She reaches me as I stand, and we wrap our arms around each other, squeezing hard. I let go first, knowing we're both on the verge of losing control. We could collapse in on each other and weep for years, but what good would that do? It won't bring Kato back. And it won't win our war.

Kaia's teary eyes take in my wings as she draws back, but she doesn't say a word.

Prometheus rises to stand beside me, towering over us both. Over the guards. Over everyone. He even towers over Flynn, who arrives in the courtyard followed closely by Jocasta. Carver sprints out on their heels. My heart swells to near bursting at the sight of them—all hale and whole.

They surround me. Then the crushing, joyful, heart-wrenching hugs begin. I revel in them, in the human contact, in the love I feel. This is my family. This is where I belong.

But the most important person for me is missing. *Where's Griffin?*

I glance up, ignoring the battery of questions—*Are you okay? Who is this? Where were you? What happened?*—and my eyes find Griffin's as he stares down at me from the darkened window of the marble tower. My heart breathes a sigh of relief, and I suddenly know with absolute certainty that this castle will be my home. This is where I'll raise my family. This is where I'll *live* instead of just exist.

Griffin is like a statue framed by the shadowed alcove, unmoving, his hands braced upon the windowsill, his eyes burning dark. He looks down at me. He stares and stares like he sees both a dream and a ghost.

My chest tightens, and my eyes grow hot. There's such a rush of emotions inside me that I couldn't ever begin to define them all. The combination, though—it's happiness unlike I've ever known.

Anatole and Nerissa fly toward me, and I tear my eyes from Griffin's so that I can embrace them both. I hug everyone again—Jocasta, Flynn, Carver, Kaia—just because I want to and I can. When I pull back, though, it's hard not to fall into the gaping hole where Kato should have been, completing our circle with his light and humor and selfless loyalty.

Bellanca stomps over, saving me from fracturing from Kato's loss all over again.

The Tarvan ex-princess awkwardly pats my shoulder with a heavy, thudding hand, her eyes cruising over my white-black wings before meeting my gaze with frank annoyance. "I could punch you," she says.

I circle her wrist with my fingers and squeeze, stopping her clumsy pounding. "I missed you, too." Some of the time. I ignore any lingering feelings of betrayal. Her time with Griffin was an illusion, a lie that was neither of their faults.

She scowls. "It's been almost a month. You scared everyone. Your husband's a mess."

I huff, smiling faintly. Trust Bellanca to tell it like it is. I have a feeling I can thank her for holding a lot of things together while I was gone. She's a rock. A blunt, hard, strong-as-granite rock.

I let go of her wrist. "Thank you for being here."

She looks shocked at first but then shrugs, as if whatever

she's been doing is nothing at all. Briefly, I wonder where her sister is. Little Lystra. Probably still hiding in her room.

I look up at Griffin again. He hasn't moved. Our eyes meet, and as anxious as I am to wrap my arms around him and kiss him until I can't breathe, we'll both have to wait.

Among us, there's only one person who has truly lost her anchor. I'm going to give her a new one, different, but desperately in need of someone right now. And I know for a fact he weighs a ton.

"This is Prometheus," I announce.

Everyone gasps—the family, Beta Team, the guards. Since stealing fire from Mount Olympus and giving it to mankind was kind of a big deal for humanity, thus birthing Fire Magic as well, the old legend of Prometheus and his gory punishment at the hands of Zeus is one that people actually still talk about, hear, and share.

"Prometheus"—I gesture widely, encompassing all the people for whom I care so deeply—"this is my family."

The Titan, an ancient *God*, looks carefully at the men and women he saw me embrace, and I know he's memorizing the faces of the people he'll watch over for generations, them and their sons and daughters beyond. He's been tortured for eons. His brethren are all in Tartarus, either tormented or horrifically bored. All separated. Just memories in his sea of endless pain. His past. Ahead of him, he has an infinite expanse of life, a new home, and no purpose—except for us.

"Kaia, I need you to bring Prometheus to the bathhouse. While he's bathing, oversee preparations for a room in the family wing and make sure there's food." The big Titan's stomach growls for the first time in millennia at the mention of a meal. "Lots of food. And find him new clothes." He only has a scrap of a bottom, and that's bloodstained and worn. Finding something big enough might be a challenge, though. Even one of Griffin's or Flynn's tunics would probably split right down the back the second he moved.

Kaia nods, her blue-gray eyes less vague and shattered now that she has something to do. Her quiet voice is still noticeably rough, though. "I'll have some things made up as soon as possible. I know who to ask."

"It might not be easy for Prometheus to adjust to life here, with us, to being with people again. Can you help him with that?" I ask.

Kaia nods again, but she's not the only one. All my friends and family will help.

Prometheus may look like a solid mountain of a male, and I have no doubt he can snap heads with one hand if he wants to—and I'm kind of counting on it, to be honest—but after what he's been through, there are bound to be layers of fragility underneath.

"I left my tutor behind just when he was getting to the War of Gods. Maybe you can tell me what happened?" Kaia's voice gains in strength, and she looks hopefully at Prometheus now.

It's Prometheus who nods this time, gravely. I wonder if he, like me, sees in Kaia both the gentle hand he needs right now and the irrepressible spirit that's going to help his gray-seeing eyes adapt to the brightness of our world.

A few flaps of my wings bring me up to Griffin, and I can't believe I managed to take care of Prometheus first. I fly through the window and plow into my husband, wrapping my arms around his neck and my legs around his waist. He stumbles back, catching me and holding on tight.

"Oh Gods, oh *Gods*." His ragged exhale breaks over my

neck as he clamps me hard against his chest. "I was afraid it wasn't real. That you weren't—" His words falter. Griffin breathes hard and fast, a staccato, manly sort of utter break-down I feel both against my skin and deep inside. "You're real. My Gods, Cat, you're real."

I find his mouth and crush his lips under mine. I want to get closer still. I want him to be all I can feel.

He kisses me back, but it's through a broken sound that's both of ours. With each touch and breath and brush of lips, we put each other back together again from the soul out. In Griffin's arms, I finally feel whole again.

I clasp his face in my hands. His eyes open, two bright, magnetic storms in the predawn light.

"I will *always* come back to you." I repeat the vow I've made to him before. Magic roars to life in my veins, sealing the pledge all over again and making me realize it held no weight in Tartarus. I welcome the jolt from the binding promise. Griffin is my glue. And despite my dark edges, I'm his light.

Griffin sets me down, and his hands rise to cup the sides of my head. His grip isn't too hard, but his touch isn't truly governed, either. It trembles. "Your hair is short."

"The God Bolt fried most of it off."

"I was so scared."

A spasm jerks my chest. "I'm all right."

"And Little Bean?" he asks hoarsely.

I take his hand and place it low on my belly. I send my life force swirling around her, and Little Bean thumps outward in return. Griffin's eyes widen and then glisten in the low light. His smile is like the sun breaking over a hard winter frost—joyous and blinding.

Despite his obvious happiness and relief, his voice stays low and raw, his emotions riding every word. "Where were you? Where did you go?"

"Tartarus."

Shock wipes his face blank. He pales. "Oh my Gods! Are you all right?"

"Yes." I lift both hands to his chest, trying to reassure him, or at least comfort him. "It wasn't, you know…fun." And I doubt I'll ever tell him more than a very abridged version of what happened to me there. I don't need to hurt him with all the things that hurt me. "I broke Prometheus out."

Griffin glances toward the window, although we can't see down into the courtyard from where we now stand. He looks back at me, his expression tight with worry. "Zeus won't be angry?"

After everything Zeus has pulled, I don't really care. I don't say that out loud, though. I still have some sense of self-preservation in me.

"I don't think so. I think Prometheus's punishment was over, and I was supposed to get him out. I think that's why we ended up as neighbors there, and I'm pretty sure the main trio of Gods approved the escape while we were on our way out."

Just a blink floods my mind with their images again, power incarnate, all-encompassing, letting their blessing wash over me in the tunnel of light. In my life, I've experienced their benevolence, their manipulation, their help, and their punishment. My head spins with it. Frankly, it's hard to know which foot to stand on with Olympians. All things considered, I think I'll just stand where I want.

Griffin frowns deeply. "How did you get out?"

I flex my feathers, knowing I can fold them away inside me now whenever I want—and also get them back out. "A door made of lightning and these pretty new wings. I finally figured it all out."

His eyebrows lift. "*All* of it?"

I make a face. "No, not *all* of it. But enough."

He traces a finger over the arch of one wing. "I like the new colors."

I smile. I thought he would.

"Was Kato with you?" he asks.

My smile crashes to the floor. "What? No. He had no reason to be"—*punished*—"in Tartarus." I wrap my hand around my ice shard necklace, remembering the day Kato, Flynn, and Carver gave it to me. Barely able to push words past the wedge of sorrow in my throat, I ask, "Where did you bury him? Are you sure he had his coin?"

Griffin stares at me in confusion. "We couldn't bury him. There was no body. He disappeared with you."

My eyes widen. I knew he disappeared out from *under* me, but I never thought he disappeared *entirely*. "That's not possible."

Griffin shoves a hand through his hair, grating out a curse. His distress and bafflement seem to equal mine. "I swear to the Gods, Cat, we got everyone out. The soldiers. The dead. There were two people missing. You. And Kato. Not even Lycheron could pick up your scents."

Shock immobilizes me, even though I already knew some of this from watching Ianthe. What I didn't know is that Griffin and Lycheron had worked together, and that Kato had vanished without a trace.

"He..." I shake my head. "He must have been transported straight to the Underworld." To the Elysian Fields, if the Gods are in any way just. Unfortunately, that's wholly debatable. "There's no way he would have gotten dropped in Tartarus. That was..."

Griffin's eyes sharpen on me. "Punishment? For what you tried to do?"

I nod.

"What were you trying to do, exactly? Bring Kato back?" The question is quiet, without censure. And pitched like he thinks I could have done it.

I nod again. "I had to try. I couldn't...not."

His expression mirrors my heartbreak and shows no reproach, although he does say, "Is his fate something you should try to alter?"

I slice my hand through the air with sudden violence. "To the Underworld with *shoulds* and *should nots*! Frankly, I didn't much care. And I still don't. I'm not sorry. I wish to all the Gods and magic on Olympus it had worked. The fight was over. He didn't need to die." The bitterness in my voice sours the air between us.

"Cat..." Griffin pulls me into his arms again.

I go willingly, but I want answers now more than I want comfort or care. "I don't understand. Even when we die, we leave a physical form here."

Griffin shakes his head. "I don't know any more than you do."

What could have happened? This makes no sense!

But one thing does and always will. I press my hand against Griffin's heart, needing that proof of life and vigor. "Home," I say firmly.

He covers my hand with his. "Wherever you are, *agapi mou*."

Despite our confusion over Kato's missing body, certainty settles inside me like an anchor. I've been adrift for too long. "It's time to finally finish this fight with Mother."

Griffin tenses under my hand. "Are you ready for that?"

"*We're* ready." I lift my eyes to his. "Our army is ready. Thalyria is ready, too."

"We won't just fight, Cat. We'll win."

I nod. I believe him. We'll go together, because we're

strongest that way. And I have a plan now—a plan that might not even require bloodshed.

"I know what to do." It's what I've wanted to do since the moment I realized it was possible.

"Tell me," he says gruffly.

"Later." I reach up and smooth back his hair. "Right now is for us."

Griffin's hands circle my waist. Our bodies gravitate closer together. "What do you need?" he asks. "A bath? Food? Sleep?"

"You. The only thing I need is you." Tugging lightly, I bring his head down to mine and kiss him with all the sighs I built up in a dreary gray prison on a high-up shelf of rock. Their weight leaves me through our lips.

"*S'agapo*," I whisper against his mouth.

Griffin lifts his head, recognition flaring in his eyes. For questions of the heart, Southerners have always honored the old words, the ones with power, even though their Hoi Polloi blood carries no magic through their veins.

"I love you, too." He answers me like a Northerner. Plain. Simple. The truth.

"Forever," I vow.

"*Gia panta*," he echoes softly, and the exploding arrow straight to my chest proves that words are the most binding of all promises, especially in their oldest form.

Griffin's eyes sear me. The love and passion I have for him must sear him right back. He swings me up into his arms, and I know he'll sweep away the misery of Tartarus with his own healing touch.

CHAPTER 30

"WE HAVE ALL THE ACES IN OUR HAND," I INSIST. "A READY fighting force. Lightning. Elemental Magic. Wings. I can fly right through her window. I can do it invisibly if I choose."

Griffin's eyes narrow. He knows as well as I do that I'm not a sneak in the dark who assassinates people from the shadows. "That's not what I call going to war."

"War's not necessary. At least not yet. What we need is a show of force."

His lips purse. He doesn't look wholly convinced, but he does look ready to keep listening.

Alone together, we sit at a small table, what's left of a light meal still between us. I'm clean, fed, and renewed. My loved ones are nearby, Little Bean is well, and I'm certain of what we need to do. But this is still Griffin's and my decision. Together.

"Picture it, Griffin. We bring the army to her doorstep. We get Lycheron and the Ipotane to come. Beta Team commands the forces. Mother will look out her window and see the future of Thalyria. She'll know it's not her."

"What you're proposing requires a person who can be reasoned with. She's megalomaniac to the core," Griffin points out. "She might not see anything the way you want her to."

"That's true," I admit. "But there's precedent. I'll control her with superior magic the same way Galen Tarva did. Now that I'm finally in full command of my power, I'll show her I can beat her—just one-on-one."

"And you're sure your power outweighs hers?" Griffin asks.

It's a reasonable question. He's seen what Mother can do, lived it firsthand. But I'm sure. My problem all along has never been *having* great magic, it's been *mastering* it.

I nod. "This is why we needed my magic to be reliable and consistent. It's why we went to Frostfire in the first place. This is the benefit of finally figuring it out. We *do* have an army. But we don't have to have a war."

"And then we do what with her?" he asks, spreading his hands. "Leave her there like Galen Tarva did? Ruling Fisa? Forever a threat?"

My plan sours a little in my stomach. "No. We all know that won't work. We'll bring Fisa into the fold. We'll reunite Thalyria, just like we planned. As for what happens to Mother… That's up to her. I'll do what I have to in the end."

"You have to be clear, Cat. You have to know what you're willing to do." Griffin looks at me hard. "Do you know?"

Mother's fate is probably the thing I spent the least time thinking about in Tartarus, and yet the answer is perfectly clear. "I know what I'm willing to do." In fact, I'm betting my life on it.

Griffin still looks troubled. "If you can fly in, then you can also fly back out. If your plan fails, we have a plan B."

"Oh, I even have a plan C."

"And what's that?" he asks.

"Prometheus."

His dark eyebrows creep up his forehead. "I'm not sure he's ready for war. Or even for the outside world. He startles at just about everything."

"Which is why he's our plan C. And why he'll stay here to protect our family and the royal seat."

Griffin looks torn, both skeptical about Prometheus's mental state and interested in utilizing the Titan's great power. "He'd be an asset."

"He is an asset," I agree. "Here." With the army gone, Prometheus will be a one-God battalion in Tarva City, protecting people and a place his giant heart has already wrapped itself tightly around. "He'll take care of any threat to the palace while we're away."

Griffin eventually nods. "I think you're right." He reaches for me, taking my hand from across the table. "If part of our show of force and power is you flying into Castle Fisa like Winged Victory, then how do I get in with you?" Griffin asks. "You can't fly me up."

And that's the final question. Because we're in this together. Even when I didn't realize it yet, we were in it together from the start.

"I'll fly around Castle Fisa and the city to make sure everyone sees me, especially Mother." If eyes can sparkle, I think mine suddenly do. Eleni and I escaped so many times, and Mother never knew how. You can't have two powerful kids and what turned out to be their Olympian protector without them digging a tunnel. It was a given from the time we could crawl.

I skirt the table and slip into Griffin's lap, bringing my arms around his neck. "But you and I, my love, are going in through the back."

CHAPTER 31

OUR FORCES SURROUND CASTLE FISA. IPOTANE HOOVES brought down the previously unshakable gates of Fisa City. Ianthe screamed triumph from Lycheron's back. She leads the creatures with their Alpha. Beta Team commands thousands of men and women at the ready, Bellanca now in charge of Kato's forces. Each leader raises the new standard of Thalyria: a banner, white and green. Peace. The olive branch. Hope and victory in a spray of leaves.

Mother witnesses the takeover of her kingdom from the high-up balcony of her throne room. We come in force, mighty, united, and not a Fisan soldier fights. Not a citizen resists. The city falls to us without bloodshed, and all Alpha Fisa can do is watch. Not even her great magic can reach everyone, or destroy everything. She knows it, and maybe ruling over death and rubble holds little appeal, even for her. In perhaps one of the only moments of decency of her life, she chooses not to try.

Instead, she watches me fly over walls and rooftops. I rally everyone, addressing not only our brave troops but also the Fisans of the city and Mother's own soldiers still on her battlements, unresisting. I tell them that today is a new beginning. I ask them to stand with me, with a new and unified Thalyria. I shout that this is the day that might meets right. I cry out that we bring peace, not war. I tell them that Elpis fights for them.

Finally, with Elpis's name ringing on all lips, I find Griffin, take his hand, and turn us both invisible. With only Beta Team knowing about this final portion of our plan, I guide us toward the now-crumbling exit of the narrow tunnel Eleni and I made. My sister burned it through rock and earth, and I laughed in her wake. We had to crawl out then, and Griffin and I have to crawl in now, my wings tucked safely back inside.

We emerge in a shadowed corner of the storerooms. There's no one here. Out of caution, we stay invisible as we make our way through the castle, moving toward the great galleries of the upper levels and Mother's favorite room—the one where she lorded over us all. There's only one throne. Father never merited a chair.

Castle Fisa is all but abandoned. A few servants flit here and there, looking as scared as rabbits and unsure. I don't see any guards. Maybe they're all up on the battlements, watching the new tide wash ashore.

We reach the throne room's heavy, high doors, and I let go of the invisibility that has been cloaking us for little reason.

Griffin looks at me. He lifts his hand to my face. "You are the Queen of Thalyria. And the Queen of my heart."

Emotion swells in my chest, warm and wonderful. Like Lycheron and Ianthe, Griffin and I are so different now, so much stronger and more balanced together—as one. "I love you. You've helped me become the person I want to be. I see the future before us."

Griffin lets his hand drop. He takes up his sword instead. "Claim your destiny, Cat."

"Claim it with me." I leave my weapons in my belt and let lightning heat my blood.

Griffin nods. Centering myself is so easy now, and I let my Elemental Magic swirl and build. Then I use a great, howling blast of wind to throw open the throne room doors.

Mother is about to taste my force and fury. And my mercy—if she's willing.

CHAPTER 32

ALL IS SILENCE. THERE'S ONLY THE SLIGHT RASP OF GRIFFIN'S and my breathing.

The throne room is empty apart from Mother. No court denizens occupy the long and ostentatious space. I don't see Father, but then again, I hardly ever did. There's not a single guard. Only Alpha Fisa, who watches us from her gilded chair. The room seems cavernous without anyone in it, and as heartless and cold as it's always felt.

A small smile plays at the edges of her mouth. It reeks of cool satisfaction, and my pulse picks up a notch. The lack of an immediate fight makes me wonder about an even more devastating clash to come.

But I'm not scared anymore. My mind, my body, and my magic are finally ready for this confrontation that's been my whole lifetime in the making.

Griffin and I stride forward, and I take in Mother with the same critical eye I've always had. Ivory gown. Loose, dark curls. A wide circlet of fat Fisan pearls. If her green eyes weren't so hard and her expression so cold, I could be looking at an older version of myself.

Even so, I don't feel the similarities between us like I used to, like a corrosive weight inside me leaking poisons into my system. Our paths diverged—far longer ago than I ever let myself believe. I don't fear becoming her anymore, but I do still recognize the need to check myself at times, and to have people in my life who will do it for me.

She rises, fluid and self-assured, and we stop walking.

Instead of moving toward us, though, she turns to a large, paneled screen on her left. An itch starts beneath my skin. There's no reason for that to be hiding part of the wall.

"I've been waiting." The confidence in her voice makes my stomach cramp. She grabs the edge of the panel and pushes it over. "They've been waiting, too."

I don't even hear the crash of wood on stone. Blood roars in my ears when I see the three iron cages backed up against the wall.

Aetos and Desma sit huddled together in the first cage. She looks okay—too thin, though, making her pregnant belly stand out like a disproportionate lump. He's a brutalized mess. Despite Aetos being covered in swirling blue tattoos, there's no hiding the bruising, and I can barely breathe through the sight of his battered face. They look at me, hope and relief exploding into their eyes. I see in an instant that they forgive me for this situation I didn't even know about, but I may never forgive myself.

I swallow hard.

In the next cage, Vasili holds his wife. One of Vasili's eyes is caked with blood and swollen shut, leaving three eyes to focus on me with unconditional love and to break my heart. I've never seen Phaedra cry before, but her eyes glisten now. A tear tracks down one of her weathered cheeks, and I can almost feel the ghost of it on my own skin.

Vasili and Phaedra were the first people to show me kindness when I needed it the most. Without them, I don't think my broken heart would have ever stood a chance.

Looking at them, rage starts to pierce a hole through my anguish. How did Selena—*Persephone*—let this happen? These are her people as much as mine.

I force my gaze to the third and final cage, the one closest to me. It holds two people I hardly know but recognize anyway. My youngest brothers, Laertes and Priam. I have no idea of their worth. They look at me with some curiosity—and no hope at all.

My nostrils flare on a tight breath, and the look I turn on Mother is one of pure, scorching wrath. Lightning boils inside me, and I clench my jaw so hard it hurts. How did I not know about this? How did *no one* know about this?

"Your choice, Talia," Mother says. "You enter one cage, and the people in it go free."

Anger pounds through me. I want to snap and snarl, like I've done all my life. Instead, with utter calm but raging with Elemental Magic and volcanic fury underneath, I say, "You don't make the rules anymore."

Ignoring that, she gestures toward the cages. "Save a pair of them, or save yourself."

"Don't do it, Cat!" Desma yells.

Four of the most precious people in the world to me start shouting all at once from too-small prisons stained with their own blood and filth. They want me to save myself. My heart burns in my chest.

Two people remain silent. My brothers. They're not that much younger than I am. Their faces are blank, their shoulders curled in. They know there's no hope of my choosing them. My affections are already divided between the other captives.

There's ice in my words. A storm in my veins. "I will not enter a cage, and you will not harm them."

"You don't make demands," Mother snaps.

"I do. You listen to *me* now."

She chuckles, but her low laugh reveals a hint of frayed nerves underneath. Her eyes dart to Griffin and then back to me. "Who's holding the leash now? You or your Sintan dog?"

Finally recognizing her acidic barb for what it really

is—jealousy—I take Griffin's hand in mine and then move closer to my friends, placing us in front of their cages. Mother doesn't miss either movement, and I didn't intend her to. I have what she doesn't. What she's always refused and pushed away.

"There is no leash," I answer. "There's a partnership. And trust."

Something in Mother's eyes seems to waver, although her expression remains hard. There are harsh lines around her mouth that I don't remember from before, no doubt pinched into her face by years of unhappiness.

Some of my anger starts to fade, my emotions taking a different form. "I feel sorry for you. You rejected everything good in life until life rejected you."

Mother goes so pale that I know my words struck hard and true.

"Where's Father?" I ask. I don't need a blade to drive a knife right into her. I see that now. And I need to pierce her hard shell deeper than ever before.

Her chin lifts. "Six weeks in his grave."

Huh. I feel nothing. "Did you send him there?"

Her features, cold and brittle for so long, abruptly shift into something that makes her look almost human for once. "No. The healer said he had a weak heart."

"He had a weak everything, if you ask me."

Her eyes narrow, almost as if she wants to defend him. She doesn't.

"Are you lonely now?" As far as I know, when Mother wasn't sleeping around, they didn't sleep apart. It always seemed odd to me that she wouldn't share anything with him, and yet she kept him close.

I've never known her to answer a question like that. I'm shocked when she does.

"There is a void now. It's unexpected."

"Unexpected because you didn't love him, or unexpected because you didn't even feel that void when you killed your own children?"

Her expression hardens once more. "I never killed my own children."

While that's technically the truth, I nearly choke on the absurdity of her claim. My anger flares again. "You certainly orchestrated their deaths, especially Eleni's. And you tried hard enough with me, or are you forgetting about Frostfire and the pit?"

"Forget Frostfire." She flings a hand through the air, as if to shove aside the whole horrific incident. "Apart from that, I've only ever tried to bring you back!"

There's no lie in her words, and I know them to be the truth. But Frostfire isn't so easily forgotten, and I know the real reason she always wanted me back.

My laugh is dark. "Only to ensure your own survival. You sold me to keep your kingdom. Was your deal with Galen Tarva worth it?" I ask.

She draws slightly back. "Yes. As it turns out, I'm the only one who benefited."

Disgusted, I ask, "Do you have any idea how that monster treated Ianthe? What he did to her?"

Something flickers in Mother's eyes again. It's fleeting, but I saw it. Through selfish, unfeeling actions, she lost Ianthe, too, and she knows it.

Griffin squeezes my hand. "Make your offer, Cat. Finish this."

I nod, but before I can move or say anything at all, Mother's telekinetic magic rips me away from Griffin and slams me up against the nearest cage.

For a moment, my ears ring, and I can't breathe. But I

don't need breath or hearing to lift both hands and let twin bolts roll off them. I aim for her feet, and she leaps back from the charred stone, the hem of her dress singed.

My friends and brothers gasp. They didn't know I could do that.

Growling his fury, Griffin helps to steady me. He looks me over with concern, but I'm fine. It takes more than one hit to rattle me.

Straightening away from the bars, I tap into Little Bean's zip and zing to make sure she wasn't too jostled. Her magic answers me reassuringly.

My own magic ignites. Lightning coils down my arm and gathers in the palm of my hand. I cock my head. "No potion needed. Your reign of terror is over, Mother. You've done enough harm."

Her eyes dart beyond us to my friends. Power gathers around her, and she lifts her hand with clear malicious intent.

I send a lightning bolt straight through her raised palm just as the cages begin to rattle and rise. My aim has always been impressive. Mother cries out in pain.

"Don't even think about it," I say. "Or you won't survive this."

Breathing hard, she cradles her smoking hand against her chest. She still manages a scathing look. "Survive this? You're as stupid as ever if you think to let your enemies live."

"It's not stupidity, Mother. It's compassion."

Her face goes momentarily blank. "Compassion? Why waste any of that on me?"

I huff. I can't help it. "Truthfully? The damage you've caused and the lives you've taken make it very hard to choose this path. But I don't think you would even ask that question if you weren't craving compassion from someone."

I glance at Griffin, so strong and solid by my side, letting me handle Mother the way I've chosen to. When we first found each other, I was a mess, full of conflict and fear. His steadfastness and unwavering faith in me helped to save me from myself, and from what I could have become. Right now, he'd kill Mother for me. Or he'd watch me kill her myself. He also understands this choice and how it's a part of me—if Mother lets us make it.

I level a steady look on her. "Compassion has no rules. And Elpis abandons no one."

She stares at me. I don't think she breathes. I see her swallow.

"I don't hate you anymore, Mother. That feeling has passed. I know joy, and you don't. I'm sad for you. I'll help you if I can."

Her mouth trembles ever so slightly, and then she clamps her lips tight.

Where Mother is concerned, part of me thinks my choices should be more black and white, but instead, I feel like I'm still in Tartarus and see only in shades of gray. Maybe that's what forgiveness looks like, or at least acceptance. Maybe that's why Griffin likes my two-toned wings. Maybe that's why *I* like them as well.

"Swear a binding vow to do no more harm," I offer, "and I can let you live."

Slowly, she shakes her head. "I can't live in a cage of my own making."

"But don't you see?" I let lightning grow and crackle from my head to my feet. Thunder rumbles around me. "That's the *only* way to live."

"I'm already a prisoner," she murmurs, her voice not quite steady. Her eyes meet mine. "I don't even remember a before."

Her unexpected words, a confession of sorts, nearly rip

me in half. They're the encouragement I needed from her. And the closest to an apology she's ever given.

"What happened to you?" I ask. "What made you like this?"

Her gaze jumps to the cages still holding my friends, to Griffin, and then back to me again. For the first time in my memory, her face twists and her stony mask really cracks. "I never had anyone. Nothing like this." Her good hand flies toward us but without any harmful magic this time. "I saw only one path."

I step toward her, and to my undying satisfaction—no matter my capacity for compassion—Mother takes a step back. "Then you were blind. I would have helped you. Eleni would have helped you."

She sucks in a sharp breath. "You hated me. You both did."

"You gave us every reason to despise you. And then you did everything you could to nurture our hate."

Her eyes start to glisten. I didn't think Mother could cry. I thought it was anatomically impossible.

She blinks all traces of wetness away, and her voice hardens again. "It's too late."

"It might be," I agree. "But that doesn't mean we can't try."

Her gaze darts over me, over the manifest power at my command. "Your magic is impressive." There's nothing grudging in her words, almost like she's relieved to see me finally coming into my own.

I nod. "You can't win. I know it. You know it. Give me your binding vow."

All artifice seems to strip from her face. Her voice drops in pitch. "Who are you?"

With that question, she might actually be seeing me for the first time. But I think she already knows. She's used my humanity against me so many times. Some think I have too little. Others think I have too much. No one can decide, least of all me, but it's there, and it *defines* me. Mother couldn't take it from me, or make me into a different person. Empathy is a part of me, even now, when the stakes are at their highest, and it's an all-or-nothing game.

Something I said during the Agon Games comes back to me. It was true then, and it's true now. "I am mercy, but I am also death."

She must read everything she needs to on my face. I've never wanted to kill her. But I will, if it comes to that.

She takes a deep breath, almost a sigh. "I envy your choices. Now, when it's too late, I wish I could have made them myself." The habitual scorn is absent from her words, and a look comes over her face that I hardly recognize on her usually hard and unfeeling features. Something selfless. Something close to peace.

Emotion bands around my chest. "It's not too late," I whisper.

"I've taken from you. So much. I understand that now." She backs up another step. "It's over now, Talia, but I can still give you one thing."

Years of suspicion rise up in me. I try to find the twist in her words.

She pulls a dagger from her belt. Does she think she can kill me with that? Kill any of us? I'll char her to dust first.

Mother lifts the knife but then abruptly turns it and drives it toward her heart.

I gasp in shock. My lightning stops raging around me, and the cavernous room dims. Sudden silence descends after the startled noises from Griffin and my caged brothers and friends. Mother staggers and then falls. Her hand drops to the side, leaving the dagger in her chest.

I lunge forward, crouching next to her. "Mother?"

Turning her head toward me, she lifts her good

hand—the one I didn't send a lightning bolt through—and then brushes her fingertips against my cheek. It's the only time she's ever touched me with affection. The softness in her face is so different, so bright.

My knees hit the floor, and I bend over her, my throat squeezing tight. Griffin kneels down next to me, his warm hand a comfort on my back. I thank the Gods he's here. Without him, I might break.

My obligation was clear. Griffin knew it. I knew it. Mother knew it. Extract a binding promise from her to do no further harm, or strike her down. She refused the vow. Mother's only gift to me besides life and my sisters was taking this terrible duty out of my hands.

With her last breath, she exhales words I never thought I'd hear. "I'll tell Eleni I'm sorry."

My vision blurs as her eyes dull into the sightless stare of death. All is quiet around me, and Griffin is a strong, silent, consoling presence by my side.

We won. Thalyria is ours. Only one life was lost today.

Love is weakness. It's what Mother always said. It's what's true, in a way.

Merciless Cat. Griffin had it right, too.

Compassion and ruthlessness have always danced around each other inside me like wary partners, but I know the music they spin to, and I'd rather have a heart to break than no heart at all.

I'll never believe that Mother chose this path today because she knew I could beat her and that her kingdom was lost. If she'd wanted to, she still would have fought to the bitter end, would have forced me to kill her. But in the face of my mercy, something inside her shifted. Elpis finally touched her heart.

My breath shuddering, I pat down Mother, looking for

her obol. Finding it, I force the tremor from my hand and pull the coin from her pocket, gripping it hard.

Her life force has only just left Thalyria. She's just now seeing the other side.

I stare at the coin. I could doom her to Asphodel. I could take her payment for passage across the Styx.

I rub the coin between my fingers. It's not even gold. It's nearly worthless on our plane of existence. But take it from her? Some days, I despised her enough to do it. I'll always struggle with the darkness in me that sometimes sways the scales and will always fringe my wings and shade my actions. But today, I have no desire for revenge, and the choice of where Mother goes next isn't mine to make.

I tuck the coin into her still-pliant hand and then fold her closed fist across her chest. I judged her plenty in life. Charon and Hades can judge her in death.

And if she gets that far, Eleni can decide if she wants to forgive.

I sit back on my heels, taking a deep, steadying breath. Then, turning to Griffin, I gently kiss his lips. "I can't believe it's over."

"It's over," he says, cupping my jaw. "And you were amazing and strong."

I tilt my head, studying him. "You were awfully quiet through all that."

A small smile lifts his mouth. "You did everything you needed to all by yourself."

He's right. Today I mostly needed him supporting my choices, watching my back, and showing Mother that together is so much better than alone.

Aetos clears his throat, and I pop up, turning to my friends.

"It's time to get you out." I only waited this long because I figured they were safer from Mother behind bars.

I go to Desma and Aetos first, grip two bars of their cage, and then let my hands heat with the extraordinary power of Zeus himself. The metal glows red-hot, but no part of my own magic ever burns me, and I pull outward, easily bending the iron. I yank extra hard, knowing that Aetos will need plenty of room to get his big body out.

Desma stumbles out of the cage first and straight into my waiting arms. The swell of her growing baby bumps lightly into mine. She hugs me hard, even though she must be bone-weary.

Drawing back, she looks at me, her eyes as damp as mine. "I understand why you lied to us now, Cat. All these years. I don't blame you for wanting to protect us."

Aetos shimmies through the bent bars after her, and Desma leans against him. Somehow, he hugs us both at once, and for a moment, I also lean into his familiar, tattooed frame. Then I step away and turn to the next cage.

Vasili and I look at each other, and my heart turns over achingly hard at the sight of his abused face. There's dried blood in his mustache, making it lopsided and crisp. His eye is puffed out and tight, the skin around it a terrible color. He needs a healer as soon as possible, or his vision might suffer, and he may never throw a knife as accurately again.

With his good eye, he stares steadily into my face. "I don't regret a thing."

Beside him, Phaedra nods her silent agreement. Their love and acceptance transport me back in time to when they first found me. In their wagon home, the red and gold paint forever coated in a fine layer of Sintan dust, they were the first to give me food, shelter, and clothes, knives to replace mine that had already seen too much blood, and a place to lay my head where I wasn't terrified something was going to jump out at me.

I don't regret a thing. Vasili isn't only talking about this terrible, recent trial. He also means the beginning—the day he first saw me, weak and wandering, and quietly coaxed me toward him, and I went. I saw him, his hair already graying, his mustache wide and bushy, and his eyes so strong and kind, and my weary feet simply carried me toward him, and then he carried me to my new circus home. If I hadn't been so bristly, he and Phaedra would have taken me in as more than just a friend. I'm the child they never had, but I was too damaged to let them have me, either.

I break Vasili and Phaedra out of their cage in mere seconds.

"I love you all," I say, because it's not something I say enough. "You're my family, and I love you."

"Oh, Cat." Phaedra's voice cracks, and Vasili wraps his arms around her.

"How did this happen?" I ask. "Why are you all here?"

"We heard you'd gone missing," Aetos says. "We figured she must have had you."

"We walked right into this trap," Desma says sourly.

Good Gods, she's pregnant, and she came to Castle Fisa *for me*? "Are you insane?" I hiss. Not that I'm much better. I pretty much did the same.

Aetos actually smiles, showing a touch of dry mirth. "You were with us for eight years. You must have rubbed off on us."

I snort. "I've decided to stop charging recklessly into dangerous situations. That's now a bad habit of the past."

There are raised eyebrows all around. Griffin's are the highest.

My husband slides his arm around my waist. "You really think you can do that?"

I wrap my arm around his waist, too. "I can try."

Griffin's eyes dance with humor as he looks down at me. And despite everything, we all laugh together, because that's what friends and family do.

Finally, I turn to my brothers and open their cage. Laertes and Priam step out, watching us warily. I don't ask them for a vow. I don't ask them for anything. I say only, "Choose your loyalties carefully."

"Good advice," a calm, smooth new voice counsels from the side.

I turn to see Persephone, Selena amplified to her Olympian form.

I scowl. That she let these people—her *friends*—suffer still infuriates me. There's obviously more Goddess in her than I thought, more of the deity and less of the person I believed I knew.

A loud boom accompanies Ares's entrance. He always did like a show.

Everyone but Griffin and I looks stunned and confused by their sudden arrival. We pray to the Gods, we make offerings, but no one ever really expects them to answer, let alone appear. Added to that is the fact that Selena is so obviously more than my circus friends ever could have imagined she was. It must be hard to take in.

"You risked big," I say in a careful monotone. She must know how furious I am.

"We all gained bigger," Persephone answers, her tone just as flat.

And that's the difference between my Olympian ancestors and me. My view is finite, and theirs is too vast for me to see.

"What did you say that night in the arena before the Agon Games?" I abruptly ask. "What were those words that knocked me down?"

Her bottomless blue eyes pulse with that otherworldly light I now know is the Goddess in her, not some magic I can try to define or comprehend. "Direct passage to Elysium for all of you, in the event of death."

Shock widens my eyes. Only Hades's cherished wife could manage that—an utter bypass of all the Underworld's rules.

"But Carver," I say. "The Styx."

"Carver wasn't dead yet. Cassandra is there," she adds.

My chest clenches painfully. "And Kato?"

"Kato is also where he needs to be."

Her even expression reveals nothing, nor does her level voice, but that answer is off-target and frighteningly vague for my taste.

I'm about to tell her so when Ares strides toward me, turning into Thanos as he moves. Even muted to human proportions, he's still larger than life. He's always been a God to me.

My childhood protector and teacher looks at me, not smiling, but his approval is there for all to see. "I'm proud of you, little monster."

My heart does an unruly flip. "Is that why you never killed her for me? You knew she would kill herself?"

He shakes his head, his wide-set eyes full of love and lessons and a shared past that marks us both. "I never killed her because I hoped you could save her. Her last seconds were the best of her life."

An unexpected sob tries to break free from me, and I clamp down on it hard. Mother and I had to reach the end of our tortured journey by ourselves, together, for both our sakes.

"I'll bring them home," Persephone says, meaning Aetos, Desma, Vasili, and Phaedra.

I nod. She'll heal their wounds, and they'll be fine. I'll see them again soon.

Thanos suddenly grins at me, the change in his countenance surprising and abrupt. "And I'll get the people of Fisa City to tear down this castle stone by stone until there's nothing left."

I nod again. I'd like to see this house that was never a home razed to the ground. Then something better can be built.

"And my brothers?" I ask.

He winks at me. "They'll help."

I nod again. It's all I can seem to do. And then they're gone—my friends home to Sinta with Persephone and my brothers somewhere with Ares, I presume.

Taking Griffin by the hand, I turn and go to Mother's throne, averting my gaze from the body on the floor. In a special compartment on one side, carved right into the marble and hidden by a clever panel, I find what I'm looking for. A golden scepter with a large red ruby on top. A crown of Fisan pearls. The Origin's own regalia. Now Griffin's and mine.

I hand him the scepter. I'll wear the crown. Little Bean kicks to remind me that she's there, too, and I silently thank her. Her light and warmth bring me constant joy.

The crown on my head and the scepter in Griffin's hand, we walk toward the high balcony that overlooks Fisa City, our people, and our army.

Coolness hits my cheeks, and I welcome the vivifying jolt, opening myself up to the bite of magic on the brisk northern wind. A huge crowd has formed, despite the chill of the season and the sharp hint of first frost in the air. By morning, ice crystals will have laid down their delicate pattern on the ground, and the rainy season will start giving way to winter—and then to a new year. A new year for a new Thalyria.

I've never seen so many people so silent, all waiting for me to speak. And when I do, it's with Griffin beside me and in a voice that doesn't waver.

"Your lost princess has returned. Alpha Fisa is dead." I wait for the noise to settle down before speaking again. "I am Catalia Thalyria. The seat of our new kingdom is in Tarva City, as was the Origin's. We are no longer a divided land. Thalyria is reborn as the unified and peaceful kingdom it once was."

The noise grows deafening. Griffin squeezes my hand. Finally, I can speak once more.

"You have a good and generous King, Griffin Thalyria. Between us, we are your sword and your shield. We will fight for you and protect you. Bow to us today."

And they do, because that's our right.

"And we bow to you in return."

And we do, our humility a new promise for a better world.

And then in front of thousands of hopeful, happy people, Griffin and I turn to each other and kiss. We'll rule together. Our children will follow us. It's a day to rejoice. It's over. And in a way, Mother and I even made our peace.

To cheers and elated shouting and trusting that Ares will settle things here for the time being like he said, Griffin and I turn back to the throne room. We'll find Beta Team, Ianthe, and all our friends, and then we'll celebrate before returning to Tarva City together.

As King and Queen we walk, but my wings long to unfurl, and I feel like I could soar. My heart feels light and bright and a million times too big for my chest. I'll count its every beat until Griffin and I are back with the family I've always wanted, and in the home I can finally have.

Now for a sneak peek at Amanda
Bouchet's stellar new series

THE ENDEAVOR TRILOGY

CHAPTER 1

I SAT BACK IN MY CAPTAIN'S CHAIR AND BREATHED, SLOW AND deep, letting my body adjust to traveling at a normal speed again. It was risky to come here, but maybe we'd finally get a break. We needed one. So did the ship.

Beyond the bridge's windows, stars winked back at me from the endless Dark. The view didn't look much different from anywhere else we'd been to in the galaxy lately, but no one in their right mind would be here. I was counting on it.

It never ceased to amaze me how vast space was—and yet not a single corner of it was free. No technology existed that could get us beyond the Overseer's reach.

A red light sputtered to life on my console, and I shot forward in my chair and stared. *Communication open/outside channel* blinked back at me on repeat.

My heart rate went from normal to warp drive so fast it hurt. "Who the hell is in Sector 14?" I asked in shock, turning to my first mate.

Jaxon looked pissed off and surprised, but not worried.

Jax never looked worried. "No one's ever in Sector 14. Half of it's the Black Widow."

"Well someone's here now," I answered more sharply than I'd intended, eyeing the blinking red com button again. This part of the galaxy was off-limits. Usually, I was the only one not following the rules.

I scanned the views outside the enormous window panels again, not seeing the ship that was reaching out to us. I did see the edge of what everyone tried very hard to avoid and felt a little queasy in the pit of my stomach—only half of which I could blame on the jump we'd just made.

The Black Widow was the reason we'd come to Sector 14. The dicey location was a last-ditch effort to lie low and recharge after three days and seven Sectors of hot-on-our-tail leapfrog with hostile Dark Watch vessels.

I was no automatic pessimist, but this couldn't be good. The *Endeavor* was out of juice, and the Sectors were crawling with government spacecrafts looking for the stolen vaccines—because of course no one but the military was ever allowed to benefit from them. Instead of emptying the lab's contents into our own cargo holds, I'd nabbed the whole thing with a vacuum attachment when patrol ships had starting popping up in the same Sector. Now it was sticking out like a sore thumb, weighing us down, *and* about to get us all sent back to jail. Or worse.

I even had an enormous, leather-clad, bearded man who'd accidentally come with the floating lab. *Shit!*

My fingers tensed around my armrests. There was no way I was reaching for that com button. Whoever was hanging around Sector 14 and a freaking *black hole* was going to have to talk first.

Or maybe they would fly right on by…

"Cargo Cruiser model 419, please identify yourself."

Damn it! They talked.

I stared at the panel in front of me like it was a poisonous snake from one of the green planets.

"I repeat, Cargo Cruiser model 419, please identify yourself."

I almost physically recoiled at the tinny, no-nonsense male voice that burst out of my console again. Interference from the Black Widow made the communication shriek like the five a.m. wake-up whistle in prison. I'd hated that whistle. It made my stomach hurt.

"Answer him, Tess," Jax hissed, nodding to the flashing button. "The longer you wait, the more suspicious they'll get."

"They're already suspicious." Only a ship up to no good would ever be anywhere near here.

I looked from Jax to Miko. Miko's good hand still hovered over the navigation panel, her elongated, dark-brown eyes bigger than I'd ever seen them. She looked like she hadn't moved a muscle since typing out the coordinates for Sector 14—where *no one* was supposed to be.

Taking a tight breath, I turned back to my controls and pressed the flashing red com button. "This is Cargo Cruiser model 419. It's only polite to identify yourself first." Even space had etiquette. Granted, I usually ignored protocol, but I could still cite it when necessary.

Jax groaned softly. Miko looked like she was about to pee her pants, which was odd, because I knew exactly what the small woman could do.

The same sharp voice came through in immediate response. "This is Dark Watch 12. Captain Bridgebane speaking."

Shock jolted me—and fear. Battleship 12? And Bridgebane? He was a high-ranking galactic general and a science freak who'd come close to carving me up when I was a kid. All the higher-ups had wanted to know what made me tick differently from everyone else.

Maybe it was having a freaking heart.

There was no doubt in my mind that Bridgebane would recognize me. I'd grown up, but I hadn't changed that much. I still had the same straight, reddish-brown hair, wispy bangs, and blue eyes that stood out from a mile away. Before she died, Mom used to tell me that my eyes made her dream of the great oceans and blue skies she'd never see. And she never did. Dad had kept us both under lock and key.

And now ancient history was coming to bite me in the neck and shake me hard. Dark Watch 12 was one of the Galactic Overseer's premier warships and could blow my faithful little *Endeavor* to pieces with just two or three direct hits. It was a fully armored beast. And I knew my way around it. Without my oddities—and my conscience—DW 12 might one day have been mine.

"Please identify yourself at this time," Captain Bridgebane demanded, "or we will be compelled to board your ship and ascertain your identities ourselves."

And there was the galactic military in all its glory—polite, even while putting a gun to your head.

I swallowed the panic rising in my throat. There was nothing on my ship that wasn't stolen. Hell, even the ship was stolen. Even the *crew* was stolen because, well, *jailbreak.*

I reached out and pushed the communications button without letting my hand shake. "This is Captain T. Bailey. You're looking at the *Endeavor*," I answered in the flattest voice I could muster.

"Captain Bailey, Sector 14 is a no-fly zone. What are you doing in this area of the galaxy?" Bridgebane asked.

I wanted to shoot back an acidic "What are *you* doing in a no-fly zone?" but managed to refrain. I pressed the com button again and calmly said, "Taking in the view. The crew wanted a peek at the Widow."

I lifted my hand, cutting off all sound from our end, and the longest few heartbeats of my life passed in total silence as the bridge crew stared at me, waiting for their orders.

My mind bounced from one possibility to the next. I'd given my usual false name—Bailey was one of the most common surnames in the galaxy—and the *Endeavor* had fake ID numbers stickered on both sides. I could peel them off and get new numbers up in less than forty-five minutes, even with the necessary spacewalk. But I couldn't do it with Bridgebane watching.

"Power up, Jax. Time to jump us out of here." The only problem was, we hadn't found a safe Sector in days. "Miko—move us closer to the Outer Zones."

"We can't, Tess." Jax shook his head. "With hauling the extra weight of the lab and that huge last jump we just made, we don't have enough power left to get us out of 14. And they've locked on to our com channel now and can follow short-range leaps, even if we jump around the Sector."

I stared at my first mate. I'd known we were low on juice, but that was very bad news.

The red com button flashed again, and then Bridgebane's voice came through to the *Endeavor*'s bridge like he was sitting right there. "We see you have three cargo holds and a vacuum attachment that looks like the lab that was recently stolen from the Lyronium System. Prepare your starboard port for a boarding party. Any lack of cooperation on your part will be taken as hostility, and we will not hesitate to fire to recover the lab by force."

The communication went dead, and my heart slammed

so hard against my ribs it left me short of breath. I leaped
out of my chair and searched the upper, lower, and side
windows. No Dark Watch 12 in sight. Bridgebane must
have been hovering behind my ship—and looking straight
at the stolen lab.

"Jax! Power up with what we've got. And tell Miko her
jump range the second you know it," I ordered.

"It won't do any good." Jax started flipping the necessary
switches anyway. "They'll just follow us and start shooting."

I glanced out the windows again and then pressed my lips
together, trying to hold back what was probably the worst
decision of my life. "Then jump us closer to the Widow."

"What?" Miko squeaked. "We'll get sucked in."

"Well don't jump us *that* close!" I kicked the lock on
my chair and then shoved the whole seat back and out of
my way. I didn't plan on sitting down again while taking
four other lives into my hands and also protecting the vaccines that could save thousands of people from the diseases
that still ran rampant in the galaxy's civilian populations.

I watched to confirm that Miko's hand was flying over
the navigation controls before I punched my own hand
down on the yellow internal communications button.
"Shiori! Get to the bridge. Fiona! You too! Do *not* stop to
collect your plants. This is an emergency."

I swung my eyes back to Jax, nerves riding my spine
like an icy comet. "Tell us when we've got the juice."

"We're good to go," he answered. "At least to Miko's
new coordinates."

I nodded. Now we waited for the other two. Usually, I'd
just tell them to brace themselves for a jump, but right now,
with the Dark Watch threatening to fire on our back end, I
wanted everyone up on the bridge.

Every second lasted an eternity with the warship DW 12

and Captain Bridgebane breathing down the *Endeavor*'s comparatively minuscule neck. I stood there. I didn't shake. I didn't move. My head felt numb. But I wanted to scream at the top of my lungs. Not in fear, although there was plenty of that, too. No, it was *rage* boiling in my chest.

Shiori finally rushed through the bridge doors first, her fingers gliding along the wall. Miko ran to her grandmother, took her by the hand, and then quickly guided the older woman toward my abandoned chair. With her good arm, Miko practically threw the tiny Shiori into my captain's seat, strapped her in, and then locked the chair back down again, not leaving me much room at my console.

Miko raced back to her navigation controls. Shiori blindly reached out to me.

"I think I got us into big trouble," I said, taking her fragile hand.

Her skin felt paper-thin, and the veins stood out, but Shiori squeezed my fingers with surprising strength. "We've been ghosts for five years already, child. You gave us many more days."

The heat of unwanted emotion climbed up my throat just as my console flashed with new information. *Incoming cruiser—starboard side. 200 meters.*

I shot a look at Jax. "We can't wait." Fiona was going to have to deal with taking a fall.

He nodded, and I grabbed the edge of my console for balance.

"Go!" I cried.

Jaxon hit the small, round button that had saved our lives too many times to count, and everything went dark and weightless as the *Endeavor* shot through space. My bones seemed to crunch and shudder and then bounce back to normal again as the ship slowed practically before it got moving. That was the shortest jump of my life.

I shook my head to clear it and then studied the view outside the bridge's windows again.

Mighty Powers that Be... The Black Widow was all I could see.

"You're certifiable, Tess," Jax murmured.

Yeah. I kind of had to agree.

I swallowed hard. "They won't follow."

The com blared like that awful prison whistle again, sending through Bridgebane's clipped voice. "Captain Bailey, you are now under military arrest. Jump again and all crew members on board the *Endeavor* will be deprived of a trial. Our boarding cruiser jumped after you, and DW 12 followed. Prepare for entry on your starboard side."

I cursed. How could I have forgotten that Bridgebane was as ballsy as I was?

Fiona burst onto the bridge, spitting mad. She was barefoot and wearing leggings and a tank top, which probably meant she'd been in a hazmat jumpsuit a few minutes earlier and had needed to get out of it before leaving her secure lab. No wonder she hadn't shown up in time for the jump. At least she'd listened to me and hadn't stopped to collect her specimens. The botanist had her priorities, and they were plants.

"What the hell is going on?" Fiona demanded. "I just cracked my head on the wall when you *jumped* without even telling me to brace myself. And I swear, I'm *this* close to finding a cure for Shiori's blindness. Those vaccines are full of good stuff—like superpower stuff."

"Those vaccines just got us followed practically into the mouth of a black hole," I said, sweeping my hand at the bridge windows.

Fiona looked around, and her eyes widened. "Holy shit!" She stumbled back. "Are you crazy?"

I gave a small shrug. "The Dark Watch was breathing down our necks."

"The Dark Watch is always breathing down our necks!"

"Yeah. Well this time, they're trying to board us as we speak, and a warship got close enough to get visual confirmation on the stolen lab."

"So jump the hell out of 14!" Fiona cried.

"We *can't*. The *Endeavor*'s power is too low to do anything other than play cat and mouse around the Sector until we completely run out of juice."

Fiona snapped her mouth shut.

"And then they'll either board the ship or blow us up," Jax said. "Either way, we're toast."

I caught Shiori's serene expression out of the corner of my eye as I swiped my overlong bangs back. Shiori was always asking me to meditate with her and Miko, but I never wanted to sit still. Maybe I should have. She looked a lot calmer than I felt.

The *Endeavor* jolted from the hard bang of Dark Watch 12's boarding cruiser latching on with a vacuum seal. Obviously, we hadn't opened the port.

"Starboard side has our most solid door," Miko said. "It'll take them a while to break through."

I nodded. But break through they would. They had all the tools.

"I don't get it," I muttered out loud. The intensity of this chase was baffling. Vaccines were important, yes, but it was as if these ones were liquid gold.

I turned back to Fiona. "Has the big guy said anything about the vaccines?" He hadn't threatened the crew in any way after we'd carted him off by accident along with the floating lab. He hadn't tried to reach the bridge. He hadn't even asked for food or water or a freaking loo in the three days we'd had him, or complained about the near-constant jumps. I'd offered him the basics more than once, but he never took me up on anything. He was big, quiet, and stoic in the extreme. I liked him. And I'd better go get him.

Would he even fit into an escape pod?

Fiona shook her head, the tip of her dark ponytail sweeping her shoulders. "He left the lab only once, and I couldn't stop him from poking around the cargo holds. He wanted to know where we were taking everything."

Nowhere anymore. At this rate, those things had no chance of getting to where they needed to go. The food and seeds were for the dirt-poor colonies out in Sectors 17 and 18, which would never recover from the war. The books were for the Intergalactic Library's rare and archaic section, and the drop-off I'd had planned would have been stealth itself. The vaccines were for the orphanage on Starway 8. Abandoned kids never got cure-alls. I would know.

"What do you mean 'superpower stuff,'" I asked, suddenly zeroing in on what Fiona had said.

"I mean give a few rounds to Jax, and he'd be unstoppable. Strength. Speed. Boosted healing." Fiona huffed. "Hell, give some to Shiori, and she'd kick ass like she was twenty years old again."

I felt my jaw loosen. *An enhancer? The* enhancer? I'd thought that was a myth. Or a dream. Or something that would never work.

And then it hit me. No wonder the lab had been so discreet, so empty of personnel that it shouldn't have drawn a single eye as it floated around out in bumblefuck Lyronium. That was how the Overseer worked. Hide your best science. Destroy what you don't understand.

Shit! I'd almost genetically modified about three thousand kids.

"We can't give that to orphans!" It was the abomination the galactic government had been working toward for years.

Fiona shrugged. "You can if you want to turn people into super soldiers without telling them and call the drug a vaccine."

I gasped. Wasn't the military already unstoppable enough?

An ear-splitting hammering started on the starboard side. I closed my eyes.

They're going to tear apart my ship.

I inhaled slowly and then glanced up, seeing the edge of the Dark Watch ship come into view. Too bad I couldn't incinerate it with only the heat of my glare.

The galactic generals weren't just lying to civilians anymore. Apparently, they were lying to their own.

Furious on behalf of just about everything that lived, I slammed out a combination on my console. "I won't give it back. I'll die before the Overseer gets his drug back and uses super soldiers to terrorize the Outer Zones even worse."

The bridge lights flickered from the sudden power drain, and the hammering abruptly stopped.

"I just electrified the whole starboard side." Best case scenario? I fried their jackhammer, and they'd have to return to the warship for another. Worst case? We were pretty much already living it.

Bridgebane's voice barked through the com again. "You are now accountable for an attack on the military, three burn victims, and a damaged Type-4 heavy armor hammer. Also, galactic records show no Captain T. Bailey

and no Cargo Cruiser *Endeavor*. We've definitively identified the floating lab. We will fire on the bridge if you
continue to resist."

Jax looked at me. "They can blow up the bridge and still
recover the lab."

I watched the behemoth warship hover over our starboard side. DW 12 definitely wasn't behind us anymore.
"If they board, we're dead."

We were all repeat offenders. With the vaccine heist, I
had four black marks against me. Now I had an attack on
the military as well. Five offenses meant no jury, no trial,
and no more wasting food and space on a criminal like me.
Jaxon was in the same situation, but not for theft. I called
what he'd done in the Outer Zones heroic. The galactic
government called it murder, because they'd won.

I wasn't sure where Shiori and Fiona stood in terms
of black marks, but Fiona was a bio-criminal who'd created at least three major airborne plagues when she'd
been fighting with the rebels out in 17, just like Jax.
And Miko had cut off her own left hand to get out of
shackles, so I was pretty damn sure she didn't like being
chained up.

I glanced over at my navigator. Miko's brown-skinned
beauty had landed her in a position she didn't want to be in
when she was nineteen years old. I didn't have the details,
but Miko's sporadic comments about the violent appetites
of powerful men spoke volumes. And Miko's death sentence spoke volumes about her violent response. She'd
escaped with her grandmother's help the night before she
was slated to die, and Shiori went where Miko went, even
if that was a galactic prison or a cargo cruiser that looked
like a good place to hide.

Five years together now—Jax, Fiona, Miko, Shiori, and

me—and my obsession with orphans and their health was about to get my loyal band of misfits killed. If I hadn't taken the whole floating lab, no galactic warships would have been looking for us. There wouldn't have been a Dark Watch frigate in Sector 14. Captain Bridgebane would have been stalking someone else.

I looked out the windows at the looming Black Widow and curled my hands into fists. Such nothingness was terrifying. I could almost feel its unholy pull.

I should have stayed away from the vaccines—the *super soldier* serums. I should have known the almighty Galactic Overseer could never produce anything good or pure.

The ship lurched—the DW's boarding cruiser latching on again with new equipment. Probably insulated this time. My tricks never worked twice.

"I'm getting some of those vials before it's too late," Fiona said, racing for the door. "I can work backward and figure out the organics, I'm sure!"

"Stay put." My voice rang out over the bridge. "I'll get the samples. And the big guy."

Fiona pulled up short. At least everyone here listened to me. When I said *stop*, they stopped. When I said *move*, they moved. My father may have stripped me of my identity and tried to get rid of me when he couldn't figure out what was wrong with me, but I'd obviously inherited his imperial vibe and knew how to use it, despite eighteen years of abandonment and four Sectors of separation.

I looked at my crew one by one. At my friends. My real family. "Anyone in an escape pod when I get back can take their chances with the authorities. If you're still on the bridge, you're dying today with the *Endeavor*, me, and a hell of a lot of super soldier serum. You have less than five minutes to decide."

@

I quickly worked my way through the succession of air locks and the vacuum seal and then strode into the stolen lab, spying the massive man immediately. He was two heads taller than anything else in the room, including the dozens of metal shelves stacked with *vaccines*.

I took him in, surprised all over again. No one was naturally that big. Maybe he'd been shot up with super soldier juice, and this was the result.

He looked up at my entrance and then set down the vial he'd been holding. It wasn't a vaccine. It was blood.

Where did he find that? I'd searched the lab from top to bottom—with him watching—and found nothing but the thousands of false vaccines.

We both ignored the booming and sawing as Bridgebane's lackeys worked on breaking through the starboard door. The *Endeavor* was a good girl. She'd hold them off for a few minutes more.

Luckily, the lab was connected to the rear door, which was the weakest of the three and disconnected from the rest of the ship by a series of air locks that made vacuum attaching easiest here. If the DW's boarding cruiser had been able to latch on to the rear port, this would all have been over by now.

I grabbed a medical satchel stamped with the galactic government's seal and started filling it with as many vials as would fit, excluding the test tube of blood, even though that was what I really wanted.

"Come with me if you want to live," I said.

The man didn't move, and I mentally gave him ten seconds before I turned on my heel and left. But I hoped he'd come. There was something about him that appealed to me.

He exuded fortitude and calm, although I couldn't tell if the impression came from physical traits, his age, which was easily twice mine, or something else.

I beckoned with my free hand. "Move it, Big Guy. We don't have long." It was time for my accidentally stolen goods to squeeze his big, bearded, and possibly enhanced self into an escape pod.

He stared at me with dark eyes. He stared as though he could see right *through* me.

"Look, I don't care if you're military or civilian or a scientist or a victim or whatever," I said. "You came with the lab by accident. The Dark Watch is about to board my ship, so unless you're one of them, you'd better get off it if you want to live."

I watched him for a reaction. There was none.

"You think they'll destroy the lab?" he finally asked, his voice gravelly and deep. It sounded like he didn't use it often.

I shook my head. "They'll do everything they can to avoid damaging it. But it might not remain fully pressurized. Or the Dark Watch goons could have really bad aim." And there was another possibility bumping around in my mind. "Or I might just take it out of their reach forever."

He didn't react to that, either. Instead, he simply asked, "Are you offering me a pod?"

I was having trouble getting a handle on his accent, and I'd been around the galaxy more than once. Plus, the kids in Starway 8 came from all over the Sectors. I should have been able to place him, but I couldn't.

"Yeah, I'm offering you a pod," I answered. "Let's go."

As I turned to leave, the man lunged forward and snatched the medical bag from my hand. He'd moved fast. Super soldier fast.

I swung back to him with a glare. "I need those." Well, Fiona did. If she opted for a pod and actually managed to escape, I had no doubt she could eventually figure out the organics and maybe use these samples for something good, like helping invalids left crippled by the war.

Shaking his head, he carelessly tossed the bag onto the metal table behind him and then blocked my access to it with his huge body. I tried twice to grab it again, but he was like a freaking building, incredibly quick, and impossible to get around.

"You're wasting time," I ground out, unable to ignore the pounding that was coming from the starboard door. It was getting louder. They were probably most of the way through.

"You don't need those right now." He jerked his hairy chin toward the exit in a get-the-hell-out-of-here type of way.

Metal cried out like it was in pain, and the *Endeavor* gave a sickening groan.

Fuck it. I didn't reach for the bag again.

"Let's go," the man said, herding me toward the door.

I was pretty sure that was my line, but we were heading in the same direction anyway. It seemed pointless to argue.

We worked our way toward the bridge to a deafening chorus of hammers and saws. The bridge doors slid open and all four of my crew members looked over at Big Guy and me—even Shiori, who couldn't see.

This was it. The end of the line. They'd chosen, and not one of them had gotten into an escape pod. I couldn't tell if my heart soared or sank. It definitely swelled.

"Where are the vials?" Fiona asked.

"It doesn't matter." Not if she wasn't getting into a pod.

She opened her mouth to argue, and I held up my hand.

"I won't let the military take them back. If we stole their

secret lab, hopefully that's their only batch. They'll need decades to figure it out again."

Fiona's brow furrowed.

I ignored her unasked questions and told them what I'd decided on the way back from the stolen lab. "I'm taking the *Endeavor* and the false vaccines into the Black Widow. If you don't want to come with me, you need to get out *right now*."

The crew all looked at me with little surprise. We were out of alternatives. Capital punishment or, if someone was feeling *very* generous, life in jail were our only options. It was really a no-brainer, at least for me.

The ship groaned again, and my console flashed to indicate an air lock breach at the starboard door. The Dark Watch goons still had to get through the safety lock, but that door wouldn't last long.

Bridgebane's voice barked over the com. "I'm taking the Overseer's lab back, and you're all going to be court-martialed in Sector 12."

"Tell him who you are, Tess," Jax whispered, the scar on his cheek whitening from the tension in his jaw. "Your name alone will stop him. Your father—"

I laughed. It burst out of me, awful. Then I squared my shoulders and told my best friend and first mate the one thing he still didn't know about me.

"My father handed me over to Bridgebane when I was eight years old and only three days after my mother died, with strict orders to keep me in an air lock on Dark Watch 12 until the ship was out of my home Sector and then float me into space."

Jax's jaw dropped. Miko gasped. Shiori stayed silent.

"Who the hell is your asshole father?" Fiona snarled.

"Bridgebane took me to the Starway Orphanage instead.

He said if he ever saw me again, he'd do what my father first asked."

Jax cursed. "You mean Bridgebane is the good guy in all this?"

"Bridgebane is a bastard. And I mean that my name will only get us all killed faster than we're going to get killed anyway."

"Who the hell is your asshole father?" Fiona practically shrieked.

I wanted to shriek back what had always been in my heart. *That man has never been my father!*

"Who the hell are *you*?" Fiona demanded.

My pulse pounded hard, so hard I could hear it in my head. Tess Bailey was about to die along with the rest of us. "I'm Quintessa Novalight."

My friend stumbled back against Jax's broad chest. That was the power of a name.

The blood visibly drained from Fiona's face. "As in *Galactic Overseer* Novalight's dead daughter?" she choked out.

Clearly, not so dead after all. Yet.

Nodding, I owned up to the name I hadn't used in years and the family I wish I didn't have. "Daddy is the evil overlord of the galaxy, and Bridgebane is my uncle."

Everyone stared in shock, even Jax, who already knew who I was.

"Soooo... No one's leaving?" I eventually asked, not surprised, but not happy, either.

No one spoke. The *Endeavor* rattled like a sick metallic animal and then groaned again—*hard*.

"We're as dead out there as we are in here," Miko finally answered. No one contradicted her, so I figured she spoke for them all.

I nodded. "Big Guy?" I asked, turning to the bearded man.

He just shook his head.

Fine. His choice, although I had no idea why.

"Power up, Jax, and get ready to punch it. Miko—set us thirty degrees to the left." Portside was nothing but the Black Widow. The huge, lightless area gave new meaning to the oft-used expression "endless Dark."

I turned away, my stomach knotting. I feared the unknown as much as anyone else.

Focusing once again on my crew, I announced, "Strap in. Don't strap in. It doesn't really matter at this point."

We'd never been much for emotional speeches, so I didn't give one. Shiori got out of the captain's chair and felt her way to Miko. The two women stood side by side by the navigation controls, holding hands. Fiona and Jax stayed close together. I was alone. Except for Big Guy. He stayed pretty close.

My gaze returned to the Widow, as if drawn by its massive gravitational force. Twenty-six years, and it hadn't been a bad life, even if a lot of it hadn't been fun. I'd wreaked more havoc on the galactic government than most rebels could manage in five lifetimes. With the help of my crew, I'd kept the Outer Zone colonies from true starvation for years. And everything else I ever had, I gave to the kids in Starway 8. I didn't regret a thing.

And I was a Novalight. I wouldn't go out like a sigh in the Dark. I'd go out like a fucking bomb.

I reached for the external com and opened the line to Bridgebane. "Your boarding crew has thirty seconds to detach. After that, I'm taking the *Endeavor* and your *vaccines* into the Black Widow. Everyone on this ship would rather die than see that serum back in the hands of the

Galactic Overseer." I lifted my finger but then pressed it firmly back down on the button again. "By the way, this is Quintessa, and you can tell my tyrant father that I hate his fucking guts."

I pulled my hand off the com. The line went dead, then blinked red again.

"Quin?" Bridgebane said.

I counted down in my head. *Thirty, twenty-nine, twenty-eight...*

"Let's talk, Quin," my uncle said. "Give me the lab, and I'll see what I can do."

Fifteen, fourteen, thirteen...

"I saved you, Quin. You owe me."

Five, four, three, two...

I turned to Jax, seeing the Black Widow looming through the wall of windows behind him. I felt a lurch and hoped it was the boarding cruiser beating a retreat.

"Quin!" Bridgebane yelled over the com.

A second later, the Dark Watch frigate fired on us. The resulting jolt nearly knocked me off my feet. Alarms flared all over my controls—pressurization compromised in three zones. Another blast like that, and they might disable us enough to hold us in place.

I gripped my console. The *Endeavor* was a good ship. It was too bad I had to take her out.

My heart pounded so violently that each beat felt like an explosion inside my chest.

Some ends are just a new beginning...

My mother's words to me, when she'd gotten so sick. Too sick for anyone to save her.

The Black Widow stretched before us, ready to snare us in her web. Nothing escaped a black hole. Not light. Not matter. Maybe not even a soul.

I swallowed. Some ends are just the end.

"Hit it, Jaxon." I nodded to my first mate.

Jax looked at me one last time. Our eyes met, and seven years of shared history struck me in a bittersweet rush. Then he grabbed Fiona around the waist and threw the hyperdrive switch with a cosmic roar.

I inhaled sharply. Everything blurred. My bones crunched, and my chest folded in on the thousands of things I'd still wanted to do as the *Endeavor* shot toward the event horizon—and the end of us all.

CHAPTER 2

SHADE GANAVAN FLIPPED THE SIGN ON THE DOOR OF GANAVAN'S Products and Parts to *closed* and locked it. He didn't care who might need a spare part today, tomorrow, or any fucking day. He cared about Tess Bailey and her little stream of lies.

Under her pale skin, her fireworks of a blush, and her rabbiting pulse, there was a woman running scared. She looked like she'd been that way for a while, like she never stopped. Never came down. No one got that white unless they spent all their time in the Dark.

Shade strode into his office, tension like he hadn't felt in a while whipping through his body.

Sitting at his desk, he powered up the tablet that might give him some answers. He typed in the passcode to the secure database only he and about a hundred other people in the galaxy had access to. This was where shit went down. This was where he made his money.

He scrolled through the latest entries first. Rebel. Rebel. Rebel. Escaped convict. Kidnapped scientist. Rebel. Priest.

Priest? His eyes stopped for a moment. That was unusual. Not many people fucked with the Powers, just in case they were real.

"Not interested," Shade muttered.

Going to the search bar, he typed in *Tess Bailey*.

No matches came up for a current job. No bounty. No info.

Pursing his lips, he typed in just *Bailey*.

Again, nothing.

He tried *Baylee*, *Bayleigh*, *Bailee*, and *Baileigh*, all without a hit.

Good. She wasn't anywhere on the up-to-date Wanted or Retrieve lists. That brought a little relief to the tension in his gut.

Shade switched databases to hunt for birth records, looking for women under thirty.

After a long wait, about two kabillion Baileys popped up.

He groaned. It'd take forever to sort through all that. She'd probably given him a false name anyway. This was a wild goose chase.

Shade ran a hand through his short hair, still not used to feeling it so close to his scalp. The movement wasn't very satisfying with nothing to shove back.

"Well, shit. Who the hell are you, starshine?"

He hadn't expected his tablet to answer, but all of a sudden, there she was, filling his screen as a new message came through from the first window he'd opened to the private database. His eyes widened, and adrenaline ripped through his body.

He stared at the enormous *WANTED* above her head.

The sum below it of two hundred million in universal currency made his jaw drop.

Shade stood up, thunking both hands down on his desk and glaring at the tablet. He leaned over for a better look— and to make sure he was reading this right.

He'd never seen that much money offered for anyone. Ever. If he was seeing this new post, other people were, too. There wasn't a bounty hunter with access to this list that wasn't pissing his or her pants right now with excitement, but Shade felt like he was about to throw up.

His shoulders tensed as he pushed away from his desk, straightening. Those others, though, they didn't know where she was. The *exact platform* where her ship was currently docked. They had no idea where to start looking for *Captain T. Bailey* in the whole fucking galaxy, but he could walk right up to her and she wouldn't even wonder why he was there.

Shade swallowed the bad taste in his mouth. *Two hundred million.* He could buy back his birthright and live like a king forever on that. Never compete for another job in his life.

He studied the picture again before looking at the rest of the info. It wasn't an exact likeness. Someone had taken an image of a kid—less than ten years old, if he had to guess—and then used algorithms to transform it into an adult woman. They'd gotten the blue eyes and straight brown hair right, but there were no freckles where there should have been.

He turned his eyes to the text. *Names may be false.*

He snorted.

Shade glanced at the top of the screen to see who'd sent out the post. Captain Nathanial Bridgebane, Galactic General, Dark Watch 12.

For fuck's sake, this just kept getting worse. They'd brought out the big guns. Bridgebane was the Overseer's right hand. His brother-in-law. And he either had no idea who Tess was, or he knew, and he didn't want to tell anyone.

Captain T. Bailey.

Cargo Cruiser model 419—Endeavor.

Subject presumed dead.

Shade frowned. "Then why are you sending this out?"

Last seen in Sector 14 in possession of highly sensitive government materials.

Shade's eyebrows nearly flew off his head. He'd seen hints of fragility in her, but she must have had balls of steel if she'd been zooming around Sector 14 with the Dark Watch on her heels.

The bounty will be doubled for recovery of the stolen goods. Bonus for a live capture.

Shade's heart stopped. Holy Sky Mother, the galactic government wanted Tess and whatever she'd taken more than it had ever wanted anything since its inception, as far as he knew.

And they preferred her alive. Some of the sick feeling inside him eased.

Unless they just wanted to torture her for answers? The sick feeling grew again.

What had she taken? Bridgebane didn't want to say outright, that much was clear. He was dangling bait, and the hunters had to figure it out for themselves. If they found her, they probably found it.

The photo blinked out, and Shade lunged for the tablet, picking it up. Bridgebane couldn't have taken down the job already. No one could have found her that fast.

A sort of rage-filled panic had started drumming against his ribs when another image finally popped up to replace the first one. It was a mug shot. In the time he'd been reading, they'd traced her to where she'd been—he looked at the date on the photo—seven years ago.

Tess Bailey. It might not have been her real name, but she'd been using it for a while now.

He looked at her birthdate. A quick calculation told him she was twenty-six.

The sentence stamped in red across her mug shot said *Life*.

He cursed. Fucking nineteen years old and sent to

Hourglass Mile. What had she done to get locked up? He knew what they did to the inmates there. The mines. The whips. The pairings.

The lunch he'd eaten earlier turned to lead in his stomach. Who had they forced on her? What had he been like?

How the hell had she gotten out?

Then he remembered the explosion about five years back. A bunch of prisoners had died. In the confusion, some had managed to escape. No bounty had ever been offered for any of them. The galactic government had probably been too embarrassed by the chaos at one of their maximum security prisons to post.

Beautiful. Ballsy. And Brave.

A wanted criminal.

Fuck!

He worked on the fringes of the law, dipping his toes into the murky side of the system, but he was still part of the galactic machine of all-encompassing order. He knew who signed over the checks. One big job like this, and he could leave it all behind, set himself up for life.

Indecision clawed at Shade's chest. His mind worked. He knew where she was.

The easiest nab and grab of his life was waiting for him on the three hundred and fourteenth level. He could land two hundred *million* in his account.

Double that if she still had the goods.

COMING SPRING 2019

ACKNOWLEDGMENTS

I am so grateful to so many people for helping me accomplish my goals and make my writing the best it can be. First and foremost, my family. You are a huge support, a huge help, and I couldn't do this without you. I love you.

My thanks also to my agent, Jill Marsal, and to my editor, Cat Clyne. My heartfelt thanks to the whole team at Sourcebooks for all of their hard work and support. I'm so lucky to be part of such a dynamic publishing house. My thanks to Dominique Raccah for taking a chance on this series, to Stephany Daniel for being a dynamo publicist, to Rachel Gilmer for her eagle eyes and for being incredibly understanding when I freak out around deadline times, and to Sara Hartman-Seeskin for working on audio and international rights. Also, I am sure that I have the most beautiful book covers ever created, and I'm very grateful to the Sourcebooks Casablanca design team, to Dawn Adams, and to Gene Mollica, for giving them to me.

There's a core group of people who help keep my stress levels from exploding. Alexis and Callie, you are the best friends and the best beta readers a person could ever have. I would be lost without you. Adriana, Rusty, Heather, and Lynn, I'm so lucky to have found you and to have you in my life—for writing and whatever else. And Katerina, I value our friendship, and I'm so fortunate to have you as a resource for all things Greek.

Finally, my sincere thanks to readers and reviewers. Books would go nowhere without you. And my warm thanks to the authors who have so generously supported my work. That remains a thrill for me, and I'm sure always will. The reading and writing community is truly remarkable, and I'm so grateful to be a part of it.